This one is for the bar...

...next round is on me.

This is the boring legal bits:

As of the time of initial publication, the URLs displayed in this book worked. They totally linked to the things they claimed, and the world, for lack of a few short comings, made enough sense to read books for fun. If this is no longer the case, it is mostly likely something you did. But who knows? I don't. I am only responsible for yesterday.

If you think this book is about you, it is. It's about everyone who has a piece broken from them. If anything seems *too* relatable, like you lived it, well, what can I say, let's call it coincidence and move on with our lives. That's the point of the book, isn't it? Moving on. Or is it just my final lament so I can get back to this drink, one breath closer to closure? Love is funny. Ha. Ha. Ha.

If at any point you are taking anything too seriously, may I recommend having a calm. This is a work of fiction printed for the purpose of entertainment. Everything in it, technically, is all made up. I was having fun wiring it. So have fun reading it. Or read something else.

Library of cosmically cataloged publication data:

Paperback ASIN: BOCP6LRB6M

Cover design by Woolly Willie

Woollywillie.com

EMPTY BOTTLES

Written by Willie Alsedek

I
OUR STORY BEGINS

Alcohol eased the car's sway over the dividing line and back. The driver danced with the yellow strip that cut the road down the middle. Darkness owned the path ahead and swallowed the space left behind. The driver's hands hung heavy on the steering wheel, pulling left and pulling right. Wondered what she would think of him in this moment—the real her.

The original her.

Seeing him like this, seeing how it all ended up. Go back in time, and they could watch him self-destruct. Watch the pain ripen. She would hold his hand and probably cry. Weep and tell him how sorry she was.

What a thought.

Changing lanes, the driver laughed at the thought of time travel. Swerving back over the wobbling yellow line, he laughed at the power boundaries had on the world. Laughed at life and all the lines we draw, the plans we make, sides we take. Things we lose. His life was just a blur. A blur of tiny light screaming down a narrow path some stranger carved across the earth long ago. A line drawn in the sand. Who knows the names of the people who paved the paths, the ones who rolled out the asphalt? That's what the driver was thinking.

Who the hell painted this line?

What side of life was he on, the driver mused. Laughing at his pain as he mocked the roar of the engine with his voice.

Growling at the motor, he wondered whether he was coming or going. Was the line an illusion? Are we all only ever going?

The driver's headlights burned a small window into the night ahead. A sudden and fleeting glimpse of what's to come. Only, the car couldn't match the speed life truly harnessed. The flash of importance we know to be ourselves. The pain didn't feel brief. It felt everlasting. Felt like he was just getting started. Like the tragedy was simply the prologue to a growing epic tale of suffering. Something a drink helped him embrace. The driver liked being lost in the dark. Alone with his thoughts. Alone with the power of the car flying into nothing. The night sky in the desert was an extraordinary sight to behold—an unobstructed view of the vast unreachable expanse.

Tipping a bottle back, he swallowed more beer. Sighing with a sense of relief as if it were a bottle of fresh air, and all he was doing was breathing.

Each drink another breath.

He had been driving for a while when the red and blue lights finally filled in through the back window. Red and blue lights glinted in the side mirrors, blinding him in the rearview. Reaching up, he bent the mirror down to save his sight, a cigarette burning between his fingers. The driver wasn't giving the cigarette much attention. Ash fell wherever it needed to. Camouflaged within the stained upholstery. The years of neglect had rotted the car from the inside out. Taking another breath from the bottle he leaned into the backseat and spoke to no one.

"What do you think he wants?"

Nothing answered.

Letting his hands play with the wheel, Caesar jerked the car around for a few big comedic swoops before cutting into the desert. The driver's name wasn't actually Caesar. It was Julius. Everyone just called him Caesar because of that famous Roman guy from history class. Nowadays, he just introduced himself as Caesar, so no one had to waste time putting it together.

The rumbling terrain shook from below with a fierce and disapproving roar. The four wheels begged for the return of smooth pavement. Caesar let a note sail out from his voice so the shaking car could rattle it. He was happy to find that it was still fun to be childish. Proof that part of him was still alive.

There was still a reason to continue his suffering.

3

Caesar didn't go far before stopping the car. He was spilling too much air from his bottle to justify the off-road excitement any longer. The cop parked behind him. The officer didn't bother running Caesar's plates. He immediately stepped out of his highway patrol car with his knee-high boots and marched right to Caesar's door—strong, precise steps. He ran his fingers along the brim of his stiff trooper hat, the strap snug on his chin. He liked touching his hat. His fingerless leather driving gloves made him feel like a badass. The uniform itself provided him with powerful confidence, but the gloves added a sort of Hollywood blockbuster flare that filled his head with a juvenile sense of reality. The cherry on top of the whole badass package that he knew himself to be was that fuzzy worm gripped strong to his upper lip. The officer's was classified as a handlebar mustache, so it turned around his lips and traveled down a bit. Facial hair can do wild things to a man's ego. When he wasn't wearing his hat, he'd pet his mustache. Sometimes, even with the hat, he would pet it—sometimes he'd finger both, fiddle with his badge, tap at the gun tight to his hip, fantasizing outlandish heroic scenarios.

Caesar was already rolling his window down. His hand was reaching out just as the officer stopped at his door. Caesar was holding a beer out, asking the officer if he wanted a drink. The cop took the beer and scratched his head, telling Caesar, "I was sorta' look'n forward to tapping on your window, giving it the old cliché knuckle, ya know, like in the movies. I just got these awesome gloves, man, I feel like Stallone or something." With a long, somewhat painful expression, Caesar asked, "You want me to roll my window back up so you can... come up to the car again?"

The officer looked back to his flashing vehicle and sighed something hopeless. Then, abandoning the invitation, he exhaled, "Nah, the moment's passed."

He hooked the beer bottle on his belt and popped the cap. Leaning against Caesar's car, he took a big gulp. It was his favorite beer, and he told Caesar this. He always did, always complimented him on his taste in drinks. The officer took another drink and looked up to comment, "Beautiful night, Caesar." With a deep breath, he added, "Nothing like a cool summer night in the desert, the air's so fucking crisp, so sweet. I just about wish I could scoop a spoon through it and take a goddamn bite." Taking another drink, he smiled. Caesar took a drink as well and suggested he turn off his flashing lights so they could enjoy the view better. The officer smiled at Caesar, tapping his beer against the car to toast the idea.

They were both a couple of pasty white boys. Harmless Caucasians with mixed heritages they knew little of. American mutts. They sat on Caesar's hood leaning back against his windshield, looking up to the vast explosion of lights that seemed to hang impossibly above them. Caesar was pretty drunk, so his eyes weren't open so well, but he was still enjoying the sight. The cop's name was Frances. Some people called him Frank, some didn't. Like Caesar, he enjoyed a drink.

Frances was talking to Caesar about the moon while they drank. It was just about half full and looking down at the two with a bright face. Frances was wondering why they only ever landed on the thing the one time. "Why haven't they built something on it yet? It's been long enough since they reached the goddamn thing, you'd think somethin'd be fuckin' built on it by now. Ya'know?"

Caesar smiled up to the big pale rock and shrugged. "What makes you think shit's not built on it already?" Frances waved his hands in a disapproving manner. "*Bah*, fuckers are sneaky, I'll give you that, but don't forget the fuckers are dumb as rocks, too. They ain't up there. Too hard to hide a thing like that. All those nerds with scopes in their yards stargazing."

Caesar laughed a little, and Frances pushed at him, asking him what was so funny. Caesar shrugged and asked him how many satellites he thought were flying over them right then and there. Frances looked at Caesar with a narrow eye, doing this thing he did with his tongue and his front teeth where he sucked in air. It made a squeaky noise. He did it when he was thinking hard. Looking up to the stars, he really gave it a good squeaky-toothed thinking before he said, "I don't fuckin' now, like fuckin' four or somethin'."

Caesar shook his head, tipping his beer back for a breath of air as he told him, "More like a couple hundred." Frances sat up quickly and belted out, "Shut up!" with a wincing skepticism glaring from his expression. Caesar smiled as he took a long breath from the bottle and sighed, "Actually, it's probably more like a thousand, plus." Frances pushed at him, excited, saying, "You're fuckin' with me, *over a thousand?* How they not fuckin' crashin' into each other? Fuck you, a thousand, plus."

Frances had a big smile, looking to the stars and back to Caesar, not sure if he believed him or not. Caesar had no idea how many satellites were orbiting the planet. He just remembered reading once that there was a lot. Didn't care if he was feeding Frances false information. Had he known the actual number, he would've embellished regardless, because he enjoyed messing with him. Frances was the fun kind of gullible. Never got mad when he found out he was being played, and he never wised up to the fact that everyone around him took constant advantage of his gullibility. Frances was a hard person to upset.

Settling back against the windshield, Frances decided a thousand-plus satellites was pretty amazing. He even whispered to himself as he reached for another drink. He whispered, *"Fuckin' thousands of'm."*

Caesar pointed to a dot moving through the stars and tapped Frances on his arm, telling him it was one of the thousands right there. Frances lit up, and Caesar smiled at his friend's excitement. He did actually know that what he was pointing at was a satellite. Something his ex had shown him. Satellites blink, and stars sparkle. Moving his hand, he pointed out another. Frances made a happy humming sort of sound, pleased with the night's discovery. He already knew about the traffic of planes increasing in the sky each year, so the number of satellites was easy to accept.

Frances wasn't dumb by any means, just trusting and maybe slow at times, but only because his excitement always took the lead on most of his thinking. He was divorced with two kids. His wife finally came to terms with her homosexuality two years ago – something their church convinced her to ignore her whole life. After a year of couples therapy, they both stopped going to church altogether. They still lived in the same house, and will until their kids get older. Frances was happy for her. It left him a good shade melancholy. Drinking helped.

Drinking with Caesar helped more.

Frances smiled really big again when he spotted another satellite. Pointing, he called it out to Caesar's attention, but

Caesar had fallen asleep, a cigarette hanging from his mouth still lit. With a chuckle, Frances tapped Caesar's chest. "Hey, come on. Let's get you home." Caesar rubbed his eyes as Frances slid off the hood. One of Caesar's flip-flops had fallen off as he woke. Frances picked it up.

"You lost your flop, buddy."

Caesar moaned, "Just leave me to sleep here. I can't drive. I'm drunk." Frances slapped the flop onto Caesar's belly and chuckled. Playing with his hat, Frances said he'd follow him, make sure he got home safe.

He always did.

"Besides, I'm a little loose myself. How's the saying go? Friends don't let friends drink and drive alone."

Caesar started to laugh and shake his head. Slipping off the hood, he told him, "That's not at all what's said. You're a bad cop."

Frances helped his stumbling friend into his car. Gave his shoulders a stern, sobering rub as he strapped his seat belt around him. "Drive slow," he told him, "I'm right behind you," and then he closed his door. Caesar started the car and gave his friend a drunken smile. "You're my best friend, Frank. You know that?"

Frances was playing with his pistol, spinning it around his finger as he answered, "I know I am, buddy." Caesar turned his headlights on and sighed, "Where would I be without you?" The question was rhetorical, but Frances answered anyway, telling him he'd probably be dead. Caesar laughed at the truth of the statement and turned to Frances with an idea for a band.

"What kinda band?" Frances asked, still playing cowboys with his pistol. Caesar bobbed his head to the imagined music as he explained, "It's a found instrument band where we find shit on the way to every show to be our instruments, and we come up with all the songs live."

Frances holstered his sidearm and laughed, "*Ha*! I like that. What's the band called?"

Caesar pondered for a second before saying, "Coke Rodent."

Frances smiled, "I'm already their biggest fan."

II
ATTACKED BY PANIC

The first ticket of the day was stabbed into the long metal grip that hung over the kitchen window. Amber took the order, stuck the order, and called out, "Huevos Rancheros, eggs simple."

All the servers used the same blue notepads to take down their orders. When a line cook took a ticket from the window, they'd read the order out loud again so the other cooks could know what to start. Crystal, the cook who plucked the day's first order from the window, blew a minty cloud of weed vapor over the blue sheet as she translated, "Deadeye party chips, hold the tears. Two eggs wrecked, strips and pilgrims, sub bricks."

"Deadeye" meant the eggs on the Rancheros were over-easy. "Hold the tears" and other crying references referred to onions. "Wrecked" meant the two eggs in the second order were to be scrambled. "Strips" meant pig bacon, "pilgrims" meant turkey sausage, and "bricks" were biscuits substituting the usual toast that came with the two-egg standard breakfast—Amber and the other servers called the order *eggs simple.*

Two eggs with a side of meat and a slice of toast.

The standard all-American diner breakfast.

Coffee was included with any meal.

Caesar was behind Crystal in his flip-flops, an apron, and a hairnet. He was cracking eggs into the appropriate places, dialing the needed heat to the proper degrees, and raising his flask to give Crystal's vape pen a toast. Crystal was a bigger woman, but she could move and groove, and she could also just as well sit and pack a bong. She'd arm wrestle just about anyone and beat just about most of them. She had a funny draw towards violence. But her real passion in life was smoking people up. When her kids got old enough, you bet your ass she would be smoking them up too.

The diner was attached to a motel and a bar. The three services all existed under the same management and the same sign: Renaissance Inn. The motel had a pool and a few barbeque pits. The bar had big barrels of peanuts and two pool tables. All of it owned and operated by Teddy Mustafin.

Teddy was from Uzbekistan. His actual name was Tursunmurod, but so many people chewed their tongues off trying to pronounce it during his first few years in the States, he just started saying his name was Teddy. He had a big forehead, big brown eyes, and a heavily receding hairline. A little pouch of hair sat isolated on the center of his head like some remote island where his youth had been left stranded. He was shorter than most men, and when he smiled, his eyes squinted. When he laughed, his eyes just about closed all the way. He spoke Uzbek, Russian, a little Arabic, and his English was mostly unaffected by his accent.

Almost.

His grammar was where things got challenging—with the accent, he was, at times, completely useless. In some instances, his words become a cryptic code, imploding upon delivery. It was really only an issue when he was stressed or flustered. The thing was, he was easily flustered and often stressed. He had two kids that were all grown up and out of college. His wife passed away a few years back. Caesar was sober for the funeral, out of respect. Teddy's wife hated drinking.

Which was why Teddy and her never had much of a hand in managing the bar on their property. A man called Lucky ran the bar. Lucky was from Texas and was missing one of his front teeth. He could whistle louder than most teapots because of it, and when you got him laughing, you couldn't get him to stop. The man just about laughed himself to tears every day — hence the nickname: lucky to be so happy all the time. Some days you could get him laughing just by looking at him. No one knew how or why, and he couldn't tell you himself. Life just cracked him up. Crystal had yet to beat him in arm wrestling and she was far from ending her attempts. Lucky would always buy her a drink after he won, and when she came into the bar, he always eyed her up, wondering if she'd come to challenge or just to chase her high with endless peanuts.

The Renaissance Inn was a few turns off Route 66, a couple of miles after the famous *Mysterious Sand Mummy's* attraction. It was a little museum of speculation that took you around a series of assumed histories that led to the mummies themselves. Were they aliens? Were they Egyptians who fell out of an alien spacecraft? Were they Vegas gangsters buried in rags by their competition? Or were they gamblers buried for outstanding debt? Maybe coppers who crossed the ginny? Feds who took too much off the top? Or alien gangster Egyptians who never got that ride home? Most of it was Vegas-themed.

Vegas *was* only a few hours west.

Miles past the Inn, there was a biker landmark. A rite of passage for some of the leather-strapped road warriors. The diner fed a lot of bikers because of this. It was a pair of bikers who put in the first order that morning. As more rolled in, their bikes woke up whoever was still asleep in the motel, and the diner filled up with bikers and tired families.

Tickets lined up in the kitchen window while Caesar nipped at his flask. Twelve stools lined the bar facing the kitchen window. The space between the bar and the kitchen was referred to as the trenches. Two espresso machines would be pulling endless shots, four coffee pots would empty all day, and trays of food would forever take off into the server traffic.

On this day, like so many, Crystal and her vape pen were in the pilot's seat. For the kitchen, this meant she was calling out tickets, double-checking orders before they'd be set for expediting, and handling all the cold and pre-prepped food— turkey clubs, soups, salads, or anything that used the blenders. Caesar was "*Sitting-Fire*," running the stoves and the ovens. There were usually two people in the hot seat, but Caesar could manage on his own and preferred when no one was in his way. There was, however, always a floater: someone who danced between stations and prepped for backstock. There were enough burners and skillets to cook ten omelets, twelve pancakes, and twenty strips of meat at once. Enough toasters to pop a dozen slices of toast at a time. There was also a microwave for quick fixes.

On a day like this one, every burner was on.

It wasn't an overwhelming rush, but the orders were steady. The only actual struggle was the floater, Neil, a man who was only ever scheduled as a floater. Covered in nonsense tattoos, he was fidgety and scrawny. Caesar called him Pop-Up because his tattoos reminded him of internet pop-up ads: obnoxious and out of place. Neil was always making things into drums, always telling a story, always talking a big game no one ever saw him play. He had a goatee to hide his weak chin, and he womanized to hide his missing sex life. If murder were legal, someone probably would have offed Neil long ago. Then again, if murder *were* legal, Neil might not talk so much.

Neil was mindlessly pushing potatoes around a frying pan and talking his usual game. Caesar had to remind him to flip the spuds and add spices as he cooked because he talked so much he wasn't paying attention. Talking about how two girls were fighting over him the other night. *Technically* they were. Neil had squeezed a girl's ass and said something vulgar. The girl's reaction was to beat him with her phone. When the phone broke, she beat him with her fists. The other girl who stepped in on Neil's behalf was presently four months pregnant with what she claimed was his child. She didn't like Neil, but she was damn sure going to see to it that he contributed financially to the child's life. So, to be fair, the fight *was* over him, just not in the way he was telling it.

Neil was grabbing at his crotch while he told his version of the story, saying, "They can smell that potent juice I brew, *ha-ha-ha*, drives the ladies crazy, man. Nothing I can do 'bout it. I don't mind share'n, you feel me, but they want me all to themselves. *Ha-ha-ha!*" Crystal rolled her eyes and gave Caesar an irritated glance. Caesar returned the look with a dead glare. He couldn't stand the guy or anyone who talked like he did about other people. Like everyone should be jealous. Like they were all beneath him.

Crystal waved a ticket at him, saying, "Nobody wants your juice, Neil. And stop grabbing your dick. You're touching people's food. It's disgusting." Then she read the ticket: "Veggie

11

omelet, no tears, side of logs… and change your gloves before you touch anything."

Neil tossed his molested latex into the rubbish, tugging a new pair out of one of the boxes behind him. He was making a sexually suggestive face and leaning towards Caesar, saying, "I'm telling you, man, ever since I knocked up Georgia, the ladies have been *dying* to get stabbed. I'm *actually* tired, *ha-ha-ha*." His new gloves snapped on, a childish grin plastered across his face. Caesar focused on the eggs and veggies he was mixing for the new omelet order, plating the others Neil was neglecting. Caesar didn't care to entertain Neil's desire to talk about anything. He wished the guy would screw up his probation and disappear.

The way things went, Neil got uncomfortable easily. Caesar ignoring his arrogant performance left him feeling vulnerable. His big stupid grin straightened into a fine awkward line. Attempting to recover, Niel stepped closer to Caesar and looked out over the working pots and pans, asking what he could do to help. Caesar poured the egg mix into a hot pan and huffed, "I need you to stop talking about your dick. I have absolutely no interest in ever knowing anything about it." Caesar took the pan of frying potatoes Neil had abandoned and gave them a toss, then pointed a spatula at an empty pan and told him to cook the sausages for the order Crystal had just called. Then he jabbed at Neil's ears, suggesting he listen to the tickets.

Neil moaned, "I didn't know you were gay, Caesar," on his way to the fridge, attempting to defend his ego. Baffled, Caesar shook his head, asking a sharp, "What?" Neil pulled a pack of links from the fridge and shut the door, explaining with a smug shrug, "You don't wanna hear about all the tail I'm slaying — I get it — 'cause you're gay. Ladies don't interest you. No judgment, my man. It's cool." Caesar flipped the omelet and laughed, "Yes, I'm gay. *That's* why I don't want to hear about your dick. Makes sense, Pop-Up."

Neil dropped the pack of sausages into a pan as he looked at Caesar with a strained expression, and attempted to explain himself. "No, man, you're gay 'cause a'like, like you don't want, like… man, why you twist my words around like that? And why you always be calling me Pop-Up?" Crystal pulled another ticket from the window and commented, "Maybe he likes you, Caesar."

Neil looked up from the sausages with a wide eye. "The fuck you say'n?" Crystal kept her smile hidden as she carried on, "You keep telling Caesar about your ding-dong. Seems like you might want him to hold it for you. Take it for a walk. Why else would you tell him so much about it?"

Neil, made instantly uncomfortable by Crystal's comment, desperately attempted to make his sexual orientation clear by hollering, "NO ONE'S TOUCHING MY DICK."

Caesar took advantage of Neil's choice of words, and he played against the defense to confuse him further, asking, "So then what was all that talk earlier?"

Neil huffed, "What talk?"

"You just said no one's touching it, but earlier, you said people were. So, which is it? Are you not actually getting any? Have you been lying to us all this time?"

Neil grunted, "No, I meant guys, no *guy's* touching my dick."

Amber poked her head in from the trenches to tell Neil not to talk so loud about his wiener. Customers could hear him. Embarrassed, Neil tried to defend himself again, but Teddy was looking in from the back and speaking over him with a stern boss tone. "Neil, god-damnit! Why you have to yelling about your private parts always?"

Neil moved to defend once more, but Crystal spoke over him, "Ya, man, they're called 'private' for a reason."

This time it was Amber who cut him off by leaning in from the trenches with a big smile. "You know what they say about men who can't stop talking about their peckers?" She stuck a new ticket in the window while everyone leaned an ear in to hear what was said about people like Neil. Neil wasn't interested. He opened his mouth, only to be spoken over once more by Teddy, who was flustered and unamused by it all, demanding everyone stop talking about dongs and balls. Everyone but Neil got a laugh out of Teddy's choice of words. *Dongs and balls.* The laughter frustrated Teddy more, and he left the kitchen with his arms up in the air and his head shaking out something in Uzbek.

Neil had folded his arms to play victim, asking why everyone was teasing him. Crystal apologized to Neil to shut him up so she could read the ticket she was still holding along with the other hanging in the window. As much fun as it was to mess with Neil, they were busy. Caesar cracked more eggs and told Pop-Up there wasn't any need to explain why they teased him, just that it was important they did it as much as possible. Neil pushed at the sizzling sausages and swore under his breath. Pouting, he told his coworkers he was going to be a father, and they should show him some respect. Caesar rolled his eyes and took an irritated breath from his flask. He wanted to fire Neil, but Teddy wouldn't let him. Teddy was the only one who felt bad for Neil.

When the breakfast rush slowed down, Caesar lit a bent cigarette he had pulled from his pocket. He was smoking to slow down his drinking. His flask was losing weight, and he was hoping it would have a few breaths left once his shift was done. Caesar didn't care to get drunk before it was time to fall asleep. He liked to chase the buzz throughout the day—tip-toeing in and out of tipsy. Working with Neil, however, well, that tended to hollow out a flask faster than intended. Neil had only been there six months and already it felt like a lifetime.

Teddy, in a nearly incoherent fury, was back in the kitchen doorway, looking at Caesar shocked, saying, "You can't smoke in here, Caesar, Jesus fucking damnit. And the feet, for god-fucking with you flip-flops. How many now I gotta say at you already to have to do shoes. I tell you this. *I tell you, I tell you, I tell you.*"

Caesar put the cigarette out and pocketed what was left, pointing to the vent over the stove, telling Teddy he kept the smoke out of the food. Teddy didn't care. "Put on shoes, or you're fired," he told him.

"I don't own any shoes," Caesar confessed.

It was true.

Just flip-flops.

Teddy left the kitchen with his arms in the air, shaking his head in a tired rage, saying, "Then you're damn fired."

Crystal immediately, and with joy, reached over and uncapped a marker off the dry-erase board beside her and added a tally to the '*Fired*' list.

Caesar was fired a lot.

Teddy rarely followed through with it, and when he did, Caesar would come back to work his next shift anyway, and nothing would be said. No one remembered the first firing—it had been happening for as long as anyone could remember. So, he was fired, and work carried on as though he wasn't. Caesar plated orders, Crystal slung them out the window, plucked fresh tickets—the cycle went around and around. And today would have kept going around and around if it hadn't been one of those rare days that kicked Caesar into a spiraling panic attack.

Caesar was plating an order for Crystal to finish when he froze in the first wave of the panic. Crystal didn't notice him stop. She was prepping salads and making a joke about Teddy. Caesar didn't hear it. Through the window, he was paralyzed by the sight of a woman at one of the tables. He could only see the back of her head. Her dark hair pulled into a familiar ponytail. *Her* ponytail. The hair he married.

Everything about this woman was familiar. Felt like *she* was right there. Like *she* never left. Like he was just coming from the bathroom, steps away from sitting next to his wife to decide who was going to pay and who was going to tip. The moment he saw this woman, he felt himself shrink, felt the kitchen around him pull in. His lungs clenched like fists around his chest, and his heart bashed against his insides so hard you could just about see the thing beating under his apron. Caesar hadn't seen her in eight years. Hadn't so much as uttered a word in her direction.

What were the odds this really was *her*, he wondered?

She didn't know where he was. No one knew where Caesar was. Eight years ago, he left his life and told no one he was going. There was no plan. He just left. He worked a deal with Teddy, so he wasn't on the payroll. They traded him room and food for his labor. Tips covered his drinking and smoking habits. With all the experience he had managing kitchens, they were happy to have him and used to hiring people looking to get away from their past. He had no phone. His car wasn't insured, and he mostly drove it when he was drink-chasing Frances in the dead of night. Caesar was as unfindable as he could manage. Not that he thought she would ever come looking. It was everyone else he was hiding from. Everyone from that broken life he couldn't stand to be around—all reminders of the awful truth. All that pain.

But who was this person with her hair?

People *did* go on vacation, and they were always stopping along the highway. They traveled, they stopped at diners, and stayed in motels. She *was* a person. It could be *her*. It could be the woman who stood at the center of his grief and self-pity. Whomever this woman was, she had her hair, wore it just like she did. But what were the odds she still had the same haircut after all these years? Still wore it up like that?

She reached out for water, and her hand was even the same, her shoulder, the motions she made —it was all too familiar. His heart was beating with such a terrifying force he felt he might fall over. Was it still pumping blood, or was it choking to death? He couldn't tell. He could smell it burning. Smell his soul melting in a hopeless pain. Could even see the smoke clouding his vision from the fire inside him. Thick black smoke drowning him in sorrow.

Smoke he was choking on.

Neil pulled him from his hypnosis to the burning pans he had forgotten were cooking. Everything was turning black and smoking. Neil wasn't helping any. He was just laughing at Caesar, using the opportunity to get back at him for being mean earlier. Caesar cursed himself as he tried to salvage what he could—rushing around the burners, coughing through the smoke, his eyes burning as he reached up and ripped the smoke detector out of the ceiling. He tried to plate what he could, but none of it was edible, and none of it went where it belonged. Caesar couldn't remember what was ordered with what. His mind was running circles, trying to figure out what he should do about the woman. Trying to peek back to see if she was looking into the kitchen.

Had she come back for him?

Crystal was yelling, trying to make sense of the mess, repeating the orders, swearing, telling Neil to shut up and help. Caesar was apologizing, throwing things out, trying to hear the orders again, trying to get back in his groove, trying to watch the woman with that familiar ponytail. His mind was calculating every scenario that could put her there. If it was her. He wondered what she had ordered. Did he make anything today that stood out, something she used to get?

Had she already eaten?

Was she waiting for the check? Soon to be out and gone? Out and on her way, never to return. This one-off chance ending the moment it was found. Should he talk to her? Should he ignore her? Should he push his face into the burner? Let the flames burn through his skull and calm his mind.

Neil held up a pan of charred bacon, raising it high and laughing, calling attention to Caesar's mistake with a childish smirk. "The fuck, man? I look away for a minute, and you burn the house down, the fuck?"

Caesar scraped some burnt pancakes into the rubbish as he barked, "Help me! Fucking jack-ass."

Neil rolled his eyes. "No need to yell."

Teddy was back, his hands digging into his head, stress and frustration falling out of his face. "What's this damn shit smoke! Everywhere we are burning! What're you done this now? How come how many you do?!"

Caesar tossed the burnt pans into a wash bin and shoved them at Neil, telling him to give them to the dish pit, and telling Teddy that his stress wasn't helping. Teddy took a step in, wafting away the smoke and filling the kitchen with more unnecessary and encrypted commentary. Crystal was going over the tickets, helping prep, trying to push Teddy out. Caesar was forgetting everything he was doing, everything Crystal was saying. He couldn't hold onto anything being said. The woman kept invading his mind. His attention kept returning to the diner, looking to see if she had turned and revealed her true identity.

Teddy was over his shoulder, his stress tangling nonsense into Caesar's ear. Caesar was mixing bowls and yelling at Neil to pull meat and cheese out of the fridge, to shut up, and put gloves on. Crystal was in the line pulling out onions and peppers and mushrooms and tossing them into the bowls Caesar was mixing. He kept screwing up what she was telling him, which was pissing her off. She was trying not to yell at him, but it was hard not to.

Caesar couldn't breathe.

Was this some freak chance? Could it be her? Just happened by? What if she found out he was here and she came to see him? What if things were different? *Jesus fucking Christ*, he thought.

What if she *was* looking for him?

Crystal jumped into his attention. "How many fucking pancakes are you mixing in that bowl, Caesar? Fuck, man, wake up!"

Caesar stopped mixing with a silent look, a look that said, *Fuck if I know*. Christ, there were eight omelets he had just burned, nine pancakes, four orders of hash browns, who knows how much meat. How long had he been standing there staring at her ponytail? What order got the cheddar BLT, and how the hell didn't it get burned? *Oh right*, he remembered.

Caesar had made himself the BLT.

Looking away from his smoking disaster, he couldn't see her. Caesar's eyes widened, and his breath shortened. She was gone. The mess he made reached up from below for his help, but he was miles away. Was she in the bathroom? Was she taking a call? Was she leaving in her car, turning the key and looking down the highway, the diner vanishing in her rearview mirror, never to return?

Caesar bolted from the kitchen, abandoning Crystal, dismissing Teddy's red-faced panic. Stumbling into the dining area, his eyes tripped over everyone, scanning faces, studying every table. She was gone. The place where she sat was all empty plates and a bill with no signature. Paid in cash.

Rushing outside, his heart fell over itself to learn every car in the parking lot. He scanned license plates to see where everyone had come from. What if she had moved? Did he even want to see her? Why would she be coming to see him? Things would never be different. Even if she changed back, she wouldn't come all this way. It'd been too long. Or had it?

What was he doing?

Sweating and panting, Caesar didn't want to talk to her. Had no idea what he'd even say. He was drowning in the image of that ponytail. The back of some mysterious head. Drowning in the memories it forced down his throat. He needed to know if it was her or not. Standing in that parking lot, struggling to breathe, Caesar felt all the feelings he ran away from all those years ago come swirling back up around his neck to strangle the life out of him.

Crystal rushed around the kitchen to fix the burnt orders. Crystal flipped omelets, flipped pancakes, cursed Caesar, and worried about Caesar. She pushed Teddy to get him. Teddy stood in the parking lot, biting his nails and looking for Caesar. He wasn't sure if he should be mad or concerned. Everyone knew Caesar was unstable, emotionally wrecked, an alcoholic liability they couldn't help but want to protect. A lost dog really, that's what he was to Teddy and, in a way, to Frances as well. Caesar was a lost dog who just needed food, shelter, and a friend. Most everyone who worked the inn understood well enough the tragic tale that was Caesar, the reason why he chose to drink. Only a few ever got to hear the details.

Those who didn't know not to ask.

Remembering was a bad thing. Bringing up the past put more holes in Caesar's ship. Sharing those stories just sunk him deeper into that helpless, hopeless sea of self-destruction. Teddy scavenged around the parking lot with the same fear he'd feel for his children—or something close to it. He dropped to his belly to look under cars. Eyed up and down the highway. Yelled into bathrooms. Checked his pulse and wiped his forehead clean from the panic slicking his skin.

The only place he didn't check was Caesar's room. It just seemed silly to him that he would go there, which in itself was silly. Where the hell else would he go?

It was exactly where he *had* gone.

Caesar was in his motel room. The place he had lived in for the past six years. His hole in the wall of everything and everywhere. He was hyperventilating, digging into his kitchen cabinets for a breath of fresh air. Fresh air from a bottle of spiced rum.

Glug-glug-glug.

And away went the memories.

III
KARAOKE &e CIGARETTES

The cigarette hadn't moved since it was lit. It was nothing more than a smoldering stick of ash with a filter resting in his fingers. His hand was dead on the bar. A moment frozen in time. Caesar was passed out on his face, his cheek smooshing his lips out funny, a half glass of stale beer sleeping beside him. The bartender had moved an ashtray to rest under his cigarette. The ash just never fell.

Crystal and Amber were stacking coasters on him. Caesar had towers of bar coasters resting on his head, his neck, his back, and shoulders. They stacked so many that it stopped being funny and started becoming a serious challenge. The stacks were becoming so serious the bartender had to go in the back to get a box of extra coasters.

They weren't at the Renaissance Inn's bar. They were a few miles down the road at a bar tucked into a little glowing strip mall. There was a convenience store, a small grocery store, a pizza shop, a Tex-Mex style restaurant, a generic clothing store, a few vacant spaces, and the bar. The place was called Bar.

Just "Bar".

Bar written in red neon lights.

The place played up on all the roadside gimmicks famously entertaining travelers across the USA. They had drinks named after every attraction. The Big String Martini, the Jolly Green Gin-arita, Giant Garden Gnome-Fashion, and the Frozen Alien Colada—things the locals never ordered. There was a small town not too far off the main road and a few trailer parks where most of the service workers took up residency. The bar named Bar was the locals' spot. It was where most everyone punched out for the day. It wasn't your usual gimmicky watering hole. There was more dust on the walls than there was decoration, and there was more decoration than walls.

A big crew from the Inn would go there for the karaoke every week, if not several times a week, which was why Caesar wound up there. He blacked out, and his legs carried him along the usual Caesar current. Polly was on the mic singing "Raspberry Beret." He always sang Prince. Polly was a slim Cuban man in his early sixties who was never without a fedora, even when he was waiting tables in the Inn. Even when he went for a swim in the Inn's pool. Friends joked he showered with a fedora. If the wind were to blow it off his noggin, there would be another one already on his head. He had a deep smoky voice that crackled when he went for the high notes but never actually got much higher than his low notes. He always sang with a big smile and a lively sway. Ever since he got his new hip, he'd been swaying bigger and braver.

When Frances entered the bar, he walked right to Crystal and Amber. He dramatically clasped his heart at the sight of Caesar, sinking a bit with each of his final steps up to the bar, saying, "My sweet Caesar pie. What happened? I heard he freaked out." His hands danced out in the air around the towers of coasters, asking, "What's this witchcraft you got go'n here? This seems mean, but I can't tell yet."

Amber shrugged and handed him a coaster. Frances waved it in the air and laughed under his breath. "You guys... this poor man doesn't deserve this. He needs love and affection. Not childish dorm room shenanigans." Examining the coaster construction, Frances carefully added to the stacks and clicked his tongue in his cheek to express he was impressed with the work they'd done. He asked how long Caesar had been sleeping on the bar, which was when he saw the cigarette—or rather the ash that hung where a cigarette once was.

"Jesus Christ," he uttered—sadness in his voice. Looking at Crystal with a heavy sigh, he picked up another coaster. As he added it to the stack resting on Caesar's head he said, "What a sad man." The bartender asked Frances if he was on duty, and Frances smiled. "Shift just ended, amigo, pour me a tequila."

Crystal liked Frances, liked him even more in uniform. She was happily married and would never cheat on the father of her children, but nothing would ever stop her from flirting. Especially with Frances, *especially* when he was in uniform. Odds were good they would both be dancing together before the night was done.

Crystal tugged on his sleeve and smiled at him. "So, how's the dating going? Your wife still playing matchmaker?" Frances took his shot from the bar and leaned into it, giving Crystal a playful look at his profile as he explained his ex-wife was getting him laid but not finding anything that stuck.

"Which, I mean, I'm not complaining, just surprised it's going the way it's going, ya know? I mean it's the woman I've lived with for over *fifteen years* — sure she was gay the whole time — but we were still close as puppies, ya know? And raising our two healthy boys together, we're a team. You'd think she would know me well enough to find a gal that fits me. *Well, shit, maybe that's the idea.* How the hell should I know? Maybe my ex-wife just wants to get me laid."

Frances laughed and raised his shot, summoning Crystal and Amber to do the same with their drinks. He praised his sex life with an "Amen!" and the three tapped their glasses and had a drink.

The first song Frances sang for the night was "You Dropped a Bomb On Me" by *The Gap Band*. Crystal molested him with her eyes while he sang. Some of the other women drinking that night were enjoying the man in uniform as well. Frances was hamming it up. He knew he was a looker. The handlebar mustache wasn't everyone's cup of tea, but it made it work.

He'd tell ladies, *"Grab me by the handlebar mustache and ride me like a motorcycle."*

It usually got a laugh. Sometimes got him more.

When Teddy showed up, Polly was back up on the mic singing more Prince, this time "When Doves Cry." He was really getting into it, closing his eyes, clenching his fist, swaying. His fedora tipped to the side. Teddy gave the coaster-covered Caesar a heavy sigh. He thrust his arms out, sort of hopeless, chastising the game his employees were playing on the broken Caesar. "What is this? Why do you do this to him?" Teddy asked, his grave, disappointed tone bearing a sincere weight. Removing coasters and shaking his head, Teddy almost wept. Teddy dropped the coasters on the bar and sighed again, condemning the game further. Crystal smiled at him. "You know he'd think it was funny." Amber chimed in, "And he'd do the same to you. Don't act like he wouldn't."

Teddy sipped his beer and sulked over Caesar. "I was worried about him all day. Burning all that food and running out this morning. I came over the moment I heard he was here." Crystal returned a coaster to Caesar's head, saying, "Seriously. He was on another planet. Whatever happened, it ran him right into a bottle." Teddy asked the bartender when Caesar got there. She said he showed up drunk just before sunset. Had a few beers and some cigarettes in silence and fell asleep. Been asleep for three hours.

Everyone talked about Caesar, standing around him, adding coasters to his restful figure. Even Teddy started to add some after a while. All of them picked songs to sing, writing their names on slips, and putting them into the hat for the DJ to pick out. Crystal sang "I Will Always Love You." Amber sang Queen's "Another One Bites the Dust." Crystal sang Joplin's "Me and Bobby McGee." Teddy sang "Jungle Love" by The Time. Frances did "Sweet Caroline" and "Wagon Wheel." Some other regulars went up, some road trippers, even the bartender sang a song—Bowie, Madonna, Blondie—typical karaoke goodies, nothing too obscure.

Polly sang more Prince.

When Caesar's name was called, everyone looked to him, still lying where he was, coasters still stacked on him. Had he added his name before he passed out? His name was called a second time, and the only part of him that moved was his fingers, flicking the ash stick into the ashtray. Frances was on the stage. He'd just finished "Respect." He had his shades on, but he still raised his hand over his eyes to get a good look at Caesar through the lights. He whistled a sharp hoot and said, "Caesar, buddy, you're up."

Caesar's head popped up abruptly as coasters spilled onto the floor. He stuck the dead filter into his mouth, patting at his chest pocket for a lighter while he dragged himself to the stage with one eye open. Frances handed him the mic and told him he was looking good. Caesar laughed a little, taking the mic and patting Frances on the shoulder. Finding his balance, Caesar realized he was trying to light a filter, and shook his head at himself. Tucking the mic under his arm, he dug into his pocket, pulling out a broken cigarette and lighting it while his friends cheered for him. Led Zeppelin's "Over the Hills and Far Away" started to play. Caesar smoked and belted out the lyrics. He wasn't the best singer, but for karaoke, he was golden, and his Robert Plant was arguably on point.

Caesar didn't remember finishing the song, and he didn't get off the stage on his own. He fell over flat on his back when he moved to bow and blacked out before his eyes closed on the way down. He woke up in the back of Frances' squad car. Frances was singing "I Shot the Sheriff" along with the tape deck. Caesar pulled another broken cigarette from his pocket and pushed his face into the cage, the cig in his lips poking through the metal mesh to the front. Frances smiled when he saw him, pulled a lighter from the dashboard, and toasted the tip of Caesar's cigarette.

"Morning, little buddy."

Caesar made a gesture but hadn't the strength yet for words. He just smiled and patted the cage. When the line in the song said "But I didn't shoot the deputy" Frances would sing "But I didn't shoot myself." This always made Caesar laugh. He laughed then, pushing himself from the cage, blowing out smoke as he settled back into the seat.

Frances was bubbly, telling Caesar, "You really tied one off today. You're gonna love the pic Crystal snapped of you. It's definitely wall-worthy."

The wall he was referring to was the back room of the local liquor store where they played poker. It was covered in pictures of friends and family when they were passed out. Both Caesar and Frances were on it more than once.

Frances put his fingers up to the cage. "Let me bum a pocket ciggie from ya, buddy."

Caesar labored over to reach into his pocket, pulling out a few, selecting the least damaged cigarette to hand over. Frances thanked him, lit the stick, and rolled his window down a bit, blowing the smoke out and singing, "But I didn't shoot my seh-eh-elf."

Caesar laughed more and let his drunken state settle him against the window as he sang with his friend. The tape changed songs, and they both sang together, singing like nothing was wrong. When Frances parked and helped Caesar walk to his door, they were both humming, "*No woman, no cry.*"

Caesar's home at the Inn was one of the smaller rooms. His unmade bed was pushed off to the left. The sort-of kitchen was to the right. In the middle, there was a futon slouched before a wall-mounted television next to the bathroom door. Caesar never turned it on. There was a picture taped on the screen he cut out from a magazine. It was an ad for the same television. He couldn't remember putting it up. The kitchen wasn't much to look at. It was a fridge and a toaster oven with a small counter and a smaller sink. The microwave's screen no longer lit up, but the thing still worked. The tiny kitchen area was floored with linoleum tile that poorly mocked some type of stone. The rest of the space was carpeted. Caesar's usual paths were forever stamped into the floor from door to bathroom, from bed to kitchen. Caesar had been living there for six years. Six years of footprints. The walls were dented and patched, scuffed and scratched. Piles of books outlined the small space. Caesar read a lot to keep his mind occupied. Mostly non-fiction, mostly history.

Other people's lives.

Lives already lived.

Caesar fell onto his futon, his cigarette still smoking in his lips, smile still on his face, "No Woman, No Cry" still in his head. Frances went right to his fridge. It was full of beers, condiments, and leftover containers from the diner—no produce, no ingredients, nothing that required work. Caesar was a well-paid chef before everything happened. Before his heart was wrecked, and his life ended but kept on going for some hilarious reason he had yet to discover. No matter how loud he screamed for a reason, the punch line always seemed to be something he was performing and nothing he was required to understand. His pain must've been a joke that was too funny for the gods to look away.

Frances took a beer from the fridge and dug out a bottle opener from a kitchen drawer. Caesar never drank beer where the cap could twist off, and he never drank anything from a can, although he loved the sound a can made when the tab punched its way in. Caesar just preferred glass. And he drank pricier booze because of the hangovers. Cheap poison hurt more in the morning. Not to mention, expensive alcohol really did taste a great deal better.

Or was it just all in his head?

Frances took a big gulp of beer and shared his usual praise for Caesar's taste. Caesar, slouched over with his head on the armrest, cigarette dying in his lips, eyes closed, softly said, "That's because I'm fucking awesome." Frances plopped himself on the futon, pushing Caesar's feet out of his way. He wanted to ask Caesar why he ran out of work, but he didn't want to upset him. Wiping beer from his stash, he told him, "You know you can come to me with anything, you know that, right? I will drop *any*thing if you need me, buddy."

Caesar smiled. "Liar."

Frances took a thoughtful breath and said, "Of course, my kids come first, but hell, I'd add you to the loop, man. If they had a doctor's thing or something, you could wait in the waiting room with me. I'm just saying, fucking, like, I'd add you to the process no matter what. You get me? You don't have to think if I got my hands full or whatever, I wouldn't be accessible."

"Even if I was a drunk mess?"

"*Especially* if you were a drunk mess. Sick all over your chin and your shirt all nasty with bad choices. Kids need to see that crap, so they don't fuck up their lives. You'd be a good role model in that regard. A warning sign on how not to live. A walking PSA."

"Piece of shit asshole?"

"Shut up."

Caesar smiled and reached his hand out to tap Frances, but he was too far away, so he just patted his own leg and said he would puke on himself for the kids anytime. The cigarette had gone out, but he kept it in his lips and continued to pull on it with his breath. Frances repeated, "I'm serious, man, you have my number. I could'a come and picked you up today, and we could'a, I don't know, fuckin' anything really. Just want you to know I'm always here for you, is all. Don't gotta be alone, not when you got me." Caesar kept his eyes closed, still smiling, his hand reaching again but not quite reaching as he managed to say, "I love you too, Mr. Policeman."

Frances patted Caesar's leg, smiling and drinking, grateful for the silly drunk and the friendship they'd formed. Despite the mess Caesar was, he was a good friend. He always opened his door when Frances needed to crash. When it hurt too much to sleep at home. Sleeping on that same futon was how their first night of friendship began. When their miseries first found company. Caesar had been on a bridge with a bottle in his hand. Frances responded to a call of a man on a bridge.

He hadn't been there to jump.

Just to drink.

And for whatever reason, Caesar felt compelled to share his story with the stranger in uniform. Frances sat on the bridge with him and started drinking after he heard it. Had a few drinks and shared his own heartbreak story right back. It was that night they had their first drink together, emptied their first bottle.

Frances didn't feel like he was helping Caesar, at least not as much as Caesar had helped him. Frances was always just his escape. But he never seemed to get any better. Caesar was a part of his family, in a sense. Frances was counting all the ways Caesar had helped out with him and his kids over the years. Some of the best dinners he'd had with his family, Caesar was cooking. He wished he could think of something he could do for his little buddy. This was when Caesar farted and started laughing. Frances smiled at him and said, "You may want to wash after that one."

"At this point, I don't think anyone would notice," Caesar told him, his eyes still closed. Frances shook his head. "People always notice a dude with his pants full'a shit. Can't hide shit."

Caesar huffed, "I am shit."

Frances turned to Caesar with a bothered look, his tone disappointed. "Come on, man, that's not funny."

Hearing how upset his joke left Frances made Caesar feel bad. But he didn't apologize or attempt to turn things around. Caesar didn't want to cheer things up. It felt right that the fun atmosphere was returning to its normal discontent. That woman in the diner who had his ex-wife's hair, who moved as she did — her image kept turning to look at him but never making it all the way around. His mind spun around delusional fantasies of an impossible reuniting.

Caesar rolled over and said painfully, "I'm just a pair of shit-filled pants." Frances pushed at him, "Don't talk about yourself like that." His tone was moving from upset to annoyed, almost angry. Standing up, Frances expressed his detest for Caesar's self-bullying, telling him, "It's not good, talking about yourself like that. I can't stand it. You're my friend, so if you keep talking about my friend like that, I'm gonna have to kick your ass."

"I was just joking."

"No, you weren't, man."

Now Caesar felt guilty. Frances had a genuine pain straining his face. A pain that inspired Caesar to apologize.

"Sorry," he said, aiming the blame away from himself by adding, "I hang out with Crystal too much. She loves the self-deprecating jabs." Raising his beer, Frances replied, "Well, Crystal's sense of humor is fucked up." He took a swig and thought out loud, "As motherly and kind as she can be, the woman's twisted. No offense to her." Taking another swig, he mumbled into his bottle, "If she was single..." Standing still for a moment, the bottle to his lips, eyes floating from the room, Frances fantasized what it would be like to follow through with Crystal's flirtatious friendship.

If she was single.

Taking another swig, he dug up a blanket from a pile of things in the corner and covered Caesar. Caesar apologized again for his jokes. Frances smiled at his sad little buddy.

Caesar asked him, "How do you do it, sleep with someone else?"

Frances shrugged. "How do you mean?"

"When you've loved someone, you don't lose that. Two people getting together who have loved others, like... they both have to know, there are parts missing. You know? Like, they gave all this to someone before. A seat was made in their heart that can't be unmade. It doesn't fit anyone else. The spot is eternally reserved. They're in there even when they're not. You love someone, they're here in the world, but people move on to other people, hold someone else. You were just holding them. Now you're holding... *not them.* Holding people who held other people. Seems like you're less and less complete with each person. Just keep lining up empty seats inside yourself. How do you make room? Is it just me? Do I not have enough space in my heart to make another seat? Or do I really just not want to? I don't know what I'm trying to say."

Frances laughed a little. "I get what you mean. It ain't easy. First person I slept with after my wife, you know, I, uh, well, I couldn't keep it up... my dick couldn't stay hard. Only time it's happened. And it was because of exactly that... it was someone else, you know. First person after all those years with just my wife. I couldn't get over it. Couldn't stop thinking about her. Felt like I was cheating even though I wasn't. Felt wrong. Like, it wasn't fun, you know. It was just sad. I was accepting that it was over, that's what the sex was, and well that just really didn't turn me on. I didn't want to be with anyone else. Didn't want to believe it was over. Couldn't stop thinking about her and how it was supposed to be her. It was an old friend, too, the one I was try'n with. Probably why it got so far. Already comfortable and all that. Old high school friend I ran into. Wonderful person. Ended up looking at old yearbooks all night instead'a fucking. Gets easier, though. Changes it. Everything's changing. Part of you stays behind, like you said. How could it not? When you love someone, shit, you'll always love them no matter what. But yeah, it's not easy to move on. I don't know. It all sucks, man. Fuck. Why you think we drink so damn much?"

Frances cleared his throat and emptied his beer, then got another one out on his way to the door. Caesar watched him, not knowing what to say and thinking to himself that Frances was a better friend than he was. He felt he only added burden to Frances' life.

Frances opened the door and said, "You sleep tight now, Julius."

Caesar had his eyes perched up on the edge of the futon to see Frances off. He cringed and winced before saying, "*Julius?* I can't like that."

Frances smiled and tipped his beer to him. "Light on or off?"

"Off."

The light went out, and the door closed. Caesar sighed a breath of failure, feeling like a worthless friend. He sighed, knowing he wasn't going to fall asleep. He pulled a broken cigarette from his pocket and lit it. His hands appear in the flash of his lighter and then vanish. The cherry tip of his cigarette floated in the nothing before him. The only thing to see was the little dot of fire in a sea of blackness. It felt comforting to think it all ended up in a place as simple as nowhere. A placeless place.

It just took too long to get there.

The mystery ponytail returned to his mind, only it managed to turn all the way around, and he could see her face. Her smile, her big brown eyes. The way they shined when she looked at him. He was in those eyes. She held him there because she loved him. What greater place was there than in her view? Being the person that made someone smile like that. What a feeling that was. Eternity passing by in brief little moments of silent bliss. The comfort of such a look. Being loved and loving back. She was so vivid in his mind. He could see her, but he couldn't reach her. The warm loving feeling recoiled with an abrasive jolt. Like he slipped and fell. Some proverbial rug yanked from under his feet.

His breath shortened, and his heartbeat stumbled out a troubling rhythm. The gap in time spent without her seemed to unravel before him, pulling a noose tight around his throat as he felt the years of her absence drain the life from him. Like he had chosen the wrong path. Took a wrong turn somewhere. Lost out on what should have been. A desperate urge to reach out and hold on flushed his skin with a cold sweat.

Caesar pulled a bottle of rum out from under the futon and popped the cork. He didn't take a drink right away, but just tucked it close to his chest and pulled a drag from his haggard cigarette. Smoked to stop himself from crying. He couldn't help but think the woman in the diner was her. That he had a chance to see her again. That he could have done something.

Tell her again how sorry he was.

Ask her if she thinks about him.

If she remembers him sometimes and smiles.

Taking a big breath from the bottle, he asked the rum to help him think about anything else.

IV
WALKING DEAD

Caesar woke up damp. The only ground for miles that ever seemed to hold any moisture was the well-groomed landscape of the Greenwood cemetery. Caesar sat up, wincing into the sky, wondering what time it was. The sun wasn't too far off the ground. Still, he had a good feeling he was going to be late for work. What a way to start the day, failing before you're even up. Today would be a series of disappointed looks emotionally veneered with the aging concern his friends always try to hide. The elephant Caesar was in all rooms.

Fuck me, Caesar thought to himself.

The bottle of rum he had pulled from under his futon was empty beside him, along with a few dead cigarette butts. Caesar plucked around the moist grass, pocketing the used ends. Heavy sighs spilled out around his efforts in these sad, bitter heaps of breath.

What kind of life was this?

Spinning himself around, he wanted to see whom he had spent the night with. The engraving on the tombstone was worn, but the name and date were still legible. It was some fellow who had passed in his eighties. Kicking the bottle, Caesar smiled at the grave. "How much'a this did you have?"

Caesar picked himself up, empty bottle of rum in hand, exhaling a painfully hungover breath. Wobbling as he managed to get his feet upright, a burp rolled from his gut that caught the inside of his cheek like a ship's sails catching the morning deciding winds. It hinted at some distant need to vomit.

Caesar needed a drink.

Looking at the tombstone, he glared and said, "Don't haunt me." With a dying cough, he dug around his pocket, pulling out a few smoked cigarettes. His fingernails caught his eye. They needed to be cleaned and cut. They looked like he'd been burying bones in someone's yard. Or perhaps he had just climbed out of his own grave. Caesar, the Walking Dead.

Poking around at cigarettes in his dirty palm made his mind drift. He didn't really care to smoke any of them. Didn't have the energy to get a lighter out, to raise his arms to spark the flame and breathe in. Caesar didn't want to bother moving his legs to carry himself to work and labor through orders. He didn't even have it in him to summon the force to sit back down, which was all he wanted — to be down on the ground laid out on his back doing nothing.

Absolutely nothing.

No one waiting around, no obligations, no responsibilities, no plans. Nothing but nothing. But he couldn't even see the point in lying down to start the nothing. Standing still, not moving, was already so much nothing. This was going to be a bad day. Odds were strong someone might try to get him to talk about his feelings. The last thing he wanted was to talk. He had tried that before. It didn't help. Caesar just wanted nothing. Complete and utter absolute zero.

A familiar voice interrupted Caesar's sunny, inner discord.

"I should start charging you rent," the voice said, a hint of humor in its delivery. Caesar kept looking at the mess of cigarettes in his palm while he answered, "Rent? Henry, I thought we paid with our lives to get into this resort of yours."

Henry laughed, "Yeah, that's one way'a look'n at it."

When Caesar turned to greet Henry, his eyes strained to focus. They were sore. Heavy lids worn raw from a long night of missing things long since passed. Henry noticed right away. Sympathy leaned into him, and he shook his head at Caesar's sad, puffy eyes. Henry was a slim Black man in his mid-sixties with a long wrinkled face that he wore clean-shaven, big, purple bags under his eyes, and dark gray hair he kept short. He always wore suspenders.

He was sitting in a golf cart, leaning on the wheel with his elbow, his chin set in his hand. His expression hung as he noticed the empty bottle and the handful of used cigarettes. Making a friendly but still judgmental *'tisk-tisk-tisk'* sound with the back of his throat, he commented, "You've been sleeping in my cemetery for four years now, haven't changed much."

"Christ, it's been that long?"

"I should start charging you rent."

"You made that joke already."

Henry patted his chest pocket, laughing and saying he wasn't making a joke. From his chest pocket, he produced a pack of smokes, made a motion with his hand, and one of them stuck out as an offering. Caesar pocketed his butts and took the fresh stick from Henry's pack. Henry told him to join him. Told him he had some fresh coffee he needed help drinking.

Caesar lit the cigarette and took a long drag before replying, "Raincheck. I'm pretty sure I'm late for work. Got a long sober walk ahead of me."

"Hell, I'll take you to work. Coffee first."

Caesar stood for a moment, smoking the cigarette and considering the offer. He wasn't yet ready for the world. Still a little drunk, but not enough to dull the pain from his long night. Caesar's brain wasn't quite awake. It was mostly the idea of having to interact that had him considering rejecting the offer. Did he have it in him? It wasn't a long drive to the diner, but it wasn't a short drive either — not for the condition he was in. He and Henry had never had a conversation that lasted longer than twenty minutes. This was also his first invite to coffee. Typically, they just joked and smoked cigarettes, and Caesar went on his way. Henry insisted. "Hop on Caesar, I need to get something to eat anyhow. I'm craving that Reuben you all make. Ted's sauerkraut. Whatever he does, he does it right."

Caesar smiled a bit. "No one does sauerkraut right."

Henry sat up. "Not a fan?"

"Sauerkraut is the puke of food."

Caesar climbed into the cart, the fresh cigarette smoking out from his lips, an empty bottle in his lap. Henry was more than just the groundskeeper for the cemetery. He also owned and

ran the Greenwood Funeral Home that filled it. Henry Greenwood, son of Nathaniel Greenwood. There were twelve Greenwood's buried in the field. Caesar jokingly called Henry "the Reaper" up until they officially introduced themselves a year back. Henry enjoyed the nickname, often waking up Caesar to tell him he wasn't ready for him yet. It always got a laugh.
The cart took off, and Henry didn't wait long to ask something he'd been wondering.

"How long's it been since you went to see the actual grave that keeps you coming back here?"

Caesar blew his smoke away from Henry as he replied, "What makes you think I'm here for someone?" Henry laughed under his breath, almost rolling his eyes, ignoring Caesar's deflection. Turning the cart, he kept at him, asking, "Ever think about going to it? Pay your respects. Maybe get some closure."

Caesar shook his head, wishing the conversation would end, taking another drag, blowing the smoke away from Henry. Keeping his sights out over the graves, he answered with a heavy breath, telling him, "No."

Henry gave him a close look, curious. Looking back to the path, he explained, "You drink yourself here so often, seems you might need to." Caesar was silent, his sore eyes keeping watch over the graves. He didn't want to talk about himself and hoped his silence expressed that.

Henry felt he might have jumped ahead of himself, with their friendship being what it was, and apologized. "I don't mean to pry. I know it's none of my business. It's just... Well, I've seen a lot of grieving faces. Yours doesn't seem to change. And you're the only person I've ever known to sleep over in a graveyard and to do it frequently enough to call it a habit. Must be something heavy you got locked away." Caesar put the cigarette out and pocketed it for later. Politely he asked if they could talk about anything else. Henry was quick to accept and said he meant no offense.

"None taken, Henry. I appreciate you not kicking me out for *sleeping over*. I've never really explained myself, so I understand why you'd ask."

After a few silent breaths, Caesar decided to open up, just a little, sharing, "There *is* a sort of tombstone I don't visit. It's very far away. Try not to think about it. I drink, I blackout, I wake up here. Never even knew there *was* a cemetery around here 'til I woke up in your backyard. But I think that's all I'm able to say about that now." Caesar choked on the end of his sentence, squeezing the empty bottle in his lap telling himself, he just needed to get a drink. Take the day's first breath. A breakfast shot to get him out of his head and dull the hangover.

Henry was nodding. "I understand. I've been at this my whole life, good at it, too. Some people take a long time to find the words they need to talk about loss. Some just need to sit with it."

Caesar cleared his throat. "Now there's something we've never talked about."

Henry smiled and asked, "What's that?"

"Your funeral home. I wonder sometimes… when people come in, like, when a family member's died, and they come to you to organize the… all that shit. I don't know, like, how do you make it feel like it's not just a business transaction? Sort of a fucked up thing to charge money for."

Henry shrugged and leaned back, answering, "Every death is different, just gotta feel people out. Never push, never suggest one way or the other. Just show them the options, explain, and let them decide. The important thing is to listen to them. Really, it's just about letting them know you're there for them, to do all the work so they can focus on saying goodbye."

Henry stopped the cart behind the funeral home, talked about grabbing his coffee, and asked Caesar if he needed to use the restroom. He did. It was his first time in the funeral home. It was a clean building. Everywhere Caesar went was usually dirty. Working kitchens, bars, liquor stores, his messy room. Clean places stood out. Made him think again about his nails.

They entered through the kitchen. Henry lived in the building with his wife who was in the kitchen doing something with a shoe. She looked up with a warm smile as they came in, and, glancing to Caesar, asked Henry who his friend was. Henry made his way to the coffee pot as he answered, "This is that Caesar fella."

Her brow narrowed on Caesar. "You're the man who's always sleeping out there with *them*, huh?" Caesar awkwardly nodded his head, unsure how the woman felt about him. She made a face that could go either way before she turned her attention back to the shoe, saying nothing more. Caesar's full bladder quickly turned to Henry, who pointed and said, "Bathroom's right around the corner."

The restroom was next to a casket display. All of it was very clean. It was a unisex bath and the lock told you if it was occupied so you wouldn't tug on the door when someone was pants-down on the toilet. Caesar wished more bathrooms had this kind of lock. Few things in life are as unsettling as someone yanking on the door while you're dropping a load.

This bathroom had a tall urinal and a bowl with a handicap rail. There was even a place for changing diapers, but it wasn't the plastic folding shelf typically seen in public restrooms. It was wooden and even had a pad for the baby's comfort. The urinal had a cinnamon-scented cake that foamed up at Caesar's feet as he relieved himself. The smell bothered him. It was the fact that it was his piss that activated the aroma. Urinal cakes always made him feel like he was pissing into his nose with a lie.

As he flushed, Caesar got a better look at the dirt under his nails. It stood out even more in contrast with his neat and tidy surroundings.

While he washed his hands, he noticed band aids above the sink along with lotions, mints, and tampons. Caesar wondered if there was an incident with a client that inspired the offer of tampons. How often was a tampon taken because someone *actually* needed one? He wondered how many people would feel comfortable taking one for later—taking one while considering the chance they might be stealing it away from a human in a future dilemma. He pictured someone finding themselves having one of those days — filling out the paperwork to bury a loved one, heartbroken, bloated, cramping, breasts aching, and just to seal every exit, another egg dies in the middle of it all. Against their consent, future life evacuates from the body in a puddle of blood — clean-up in aisle thighs. Given the circumstances, they'd be too preoccupied to consider the possibility of a visit from old Aunt Flo. There's no casket for a period. No paperwork to fill out for the newly-micro-departed. Just a shelf in a funeral home with no more tampons. An awkward predicament and a dusty outline around a stolen gesture.

If, of course, there *were* people like that—tampon thieves.

Caesar figured they probably stocked the supply regularly. The way Henry seemed to operate, they were most likely prepared for the occasional non-menstruating tampon harvester. Caesar used to always have a spare tampon on him back when he was married. Never left the house without one. He couldn't figure out why men were so uncomfortable when it came to handling feminine products. Seemed idiotic, this silly stigma his gender embodied. Was it fear of male ridicule or some sexual orientation superstition? Maybe if they held a tampon for too long, their dicks would invert and start bleeding on a monthly routine. He remembered the first time he picked up a box for his wife. It was early in their relationship. She was impressed with him. He could see her face scrunching up, delighted, and surprised.

Happy.

She was always so happy to see him.

Caesar was trying not to think about it.

V
ROCK BOTTOM

Caesar's fluff of receding hair was enjoying the fifteen-mile-an-hour wind of Henry's golf cart. The little electric motor took its time down the back road. The passing traffic seemed to drive right through Caesar's hangover. Occasionally a car would honk at them, filling Caesar's skull with a horrendous pressure. His eyes would bulge, brain would moan, and the radio would disappear under another roaring engine. As the cars passed, Caesar wished he had asked for a drink back at the funeral home. Every morning, usually before breakfast, Caesar would have his first drink. The first drink of the day was the most important drink of the day. It eased the aches and tamed the shakes. Thankfully, Henry didn't try to talk. He just drove Caesar to work. Parked and smiled.

Caesar climbed out of the cart, thanking Henry again for the ride, and telling him to enjoy his vomit sandwich. Caesar wasn't going in just yet. He wanted to grab a drink from his room before beginning work. Drink a beer and fill his flask. Maybe have a screwdriver. Maybe eat some of the cheese that was still in his fridge. Cheese or not, the screwdriver sounded nice. And it would've been. Henry opened the door before Caesar was clear, leaving him exposed to his coworkers inside.

Amber spotted Caesar while Henry held the door open, and she saw him see her. The window of time to play dumb and turn away was long gone. There was full, undeniable eye contact. Caesar gave her a look that said, *You don't see me*. But she did see him. And he could see in her eyes the weight of concern. Emotion and compassion and an ocean of questions already pulling him toward her. If he could evade the conversation, there was booze stashed in the kitchen. Caesar needed that drink, any drink. It couldn't be stressed enough— breakfast is the most important drink of an alcoholic's day. It would take every ounce of his will to not be an asshole to anyone before that first drink. Keeping things as brief as possible was of grave concern.

As he got closer, the look on Amber's face made him want to apologize for getting in her life. He should know better than to bother people with himself. He should just move under a bridge and drink himself into the foundation. A drink wouldn't care so much if he was upsetting his friends. A couple of drinks wouldn't care if he had friends at all.

"Are you okay, Caesar?" Amber was hesitant with her question.

His eyes were sinking into a void of light. Dead marbles that floated in the purple bags of his lower lids, puffed and swollen with a depressing exhaustion. It was obvious the answer to her question was that he was nowhere close to okay. He deflected anyway. "Never better. I got to sleep in."

"You look like you have never slept a day in your life."

Caesar laughed, happy to see she was letting him pass. He was always grateful when someone could tell he didn't want to talk, and they didn't fight him when he tried to go.

As he passed, she sighed a playful breath, asking, "What are we gonna do with you?" Caesar patted her shoulder and smiled, "You could get me a drink." Amber laughed under her breath. "Of course. You never change."

"That's not true."

With his back pushing against the kitchen door, he shrugged. "Sometimes I change my drink order."

In the kitchen, Caesar was greeted with a mixed bag—a taunting-teasing sort of roar. Crystal was laughing, "Well, well, look who it is! What day is it? Are you on the schedule today? No. You must be confused. Or is this just a friendly pop-in on your day off 'cause you love us so much?"

"Ha ha," Caesar said.

The crescendo of his greeting roar fizzled out into serious looks. Serious looks and a serious sigh that collectively asked, "The fuck were you?"

Crystal blew out a watermelon-scented cloud of weed with the question. She leaned on the counter, her expression suggesting that he not bullshit her. Caesar couldn't tell if she was mad or worried or both. It was probably both. Another line cook had a ticket in his hand he was waiting to read. He wanted to hear the answer to Crystal's question. Caesar made his way to the sink, pushing the question away with, "I had a doctor's appointment." His mind was reaching out for the nearest vodka, wondering when a good time would present itself to take that breakfast breath.

Crystal chuckled at this attempt at an excuse, biting back, "Yeah, right, *you* at a doctor's office, and I can suck my own dick. Where's your note, huh? No doctor's note?" The other cook read the ticket in his hand, no longer interested in where Caesar had been. Caesar started washing his hands, saying the doctor told him he wasn't worth a note. Didn't want to waste the paper.

This got more laughs.

There was a bottle of vodka in the walk-in fridge, which Caesar strategized to seize. Better to drink out of sight. Not that it usually mattered. Everyone at the diner drank at work. Given the circumstances, Caesar figured since it was his drinking that made him late and that made everyone worry about him, he should hold off until he did some work — common courtesy, or something like that.

Or was he overthinking it?

How pissed were they?

Were they even pissed?

Crystal pocketed her vape in the front pouch on her apron, dismissing the itch to interrogate and instead let Caesar settle in. She told him to glove up and start cooking.

No one seemed pissed.

Caesar washed his hands and pulled two gloves from a box. Only he couldn't get them on. His hands were shaking too much. Withdrawals are quick with alcohol. Crystal noticed his struggle. Caesar could feel her watching him. Imagined what pitiful she was thinking. He wanted to scream at his fingers to go in the goddamn gloves. Crystal silenced his mind by telling him not to worry about the stupid gloves, just get some meat cooking. He couldn't bear to look at her, and instead gave her a shame-filled nod and tossed the impossible gloves aside. Whatever resentment Crystal may have had, it was clear in her tone she was more worried about him than mad. Caesar would prefer everyone to just be mad. Anger was easier to absorb, and it didn't stow as much guilt.

Caesar's hands shook more as he opened a packet of sausage, the links spilling out onto the floor, an angry *fuck* spilling out of his mouth. The other cook caught a quick glimpse of Crystal's face hanging with sympathy. His eyes asked, *What should we do?* Crystal shrugged, and he turned from the scene to hide in his prep. Caesar reached down, and Crystal told him to leave it. Looking up at her, he sighed, sort of laughed at himself, and shook his head to confess, "I need a fucking drink." Crystal smiled a painful smile and said, "No shit." They shared a brief, awkward smile.

Crystal had never seen him like this. It made her reflect. It made her realize Caesar really did have a drink in him every time she saw him. She suggested he heal himself with the bottle under the prep line, suggesting further, "Why don't you hop on the tickets." Pointing to the other cook, she asked, "you mind switching with the injured?" The cook burped and shrugged. He didn't care.

This was when Teddy entered. Caesar was still kneeling over the loose meat sticks, feeling pathetic. Now he had Teddy with his heavy sigh shadowing over him. The look on Teddy's face disgusted Caesar. *My poor lost dog,* he was probably thinking. This pity made Caesar angry. Sometimes he felt like Teddy just missed his kids being kids and held onto the feeling by looking after Caesar in the same light. At least that's what he told himself when he hated everything. That his help was selfish, and it had nothing to do with him.

When Teddy folded his arms and asked him where he was, Caesar could tell Teddy wanted to hug him, maybe tuck him into bed and check his temperature, tell him everything was going to be okay, and call him "champ." Caesar was too worn out to give him shit. He just told him he was sorry, had a really bad morning, and that it wouldn't happen again.

Teddy, being the worrying parent that he was, spoke his concern. "You tell me same last time. So how is now different?" The fatherly tone irked him. Caesar was now no longer too worn out to give Teddy shit, and he smart-assed back, saying, "There's no one here, Ted."

This was true. There was only one table.

Teddy yapped, "That's behind the point, Caesar." He clasped his hands for emphasis, adding, "You know we schedule short when you're on, and we get rushed most days. None of us we can predict when the busy happens. We need you here when you're scheduled."

Caesar forfeited the argument and surrendered to the pity, mostly wanting Teddy to calm down. His English was falling apart, and it dug into Caesar's hangover. "I'm sorry," Caesar said, "I don't know what to tell you. I woke up in a cemetery. I'm fucked up. I'm not going to get better anytime soon."

Teddy moved to pound his fist against the wall but stopped himself and tensely tapped it, grinding his teeth. His stressed expression was torn between whether he should continue reprimanding Caesar or drag him to an AA meeting and chain him to a sponsor. Crystal and the other cook shared an awkward look. Both of them mouthed the word, *Cemetery.* Caesar could've choked on the discomfort, it was so abundant. His miserable life was getting in everyone's way.

A *ding!* in the kitchen window stole the spotlight.

Amber was setting a coffee down for Caesar while she rang the bell to let everyone know that two tour buses were unloading in the parking lot. Everyone froze. It was a senior citizen group on a Route 66 landmark excursion, and they chose the Inn for their lunch break destination.

The fan, as the famous idiom so poetically foretells, was soon to be hit with shit.

Everyone turned to Teddy with the same troubled look. Crystal voiced the question they were all thinking.

"They didn't call ahead?"

Teddy slapped himself on the forehead. They *had* called ahead, a week in advance, in fact, to make sure there was enough seating for forty old sightseers, plus two guides and two drivers.

Teddy had forgotten.

The other cook's nostrils flared. He was gripping a spatula and glaring at Teddy, saying, "*God* damn it, Ted, we're not prepped for a full house." Amber reminded everyone there were only two servers. Teddy waved his hands in the air, saying he would help wait tables.

Amber growled, "*And* expedite *and* seat these people?"

Caesar had fished out a bottle of vodka during the commotion. The lid spun off, and he tipped the bottle back, his aches dissolving, anxiety washing away as the fresh air flowed through him. The bottle sailed from his lips, relieving the weight of the world from his shoulders. Caesar was now ready for the day. He rang the bell and took his place in the pilot's seat, saying, "Let's get ahead of it. How's the line look?" Crystal opened her line fridge and scanned the bins, shaking her head to say, "I'm half-full here." The other cook chimed in from the back stock fridge, reporting more of the same.

Lining the window with little ceramic containers, Caesar ordered, "I'll start chopping veggies. Let's get the basics working. Let's get eggs scrambling, spuds frying. Start cooking sausages and bacon and cut more potatoes — hash browns all day." Filling the sauce containers with vodka, Caesar asked who needed a shot. Teddy ran his fingers through his hair, nearly tearing his face off as he reacted, "What in fuck are you doing? Damn god! You can't be damned fucking real!" The other cook held a shot up right away, joining Caesar with a look of solidarity to the group. Crystal smiled. "Fuck yes, shots. Exactly what we need, Teddy. A little fire under our asses. Let's feed these gorgeous geezers." The ladies in the window both took up a shot and joined the line of faces looking to Teddy. Crystal gave Teddy a big playful grin and waved him over. "Come on, Teddy, you need this more than anyone. Plus, it'll help your English." Everyone agreed, encouraging Teddy to join them.

Rolling his eyes and huffing under his breath in his native tongue, Teddy stepped up to the window and reluctantly raised a shot with the group. He was conflicted about the drink. Everybody was. The elephant in the kitchen had poured it. They were always a little troubled with Caesar's drinking. That was just part of the Caesar package. They were all just happy to see him smiling. There wasn't any time for an intervention, so arguments aside, it was the perfect uniting gesture for the storm ahead.

The old were coming.

Caesar smiled and toasted, "To Teddy forgetting."

Most everyone chuckled. Teddy just sighed. Still, everyone tapped their drinks and shot them back.

Vodka was the kitchen's drink of choice because it didn't stink up your breath. You could hide it in any beverage and not bother anyone.

The kitchen went to work as the elderly shuffled in — a platoon of frail waddles and big, magnified eyes, chitchatting their way into every nook and cranny. Walkers rested at the ends of tables, reminiscent of baby seats. Like an omen, the walkers were symbols for the skeletal remains of their youth. One last meal before the curtain closes. Inspiration for a painting on the modern-day circle of life.

Once the orders started lining up in the window, they didn't stop. Every operation the kitchen had was in use. The diner was loud. Plates were crowding the window. Caesar was spinning in circles, setting orders when a plate bumped the others, knocking a bun off the top of a burger. Caesar grabbed a fresh bun top and spun back around to set it, grabbing a new ticket on his way back around. Spinning and reading the new order, he spun again and heard a man bark, "You fucking serious?"

The chatter in the diner dimmed slightly in response to the remark. Caesar sipped his mostly-vodka coffee, putting an eye out the window in search of the man who had just barked.

Things seemed tense.

The tension was pulling the room towards a burly white man sitting at the bar who had half a burger in his hand and some chewed food in his cheek. Keeping his mouth to one side, he barked again, "HEY! You serious?"

Caesar was the target of the "you." It caught him off guard. It was clear the man was pissed. Caesar saw Amber preparing herself to play hospitality. But he also saw that the upset man was staring *him* down — even had his hand up with a big, fat finger pointing out big and fat right at him. He had the hands of a working man, swollen from a life of manual labor. Hands that could crush a common handshake into dust. Hands that set the half-eaten burger down so all of his fat fingers could gesture if need be. He continued to call out to Caesar. "Yeah, *you*, bug eyes. You just touched that bun. You grope'n everyone's food?"

Great, Caesar thought, *now my mishaps are upsetting customers.* And he was doing so well managing the rush. At least he thought he was. Everyone was already watching him so closely. Every mistake now would only add to the weight piling onto him. He couldn't win. And he never liked the glove rule. Customer complaints about it always bothered him. He was disgusted by people who were disgusted by people. This man wasn't concerned with hygiene. There was a pile of change by his plate he had clearly been playing with. It was neatly stacked next to his food. Dirty, molested coins he fiddled with while he raw-pawed his meal into his face. Caesar thought, *Fuck gloves and fuck this man.*

Caesar pointed to himself and made a dumb face, pointing like, *Who, me?*, purposely agitating the man further. Amber intercepted, and the man turned his complaint to her. "He's touching the food with his bare hands. What is this? I mean, come on, that's disgusting."

Amber ping-ponged apologies between his complaint and Caesar, looking for some support, but Caesar wouldn't budge. There was a heart filled with years of self-resentment in need of lashing out. The lunch rush had been so busy that no one had noticed Caesar had finished the bottle of vodka. It was lying empty in the rubbish. The last few ounces of the clear spirit were swimming in what was left of his coffee.

Caesar opened his mouth and put the drink back. Coal tossed into the burning belly of an old-fashioned locomotive. Clearing his rosy nose, Caesar leaned into the window and grinned at the big man but spoke to Amber, telling her, "Don't listen to this hypocrite."

Amber froze, thinking—*god-damnit Caesar.*

The angry man stood up and squawked, "Hypocrite?"

Caesar sighed like he wasn't interested, a gesture made to further irritate the man. Turning to the steaming brute, he asked, "You wash your hands before you started eating that burger?

The man's face scrunched, and he growled, "What? No, I didn't wash my freagg'n hands. I'm not touching other people's food."

Caesar shook his head and said, "Of course not. But you touched the door on your way in, pawed up the counter, the menu, your change there. Then you picked up the burger with those hands and stuffed your face."

The man sneered, "Fuck you. You're the one working in the kitchen. I can touch my own food, asshole."

Caesar leaned in further. "You know how many people dig at their balls and then open that door? Pick and scratch their butts and then come in here fingering the place up? Their balls are all over your hands now, all over your *burger*. You're stuffing their balls into your mouth and now yelling that mouth at me."

Steam almost whistled from the man's ears as he replied with, "The fuck?" Teddy jumped over the counter like a cat pouncing on a mouse, trying to calm the man, asking what the problem was. Caesar made a patronizing face and said, "No, Teddy, don't feed this crap. It's a psychological problem this man has, and I refuse to enable his social illness."

The man spat, "What are you talking about? You can't touch people's food. It's a health thing."

Caesar sneered, "If germs bothered you, *you'd* be wearing gloves right now. Not eating in public with your bare hands, not fondling loose change. So, this complaint you have with me has nothing to do with germs. The door-balls all over your mouth can attest to that." The man gestured firmly for Caesar to join him, saying, "Why don't you come out here and talk to me like that." Caesar laughed. "So, I can smell the balls on your breath? No thanks, guy."

Crystal was pulling on Caesar, telling him to ease up. The man he was lashing out at was big and turning red. Crystal's tug gifted Caesar a fresh view of just how upset he had made Teddy. This kind of upset was a rare shape on Teddy's face. A real nerve was struck. Caesar felt he was failing in a real way. Like he was disappointing his father. This added points to the scoreboard of hating himself. But it also itched at that surrogate parental fantasy Caesar projected onto Teddy's intentions whenever he hated himself. So, it made him hate himself *and* Teddy.

In moments like that, when all he needed to do was apologize, he would either deflect the blame or make it worse, because he already felt bad enough, but he also felt so alone and pointless that he wanted to break shit. It didn't help that the rising tension was caused by this customer's complaint. *How dare you touch my food.* A disturbed blemish in the human psyche, terrified of human contact. All we want is companionship, yet all we do is push each other away. People were so stupid.

Fuck life and fuck gloves.

All these dreadful thoughts stumbled hopelessly around Caesar's tired mind, irritating and depressing him. Bleak, overcast shadows sunk him into emotional darkness — a place he considered more and more to be the truth to everything. Life is a long and agonizing tragedy.

Fuck this man and fuck his complaint.

The vodka was mixing well with his self-loathing now. His pain was finding clarity. This angry man was the perfect catalyst for complete self-destruction. Caesar's mind said, *Abandon all belief in goodwill. Disregard all signs of empathetic potential, for they are all masks. We are survival machines enslaved by hungry genes and tortured with emotional wiring. Humanity has had enough time to prove itself. To show its emotional reaction to time and space has created some value.* Today was the day. This man was the door out. Caesar would finally let go and plunge from the cliff of hope to fall carelessly into the grasp of despair. Emotions were frivolous functions grown from hunger, and Caesar was full. His mind ran again. *Life is a machine of self-awareness that has confused people into making words like "care," and "respect," and "kindness," and "love." Emotions are weaknesses that trick us into repopulating. Because we can't live forever, we force a copy of us to carry on without us.* These were the dreadful thoughts Caesar was deciding were no longer dreadful. They were simply the truth.

Fuck this man and his complaint.
Fuck my friends and their concern.
Fuck this job, and fuck you, too.

This was the only time Caesar had ever had an issue with a customer, and so far, it was arguably the worst interaction anyone had ever had in the diner. The angry customer pointed to Teddy, asking him if he was the manager. Teddy shrugged uncomfortably, telling him, "I'm the owner."

"Even better. Fire this smart ass," the angry man demanded.

The customer was glaring at Caesar, who was working up a comeback but dismissed it, waiting to see his surrogate father's next move. Teddy forced a smile and told the man he'd handle it.

Teddy was red when he entered the kitchen. Looking at Caesar with an expression that was troubled and fuming, he desperately asked, "Why are you do this with him? How it's gonna look I don't fire you? Huh?"

Caesar thought about where he had woken up. Thought about his morning and the overwhelming desire to dodge everyone. He could feel the hole his ex had left in his heart. He turned on the numb switch and began to form his quitting words. Watching the man eating with his hands covered in the world's unwashed balls, he smirked, ready to unleash his defeated view of it all. He would tell Teddy to fire him, that he didn't care. To throw something in the angry customer's face. He would have, too, but the other cook spoke over him. With a heavy hand toward Teddy, he almost snarled as he said, "You fire him, and I'll fold your sack over your body like a big fucking nut cocoon. You'll emerge in a week as a big dick butterfly."

It was obvious the other cook was feeling the pressure of the orders, which were still coming in. The lunch rush was far from over. Amber rolled her eyes at the scene, put a new ticket in the window, and said, "Hug it out already. We don't have time for this."

Crystal agreed, working while she said, "Just go apologize to the guy, Caesar. For fuck's sake, we're busy enough as it is. And put gloves on already. You know it doesn't matter how many fucking balls the guy's handled. Health code is God, not logic."

Crystal's tone agreed in all the right ways with Caesar's callous disposition. It made him feel less lonely. And with everyone talking over him, he had time to think. His anger evaporated enough. The vodka was heavy under his skin, but it was malleable. It was just as easy to keep working as it was to yell. Yelling seemed less cathartic somehow now. The vodka was no longer in the mood to give a shit. What was the point even in quitting? There was nothing to blame for the pain he felt. It was no one's fault. And Caesar didn't want to feel better. Feeling better was bullshit. It was far too late for feeling better.

Hating himself was better left to stir silently within. It wasn't a thing meant for lashing out. Lashing out was an act that indicated holding onto some kind of hope for something. She was gone. They were gone. All of it was gone. His hands were empty, and there would never be anything to hold again.

Fuck me, and fuck my life.

Caesar put gloves on and thought, *Just run the program, make the food, who cares.* And there was Teddy, pestering him to make it right with the disgruntled patron. Caesar rolled his eyes and looked out the window, catching the man's attention with an assertive nod. Just apologize to him. Why not? What did it matter?

She was gone.

All of it was gone.

The man was waiting impatiently for whatever apology Caesar was summoning. They were looking at each other, the universe resting between them.

On second thought, fuck this guy and fuck this job. Caesar raised his gloved hands, middle fingers standing tall in their latex covers.

"Here are your fucking gloves," he said, smiling.

The other cook forced Caesar out of the kitchen while Teddy rushed to the shouting customer. The other cook was pissed, realizing how drunk Caesar was as he tossed him out the back. He gave him a stern speech about respect and teamwork but Caesar wasn't listening to the let-down lecture. He walked away. Carried on around the building, ignoring him, retiring to his messy room to be alone. It was a strange victory. Strange to think of it as something victorious. Did it really feel good to push the man's buttons, to sabotage his job, to throw himself away? What was it he felt he was proving? Did he *really* believe life was so nasty?

Did he care if others agreed?

His misery was in no mood for company.

That was all he could figure out at the moment. The one thing that made sense. Caesar wanted to be alone. He should have called out of work. Should have just stayed in the cemetery.

Once inside his room, he made his way from the door to the fridge, the fridge to the bathroom. Popping a bottle open, he turned on the shower, still wearing his apron, his hair net, and the troubling latex gloves. He drank the beer as his clothes drank the water. Cold beer and a hot shower went well together. Caesar closed the shower curtain. The white tub he was standing in was plastic, and all the years of cigarettes he'd smoked had given it a yellow tint. His flip-flop pushed the rubber cork into the drain. Leaning against the tiled wall, his face started to hang, and tears fought through the slits in his eyelids.

She was gone.

They were gone.

It was all gone.

But why wasn't he?

Realizing he was still wearing gloves made him laugh a little. Laughing and crying, he swallowed the bottle whole. Caesar wondered if he still had it in him to scream. He hadn't screamed in a long time — had gotten good at being the silent drunk. The hot water calmed him, helped keep him sort of docile, kept him from freaking out. Wet flip-flops left a soggy trail to the fridge, and a six-pack joined him in the shower. He sat in the tub when he returned, drinking under the comfort of indoor rain. Caesar shut the water off before the bath overflowed. Beer kept him awake while he soaked in the steamy water, soaked in his emotional disarray. Laughter arose at times with undertones of heartbroken whimpers. Empty bottles floated around his tiny depressing ocean, life rafts void of life. Caesar drifted from the world, lost in his pain. Lost. Not so much feeling sorry for himself, but more so feeling infected with emotion. More so missing her more than himself.

Why am I still here? he wondered.

Stretching the gloves aggressively from hand to hand, he shot them out of the bathroom and into the kitchen with a sad wet *thwack*. He would sigh. He would drink. Eventually, his head got heavy, eyes got heavy. Everything heavy. Nine beers later, Caesar passed out in the tub, fully clothed, head slumped over the side, hairnet still strapped to his scalp.

One can only dance for so long atop the rocks that hold the bottom so low. Caesar was finally there. Finally, ready to just admit—the bottom had been struck.

When he woke, he woke to find he had struck gold. Caesar's impact with the proverbial lowest level of self rewarded him with a strange sense of meaning.

Rock bottom was not a place of revelation or redemption. It was not a place to rise above, to climb out of and heal, grow, or change. It was the place to be.

Rock Bottom was his home.

His motel room was almost pitch black when Caesar finally woke up. If it weren't for the few cracks in the blinds— that haze of artificial light buzzing in with its mix of red and blue — he wouldn't know where he was. Caesar rose from the now-cold tub, water rolling and empty bottles clanging in the wake of his exit.

Clothes sloshed off and slapped the ground. Caesar's nude figure shivered into something warm, plucked a beer from the fridge, and peered through the blinds. Someone was cooking at one of the grills by the pool. Caesar had to look twice because it was the germophobic customer, and he didn't believe it at first. Teddy must've made a deal with him and given him a room for the night to apologize for Caesar's behavior. Or he had already been staying there. Caesar didn't care for the reason. He was just happy to see the guy.

The perfect new friend for rock bottom games.

With a big breath from his bottle, Caesar stepped out of his room with his bare feet clapping the cement walkway around to the pool gate. Wearing a wide smile, he raised his beer, greeting the man. The brute was rotating hot dogs and smoking a cigar. He had some buddies standing around with him — a bunch of white boys in golf clothes smoking stogies. The perfect rock-bottom gang. The grill man, Caesar's new best friend, started turning red instantly. Things were still bitter within their friendship. Caesar had been hoping they were.

The man was so red that he didn't even hear his new friend's greeting, so he asked Caesar to repeat himself. His tone was guarded, ready for an apology, but also ready to fight, to *fuck shit up.* That was what Caesar was hoping for. So he repeated himself.

He said, "Shouldn't you be wearing gloves when working with your friends' food?"

The red man set his grilling utensil aside, fingered his cigar, and gestured to his friends that he had it under control. With a puff of smoke, he asked, "You gotta problem, guy?"

Caesar sipped his beer and shrugged. "No problem. I mean, who gives a shit about being a big pussy when someone touches their food, am I right?"

Caesar's new best friend tensed and asked, "What the fuck did you just say?" Caesar shrugged again, almost yawned, and said, "Nothing, everything's fine. It doesn't matter that you're a big, dainty pussy."

The man's ears were glowing red. Stepping close to Caesar, he growled, "Motherfucker, I'll bust your head open." Caesar calmly shook his head, matching the angry man's pace, closing the space between them with an easy stride. His angry friend sized him up, cigar docking back in his mouth. Caesar snatched the burning stick, saying, "You know, smoking can kill you." The man shoved him, faking a punch. Caesar didn't flinch. The man's shock betrayed his strong, angry stance, and Caesar smirked. "What's the matter? Need to put gloves on first?"

A pointer finger sprung from the grill man's fist. A finger that waved at Caesar with a threatening sway. His red face growled at a warning. "Don't touch my *fucking* face."

Caesar planted the stolen cigar's wet butt in his lips, puffing away with a grin as he antagonized the man. "You mean this face?" he said, pushing his dirty fingers into his new friend's cheeks. His new best friend didn't like it. He cursed and smacked Caesar's hand away, pushing him again before pulling his arm back, locking it into a tight spring ready to strike. This was it. His fist was beaming at the end of his flesh-and-bone battering ram. Caesar could hear a click as the man's arm cocked into place — a click and a snap as it was set free.

That was easy, Caesar thought.

The fist rocketed towards Caesar, who had a smile growing victoriously from ear to ear. Eyes closing, he inhaled a relieving breath as knuckles smashed into his nose and sent his head into the sky. Caesar's feet shot up from the ground and were taken away, his body soaring horizontally. Soaring out and over the calm pool like a dream. Letting go of everything, he was free of himself and the burden of being Caesar. Weightless in his voyage from the man's steaming knuckles, a calmness carried his peaceful shape into cold water. A deep, consuming embrace swallowed his unconscious figure into the Nothing he so sincerely craved.

Rock bottom.

VI
ROCKING BOTTOM

Stories of Caesar being fished out of the pool were swimming around the Inn in a collective distress. No one had seen him all morning and the lunch hour was creeping in. The dry-erase board archived with all the times Teddy had fired Caesar no longer held the same humorous charm. Crystal's eye kept catching on it and pausing.

Pausing and sighing.

Frances hadn't heard yet about Caesar's night. He was sitting in the shadow of Exit 40's vacant billboard. Sun-bleached letters fading across its face read *"Rent this space!"* There used to be a number to call. Now there were numbers, but not enough to ring any phone. Cigarette butts littered the dirt beside the squad car. The engine was idle, AC blowing, and Frances was reclining with his fancy, gloved hands around a Gameboy, lost in the forever-falling shapes of Tetris. Something green rushed through his speed detector. The device chirped, and he stopped his game to look.

109 miles an hour.

Frances looked up, registered the speed, caught the ass-end of the green blur, and uttered a pleased, "Hello, ticket."

The Gameboy dropped into his lap, and Frances reached down to adjust his seat, pulling it upright with a quick and rehearsed motion.

As he put the car into drive, he tossed his shades over his eyes and grinned, more than pleased with how awesome he thought he looked. Rushing onto the road, sirens singing their abrasive tune, Frances tightened his grip on the wheel, admiring his badass gloves. He caught up to the speeding car faster than he would have liked. The chase was a moment he relished. The car pulled over without any resistance.

Tapping on his reflection in the rearview mirror, Frances smiled. "Who's the man?" Adjusting his sunglasses, he answered himself, "You're the motherfuckin' man."

His knee-high boots led him to the green speeder. The driver and passenger both appeared calm. The driver's window was up. Frances had hoped it would still be up so he could reach out with his badass gloves and *tap tap* on the window. Up it stayed, and badass tapping he did. As the window rolled down, he gave his mustache a gentle stroke.

Frances leaned down, ready to ask for the driver's license and registration. He'd said it a lot in the past. Ran countless plates, scanned a great number of IDs through the system. This time was different. Instead of reciting his usual lines, he diverted from the script and spoke without thinking, his jaw sagging slightly as he reacted to the driver.

"Jesus Christ, you're fucking gorgeous," he said.
The driver blushed and smiled. She was unmistakably beautiful. A blond bombshell, she stood out. The kind of face one finds on the cover of expensive fashion magazines. She leaned a bit, looking up to Frances, who was resting his hands on the roof. The driver was playing up a bashful look, asking, "You pull me over just to tell me that?"

Frances took a long focused breath, smiling a genuinely shy look, and finally said, "No, you were actually… speeding… and, uh…" He paused, lost for words. The driver looked closer at him, saying, "I was speeding?" She smiled with her question. Frances didn't answer her. He just blushed. Blushed and laughed at himself under his breath. "Are you going to give me a ticket, then, or what?" she asked, wincing around the sunlight peeking from behind Frances, trying to see his eyes behind his shades. Frances fought around his smile and shook his head, doing that thing he did with his teeth when he was thinking, finally telling her, "Yeah, no, I can't give you a ticket." She didn't know what to say, didn't know how serious he was. The whole scene was making her laugh.

Frances, in complete awe of the woman's beauty, nodded his head and explained, "No way. You're a drop-dead goddamn knock-out. I'm knocked the fuck out. I'm on my ass dead on the road right now. Gorgeous, sexy-ass stars are swirling around my head."

The passenger leaned into the conversation with a snotty tone, saying, "You can't give her special treatment just because you want to fuck her. We could sue you for sexual harassment." The passenger was snow white with a little European in her accent. A petite, English porcelain doll.

The driver moved to hush her friend, turning to her with an evil glare. They had a silent conversation while Frances pet his mustache and laughed, saying, "Wouldn't that be something? Suing a cop for *not* giving you a ticket."

The passenger tried to talk around the driver, looking to piss her off for reasons Frances didn't care to know. Frances spoke over the passenger. "I'm not being sexist. I just think I'm having a stroke. I mean no offense by not giving you a ticket, really, but shit just ain't gonna happen. You've gotta be the most beautiful woman I have ever seen." Taking his shades off, Frances leaned in and looked to the passenger with another shy smile, telling her, "Fuck'n hell. You're pretty stunning, yourself. I'm honestly short of breath." His shades went back on. Frances was more confused than they were.

"Listen, I don't want your number or anything, not trying to play that game. Even if you offered it, I wouldn't accept. No, it's just I can't give you a ticket. I wouldn't be able to live with myself if I did. You are both... out of this world. Again, I really am sorry if I'm offending you. I honestly don't understand myself why this going the way it's going."

Frances shrugged, not sure himself what he was doing. Snow White rolled her eyes and huffed, "This is so ridiculous." The driver hit her friend on the arm and told her to shut up, saying, "He's letting us go. Would you relax?" Looking back to Frances, she smiled. "You're *really* just going to let us go? Just like that."

Frances smiled and answered, "I'm sure I'll rethink this in about thirty minutes once the shock wears off. But yes..." Stepping away from the car, he laughed under his breath and pointed down the road, saying, "You can go. But I'd slow down if I were you. The next cop you pass will definitely give you a ticket. Fancy car like this. My kind loves giving big tickets to shiny, little bullets like yours." Frances started walking away, keeping his eyes on the driver. The driver leaned out her window, curious to know more about this officer, but she didn't know what to say. So, she just watched him slowly backing away with his grin betraying his otherwise cool persona.

She watched him and said goodbye.

"You're not so bad-looking yourself, copper."

Frances waved, and turned around, still laughing to himself. Sitting back in his squad car, Frances sighed, adjusted his sunglasses, and watched the green speeder buzz off—a big old smile chewing up his cheeks. He sighed again and leaned back, wondering what had just come over him. He'd never done anything like that before. Leaning over his steering wheel, he laughed at himself more. Looking around the desert, he huffed, "Well, fuck me running. Maybe I should'a got her number."

A big, rusted, silver bus with a worn yellow top chugged past him as he sat with his thoughts. It was a funny shape and Frances didn't recognize the make or model. For whatever reason the bus made him feel understood. He felt the people inside knew exactly why he let the woman in the green car go. Wanting to talk about it, Frances flipped his phone open, and he saw a few missed calls from Teddy. So he rang him back.

Teddy picked up and told him about Caesar's late-night swim. Told him he was missing. Frances leaned back over his steering wheel, emotions aching out in long, tired breaths. He told Teddy he'd look around for him, keep an eye out, and call him back when he found him. Made sure he said—*when.*

Not—*if.*

...

Caesar was sitting on the bridge where he first met Frances. His view was overlooking a bus station. He was watching people come and go, people waiting, bags going in and out of big bus bellies. He was smoking cigarettes and breathing out of a flask. He wasn't drunk yet, but he was feeling good. He was taking his time, making plans. Didn't have anything worked out yet, but his brain was storming with directions. The theme of most of them was drinking. He was either drinking himself off the bridge or onto a bus. Drinking himself somewhere to not make friends. To drink alone.

Caesar always figured if he really was going to kill himself, it would be in a way where no one could find him. Apart from falling into a volcano, he didn't know how to pull something like that off — if checking out was to be the plan. If only there was something as simple as an off button.

His nose was a little swollen, and his eyes were held in a dark galaxy of black and purple bruising. There was a book in his lap. It was a book about aliens. Real-life stories of extra-terrestrial encounters.

When Frances found him, he was pulling pages out of the book he thought were bullshit and dropping them off the bridge. Frances watched a page float away as he asked, "Good book?" Caesar waved at him with a kind of lazy salute. France sat beside him and said, "Thought I'd find you here." Caesar just nodded and took a drag from his cigarette. Frances looked around a little before he asked him if he was going somewhere this time.

Caesar forced a little cackle. "Me? No. Just reading."

"Yeah, that's how I figured I'd find you." Frances pulled at the book and commented, "Although, didn't peg you for an *X-Files* guy. You believe in aliens now?"

Caesar gave him a dramatic look and told him, "We *are* aliens."

Frances held his hand out, asking for a drink. Caesar put on an offended expression, asking him, "What makes you think I got a drink on me?" France kept his hand out and just looked at him — looked, and waited. Caesar shrugged and pulled his flask out. Frances took a sip and coughed, "Oh damn, tequila!" He cleared his throat for another sip and wiggled his spine with a smile before taking it. They both started to laugh at each other, enjoying the company. Despite Caesar's itch to depart from this chapter in his life, Frances made him feel good. Frances nipped at the flask again, grinning and saying, "Life's weird, isn't it?"

Caesar asked if Teddy called him.

Frances nodded and said, "Yep. Told me how you got them shiners. Fucker really gave you one."

"That was the idea."

"You got him to hit you on purpose?"

Caesar nodded. Frances wondered what it felt like to seek out that kind of punishment. How hopeless was his friend?

Looking over the station, Frances relaxed into the drink and asked Caesar, "So what? No more diner? You, like, quit then?"

"Looks that way."

Frances accepted, using the flask to conduct his words, asking him, "So what are you sitting here thinking about, Mr. Dark Eyes?" referring to the bruises. Caesar chuckled and said he was thinking about the song "Mad World."

"'Mad World'?"

Caesar yawned the lyrics. *"People run in circles, it's a mad world...* that one."

"Yeah, I know it. Why you think'n about it?"

"Just thinking about how it's all circles, life. People making more people and making more people. How selfish is reproduction? The life we make can't consent to its creation. We force people into this mess. Does it give our own life validation to know something else will do it again? Like our lives are only justified if something else keeps playing human after we die. For what? We're all forced into this. Forced to walk the long road to death, again and again. To suffer the tease of joy while age wears us down and takes away everything we love one beat at a time. How many people would opt out if they could have the choice before it starts?"

Frances had a look of disgust on his face. Caesar shrugged like, *What?* Frances sunk into his reaction, saying, "Jesus *fucking* Christ, buddy. The king of the cynics would tell you to ease up."

Caesar took the last drink from the flask and shook the hollow tin as he passively commented, "You know cynicism didn't start out negative? It was a Greek philosophy. A student of Socrates started it. Rejected the established desires for success and wealth and looked for a simpler life free from possessions, to live in harmony with the natural world. Back then, it wasn't that they felt humanity's good nature wasn't sincere. They just saw the absurd bullshit in the game of social status. They knew even then that we were heading to this neglected landfill of plastic self-indulgence. They figured out then that our priorities were going in the wrong direction. Over the years, the road they saw as the wrong direction just kept being the road everyone took. Cynicism was just worn down and no longer the virtuous rebellion against the Joneses that it began as."

Frances was staring at him in silence, wondering what it was like in Caesar's head. Finally, he asked, "Is that really how you see it?"

Caesar relaxed his shoulders and turned to Frances with his answer. "We've come a long way since those street prowling days in ancient Athens. You tell me, you think human motivation is purely selfish, a hungry machine disguised in an expressive rainbow of emotional variants? Or are we just afraid of death to such extremes that we can't help but gobble up the world in a race for the greatest individual experience?"

"I think you're in your head too much."

"Sorry, all I do is think."

"No. All you do is drink."

"True."

Caesar pulled out a little hotel bottle of rum and cracked the plastic lid off with a devilish smile. Frances laughed. "You're a ridiculous person." Caesar agreed, saying, "And you're a good friend, and I suck, and I'm sorry, but... fuckin'..."

Caesar lost what he was trying to say, and Frances smiled. "Butt fuckin'."

Caesar raised the little rum bottle and agreed. "Butt fuckin'." They each took a healthy glug.

They both wanted to escape.

Frances coughed and cleared his throat, asking Caesar if he wanted to go see the mummy museum. Caesar was tipsy. "I've always wanted to see those mummies." Caesar had forgotten he was just contemplating getting on a bus and never coming back.

Frances stood up. "Come on then. We'll get tacos on the way, and half pull over people in any sports cars we pass. Which reminds me, I have a fucking story to tell you."

...

They ate tacos and sang to a Cars record on the way to the mummies. The attraction, however, was closed.

61

Frances was pissed.

He wanted to help Caesar get away from his grief. *Fuckin' son of a bitch* this and *mother fucker* that and *bull shit, bull shit, bull shit*—Frances swore his way out of the squad car, his sunglasses coming off, half a taco sagging in his hand. Just standing there with his arms resting on the open door, a look shook left and right across his face that had *you gotta be kidding me* written all over it.

Caesar was chewing, peeling away the wrapper to get at his next bite while he watched Frances standing like something would change if he was pissed off enough. Like there was some specific frequency of disappointment he needed to dial into to get the owners to open up.

"I pass this dump every day," he said, carrying on, "Never seen the fucker closed before. Fuckin' place is lit up all night, even." Giving it a final glare, still searching for that special frequency, he sighed, *"Never seen it closed...."* One final *bull-shit* flew out, and he sat back in the car, his door slamming.

With a breath, he calmed and said, "Sorry about that, buddy, the place is closed." Caesar started to laugh at him. Frances smiled and asked him what was funny. Caesar just chewed his taco and shook his head. "You just make me laugh," he told him. Frances smiled back and looked out the window, mumbling to himself, *"Yeah, I'm a funny guy."*

Watching a plane slowly drag a line in the sky, he asked Caesar again if he really believed in aliens. Caesar didn't get a chance to answer him. A call came out over the radio that struck Frances. The dispatch was calling it a 10-93. He turned from the sky to the radio. It didn't keep his attention for long before he went back into the taco box. Unwrapping a beef taco, he asked if Caesar wanted to break into the mummy exhibit and poke around. The radio was still going on about a code 10-93, and Caesar couldn't help but ask what a 10-93 was. Frances turned the radio off and said it was a robbery.

"You gotta go to it?"

"Nah. Shit's a few hours away from us. Sounds like a doozy, though."

He turned the engine back on and complained how nothing ever happened on his post. "The dead zone" they called it. Plopping his taco on the dash, he started driving back to the main road, saying, "Let's bring these tacos to the karaoke bar and smoke some cigarettes."

...

Frances and Caesar stumbled out of the Bar. They were both drunk. Both ready to break into the mummy attraction.

Back in the squad car, Frances said, "You never told me where you stand on the alien debate." Caesar laughed and closed his eyes, his head resting against the window as he looked into space. Frances laughed at him and picked up the radio, pretending to call out to some aliens.

"Attention aliens, I'd like to place an order."

Laughing more, he turned the radio on, which startled them both. The 10-93 had escalated. Dispatch was looking for all available officers. The robbery that had been too far away to consider had driven right past his post.

The dead zone was alive, and he missed it.

"Fuck me," Frances spat.

The mood shifted in that instant. The fun was over. Caesar was going to ask how serious it was, but he could tell by looking at his friend just how serious it was. Suddenly they were aware of how drunk they had gotten.

"What am I going to do?" Frances asked rhetorically.

Caesar shrugged, his mouth half-open, hopelessly silent. Frances held the radio in his hand, thinking hard about what he could say. Nothing came to mind. Caesar suggested he tell them he was singing and couldn't hear the radio. Frances managed a smile. It didn't last long, but it showed up. Squinting at Caesar, all he could manage was, "That's stupid."

Caesar shrugged. "Truth is stupid."

Frances sunk into his seat and sighed, "Ah, fuck. I mean, I'm pretty drunk right now. This ain't good, man. This is a serious chase. Armed robbery. Highway pursuit. I could'a stopped the guy if I was at my post. I'm gonna get reamed at work tomorrow."

Frances hit the steering wheel and cursed. "I just wanted to blow off a little fucking steam." He took a long breath in preparation to explain something. Caesar noticed his change in demeanor, and so he leaned a little closer to Frances and waited for him to open up.

Finally, Frances explained, "She's moving out."

"What?"

A slow nod worked his head up and down as he clarified, "Moving in with her girlfriend. Told me last night."

Frances wiped a tear away and continued, "I'm happy for her. They're great together. It's just real now. I mean, it's been done for years, but... I don't know, man. It was nice still being *the team,* you know. The parent team making breakfast happen. Sitting down for dinner together with the kids. I guess I just figured we'd keep this up until high school. I suppose that was silly."

They sat in silence for a little while.

Caesar wondered what it would be like to have Frances join him at the bottom of his rock. But Frances still had too much to hold on to. It wouldn't help. Frances was still going to be a good father. Letting him sink would be terrible. Whether or not the world was or was not shit, there was no sense in deliberately adding to the pile.

Caesar wanted to help Frances. If life really was an awful charade, then Frances was a malfunctioning human. His kindness was a genuine fluke in the otherwise selfish code that made up people's naturally greedy dispositions. When he considered what Frances had been for him over the years, drunken Caesar didn't feel like his typical contemptuous self. In fact, Caesar felt like giving back. Frances' big, beautiful, gullible heart was proof Caesar's pain belonged. *Fuck the cynics*, he thought. *People don't suck, life sucks.*

A drunken lightbulb flickered to life in his fuzzy mind. "What if you were busy with a perp? That's what it's called, right? A 'perp'?"

"What?"

Caesar winced as he explained with a devilish passion, "Say you were chasing around some *slippery drunk,* and he spilled his filthy booze all over you while you fought to take him in."

Frances lit a cigarette, waving the smoke away and shaking his head. "The fuck are you talking about, man?"

Caesar kept his thought going. "*That's* why you missed the radio call."

Frances smiled into his cigarette, sort of laughing out smoke, "Oh. Shit, well, had I actually had that, sure, I'd be fine. But I'm not about to pay some drunk to spend the night in a cell to cover my ass."

Caesar smiled and started to pour his beer on Frances, right on his head. Frances held his hands out, attempting to dodge the hoppy waterfall and keep his cigarette clear from the downpour. He gasped, the beer running down his face, his mouth opening wide in a shock-inspired O-shape. Wiping his brow clear, Frances gave Caesar an evil eye. Caesar was already climbing out of the car. Frances jumped after him, his wet arm pointing over the squad car, his words searching. "The fuck, Caesar? I should kick your ass."

Caesar took his shirt off. "I'll be your perp. I'll cause a big scene. You can take me in, drunk and disorderly. Just make sure in the days that follow, you know... the paperwork gets soggy." Caesar winked. Frances yelled, "Why the hell did you have to soak me, man?"

"To cover up your drunkenness. I attacked you with a beer to get away. I'm a slippery perp taking up all your time."

Frances almost smiled. "Hold on a second. This is pretty brilliant. You'd have to stay the night in a cell. You up for that? Should be able to get you out in the morning." His mind changed again, anxiously rubbing his mustache. "No, Caesar, we can't lock you up overnight. I won't be able to sleep, little buddy. I'm sure it'll be fine."

Caesar shrugged. "I'm unemployed. I need something to do."

With that, his pants came off, he flipped Frances the bird, and started to screech, "Catch me, bitch!" Caesar ran off, laughing hysterically. Frances shook his head and watched his intoxicated friend running away in his underwear.

Then the underwear came off.

Frances had a smile, but it went away watching Caesar fall over while he tried to run and disrobe all at once. Caesar was back on his feet quickly, triumphantly holding his underwear in the air. Frances darted after Caesar, yelling, "Caesar, keep your dick out of it. You freak out the wrong person and you're a sex offender the rest of your life." Caesar just flipped him another bird and reached for the front door to an open restaurant with his junk delightfully flopping about, ready to offend. Frances grabbed Caesar's pants and hurried after him, panicking and thinking to himself that he was far too drunk for what was about to happen.

Inside, Caesar laughed as he ran around tables, throwing around winks to blushing women. Parents covered their children's eyes. Laughter bounced around the restaurant, along with a few yelps. Some cooks poked out from the kitchen to spectate with the waiters. Frances, fighting through his own laughter, tried to keep everyone calm.

"Everyone stay in your seats. Police officer, here. I'm a police officer. I have everything under control."

He sounded drunk, but the scene was so chaotic that no one noticed. When Frances finally caught up to Caesar, he was in the kitchen trying to open a bottle of wine—digging through a drawer for a wine key, hiccups kicking out of his gut.

Frances held Caesar's pants out as he made his way toward his drunk friend, taking brief, harmless little steps. *Just put the pants on*, he urged. *No more running, little buddy*. The cooks were huddled up behind Frances, giggling, one of them taking pictures on his phone. Wine spilled as the cork popped, and Caesar cheered, the bottle swinging through the air with his laughter. "Fuck pants!" he told Frances, laughing and guzzling all the air from the bottle.

Some people might put themselves into these situations to force cops to shoot them — that's what Caesar started to think about. They might bring an unloaded gun into public and aim it at an officer to coerce them into punching their ticket for them. He didn't want Frances to shoot him. He just knew this good feeling was almost over. Frances wouldn't be around to facilitate his every rock-bottom inspiration. What would tomorrow's bottles empty into him? As liberating as the nude chase was, his pain couldn't figure out if it was an escape he was after or an ending.

With the spirit of Dionysus proudly running purple down his chest, Caesar told Frances to tase him. With his arms out, opening the target wide, Caesar became giddy. "DO IT! It's perfect. I'm your perp. Bring me down to justice." Frances paused for a moment to consult with himself. It was a short-lived review of the consequences. Caesar's expression was more than convincing. Mostly he was ready for it to be over.

Frances aimed the taser and Caesar nodded with a nervous smile, telling him to give it to him, singing out, "Electrify the demons!" Two little barbed fangs sprung from Frances' hands, biting and filling Caesar with electrical venom. His eyes rolled back, teeth chattered, and his testicles sucked up into his body as he collapsed. Frances only gave him a quick zap and ran to him immediately after.

"You alright, little buddy?"

Caesar put up a strong thumb, too dazed to speak.

Frances cuffed his hands in front of his body, got his pants back on him, and walked Caesar out to the squad car. They both caught their breath. Both feeling a great deal more sober. People were still watching, so Frances opened the door, and Caesar plopped himself into the back. Frances settled into the driver's seat, closed the door, and after a silent moment of reflection, began to laugh. Caesar laughed with him. Neither of them knew what to say.

Frances patted a pack of cigarettes on his palm and popped two sticks into his mouth. Lighting both, he put one up to the cage, and Caesar took it, pulled a drag, and sat back, blowing smoke through his big, happy grin.

Frances called the incident over the radio as he drove off. About five minutes into the drive, they both started laughing again. They laughed so hard, tears chased out after.

"You're fucking nuts, Caesar. Fucking nuts."

. . .

Caesar had a cellmate for the night, a big white boy sleeping off a DUI, but the kid was passed out. In the cell next to them was a woman in her late forties. She was a pale ginger. Her freckles hid her wrinkles. She was giving Frances hell as he locked Caesar in.

"What happened to equality?" she asked, leaning against the bars, amused with herself as he carried on. "This's some bullshit, officer, segregating genders. I should sue you for this sexist bull crap."

Caesar sat down and folded his legs, saying, "You wouldn't have fun with me anyway." The woman moved to the bars that separated their cell and smiled. "Baby doll, I'd suck your dick so hard I'd slurp your balls right outta that pecker of yours." She smiled and coughed. Coughed a little more. She had a thick smoky voice. Like she ate cigarettes.

Caesar scratched his head and looked at Frances. "Tempting offer." He said, hiding his smile.

The woman tapped on the bars to get his attention, pushing her face into his cell. "All you gotta do is slide up to these bars and let me take care of ya."

Caesar looked at her, curious. "You're an aggressive hooker."

She corrected him, saying proudly, "*Working girl.*"

Caesar gave her a weak salute. "Noted."

Frances slipped a brown paper bag into Caesar's cell and wished him and the working girl a good night. The woman watched him leave, staring at his ass. Turning to the bag, she asked what it was.

Caesar pulled a little pint of whiskey from it and laughed. The working girl asked what was so funny. Caesar sat down and sighed. "I don't know what's harder to deal with. People caring about me or people not. Which one hurts more?" The woman leaned against the bars. "How about you give me a drink of that, and we can talk about it all you want." With his eyes still on the bottle, he said he'd share if she promised to not suck his testicles out of it.

She smiled and promised, "I come in peace." Holding up two peace signs with her hands, she laughed a subtle and raspy cackle. Cracking the cap off, Caesar raised the drink to her and smiled. "You're alright, prostitute lady."

VII
CUPID WALKS INTO A BAR

"I can do it… it's fine. I'll just switch my shift. No, no, no, it's no big deal."

Frances was on the phone with his ex-wife making a gesture to the officer stationed outside the cells to open them up for him. Stepping inside, he told his wife he needed to give Caesar a ride, and then he'd be home. It was almost noon.

Stopping at Caesar's cell, Frances laughed and said he wished his phone had a camera. "You'd get a kick outta this," he said to his wife through the phone.

Caesar was asleep sitting up against the neighboring cell, the working girl on the other side. They were back to back. Frances hung up the phone and leaned on the bars. The officer who let him in asked if he thought the girl had given him a little nighttime tug. He was being disgusting and making crude suggestions with his expression, even pretending to jerk off the air. Frances just shook his head. "Caesar? Nah. Not a jail-tug kinda guy." Frances whistled, and Caesar opened his eyes. The woman didn't wake up.

"Made a friend?" Frances asked with a big smile on his face.

Caesar stood up, looking at his sleepover company as he answered, "Actually, yeah. She's a fun conversation."

Frances opened the cell, and Caesar asked what time it was.

"Well, you missed breakfast."

Frances put a stick of gum in his mouth, smiling at Caesar and leaning an eye over to the sleeping woman. Caesar patted his friend on the shoulder and motioned for him to offer up a stick of gum. Caesar chewed his way to the collections window, a funny caged closet of shelves lined with numbered bins. The officer inside thumbed through papers that led him to Caesar's wallet and flip-flops which he set on the counter. Caesar held his wallet up, bothered, waving it around as he asked where the rest of his things were. The officer scanned his papers and said there was only a wallet and flops.

"Bullshit," Caesar barked, declaring, "I had some good cigarette pieces."

The officer gave him an odd look and told him, "Sir, it says here, besides the wallet and the, uh, flip-flops, that you just had a pocket full of cigarette butts and two pencils shaved all the way to the erasers."

Caesar nodded. "I did, so where the fuck are they?"

The office blinked and plainly stated, "It was trash. I tossed it."

Caesar slapped the counter. "Fuck that. You owe me some cigarettes."

"You better get moving, Boy."

Caesar snatched a pencil from the officer's station and held it up, his eyes big and shining. "I'm taking this." The officer reached for the pencil, and Caesar pulled away. Annoyed, the officer huffed, "Come on, give it, you little shit."

Frances stepped in, telling the officer to leave it and Caesar to stop acting like a child. "You're worse than my kids," he told him. Caesar pointed the pencil at the office in his cage and told Frances the man owed him a few halves of some cigarettes. Frances pulled Caesar back. "I'll buy you a whole pack. Let's just go."

Caesar stuck the pencil behind his ear and scolded the officer in his little closet, saying, "Those were some good fucking cigarettes. Fucking asshole." Frances pulled him toward the door.

As they left, the officer leaned out of his cage. "You better keep a tight leash on him, Frances."

Outside, Caesar was asking Frances why he was rushing. He said his ex-wife needed him to watch the kids and that he didn't want to talk about it. A while down the road, Caesar thanked him for getting him out. Frances smiled and laughed. "You're the hero here. I owe *you*, you kidding me? You won't believe this, but that guy got away last night. He's in Texas somewhere now. If I was sitting under my billboard, I could'a stopped him." Frances leaned back and grinned. "But you wanna know what's really funny?"

Caesar cleared his nose. "What?"

"My shift was over long before he drove past my post."

Caesar let out a slow-paced cackle before pulling in a long dramatic breath and saying, "That's hilarious. So it was all for nothing."

Frances reached over and rubbed Caesar's shoulder, telling him, "I still owe you. That's a nice thing you did for me last night. Dumb as hell, but sweet as fuck."

"Well, you can repay me with a beer."

"Of course. Once I tuck the kids in, I'll come out and play. I'll need a beer myself."

"No, I mean right now. I missed breakfast. I need to get my shit straight."

Frances paused, weighing the dark reality of Caesar's words. There was a bitter sincerity that hung unforgivingly in his tone. His friend was an alcoholic, and *he* wasn't far from it himself. He didn't think he'd ever try to stop Caesar from drinking. Didn't see much good in it. Besides, he wasn't planning on ever going to AA himself. If he ever suggested Caesar should go, he'd feel like a jerk to not go with him. It made him wonder how much worse things would get down the road. He knew he'd always look after Caesar no matter what state he ended up in, but Caesar would start getting old. Old and sick. Maybe he wanted a breakfast beer too. *Goddammit*, he thought, *maybe I should go to AA*.

A thought for another day.

Best to change the subject.

"So, how was your sleepover with the hooker?"

Caesar spat his gum out of the window and answered, "She's the first Clarissa I've ever met. But I never stopped to ask the few Clair's I've known in my life if they were just shortening it."

"What'd you all talk about?"

"Just shared emotional scars."

"Were her's bigger?"

"No... just different."

"So, you told her about... you know..."

Frances stopped himself. Best not to say names. He'd already walked in further than he should've. Caesar kept his attention out the window and just said, "Beer would be nice."

...

Frances bought Caesar smokes and a six-pack and dropped him off at his motel room, suggesting he make up with Teddy and get back in the kitchen. *You're a damn good cook*, he told him. Caesar was finishing his first beer while he shrugged a *maybe*. He was going to drink first, then make decisions. Drink himself drunk, and then interact with the world.

With a heavy flop onto his futon, Caesar drank. He drank his thoughts into old places, and his mind drifted. He drank with old conversations and couldn't help but hear people defending the world's awfulness in his mind. His night with the sex worker reminded him of the counseling he used to attend. *Instant karma*, people would say to him in his group therapy sessions.

Caesar took part in therapy support groups for the first few months after the accident. That's the thing people do when their lives get destroyed — when their emotional foundations collapse. These people congregate with others who have fallen to discuss the directionless pit that now surrounds them. Caesar couldn't stomach the people in those places. Felt their coping was bullshit. Denial in the face of the bigger picture. An overly-prescribed spiritual blanket they pulled over every conversation they had about anything with everyone. Caesar was bitter, sure, but he couldn't see it any other way. They were all letting God get away with playing Devil.

Things happen for a reason.

That's the stupid thing they said. Victims of life said it about everything. They called it their "higher power" and said it took care of them. Watched over them. But it always seemed to be guiding them after tragedy. Where was this higher power's guidance before the shit hit the fan? What good reason could so much suffering be for? Caesar always got a laugh when these people spilled something or bumped into someone and apologized, and then someone would say something like, *Don't worry, it was just an accident.* Caesar never missed a chance to start an argument at that, asking, "But I thought everything happens for a reason?" People would tiptoe around logic when Caesar would highlight any contradiction. It was the same denial he found in most churches. Caesar's bitterness got a great deal uglier when churches were brought up. Humanity's most powerful excuse to perpetuate the horrors of the world: religion.

The funny thing was, Caesar wished there was a higher power. If there was, then he'd have a place to direct blame. There'd be something he could hold accountable.

Three beers emptied. Caesar reflected on his self-destruction. The days of being a responsible drunk were over. It was time to get drunk and stay drunk. Digging through the fridge, he contemplated nibbling on some leftover cheese. Opening a can of beans, he chopped up some cheddar and mixed the two up in a bowl—cold.

Self-destruction.

Where to begin?

With a few deep breaths from the bottle, Caesar couldn't think of anything other than drinking to fill his day. What was there to do? Hop on a bus and go where? There wasn't anything he wanted but to forget. And forgetting was impossible. The pain was a part of him. He was the pain. Stuck in the life this "higher power" let happen. Opening another bottle, Caesar couldn't feel any higher power's love. So-called angels were either sadistic, apathetic, or simply neglectful. Heaven needed to re-staff.

Someone knocked on his door, and Caesar dropped behind his futon. Peering over the top, he held his breath and waited. They knocked again. It was Teddy. He was calling out, asking Caesar if he was home. Caesar didn't respond, and he could hear him talking to someone outside his door.

"You sure you saw him?"

"I didn't *see* him. When I came down, Kim told me *she* saw him. Said a cop dropped him off about an hour ago. Figured it was Frances."

Caesar didn't know how he wanted to play his character with them just yet, so he waited until they left before he reached back for his bowl of cold cheddar beans. Thinking his way through the cold mush, he wondered what Teddy wanted to say to him.

This last screw-up wasn't like his usual.

For all he knew, Teddy was coming by to boot him. Tell him he had to pack up and move on. They had put up with enough of his crap, and it was time to move on.

Goodbye and farewell.

If only everyone just told him to screw off, then he wouldn't have to think about what to do. He could just leave guilt-free. Not wanted is not wanted. With a mouth full of beans, he raised a beer and sighed with the thought that it was life that sucked, not people. As bitter as he was and as delusional as people were, most of them meant well. They were all victims. Victims of chance with nothing to blame. Even trophies get dusty. Caesar didn't want to make things worse for anyone. He just wanted to be left alone with a bottle. Life needed a pity machine. The defeated and depressed could step in and be vaporized.

First rule of his rock-bottom life — *don't make things worse for others, it's not their fault.*

Caesar dug under his futon. A small tin box found his lap. He pawed at the lid and drank. A bottle emptied, and another opened. The tin opened. A breath shuttered through his body, and Caesar stared at the memories that filled the little metal box in his lap. Pictures and letters and trinkets. Priceless relics. There was a chocolate wrapper folded into a bowtie that Caesar pulled out. His ex loved Tootsie Rolls. She could eat a bag without stopping for a breath. Caesar held the folded wrapper up to his nose, and he smelled memories of laughter.

His fingers poked around the tin, pushing things clear to see his ex-wife's face smiling. Before he knew it, his six-pack was empty. Sadness carried him into the kitchen for more to drink. The bottles in his cabinet were empty. The futon flask was empty. Bedside flask was empty. Bathroom bottles were empty. His place was dry—empty bottles in every corner.

"You gotta be fucking kidding me," he said.

Rule two of his rock-bottom life — *always be drinking.*

Caesar peeked out through his blinds. He was on his knees, eyes poking through the bottom corner of the window, trying to be as inconspicuous as possible. He could see Kim sitting behind the motel's front desk. It was nice outside, so the doors were open. Kim was a tall, red-faced, German woman. She didn't have an accent, just the bone structure. She had the kind of white skin that was almost transparent. Too much conversation about the sun could burn her.

Kim was on the phone, her attention far away. Just as long as no one was having a smoke break out back of the kitchen, Caesar could make it to the bar without being spotted. He could drink with Lucky all day and be good and blacked out before anyone he knew would come around.

Caesar eased out of his room, double-checking Kim's line of sight, his flip-flops flopping and flipping. Sneaking a view around the corner, he saw no one out back. A few steps out, and the door opened. Amber had a bag of trash in her hand. Caesar cursed and spun, slipping and falling but recovering with a frantic crawl back into hiding. Amber heard it but didn't know what it was. She gave the little bit of dust Caesar kicked up a brief inspection as she tossed the bag and went back inside.

Caesar was sitting against a wall, panting and laughing at himself. A fresh cigarette from the pack Frances bought him docked in his mouth, and he sparked and puffed and calmed himself down.

Lucky greeted Caesar with a laugh. "Fucking Christ, he shined up both your eyes with one blast, huh?"

That was Lucky's hello.

Caesar almost smiled, telling him, "His fist was impressive. Listen, I need to do some thinking. I'm gonna post up here and keep to myself. You mind not mentioning I'm here if anyone asks?"

Lucky shrugged. "Of course. Do your thing. What are we drinking while we think?" Lucky immediately stopped Caesar from answering, excitedly suggesting, "Wait. Give me a taste of what you're here to ponder, and then I'll make you a drink to match it." Lucky loved to invent new cocktails.

Caesar pulled in a long, tired breath and said, "I don't know. I guess I'm here to think about how we're all just some chance reaction teasing a communal moment with a fleeting presence of euphoria. All this pain is not our fault, Lucky. We're all victims of life."

Lucky frowned his brow and huffed, "Whiskey it is."

Caesar sat with his back to the door — sat and breathed in whiskey. Drank and considered it was time to move on from the kitchen. Move on from friends. He swirled the dark air around in his glass, thinking to himself, *This is my friend.* Maybe Henry would let him hermit up in the graveyard. He could live amongst the tombstones. Maybe pitch a tent and drink in the woods. Get drunk and hug a bear.

Caesar laughed at that.

So far, this was a stupid meeting he was having with himself. Self-pity never seemed so pathetic. He was feeling so bad for himself he just wanted to disappear. March into the desert and shut down. If he was drunk enough, he figured he could find the courage to slice his wrists. Pills seemed easier. Or digging a hole and emptying a different kind of bottle. But how would he bury himself? Hanging was out. Not just because he didn't want to hang himself — it was being found that bothered him. The thought of a friend finding his body depressed him more than the act of a self-checkout.

First rule of his rock-bottom life — *don't make things worse for others, it's not their fault.*

His glass emptied and filled.

Emptied and filled.

Filled and sat.

Suicide bummed him out in a different way. It brought him to that numb, motionless place. His motivation to even lift the glass for another breath had left him. The Cigarette hung from his fingers, burning for nothing. What a waste he had become. What a joke. Sitting in his bleak cloud of tobacco, staring at the whiskey, someone noteworthy came into the bar.

Caesar heard feet shuffling in. His mind departed from its depressing sinkhole, and he turned to the door, his cigarette sailing back to his mouth in reflex. Taking a drag, he watched as a few strange-looking people entered. Only they weren't people. Something even stranger followed in after. It was one of those things you wouldn't believe happened unless you saw it yourself.

Cupid walked into the bar.

VIII
FUCK CUPID

Caesar and Lucky had the same dumb expression hanging from their faces. Both of them smoking, both drinking, both staring at Cupid. Both thinking, *Is what I'm looking at really what I'm looking at?*

Lucky scratched at his head and said, "There he is."

Caesar was lighting a fresh cigarette. It bounced in his lips along with his words. "Feels like this should, like, not make sense or something." Lucky raised his brow, then raised a bottle of beer to his mouth, as he sluggishly nodded his head, responding with a long, quiet, *"Yeeeaaah."*

He took a big drink and burped.

Caesar said, "But it does."

Lucky agreed with a spellbound sigh and another long, *"Yeeeaaah."*

Pulling in a thoughtful drag, Caesar blew a big cloud of smoke. "I mean… there he is. Big, fat, naked Cupid. Little wings, little glowing halo… he's real."

Lucky shrugged. "And he drinks."

Cupid had been drinking mojitos. Fourteen cocktails danced him around a smokey pool table. He was pushing three-hundred pounds. Round and hairy. Hairy and naked. His hair was tied back in a bun, a bright ring of light was floating above his head, and two little fluffy wings fluttered off his back. He was relatively graceful for the big drunk that he was. His focus on the billiards seemed to keep him balanced. That, and the cocaine. Cupid and his four friends were sniffing speed in between drinks. No one stopped them. No one even thought to comment on it. The illegal narcotic was accepted just as passively as the living, breathing Roman myth that was sniffing it.

"And what the fuck are those things with him?" Lucky asked.

Something about Cupid's companions was off. Neither Lucky nor Caesar could place it. Caesar pulled a drag and shrugged. "Too tall to be midgets, too short to be... not midgets."

Someone at the bar rolled her eyes and corrected him, saying, "'Dwarves.'"

"What?"

She leaned on the bar, casually turning their direction through her cloud of tobacco to say, "It's demeaning to call'm 'midgets.'"

Lucky scratched his head. "Thought it was 'little people'?"

She sighed, "Pretty sure it's 'dwarves.'"

Caesar pulled another drag and asked, "And what do we call you?"

"Nosey?" Lucky said, his finger on his nose.

She flipped them both off and turned away. Susan was a spunky little Black lady who drove a taxi. Her hair was thinning, so she wore wigs. She missed her real hair. When she got drunk, she felt less self-conscious about it and would take the wig off her head. Caesar had worn a few at her request in the past. They had switched hats on many occasions and sung a number of duets together at the karaoke bar. They also had an ongoing competition to see who could smoke the most cigarettes in a single lifetime.

Lucky stepped over to Susan to make sure she knew they were just joking. Lucky was always an apologetic ballbuster. It made Caesar think about his choice of words and had him wondering how many other offensive labels his drunken lips mindlessly handed out. He thought maybe he should stop joking around with words like "midget," even if there weren't any little people around. Frances was always telling him, "Best not to get comfortable saying a word that doesn't fit into every ear." Caesar made peace with Susan by buying her a beer.

Giving Cupid's strange company another study, he told Susan he didn't think they were little people, but he added, "They aren't people, either."

"Look like people to me," Susan said, wincing through her billowing chimney. Caesar examined them closer and thought, *No they don't*. But he also thought Susan was right. They did.

They did, and they didn't.

Cupid's companions were all between four and five feet tall. They shared long, slender faces, odd noses, big eyes, and obscurely tinted skin — skin that seemed to breathe. The more they drank, the more their skin appeared to shimmer with a faint, pastel iridescence. Caesar couldn't decide if they were beautiful or hideous. At certain angles, they resembled testicles, but then they'd turn into the light and appear incredibly attractive. Were they female or male? He couldn't tell. Were they tall or short? The only clear thing was that they were unquestionably wasted. Some of them could barely stand up.

It was a real party.

Caesar smoked most of the pack Frances had bought him. He was emptying bottles, leg bouncing while he watched Cupid. The chubby god was having a wonderful time schooling his four mysterious friends around the pool table. They were all good, but Cupid was stupidly good. He barely needed to look where he was shooting—even sunk a few balls with one hand. The shots almost looked careless. None of the entourage were bothered they were losing. Everyone was just enjoying the party, drinking and sniffing up bags of blow, never quite looking like one thing or another. It wasn't until they sucked Susan into their disco that Caesar's thinking moved inward. He felt an unplaced sense to warn Susan not to get close. His heart ached. It raged in his chest with a quick and unsettling tremor. All the pain he harbored, agony he juggled, all his anger and resentment—it all came rushing over him.

It was all Cupid's fault.

When the realization struck Caesar, he felt an overwhelming sense of agreement. Every voice in his mind stood with him. No opposing opinions surfaced. There he was, after all. A new fact of life. The God of Love drinking amongst the people. Water was wet, the sky was blue, and Cupid was real.

Love was not by chance. Love was forced upon people. The chubby god's guilt was the center of Caesar's epiphany. Every broken heart the world had ever known was blood on his fat hands.

Cupid's gut bounced into the bar. He was sweaty. A big, fat, happy mess slicked with sweat. His nose was more a lump of powdered sugar than it was an organ. Leaning over and waving for Lucky, Cupid didn't notice Caesar staring. Lucky asked him if he wanted another mojito. Cupid brushed a few wet strands of hair from his bloodshot eyes, saying no and shaking his head, then correcting himself by saying, "I mean, yes, of course. And another round for everyone."

"Your group or the whole bar?"

Cupid hiccupped. "The whole bar!"

His accent was hard to place. Wherever he was from, he'd been in the States long enough that his home was mostly washed out. He wasn't at the bar for a drink, though. He came over to ask about food.

"Diner next door is open all night," Lucky told him.

"No, I mean like snacks. Chips or pretzels, something like that. You know, like a little snack bag."

He kept listing things, Combos, Pringles, Funions…

Lucky pointed to the barrels of peanuts and told him there was a vending machine out front. Cupid took his new mojito and spun around, catching a glimpse of Caesar. He took a big, sloppy step towards him and rolled his brow. "Cheer up, guy, I bought your next round." He was drunk and stoned, and his smile was practically falling off his face. He tapped his cocktail to Caesar's beer and took a big gulp. He smelled awful, but it wasn't just B.O. It was like his body was leaking vodka and piss.

Marching across the bar, he roared out with drunken glee, telling everyone he had bought their next drink. A round of applause surrounded him. Cupid liked the attention. This bothered Caesar.

Seeing this creature happy bothered Caesar.

Was there no remorse to carry from his cruel career? Did he not care for the lives he cursed? Cupid slung a quiver of arrows around his shoulder, his bow joining along for the ride. The legendary weapon of human suffering. *The murder weapon,*

Caesar thought. Caesar's leg was bouncing faster. The chubby god told his friends he was going out to get chips. They all started making requests. Even Susan chimed in.

"Salt and vinegar for me."

"You got it, Susan."

Cupid wobbled out of the bar. Each step he took looked like his last. Each step was overshot, and he never moved into them with the correct resistance—you'd think he would just keep going until his face went flat into the ground. But being wasted came rather naturally to him. Cupid's drunken waltz saw him to the door without fault, and he was gone.

Caesar swallowed his beer and tapped the bar for his next. He didn't drink any of it. He didn't care for Cupid's little gift. He just carried it with him as he left the bar.

Cupid was leaning against the vending machine, singing some song in French. He was really into it, swaying with the words, tapping the machine to the beat in his head. Caesar lit a cigarette and watched him. Cupid's drink rested on top of the machine, dancing to the vibration of his chubby-palmed whaps against the snack box. Arrows bounced on his back, and the bow leaned on the wall next to the machine. Occasionally Cupid would lift up onto his toes and reach for his drink. He'd take a sip, punch some numbers on the machine, and set it back. Cupid wasn't putting any money in the machine, he was just touching the little slot where coins were fed. A subtle light would hum, and snacks would fall free. He opened a bag of chips and sang his song as he chewed through them, flashing his light into the coin slot, piling up more bags, and swaying his drunken hips.

Caesar wanted to push the machine onto him.

Cupid had his hands full of snack bags when he turned from the machine. Caesar was standing in his way and Cupid almost tripped when he saw him. "You spooked me," Cupid said with a chuckle, adjusting his grip on the mound of snacks. They were both hammered, both of their eyes bloodshot and their minds heavy and foggy. Caesar pointed up to the mojito Cupid had left on the vending machine. "Forgetting something?" he asked. Cupid turned around and laughed, then turned back, smiling a dumb grin. Looking at his hands, which were cradling the excessive mountain of snacks, he sighed. "I'll come back for it. Mind getting the door for me?"

Caesar didn't move.

He just stood there and stared at the wet, chubby god, contemplating. Cupid looked around the parking lot awkwardly and then back to Caesar and asked him, "You alright, man?" With a big drag from his cigarette, Caesar replied, "No." Cupid sort of frowned and drunkenly offered, "You want chips?"

Caesar faked a laugh. It was a short, contemptuous cackle. So many years he had spent cursing at the universe, screaming into nothing, howling his lament into the empty spaces he made of countless bottles. And now, here he was. A figure to fill those spaces. A shape. The culprit to his suffering had manifested like a gift. A big, sweaty gift. Caesar raised his brow slyly and said, "Thanks for the beer," and then he poured it out over Cupid's bare feet. Cupid jumped back and whined, "The fuck?"

Caesar threw the bottle into the parking lot. "Shut up," he growled, "you dumb, fat bitch." Cupid's eyes widened, his neck extended his head forward, and his mouth opened dramatically to express, "Whoa! What's your problem, asshole?"

Caesar stuck his finger out and snarled, "You."

Cupid's head sucked back, his neck swallowing his chin as his bare foot slipped off the curb, and he stumbled, almost dropping his snacks, stuttering, "M-me? The fuck did I do?" Caesar stepped closer, telling the wasted god, "It's you. You're my *fucking* problem." Cupid tried to ask if the bar had given him the wrong beer, but Caesar spoke right over him. "Who the fuck are you to put people through this shit? Huh? What gives you the right to fuck with people's lives? To ruin us?"

Cupid tightened his grip on the snacks but a bag slipped. He kicked it off his heel in an attempt to regroup it with the mound. Looking at it, longing for the fallen soldier, he replied, "Listen, I think you've had enough drinking for tonight, yeah? The sauce has your brain cooking the wrong direction, guy. Maybe go lay down. Sleep this off, brother, 'cause I don't know you from Adam."

Caesar took a fighting step forward and asked, "Is there some other Cupid I should confront?"

"Confront?" Cupid mumbled, juggling the confrontation along with the snacks while Caesar's approach pushed him backward. Sensing the broken heart, Cupid cleared his nose to say, "I'm Cupid. Only one of us. Of me. I'm him. Cupid. Always have been. If you have a problem with me, get the fuck in line. This shit is not up to me, man."

Caesar took a drag and flicked his cigarette, still advancing toward Cupid. Pointing again he added a stern and profound, "Fuck you." Cupid scrunched his brow and shook his head, his greasy, sweaty rear pressed against a car door. He raised his chin a bit and said, "Let me guess, someone broke your heart. Boo-hoo. Not my fucking problem. You ever think you just weren't good enough?"

Red lights blazed through Caesar's eyes. The sour pain that called his heart home solidified into a lump of dead rock. A cannonball nestled in a fresh pile of gunpowder.

Game on.

Fuck Cupid.

Caesar smacked at the snacks in the cherub's hands with a vicious swipe. Bags spilled onto the asphalt, and Cupid cried, "SERIOUSLY?! That... that is un-fucking-called for. Apologize and pick them up, you little prick."

Caesar was focused — drunk, but focused. "It's all your fault," he growled. "You're the reason life is miserable. You and your *bow and arrow*." Now Cupid got mad. His temper provoked an edgy electricity to run through his body that made him move awkwardly as he defended himself.

"You don't know who you're talking to, you ignorant twig. What a horrible, *horrible* thing to say to someone. I do my fucking best, man."

Reaching down and picking up his snack bags, flustered, he shook his head and carried on, "You don't know me. You have no idea what my life is. *I* don't break hearts. I make love. Join people together." Cupid rose with a bag swinging in his hand as he declared, "Join them together for having love. It's not *me* who fucks it up. That shit is on them." He was struggling now, his drunkenness getting in his way, and he kept dropping bags, mumbling, "Ungrateful prick." Standing up with his mound, bags still falling, he stomped his foot and professed with a grouchy, bleating tone, "I'm the goddamn fuckin' God of Love, asshole."

Cupid looked up right then and saw a fist.

Caesar punched the chubby god. Struck his sugary nose right on its sugar button. Cupid stumbled back, moaning, dropping his precious snack bags. Pinching his nose, he cursed, "You *fucking asshole*. Are you serious? *Are you fucking serious?* You just hit me. *You just fucking hit me.*"

I did hit you, Caesar thought, *and I'm going to hit you again.* Caesar took a fierce step toward the dazed god, pulling his fist back for another strike. Cupid gasped and backed away, guarding his face, threatening Caesar with a few scattered words. Caesar swung again, and Cupid flinched appropriately. His head tilting back, Caesar's fist combed the air. It was a humorous *swing-and-a-miss*—a clumsy, stumbling spin. Caesar put too much of himself into the strike and fell forward, his face slapping into Cupid's wet chest. The two tried to grapple, but Cupid was too sweaty, and Caesar slipped through his arms and fell onto his side. Cupid stood over him, puffing his chest and yapping, telling him to stay down.

"FUCK YOU," Caesar shouted as he started to kick up at him. Cupid tried to dance around his legs, whining each time he was hit until he finally fell over himself—flopping on his butt and rolling onto his back, his arrows spilling out. Caesar was half up and lunging for him the moment he crashed. Cupid yelped and kicked his feet out in a bicycle style. Caesar fought and clawed around his thick legs. Both of them squealed and panted. Neither of them could fight. They looked like children.

Caesar lost his balance and fell back. Cupid rolled over and crawled away, frantic, whimpering, and sort of snarling. Snack bags were crushed under his escape. Caesar started crawling after him, grabbing at his feet. Cupid kept kicking back at him, cursing him. Caesar got some leverage and sprung up to kick Cupid in the side — a blow that Cupid caught, pulling Caesar down as he rolled away. Both of them on their backs, they kicked at each other's feet. Grabbing a hold of Caesar's leg, Cupid bit his shin. Caesar screamed and retreated. Cupid plucked an arrow from the ground, jumping to his feet. Grabbing his bow, Cupid slung the arrow and pulled back his magical string. Caesar slowly rose, eyes burning as he taunted, "What are you gonna do, shoot me with your stupid love stick?"

Cupid pulled the bow tight and hissed, "Fuck you."

To which Caesar replied, "No, FUCK YOU!"

Cupid retorted with a more confident, "Fuck you." Caesar stood with a grunt. Mid insult, an arrow struck him in the chest. Stunned, Caesar tumbled backward, grabbing at a car to catch himself, ripping a side mirror off on his way down. Cupid leaned against the vending machine and cackled. He was out of breath, so the laugh was short. Caesar wasn't moving. He was just lying on his back, the arrow standing tall out of his chest. Cupid huffed a final worn, but victorious, "Fuck you."

Cupid wanted to gather his things and leave. His party mood had been significantly compromised. Over the centuries, he'd had his share of angry and resentful failed lovers expressing their opinions of him. Physical assaults were not common, but they did happen. His view was starting to spin a little, and his nose began to hurt. Reaching up to feel it, he saw blood on his fingers. His nose was broken. Staggering around the vending machine, he thought he was moving towards his quiver.

The spinning got worse, and Cupid moved to lean on the building, only it was a glare he reached for, and his hand fell into nothing, taking his large figure with it. Through a bush and into a shallow ditch, Cupid plunged out of sight. He crashed with a hefty whack and a crack, a thud, and an oof.

It was a shame no one was around to see it.

IX
LOST BUT NOT FORGOTTEN

Cupid's chubby body lay tangled in a bit of thinning shrubs. His broken nose had healed but left some blood dried on his face. The lights were on outside. The sun climbed up into the morning clouds. A shrill, worn voice clawed into Cupid's ears, peeling his eyes open to catch the first light of the new day.

"I found him!"

Cupid could just make out the shape of his short companion. Another joined the ranks to look down upon him. They floated over him, distant, out of focus.

"He dead?" one asked, the other laughing. "Don't think he can die."

Cupid moved, and they both cheered. It was a mildly sarcastic cheer, somewhat teasing their big, round leader. A third shorty joined the other two to make fun of the love god, joking, "I remember my first drink." Cupid sat up and rubbed his eyes, mocking a slow-paced *Ha ha ha.*

One of the shorties leaned toward Cupid and smiled. "How'd you end up here?"

Another added, "Could'a invited us."

"Yeah, we would'a liked to shrub-it-up with ya."

The fourth shorty in his entourage popped in for the viewing, wasting no time before contributing his own jeer. "So, this is where you *ditched* us."

All four of his shorties laughed at the pun, and Cupid sighed, rolled his eyes, and coughed up some phlegm. His hangover wasn't in the mood for his company's lively nature. All the bruises and scratches from falling into the shrub had healed in his sleep, but despite his body's magical healing ability, the pain remained. Pulsing sores shined up and down his lumpy shape as he struggled to his feet with a weak huff and grunt. His shorties continued to tease him. Cupid ignored their razzing as he managed to free himself from the ditch. They didn't bother assisting him up. Cupid didn't expect them to.

His company's appearance was no longer attractive. They were even shorter than they were when they had entered the bar. Their skin hung from their bones in excess. Their limbs were scrawny, their heads shining and bold with stiff pointy ears, yellow and bulging eyes, and noses somewhat shriveled and droopy, like deflated sacks of flesh. These creatures were a unique hybrid breed of imp known as a chameleon—often called changelings, mimics, shapeshifters, skin-flippers, or doublers. Shifters for short, but more often Cupid called them his shorties.

They were so skilled at changing their shape that they only needed a brief moment of observation to replicate anything new. The more similar the size of their target was to their own size, the faster the change. A mouse, for instance, would be a bit of a workout for them. As would transitioning into a small one-car garage. They couldn't duplicate anything without a heartbeat, however. If they could, they would. They never missed a chance to pull a prank.

Shifters loved a good ruse.

They were in their born form on this dry and windy morning. It was, arguably, a hideous appearance. This was nothing that bothered a Shifter. They felt all shapes belonged to them, and no one look defined them. It simply required no magical strain to rest in their born form. If there was no need or interest, they saw no need and they weren't interested. They were also naked. Chameleons were genderless beings possessing both female and male genitalia, and, oddly enough, they laid eggs. All of their private bits were kept concealed in a pouch and were even more of an eyesore than the rest of them.

They were always chipper. Drugs didn't affect them in the same way that they wore on Cupid. Pain was no stranger to a Shifter. They simply had too much energy to know fatigue intimately. Their figures were too malleable for swelling, aches, or stiffness to remain once realized.

All of this annoyed Cupid.

He was always a step behind his party troupe, recuperating from the night before — and always the butt end of the joke. He was used to being woken up in embarrassing corners and nooks by the taunting, bouncing clowns that were his eccentric entourage. They were always just too much for him in the morning. Nevertheless, teasing aside, they were always right there, putting that first cigarette in Cupid's mouth, sparking the match for his morning smoke. Cupid was their party ticket.

Making his way from the ditch to their bus, Cupid's head was low, his brain throbbing, body aching. His shorties were strutting around him, talking about their night, catching Cupid up on everything he missed. He wasn't paying attention. He just wanted to get on the bus and get a drink.

The bus wasn't much to look at—silver, a bit rusted, with a worn yellow top. It was in the shape of a big rectangle — a big, slanted rectangle like it was driving too fast — and the whole thing shifted one day when someone hit the brakes. The bus had round, protruding headlights and a few windows done up with blinds. It was bigger than most buses but didn't look like any bus that had ever been manufactured on the planet Earth. Because it wasn't.

Cupid's tour bus of love.

The bus's interior was a little messy. It was also much larger inside than it was outside. Not obnoxiously so, just a few feet here and there, an extra room or two. It was a typical spell for beings of the other side, to expand interiors. Space was relative. There was a full kitchen, a little lounge with a TV and couch, a cozy bathroom, a Jacuzzi, a tanning bed, a few closets, and a couple bedrooms in the back. The party never really stopped.

Climbing into the bus, Cupid growled at the stranger he discovered eating cereal at his kitchen table, with his favorite bowl of all things. After Cupid's night with Caesar, he wasn't in the mood for mortals he didn't know.

"Who are you?"

Cupid stood over the stranger to make her uncomfortable. The stranger was an olive-skinned middle-aged woman of average height, with a French accent accompanying her words. She had her mouth full of sugary shapes when the question of her identity came up. She crunched away a free space to answer just as Cupid's entourage boarded the bus and interrupted. She was starting to say her name was Vivianne, but the loose-skinned chameleons told Cupid to leave her alone. Cupid turned away from her with an attitude and asked, "Who is she?"

"We picked her up in Colorado," a shorty said, digging into a cupboard for a blender.

"Yeah, don't you remember?" another shorty asked, fishing out a bottle of daiquiri mix.

"She's a painter, Cups."

"Been with us a while now."

"On her way to California."

"She's been sketching us."

"Yeah, fabulous renderings."

"Don't you remember?"

"Gonna make a series of paintings."

"All about us, Cups!"

Vivianne held a full spoon ready for biting, unsure if she ought to carry on eating or if she should aid the creatures with Cupid's memory. She'd been with them long enough to know it was difficult to get a word in when the four Shifters were going on like they were. They could talk quickly, and between all of them, there was rarely a break to contribute. There was no break offered at that moment.

Vivianne took another bite as the chatter raced around her. A shorty rolling a joint at the table was telling Cupid she had been with them for a week now, which was true. Cupid had just been drunk and stoned for the past three-hundred-plus years, so the passing friends were almost completely unrecognizable to him. Much like his state of sobriety, humans were never around for long. A shorty brought Cupid an ice pack while another rubbed his shoulders, easing him into a seat at the table.

"Relax, Cups."

"Yeah, Cups, you're tense."

"Vivianne's part of the gang, mate."

The bus fired up and started driving off. The shorty at the wheel was humming some song, plucking a pair of sunglasses from the sunshade. At the table, the shorty rolling a joint asked Cupid why he vanished. Another shorty jumped onto the topic. "Yeah, Cups. We had a blast with that Sue woman. She had lots of questions about you." The Shifter puffed its eyebrows suggestively, and Cupid rolled his eyes.

Cupid put the ice pack on his head. The joint was lit and placed in his lips. Vivianne slowly crunched her sugar shapes. Collecting a breath of the grass, Cupid looked at Vivianne and puffed. "I was accosted."

"Accosted?"

Vivianne's French accent didn't get in the way of her English. The mouth full of cereal sort of did.

Cupid sat back, crossed his legs, relaxed, and told them all that some man had attacked him when he was trying to buy chips from the machine outside the bar. "He hit me in my face," Cupid said, adding, "My nose was bleeding."

A shorty looked close and shrugged. "Nose looks fine now."

Another shorty interrupted with their hands on a full blender loaded with ice, rum, mango mixer, and a few prescription painkillers, asking, "Anyone want an iced daiquiri?" The blender screamed and whirled. The shattering ice disagreed with Cupid's headache, and he cowered from it but also put a finger up requesting a drink. Everyone got a daiquiri.

Even the driver.

The party was back in full swing. Lines of cocaine shot up into most of the noses. The passing joint became a passing bong. All of it masked the noise of the ticking that Cupid couldn't stand more than anything. The ticking came from the fancy machine resting on a low table next to the fridge. A machine built for Cupid. Out of the machine spun a roll of thin, rose-tinted paper that curled onto the sticky floor with names, dates, and coordinates. His shorties knew he was in no mood for the ticking machine. They raised their voices, turned on music, and kept Cupid's goblet filled.

Cupid's purpose in life always had him reaching impatiently for the next substance to distract him. His shorties did their best to keep the conversation moving so no one would think to point the ticking out. Brainless non sequiturs volleyed around adolescent curiosities. *How strange would it be if we all ate like flies, melting our food with puke before gobbling it up?* Or *What if reproductive organs were in the mouth?* Idiotic things like that.

Vivianne was stoned on the sofa, sitting with a big sketchpad, drawing everything around her with charcoal pencils. She had been finding lots of inspiration from the magical troupe. Eventually, someone asked for more information about Cupid's assailant. What did he want? What did he look like? Who the hell was he? Pulling his chubby lips from a bubbling bong, Cupid scratched his back and exhaled a big cloud, saying, "I don't know who he was."

...

Caesar was walking east along the highway. He had some pep in his step, a little gleeful bop to his forward motion. There was even a smile on his face — an awfully big one. Chuckling on and off every mile or so, Caesar was almost floating. Joy gripped his eyes with a longing shine. Deep, elated breaths accompanied the flop and crunch of his flip-flops, munching their prance through the dirt and gravel that trailed alongside Route 66. The rising sun faced him. It complimented his warm, delightful, but out-of-character, disposition. He started singing "Wild Horses" by The Rolling Stones.

He was really getting into it.

...

Cupid was pulling another massive bong rip. His scrotum-esque entourage was cheering him on. The bong neck filled with a dense fog, and he released the storm into the massive vacuum that was his big, Cupid face. The moment the cloud filled his lungs, a shorty jumped and shouted, "HOLD IT!" The other shorties hollered with rambunctious pressure for Cupid to hold the hit. Even Vivianne chanted with them. The bus was in a joyous uproar, encouraging Cupid to resist exhaling for as long as he could. His big, chubby cheeks flushed with a blistering red blemish as he accepted the challenge. It was a red that filled his neck and chest until he finally burst. Smoke rushed out, and he coughed and laughed and peered out through his burning eyelids to witness his friends' enjoyment. Sitting across the table from him was a face he didn't recognize. Laughing and coughing, he asked, "Who are you?"

A shorty answered for the new stranger. "This is Pam."

Another shorty passed behind him, adding, "*You* told us to pick her up."

The driver laughed. "Yeah, Cups. Don't you remember?"

The shorties criticized Cupid one after another.

"It's Pam, Cups."

"Her bike was broken down, so we're taking her to the nearest garage."

"Your memory's going, Cups."

"Too much weed, Cups."

"Yeah, you need a bump."

A shorty unfolded a long pinky from its wrinkly fist. Its nail was a long, curved dish holding a little pillow of blow. "This'll bring you back to reality," the chameleon suggested, holding its pinky out before Cupid's nose. Cupid didn't hesitate. He leaned in and snorted himself upright. Sniffing and rubbing his nose, he laughed and slapped the table. Pointing to Pam, he shook his head and smiled, "Nope, we picked up Pam in Austin *last* year. You're fuckin' with me." Pam reached out and grasped Cupid's hand, saying, "I just *love* love." Still holding his hand, the chameleon morphed from Pam's shape back into its original wrinkly form. The one with the cocaine finger corrected Cupid, telling him, "We picked up Pam in Pittsburg, not Austin. You're thinking of Jennifer." Cupid turned to the shorty, asking if it was sure it wasn't Austin. That shorty was now in the shape of Pam — a tough, tattooed, leather-gripped Canadian woman with a pink tint to her white skin. The driver was also now in Pam's shape, supporting the Pittsburg fact. All four shapeshifters had taken on the shape of Pam.

Vivianne was on the couch, somewhat frozen by it all, the charcoal in her hand, waiting for herself to come back to Earth. The chameleons enjoyed their effect on her, the awe they inspired, the astonishing power their talent held over most mortals.

This game of adapting the forms of past hitchhikers was usually annoying to Cupid, and the chameleons enjoyed confusing him. They tricked him often. Sometimes it would take him days to realize the joke. What the chameleons wanted to do most at that moment was take the shape of the man who attacked Cupid, but none of them remembered seeing him. Another broken heart pointing the blame at him was all Cupid could remember of the man. Another angry lover. If anyone should be angry, it was Cupid. Cupid was the victim in all of this.

At least that's how he felt about it.

...

Caesar was pretty sunburnt by the time Frances pulled up next to him, window rolled down, eyes looking over his shades to his friend. Keeping a slow crawl alongside the pinking Caesar, Frances asked, "How we doin' buddy?"

Caesar kept on marching as he happily replied, "I've wasted all these years, Frances. Wasted them."

Frances didn't understand. His confusion and concern was obvious in his inflection as he asked Caesar to elaborate. Caesar just looked up into the sky and breathed a big, lively breath. "I'm just going to go back."

"Alright, Caesar, that's fine. You wanna climb in and tell me about it? Maybe I can give you a ride."

Caesar was silent and just kept on walking. Frances slowly rolled beside him, asking, "So, where we going?"

Caesar smiled. "I'm going to get my wife back. Not that she'll have me. It's not what I mean by 'back'. Just back in my life. You know?"

Frances couldn't believe what he was hearing. Countless questions flooded his mind, but he addressed his more immediate concern, asking, "You're just gonna walk 2,000-some miles right now?"

Caesar started singing, *"I would walk five hundred miles, and I would walk five hundred more…"*

Frances laughed under his breath, uttering a lost and troubled, *"Jesus-fucking-Christ."*

Caesar kept on singing, skipping a bit as the words made him even happier. Frances leaned close to say, "You're pretty red. Why don't you come in outta the sun, buddy?" Caesar looked back up to the sky for a thought before turning to face Frances. He smiled at him. Frances had never seen him smile like this. He seemed happy, and truly at peace with himself. It made Frances uncomfortable — sort of freaked him out. Given the context, he was worried the reason for his joy was something horrible. Walking down the highway alone with an unnatural grin, carelessly burning in the morning sun, and openly talking about his ex with a joyful smile did not paint a reassuring picture. Not to mention the arrow.

Which he had to mention.

"You know you got a big fucking arrow sticking outta your chest?"

Caesar looked down to discover there was, in fact, an arrow stuck in his chest. The sight surprised him. So much so that he stopped walking. An abrupt halt of awe and wonder opened his eyes as he uttered to himself, *"Holy shit… look at that."* Grabbing at it, somewhat in disbelief, he gave it a tug. Caesar could feel his heartbeat when he pulled at it. His pulse was abnormally present in the protruding stick. Frances watched him investigate the injury with a nervous and attentive eye, wondering what drug Caesar was on that allowed such an injury to go unnoticed.

"You piss someone off?" Frances asked, brow bent in odd directions.

Caesar looked back at Frances. His expression was straining to recall what led him to this moment—lost in a space between memories. Nothing was said. Caesar just stood there with a searching expression. Frances waited with his silence long enough before he asked him, "You wanna sit down? Maybe go to the hospital?"

Caesar shook his head with a subtle sway, saying, "No… No way, man. I need to go back. I need to be in her life. I don't care how much it hurts. I love her." Then he nodded to his own words and explained, "I don't care if she doesn't need me. We don't even have to hang out, you know? I just need to be around her. I love her, Frances. She's still on this earth, so I need to... need to just be around her."

Caesar turned as if he would start walking again, but he didn't manage the first step. Looking back down at the arrow, he started to put the pieces of his night back into a solid image. Frances parked the car and made his way around to Caesar. Giving the arrow a closer look, he scratched his head, wondering why there wasn't any blood— and still wondering how Caesar was standing and breathing. The arrow was a dead-center bullseye, puncturing his heart.

Nervous about bumping against it, he asked, "That hurt?"

Caesar shrugged, and said, "Not really."

Grabbing onto the arrow, Caesar yanked it out. Like a band-aid, he just went for it. Frances flinched and then hurried close to do something, to cover a wound, to catch him, to *something*. But there was no wound, no blood flow to stop, not even a hole in his shirt. Holding the arrow, Caesar spoke out confused, asking, "What am I doing, Frances?"

Frances shook his head, speechless.

Caesar looked around, asking where he was. Frances told him the mile marker they were at. Caesar wasn't really listening, just looking at the arrow. Leaning his butt against the squad car, Caesar shook his head, mesmerized by the arrow. "Why the fuck did I think I should go back there? That's a horrible idea." Looking to Frances, he added, "It hurts so much to be around her. I would probably kill myself."

A creaking sound pulled both of their attentions to the arrow. The sound was like the twisting bark of a thick tree stretching out an aching back. Or perhaps it was a yawn. If a tree could ever do such a thing as yawn. The arrow turned black and cracked from burnt stone to ash, blowing away from Caesar's hands in a rapid escape, littering the wind with nothing. Neither Frances nor Caesar understood what they had just witnessed. The empty space of air that sat forever before them had just sizzled with such a monumental vision that the calm nothingness that remained left them feeling misplaced.

Frances leaned against the hood next to Caesar, patting a pack of smokes against his thigh. He did that thinking thing where he sucked air through his teeth. Popping a cigarette into his mouth and holding one out for Caesar, he asked the only question there was to ask.

"So... who shot you?"

...

Cupid was puking painful throws of hard liquid into a ruby-red toilet bowl. Hard chunks were splashing back into his face with a projected sense of ridicule. They struck him as if thrown by the audience of life he had failed to amuse. The disapproving, rotten fruit of the old romantic ages echoed in the rancid splatters of bile and toilet water. Each toss of his insides left him desperate for air. Desperate for release. His mind was an orchestra of apologies, screeching inner voices begging for the infliction to stop. His eyes stung with salted self-loathing, tainted with notes of mango daiquiri. All the trails cocaine had paved from his nose through his brain burned and itched with the weight of countless regrets. There was only the awful truth to the mistakes that his decisions always became, shoveling out of his mouth into the toxic bowl of discontent. Every heave of his twisting gut taunted him with failure. Every deposit he made brought shame. He didn't seek redemption. Saw no use in forgiveness. Defeat had found him long ago. Defeat he had long since accepted.

Cupid was all too familiar with the humiliating experience of being curled up face-first with the ass-end throne-of-waste and the untamable compulsion to hurl overpowering him. The pain was always the proof that authenticated his disgrace. There was no denying his failure with such a wretched twist in his guts. He was garbage, and he was wasting himself — had wasted himself. It was too late for second chances. Cupid had lost, and he simply wanted mercy. Wanted the pain to end.

This was how it always was. Vomiting was a fight he never won. It wasn't a fight at all but a mugging. There was nothing he could do but wait for the assault to tire out and leave him to lick his wounds. Puking and whining and begging for the end. Apologizing and begging *I'll never drink again. Just let this end.* But how quickly the pain was forgotten once it passed.

Wiping his mouth dry, Cupid caught his breath. No longer possessed with the vacating obligation his grief inflicted, Cupid almost instantly returned to his well-rehearsed denial. The physical relief he felt had him forgetting mercy altogether. A cigarette and a shot of something dark was all he wanted now. The clarity the purge delivered allowed him to forget the reasons. His chubby face rested against the ruby-red seat, his cheek sprawling out, distorted, and mashed. Spitting a sort of final note to the symphony of pain that left him ravished, he uttered a slow and contemptuous, "*Ha ha ha.*"

He would live to drink another day.

The overweight god labored to his feet with terrible grunts, flushing the toilet while on his ascent to ground level. The sound of the toilet gurgling down his shame was an appropriate applause for his bogus victory.

In the mirror, he forced a smile and belched, slapped his cheeks a bit, and thought about fucking Vivianne. No better cure for his self-loathing than hiding his pain behind a good shag. It helped that he found her attractive. Not that Cupid thought anyone was ugly. He actually didn't have the ability in him. Cupid saw the beauty in everyone. Just a part of what he was. Some more than others, depending on his mood. At that moment, he was finding Vivianne a good step above his options. Seeing as she was the only thing on board aside from his shorties, his only other option was having one of his chameleon companions turn into someone for him. Something to note about Shifters: they were one of the horniest creatures in the universe — vastly surpassing even that of Homo sapien teenagers during their transformative stages through puberty. It was one of the variables that had brought them into a companionship with Cupid.

Two of the Shifters were actually screwing just then.

Cupid could hear them. They were always going at it. If they weren't going at it, they were talking about going at it. It annoyed Cupid more than it pleased him. Everything annoyed him when he was in between inebriations. The shagging would probably be making Vivianne uncomfortable. Then again, it may be exciting for her. She *had* been with them for some time now and hadn't left. Most humans who tagged along for a ride with Cupid were looking to get it on. The Shifters were always roping in groupies for that exact reason. It was really all they wanted — sex and drugs. Plus, Vivianne was an artist. Not that all artists were promiscuous. The odds were just in his favor. If he struck out, he could always have one of his shorties turn into her, or anyone else for that matter. Either way, he was going to get off, take a nap, and put all this pain behind him.

Bury his woes a little deeper.

Stepping out of the bathroom, Cupid saw Vivianne sitting in the living room, drawing on her big sketchpad. One of his shorties was posing for her in the shape of a Roman gladiator bleeding roses. Cupid turned from them to open the bedroom door that housed the present humping. It was two shorties in the shapes of fit humans, two dark chocolate lovers bouncing in each other's laps. Cupid hissed at them, "Everyone can hear you. Fuck quieter."

They humped harder and moaned louder, both reaching for Cupid, moaning, sweating, bouncing—inviting him to join them. Cupid smacked their hands away and closed the door. Their sounds carried on.

Cupid got a beer from the fridge, studying Vivianne, trying to gauge her attitude toward the shagging taking place in the next room. She didn't seem to notice it. What kind of lass was this Vivianne, this painter on her way to California? Cupid had a gift for reading romance. With a little focus, he could sense Vivianne was a monogamous lover with an open mind. She'd had few relations in her life, all of them serious. Charming her in the present atmosphere would probably fail.

Cupid casually looked over her shoulder to see her progress with the portrait. She was good. Cupid loved art. Couldn't draw himself, and he even made smiley faces look bad. With a swig of beer, Cupid awkwardly complimented her work. She smiled up at him, thanking him. She seemed strangely comfortable for a mortal in her position. Then again, she was pretty stoned. She turned back into her piece, and Cupid nervously picked at the back of the sofa. He read deeper into her aura. She was thirty. She was a pear-shaped white lady—big rusty brown eyes, slim face, not much chin, bright smile, hardy laugh, short pixie hair. She was pretty. She was spunky. Seemed pretty sharp-witted. There was an obvious confidence to her glow that Cupid could smell.

Strong-willed people had a citrus nip to their aura, often orange, but just as often lime. Good-hearted people typically smelled of mint. Nasty bastards always gave a mustard seed kick to Cupid's snout. Ginger, though, was the smell of all smells for someone like Cupid. Ginger was the scent of a longing heart. Sadly, lament carried a similar ginger spice. The more broken the heart, however, the more it smelled like cinnamon. Where the sweet scent of freshly baked cinnamon buns commonly brought those around it immeasurable joy, it only brought Cupid grief.

There was no cinnamon jazz to Vivianne's essence. Along with her orange tang, she had a powerful note of mint and an even more notable zing of hopeful ginger. It wasn't necessarily a partner that had her heart pining. It was a connection with life, in general, she was after. Breathing in her heart's colors, Cupid could sense what she wanted, what she liked and disliked. With just a sniff, he could know the perfect match for anyone. Cupid wasn't her type physically. His habits were far from her desired spectrum, as well. Cupid was a mess, and he wouldn't deny this. He *could* cast a spell to seduce her, but that was more the Shifters' style. Vivianne wasn't some floozy riding the high of Cupid's magic love bus. She wasn't like anyone who typically hitched a ride with the Love God and his slutty entourage. She reminded him of a time long forgotten.

Cupid's posing Roman Shorty gave him a teasing eye. He could tell Cupid was looking to make a move on their artist companion. Cupid glared at the Shifter, who, while noticing Vivianne wasn't looking, turned his tongue into a flaccid cock and slid it out of his mouth to taunt Cupid. Cupid's round cheeks flushed red as fresh cherry pies, and he scowled at the shorty with a fierce look. The Roman-shaped shorty flopped the cock a bit before sucking it back up and re-forming its pose for Vivianne.

Vivianne didn't notice.

Cupid sat next to her, his chubby rear moving the sofa and bumping her mid-stroke. Cupid apologized, and she told him not to worry, that it was only a sketch. She kept drawing, and Cupid watched. He looked around for cigarettes. Saw a pack on the kitchen table. Thought about Vivianne's tits. Tried to sneak a peek. She moved, and he bumped his teeth on his beer while going for a drink. The Shifter smirked. Cupid saw him laughing at him and acted as if nothing had happened.

The only sound aside from Vivianne's sketching hand was the two shagging in the other room. Muffled moans and squeaking furniture ached around the bus with a steady rhythm. Cupid coughed and called attention to the rocking boat, awkwardly apologizing for the sexual ruckus. Vivianne didn't mind and told him so.

Said, "I don't mind."

Cupid raised an eyebrow to her tone. It was all *easygoing*. Sliding a little closer, half an eye on the pack of smokes sitting on the table, Cupid tried not to make his move obvious. But he was a big, round god with little wings and a glowing halo, so Vivianne noticed. She kicked at him and asked, "You aren't getting any ideas, right?" Cupid raised his hands, retreating to his end of the sofa, and promised, "I wouldn't even think of thinking of anything. I was just looking at your drawing."

The bouncing creatures had emerged from their love shack, giggling, saying, "Oh, he's thinking it." Cupid gave them an evil glare. They were turning from their dark chocolate shapes back into their loose nut sack skins, carrying on with their comments. "He's always thinking it." Naked and slick with sweat, they were in the fridge looking for drinks.

"You kidding? Cupid *not* trying to bone?"

"That's like a cat not killing a mouse."

Vivianne started to laugh. Turning to Cupid, she asked if all gods were this open about having sex around anyone without a care. Cupid rolled his eyes. "They aren't gods. Just sex-hungry tricksters."

The ticking from Cupid's dreaded machine interrupted. The naked Shifters were in the fridge holding still. It was hard to tell where Cupid's emotions would go when the machine went off. It was an olive green box with rounded edges and a little black mouth where the orders printed — orders sent out from the highest authority in the known universe. Each tick from the machine delivered a pairing Cupid was to unite. Each ticket was first stamped with a time, letting Cupid know how long he had to shoot his arrow. Under the time were the two names he was to make fall in love with each other. Sometimes they were gods, but mostly they were the names of mortals. Under their names were their locations.

And that was all.

When, who, and where.

The "what" was always love. But the "what for," the real "why," that was thought of as something too grand to share. The reasons for the pairings were never given. It was simply expected of Cupid to play out the requests. Cupid stopped asking a long time ago. Now it was just a job, just a burden. The Almighty Architects of the Universe harnessed a power that was wise to fear. They were the great creators of life.

The Council of Ultimate Assholes, as some jested.

Gods and magical creatures alike spoke a lot of hate behind the backs of the Supreme Storytellers. They spoke about the cryptic games of politics they played from their hidden thrones. Equally arrogant as they were ambiguous.

When Vivianne asked what the machine was, the shorties tried to change the subject. Cupid saw an opportunity, however, to impress the mortal. So he patted her leg and tried to stand up from the sofa. With all the abuse he had put himself through, he struggled to stand. But he hid the strain with a supportive flutter of his little wings to aid him up.

He explained the machine. Told her how being Cupid worked. Expressed it all with a bit of theatrics, made a real show of it. Cupid could speak of love like no one else. His blood vessels were literally in the shape of hearts. Romance boomed from his chest with every thump his heart would beat. Vivianne was captivated by Cupid's way with words. He made Shakespeare sound adolescent. It was hard not to be captivated by any of it. It was love. Magical instructions curled through rose-tinted ribbons of love, draped with future romance. Vivianne was completely spellbound by the enchanting device.

A real-life love machine.

She was turned around, looking over the back of the sofa, and asked, "Was it always like this, with your little receipt pod feeding out future lovers?" Cupid shook his head. "Goodness, no. My love was a gift given but once a year. In the beginning. Back when love itself was the design. With each passage around the sun, a new true love was to bloom. A pairing picked with the utmost delicacy in calculations. Chosen to inspire love within every heart to bear witness and marvel upon pure bliss. Love for the sake of love." Cupid sipped his beer, his gut feeling better from the earlier purge. Fingering the strip of rose paper, he continued to explain, "It's funny, really. The high and mighty creators loved the stories mortals made up so much that they made them a reality. Zeus, Poseidon, Ares... me."

Vivianne cocked her head and squinted. "You're shitting me, aren't you?"

"Unlike my degenerate company, I am not fond of jokes. The power to induce ultimate love was bestowed onto my bow. The power to craft arrows which carry love's spell into the chosen heart was ingrained within my being when I was birthed into existence. The Greeks wanted gods, and so they got them. The tribes of ancient America wanted spirits, so they got them. The great Architects made many arcane beings in the vein of human imagination. And they also grew bored with them as they do most everything. Most of them are neglectfully retired."

Vivianne ignored Cupid's bitter inflection and asked with a wondrous smile, "They make gods, like, how? A big cauldron or something?"

Cupid smirked. "There are lots of ways to make gods. Gods like me are created in rituals. But my astrological siblings and I are the children of the real gods. The world I come from is much older than yours. It was filled with gods long before they were called gods."

"Gods like you?"

"No," Cupid sighed, saying, "I am a god with a role. Bound to a force of nature that binds your world and mine, tethering me to both. They call me a Story God."

"How many of these Story Gods are there?"

Cupid shrugged. "Too many. Not enough. None of which are taken seriously anymore, I'm sad to say."

Vivianne smiled and pointed. "Do they all have one of these boxes printing out orders?"

Cupid took a big swig of beer and nodded. "Some of them."

A shorty standing before the open fridge, orange juice in one hand, a bottle of vodka tipped into it from the other, said, "But only one God of Love."

Cupid sighed, "Only one love god with my gift. There are others in the same field, but only the one bow."

Cupid tore off the thin rose sheet and gave it a glance. There were five new sets of partners he was to join. Letting it roll up, he sighed and sipped his beer. He made a gesture to Vivianne, seeing if she wanted to look at the list. She lit up, bouncing up to her knees, her hands out to receive. Cupid lobbed the paper, and she cupped it with a smile. Unrolling the magical rose paper, her eyes shining with a warm light, she read the names. It was all so exciting.

"You're going to make these people fall in love?"

Cupid nodded his head, emptying his beer and tossing the empty bottle into the rubbish as he belched. He had forgotten about his urge to take Vivianne to bed. All this talk of his work made him limp. Plucking a cigarette from the table, he thought about his fight with Caesar. Another heart left tattered and broken from the Architects' careless orders. Puffing away, Cupid told everyone he was just now remembering he had shot the guy with an arrow during their fight.

The shorty making the big Screwdriver closed the fridge and asked him which guy he meant.

The shorty posing like a Roman answered for him, "The guy that attacked him."

"Oh, right."

Vivianne asked what happens when he shoots someone not on the list. Cupid smoked and shrugged. "Nothing, they just fall in love with someone."

"Don't you gotta pick someone?"

"No."

"Well, then, who'd he fall in love with?"

...

Caesar was leaning out the window, the wind blowing through his thinning hair. He turned to pull a drag from his cigarette before blowing it out of the car. Frances kept looking over to him and wondering what he was thinking. The arrow still had him puzzled. He kept pinching himself to see if he was dreaming. Caesar had told him about Cupid. That also had him puzzled. Caesar was mostly thinking about his ex. It was nice to think about her as part of his life again. To think of her as something positive. Nice while it lasted anyway. The whole ordeal left him in a sort of fresh space with the pain. So much he had been keeping in the dark was now lit up once again. Old images of her smiling at him sideways from pillows and giggling through bed sheets on lazy weekends pricked at his heart. He wanted to face Cupid again. Get a real chance to slug him properly.

Sitting back in his seat, he started to say, "You know what..."

Frances leaned in, attentive, eager—but Caesar didn't finish the thought. His eyes were looking out, seeing something far away, his mind nowhere close to them in that car. Frances couldn't take the silence, so he yapped, "Fuckin' know *what*? God damn, Caesar. Connect your mouth to the thoughts you're thinking. I'm mystified over here." Caesar apologized and took another drag but said nothing else. Frances bounced in the seat with an anxious little bop, excited and agitated. "Fuck me, man, come on, *spit it out.* You fucking fight Cupid, motherfucker shoots you with an arrow. Has you walking across the desert back to your death, and you just sit here smoking my cigarettes in some bullshit silence."

Caesar patted his pockets. The cigarette bounced in his lips as he said, "Fuck me, I lost my wallet."

Frances dropped his face asking a perplexed, "Your wallet?"

Caesar freed the cigarette from his mouth and turned to Frances. "Yeah, my fucking wallet must've fallen out when the fat ass shot me into a love coma. Take me to the Inn."

Frances rolled his hands out toward the road ahead and just chuckled. "Where the fuck else would I be taking you?"

...

Vivianne was reading names off of Cupid's love lists. There was a bin filled with unfinished matches.

"Edward Jonson and Samantha Miller, Montreal, six-month window," she said, smiling a big, warm smile. Cupid sat back in his chair, his head looking up as he exhaled smoke, and said, "Some boring fucking names there." Vivianne gave him a concerned look, commenting on his bitterness. Cupid huffed and smoked. "Oh, please. What about their union could possibly be so interesting that they were chosen out of the rest? I tell you, most of these fucking couples I'm tasked to gift love to are some of the most ordinary, basic people you will ever meet."

"But, it's love."

Cupid smiled at Vivianne with a sort of condescending nod. Pulling in a dramatic drag from his cigarette as he sat up, Cupid sneered, "Love happens every day with or without my arrows. I swear they just want to pick fights and make drama. All my arrows these days are used to entertain some childish phase our overlords can't seem to grow out of. I am the slaved conductor to their daytime soap opera."

Vivianne was upset with Cupid. Her face scrunched, displeased with his words. Cupid winced at her. She had no idea. Standing up with a big, robust breath, Cupid puffed away as he said, "I remember the old days. When my arrows were made to shape history. When each pairing the Supreme Assholes chose meant something. Back when their council was considered the most divine word in the universe. My arrows were crafted for queens. Mixing royal families to sway the direction of time. Putting arrows into kings to crumble their rule over impossible obsessions. We started wars, built empires, made your world into the way it is. All in the name of love. But somewhere along the way, they started picking nobodies for no reason and stopped talking to me about it altogether. They stopped telling me *why*. And now look at this place. It's a dump, littered with ordinary fucking people. The fights they use me to make are so vapid I could drown in my absolute lack of interest."

Vivianne heard what he was saying, but she had never known any kings or queens. She could only imagine what that world was like. But it was still love, and it was still incredible. Smiling with sympathy for the chubby god, she remained excited. And she wanted to see him get excited as well. The god of love shouldn't be anything but excited. And what better medicine than an excited fan?

She asked him if anyone could use his bow or if it only worked for him. "I know you said only you can make the arrows, but could I shoot one? I'm just thinking since it doesn't really matter, could I shoot one of these basic nobodies and make them fall in love?"

Cupid smiled and finished his cigarette, telling her, "Of course." He put the butt out in an ashtray and started looking around for his bow, asking her if she wanted to hold it.

Vivianne lit up. "I'd love to."

Marching around the bus, Cupid said how beautiful the bow was. He told her about the sacred trees it was cut from. The first trees ever made. His bow was the only artifact in the universe to be made from the sacred wood. No mortal had ever set eyes on the ancient trees or set foot in the garden where they stood. It was a real piece of art, he told her.

Vivianne was ecstatic with the prospect of shooting someone with Cupid's arrow, ordinary or not. The concept delighted her. Watching Cupid digging around the bus, lifting clothes, poking behind furniture, she thought he was teasing her, making a game of it, like he wasn't actually going to let her shoot someone, let alone hold the thing. Maybe he didn't let anyone hold it. Then again, he said he wasn't fond of jokes.

Cupid slipped into the bedrooms, and the sound of him searching carried on. Vivianne noticed the shorties giving each other looks of concern. Cupid's search was causing a racket and growing furious. Coming out of the bedroom, Cupid cried out, "Where the fuck's my bow?"

. . .

Frances pulled Cupid's bow out from the shrubs where the chubby god had slept. Looking up from the little ditch into the parking lot, he called out to Caesar, "Look at this fuckin' thing." Caesar was on his side, reaching under a car for his wallet, when he spotted Cupid's arrow quiver. The arrows had all spilled out. Frances was still talking. "This thing's gorgeous."

Caesar grabbed the quiver and pulled it so it scooped up his wallet along the way. Frances was over him when he came out from under the car. Caesar sat up and looked at his friend and the bow.

"This is a serious piece of work here."

The bow was a perfect curve. It was made from two different pieces of wood — a dark crimson wood on one end and an ivory wood on the other, both spiraling around the other in the middle. Hearts and flowers were carved along it with magnificent detail. The quiver was just as impressive, with black and red leather embroidered with the same heart and flower decoration.

Frances grinned. "This is some wild shit. You can feel it just by holding the thing, like, fuckin' feel the power. I feel like crying right now."

Caesar stood up, finding an arrow along the way. Frances pointed at it, remarking on its similarity with the one that was stuck in Caesar.

Caesar sighed sarcastically. "What are the odds?"

Frances squinted. "No need to be a dick. I was just saying."

Caesar walked around the car, filling the quiver with the rest of the spilled arrows. He complained as he did it, saying, "Why does some drunk have the power of love?" Frances held up the bow and pulled on it, mocking a shot. "Strange to think he drinks at all, or eats chips and plays pool."

Caesar laughed. "Maybe it makes perfect sense."

Waving the bow around, Frances kept thinking out loud. "Strange that he's real. Feels like we should've known already."

Caesar hung the quiver over his shoulder and looked around, deep in thought. Frances watched him and asked, "What's the look? You seem bothered." Caesar scratched his head. "I just need a drink."

"Bars ain't open yet, buddy."

"Liquor store is. I need to restock anyway. My place is dry."

...

Cupid was tearing the bus apart, swearing, and spitting, and screaming. Vivianne and his shorties kept their distance. Vivianne hid on the sofa, nervously watching his shorties huddled up together, keeping clear of Cupid's rampage. The driver was parked at a fast-food drive-through, trying to order breakfast over Cupid's commotion. He leaned out the window with a finger in his ear, and corrected, "No, I want fries with all of them."

The kitchen was ripped open—everything tossed out onto the floor, bedrooms ransacked, bathroom devastated. His shorties tried to calm him and told him the bow had to be somewhere.

"Yeah, Cups, just relax."

Cupid threw a bottle at them. They ducked as it smashed on the wall behind them. "Where is it?" Cupid shouted, his big, chubby cheeks red with rage. A trembling shorty braved a suggestion, noting, "You haven't checked the couch yet." Vivianne's spine snapped stiff, and she gulped. Cupid stomped up to the sofa, and Vivianne balled up with a gasp. The sofa lifted and tipped back, Vivianne screaming as she fell over along with it.

There was no bow under the sofa.

The driver pulled itself in from the window and yelled back, "Can you keep it down? I'm trying to order our breakfast."

Cupid sprung to the front, screaming along the way. The shorty in the driver's seat barely had a chance to think before Cupid was on top of it. His belly pinned the little Shifter to the steering wheel as his big, chubby butt filled the seat. The shapeshifter's arms flailed about from under the big gut, changing colors and textures as it remained pancaked between Cupid and the wheel. Cupid slammed on the gas, pulling out of the drive-through queue. Burning rubber onto the main road, his middle finger stuck stiffly out of the window to wave off the honking cars he had almost hit along the way.

Everyone in the bus went toppling over to the left and then back to the right. With a hard turn, the sofa went back up on its legs, and Vivianne fell off. The shorties all yelled for Cupid to calm down.

"You're gonna get Vivianne killed!"

"Yeah, Cups, she's fragile!"

A shorty took her hands and told her not to worry. "If you die, we'll bury you somewhere really pretty."

Vivianne gulped.

Everyone huddled to see who was going to approach Cupid. When he was like this, the last thing he wanted to hear was someone consoling him. No one wanted to talk to him unless they had the bow. Unless they could say, *Here it is!*

This wasn't the first time he had left the single-most important creation ever to exist in the universe behind at a bar or hotel room, or that one time where he left it in a taxi. It was always the same reaction – rage and panic.

Three chameleons all started pushing each other to the front of the bus, each of them telling the other it should go.

"You should just rub his shoulders."

"No, I think you should get him a cigarette."

"Why don't you?"

"Me?"

"Of course you, you're his favorite."

"Fuck you! He can't tell one of us from the other."

"And whose fault is that?"

"All of ours! All we do is fuck with him."

The shifter trapped under his belly freed its lips and asked where Cupid was going. Cupid looked ahead and watched the road blur past at eighty miles an hour. He didn't recognize the name of it. His chubby foot let off the gas and crushed the brakes. Shorties went sailing to the front, crumbling over each other and crashing against the front console. Vivianne tumbled over herself and used her legs to keep the sofa from running her over. The bus screamed to a halt, and Cupid pulled himself from the wheel. The crushed shapeshifter gasped for air and unfolded the wheel-shaped creases in its head.

From the pile of others came a loud, "What the fuck?"

Cupid looked to his companions, short of breath, and huffed, "Anyone remember which way that bar was? I have no fucking idea where the fuck we are."

X
A SPARK OF VENGEANCE

Cupid's bow was lying on Caesar's coffee table. Caesar was staring at it, smoking some cigarettes, sipping a beer. The quiver had five arrows. They were next to him on the couch. He pulled an arrow out and rolled it in his hand. Ran his fingers over the colorful feathers. Picked at the heart-shaped arrowheads. He walked into the kitchen space and sipped on a scotch.

Sipped and thought.

Something about the bow and arrows made him feel the cracks in his broken heart with such distinction—it was as if there were literal cracks running through his thumping organ. The pain angered him. The magic of the bow enhanced all feelings of love, even sorrow. Caesar's inner lament was a roaring forest fire, aiming to burn the roots of any future vegetation.

After much of his beer-and-scotch pondering, Caesar decided destroying the bow and the arrows was the thing to do. If Cupid no longer had his evil toy, he couldn't doom any more people to broken hearts.

Standing up with the bow in hand, he tried to break it over his thigh. The bow didn't notice the gesture. Caesar dropped it, falling back to the couch, cursing and rubbing the sore spot he had just bashed into his leg. Rocking in his seat, rubbing the welt, he puffed away on a cigarette and emptied his beer bottle.

Standing back up, he swung the bow into the edge of his kitchen counter. It bounced out of his hands and flew across the room, but not before putting an impressive dent in the counter. His hands vibrated with searing pain from the impact. He waved them in the air and shoved them under his armpits shouting, "FUCKING MOTHERFUCKER!"

From under the sink, he pulled a hammer and smiled, thinking, *This'll fuckin' put an end to you.* Stomping over to the bow, he kneeled with the hammer propped up high and swung. The hammer's head snapped off the handle and went whizzing by his face. It flew into the kitchen, smashing into the microwave. Caesar turned around to find the metal head resting inside on the turntable.

He mumbled to himself, *"Shit."*

Turning back to the bow, he looked at his hand. The hammer's handle had cracked, and there was a throbbing pain in his hand. The wood had splintered and stuck into his palm, drawing a little blood as he pulled it out.

Caesar was pissed now.

Looking down to the bow, he thought, *Fuck you.* Tossing the remainder of his scotch down his throat, he ran up to the bow and leaped into the air, growling, but Caesar's flip-flops weren't the right footwear for the decision he was making. His feet smashed onto the bow and shot a pain back up through his legs that sent him bouncing off his ass and onto his back. With his toes curled in, legs bent up at the knees, Caesar palmed his feet and swore through his teeth. Laying on the floor out of breath, he reflected on how things weren't going so well and decided it was time for a break.

Once his hand was freshly bandaged and he had a new beer to sip, Caesar smoked some cigarettes. He smoked and sneered at the bow and arrows, and poured a fresh scotch. Looking at the burning tip of his cigarette, he laughed. *Burn it*, he thought. Putting the bow and arrows into his bathtub, he fished out a can of lighter fluid and stood over the magical items. Ready to cover them in the flammable liquid, he paused.

"This is a stupid idea," he muttered.

Picking up the bow, he asked it, "Can you even burn?"

Flicking the lighter, he held the flame under the bow and watched as nothing happened. Not a mark was left where the flame touched. Caesar wasn't ready to give up. He had a little keyhole saw in his closet. With another shot of scotch, he dragged the saw across the bow and laughed as all the teeth broke off with an effortless swipe. There was no mark on the bow. Caesar plopped back onto his couch, cigarette in mouth, beer in hand, and a stumped expression all over his pissed face.

Better get some more smokes, he thought.

There was a little odds-and-ends store just past the check-in counter at the Inn. It wasn't big — little snacks, energy drinks, bottled water, batteries, tampons — things you might need on long road trips. There were also cigarettes. Caesar brought his beer with him, drinking his way across the parking lot. A troubled drunk named Mike was cleaning the windows outside. Sometimes Teddy had him clean messy bathrooms, too. When he came around asking, he traded him meals for labor.

Another one of Teddy's lost puppies.

He was a short, half-Mexican fellow. No one could figure out what his other half was. Mike didn't seem to know it himself, or care, for that matter. His father had just been passing through when he knocked his mother up. Never even knew Mike happened. Apparently, he was named Mike after the man who had just passed through. His mother thought it was funny. Mike thought his mother was funny, but not "ha-ha" funny. The other kind.

Caesar liked Mike because he never tried to cheer him up. In fact, he would typically greet him by busting his balls. Today was no different. He paused his squeegee mid-stroke on the window and smiled a gummy smile at Caesar. "What happened to your hand? Burn it skinnin' your dick?"

Caesar faked a little chuckle. "Actually, it was your dick I was skinning. Don't you remember coming over last night to cuddle?" Mike smiled and stopped Caesar just before entering the building to ask for some money. Caesar patted his pockets and sighed, "No, but I can give you a cigarette."

Mike held his hand out and waited.

Caesar laughed. "I gotta buy them first, Mike."

Teddy was at the counter, and Caesar slowed his flips and his flops. He still hadn't talked with him since he walked out of the kitchen. Awkwardly, he rubbed the back of his head, face down, dragging his feet around the only aisle in the small store. *Should I just leave?* he thought. *How long is he going to talk? How pissed is he? Is he pissed? Will he be all heady and concerned, with an arsenal of hugs ready?*

When he turned around, thinking about the bigger convenience store a couple of miles up the road, Teddy spotted him. "Hello, Caesar," he said, turning the page in a magazine he had open on the counter in front of him. Caesar poked his head up over the aisle and waved an awkward hello. Teddy kept looking in the magazine, and asked, "You alright?" Caesar walked up and rolled his fingers on the counter and slowly replied, "Yeah, I just came in for some smokes." Teddy pushed the magazine aside and looked at him, his mouth pinching with emotion and unease.

"So, you walked out the other day?"

Caesar nodded his head.

Teddy pulled Caesar's usual brand of smokes from the wall behind him and asked him if he was sure he was okay. Caesar dug around his pockets and gave Teddy a heavy look. Teddy knew it well. Pulling his hands out of his pockets, Caesar frowned. "Can you put the smokes on my tab?" Then he smiled, but it was an uncomfortable smile. Teddy was silent for a moment. Finally, with a sigh, he slid the pack across the counter. "You're lucky I care about you. Otherwise, I'd get up and hug you right now. But I know better." Turning his attention back to the magazine, he suggested, "You should go talk to your team in the kitchen. Let them know you're alright. And I know you know this, but I'm going to say it again anyway. You have friends who would love to listen. And you better be concerned for yourself because you're running out of strikes. You screw the kitchen over again like that and I'm going to have you committed." Caesar thanked him for the cigarettes and left. He had let him off easy, considering.

Too easy. He feared an intervention was in the works. Teddy's English was too good. Group hugs were being planned. He needed to run.

Mike was quick to ask for a cigarette. Reminded Caesar he had promised. Caesar peeled the pack open, gave him one, and lit it for him. Mike smoked and thanked him. Caesar lit his own, and they both smoked and watched the road, saying nothing. Caesar was thinking about disappointment. Looking at his bandaged hand, he thought about the impossible bow and the fat god. He thought about Teddy and how he would have liked that hug. But he was right. He would have fought it. He would have made himself not like it. *How pathetic,* he thought. *How sad.*

Turning to Mike, he asked if he wanted to come over and get drunk. Mike dropped his window squeegee and said a resounding, "Hell yeah."

Mike got comfy on the futon. Caesar poured them two vodka sodas — Mike's request. Mike, looking at the bow and arrows, asked, "You hunt?"

Caesar chuckled. "No." Then he sighed and added, "No, Mike, I don't *hunt.*" There was an obvious annoyance to how Caesar said "hunt" that Mike picked up on. Taking the drink he was handed, he bobbed his head defensively, asking, "Well, what *else* do you do with a bow?" Then Mike rolled his eyes toward his drink. "No straw?"

Caesar laughed. "You want an umbrella, too, Mike?"

Mike bobbed his head again and shrugged. "Yeah, that'd be nice."

Caesar huffed and turned into the kitchen, opening a drawer filled with rubber bands, some loose Band-Aids, a dead cockroach, some paper clips, a box of rainbow-colored straws, and a box of little colorful paper umbrellas. As he dug into the drawer, he explained to Mike that he wasn't annoyed with his question, just with the bow. A straw and an umbrella landed in Mike's drink. He smiled and stabbed at the ice in his cocktail with the straw before taking a sip and asking what the deal was. "It's a nice lookin' bow. Makes me happy lookin' at it."

Caesar scoffed, raising his brows. He took a drink, chewing a bit of ice as he leaned against his kitchen counter. With a big, dramatic drag from his cigarette, he told Mike, "Well, Mike, that there is Cupid's bow." Mike gave the bow a skeptical glance while he sucked up his drink through the plastic rainbow straw.

"Whaddya mean 'Cupid'?"

Caesar did a little wing-flapping gesture with his hands as he answered, "You know, big fat asshole with little wings, shoots people with arrows to make them fall in love. Cupid."

Mike gave Caesar a dumb stare before looking back to the bow, asking why he would have Cupid's bow. Caesar told him about his night, the fight, waking up with an arrow in him, finding the bow, and trying to break it. He got into the reasons why he was trying to break it, and why he fought Cupid, but then hesitated, saying, "I don't know why I'm talking to you about this."

Mike shrugged. "I don't know why anyone talks to me about anything."

"That's sad, Mike."

Caesar watched him suck his drink down and shake his head, and say, "Look at me, man. I got four fuckin' teeth, I smell like piss, and I smoke meth like it's God's cock. I don't wanna fuck'n talk to me." He held his glass up and shook it about as a means of asking for a refill. Caesar smoked with his reply. "I see what you're saying. All those things are incredibly unapproachable. At least you can still recognize those things... I guess.... That's a silver lining. Self-awareness is a dying virtue." He took Mike's glass and blew out a cloud as he added, "What am I saying? That's not even a bronze lining." He set the glass down and grabbed the bottle, asking him, "You just want the whole bottle?"

Mike thought about it and said, "Yeah, but can I still have another vodka soda?" Caesar started mixing him another drink. "Of course."

Mike smiled. "Thanks, man."

The two got drunk, shared stories of all the bad cards they'd been dealt, and smoked a bunch of cigarettes. The bow inspired it all. It plucked at the need they both had for the company. When they were good and pissed, Mike asked, "Are we friends?" Caesar smiled and talked around his cigarette. "Yeah, Mike, we're friends." Mike sighed. "Then, will you kill me?"

Caesar curled his eyes funny and said, "We ain't that close, Mike."

Mike took a drink and shrugged facetiously. "Well, shucks."

Caesar watched him for a while before asking him if he ever thought of going to the church down the road. "They're supposed to help people who are down on their luck," he told him, adding, "I think that's sort of Jesus's whole bag."

Mike growled, "Fuck that shit, shit's a bunch of fucking bullshit."

Caesar sighed, "Yeah, I hear ya."

Mike grimaced more. "The people preaching it are even more annoying than the bullshit of it all. I wish someone would just kill God already and spare us all this pain he doesn't do dick about. Big fucking scam if you ask me." Caesar froze with his cigarette hanging in his fingers, smoke furling into the air. Mike kept on venting, but Caesar stopped listening. He couldn't break the bow, but what if he broke Cupid? *Just kill God and spare everyone of all the shit,* as Mike so elegantly stated.

Caesar had made Cupid's nose bleed with nothing more than his fist. He couldn't scratch the bow, but he could scratch the god who used the bow.

He interrupted Mike's rant to say, "Hey, I gotta go."

Mike stood up with a sigh. "Yeah, figures." Caesar ushered Mike out the front door and said, "He doesn't get to do this to us. I'm gonna go kill him, Mike. I'm gonna kill Cupid." Mike was out the door, saying, "That's nice. Can I have another cigarette?" Caesar said no and started to close the door. Mike bounced up all bright-eyed with a hand out, and said, "Hey, what about the bottle?" But Caesar had already shut the door on him.

Caesar ran around his apartment filling a bag with clothes, filling a little cooler with ice, drinking a beer, collecting all of his liquor bottles, and thinking to himself how important it was that Cupid should die. How important it was for everyone. This was bigger than his broken heart alone. *Fuck*, he thought, *this is bigger than anything.*

Opening his fridge, he saw there was still some cheese, but that was it. He needed food for the voyage ahead. So he drove down the road to the bigger convenience store for some road snacks.

Caesar was pretty drunk.

He should not have been driving.

Edmond was behind the counter. Edmond was a melancholy Black man who often offered poetry in the form of advice. He and Caesar had an unofficial competition going to see who could be the most bitter towards life.

When he saw Caesar set his basket down on the counter, he raised a brow. "Never seen you buy so much food at once. And no beer? You a clone of my man? Caesar's twin brother, perhaps?"

Caesar laughed. "Yeah, evil twin."

Edmond started to ring him up, chuckling to himself. "The food doesn't fool me. I think sober Caesar's the good twin. Shit, I'da loved to meet the sober you." Caesar sighed. "I'd make a joke, but I'd like to have met you back then, too." Edmond stopped what he was doing, stood back a bit, surprised. "Damn, I'm touched and confused. Who the fuck *are* you?" Edmond laughed a little and studied Caesar's appearance. He had an air of purpose about him. It wasn't like him at all – focused, determined.

"Just seeing it clearly is all. Life is a miserable tale, Edmond. Old age takes just enough time to set in to have us thinking that it's all worth it. It's a cruel trick, and love is the jester distracting us from discovering the truth to this tragedy."

Edmond grinned and commented, "There he is."

Caesar gave him a wink and tossed a bag of chips from the snack rack onto his pile.

Edmond had a store cat, a stray he would let in when he worked. He even bought it a little outdoor cat house for the back of his store. It was a little black puss with a white spot on its neck and mitts, which made it look like it was wearing a tuxedo, so he named it Tux. The cat hopped onto the counter to greet Caesar. Tux liked Caesar, and Caesar liked Tux. He scratched the cat's ears and asked him how he was doing. Edmond said, "I'm not too bad considering, and yourself?"

"I was asking the cat."

"I know."

"Can you put this on my tab?"

Edmond laughed and shook his head, waving Caesar away with an eye roll.

The cat followed Caesar out and watched him set the bag of food in his back seat and light a cigarette. Caesar climbed into the driver's seat and started the car. A thump startled him. He looked up to see Tux on his hood staring at him through the windshield. He waved for the cat to move.

The cat didn't move.

Caesar rolled the window down and poked his head out, asking the cat to please get off the car. Tux hopped down, and Caesar pulled his head back in the car. "Thanks Tux." As he put the car into drive, Tux hopped in through the window and landed on his lap. Caesar jumped and laughed. He gave Tux a few pets and moved to pick him up, but Tux jumped out of his lap into the passenger seat. Spinning around, he sat and looked up to Caesar with what could only be assumed to be a smile. It was a smile that asked, *Where we going?*

Caesar took a drag of his cigarette and blew it out the window, away from Tux, and asked him, "What, you want a ride?"

Tux meowed.

Caesar shook his head to say he didn't think it was a good idea. Tux meowed again. Caesar reached over him and opened the passenger door. He gestured his head to the outside, telling Tux it was time to go.

Tux meowed again at him.

Caesar sighed a long exhale and reached back to close the door, "Fine. Just know I'm going to be doing a murder. You'll be considered an accomplice from this point on." Caesar looked ahead and spoke around his cigarette. "Let's go kill a god." With a final drag, he flicked the butt out of the window and looked up the road, ready to pull out. Just before he pushed the gas, he told the cat, "Also, I've been drinking, so if we get pulled over, we're switching seats."

XI
A BIG RED CAN OF GASOLINE

Tux was sitting on the dashboard, licking spicy dust off the nacho-flavored chip Caesar was holding out for him. His cigarette bounced on his lips as he told Tux he'd get him real food soon. Tux didn't seem to mind. He couldn't lick it off fast enough. His big cat eyes bulged over his tongue, excavating chip dust.

Caesar parked at a little shopping center with a sports bar. His plan was to stop at every bar and ask about the fat man with the little wings. With how Cupid was drinking when he met him, Caesar figured he was bound to stop at another bar eventually. He noticed a big billboard for a strip joint a couple of miles up the road as he got out of the car. *Maybe Cupid's getting a lap dance*, he thought.

But how early do those places open, he wondered?

Caesar held his car door open, asking Tux how he felt about strip clubs. Tux looked up to Caesar, and Caesar shrugged. "Yeah, I've never been to one either." Standing with the door still open, he motioned to Tux and asked, "You coming?" Tux hopped out and followed Caesar to the bar, where he held the door for him again. Tux went right in.

It was a smoky bar with televisions for wallpaper. Everywhere you looked, sports or someone talking about sports was playing on a big flat screen. Only one of the games was feeding sound through the bar. The few people drinking at this hour were talking back to the screens. None of the televisions seemed to hear them.

Caesar asked the bartender if he had recently served a fat naked man with wings. The bartender was a slim man with a beard. He had a funny slouch to his neck that appealed to his relaxed nature. Caesar's question made him scratch his beard, and slowly say, "How'd *you* hear about it?" Caesar leaned in, quick and curious, and asked, "What do you mean?"

The bartender waved for the attention of a husky white guy who was watching the game. He asked him to tell Caesar what he had told him. The man had a blistering red face. He started talking right away, his eyes dancing between Caesar and the game. "Yeah, so, buddy'a mine saw him, *says* he saw him. Traveling in a big rusty bus. Thing stopped outside real early this morning, and some smoking hot model-type came out to use the gas station's bathroom. I mean a *fuckin'* model. That's what he was saying anyway. A woman like he'd never seen, he said. He wouldn't shut up about it. Sat out and waited for her to come back outta the bathroom because he just *needed* to see her again. This is what he was telling me. But some man came out, he said. And get this, the man was wearing her clothes."

"What?"

"Some man came out, not a woman. And the *man* gets on the bus. My buddy saw a fat naked guy when the dude climbed on. Looked in through the door, saw a bunch'a weird shit, he told me. The fat guy was in there, the one you're asking about — little fucking wings and a halo. That's what he says to me, anyway. Said he saw *Cupid* on that fucking bus. You believe that shit? Cupid. Fuckin' been telling everyone about it all morning." The man took a sip of his beer and shook his head. "He swears, though. Fuckin' Cupid."

"Don't believe him?"

The man shook his head, returning his focus to the game. "Just some band passing through on some rock 'n' roll tour." Caesar watched the man take a big drink and burp. He went back to making comments on a referee's call. Caesar tapped on the bar and apologized for bothering his game, asking him if his buddy said which way they were going – the rock 'n' roll band. The man shrugged and told him someone from the bus was asking how far California was.

Caesar put a quarter in the bar's payphone and dialed 411 to get the number for the convenience store he was at earlier. He put Tux on top of the phone box. Tux stared at Caesar and purred. Caesar told him he was calling his owner. With the receiver wedged in his neck, he dug in his pocket for his cigarettes, and asked Tux, "Do you call him 'owner'? Or do you call him 'dad'?"

Tux just purred and blinked.

Edmond picked up, and Caesar told him, "Hey, it's Caesar. Your cat followed me. I sorta have him now." Edmond was in the middle of something, and just said, "He likes you." His tone was unmoved, as if to suggest Caesar's call was pointless. Caesar put a fresh cigarette in his lips, shrugged with a bit of attitude, and said, "So that's it?"

Edmond stopped what he was doing and sighed. "Listen, Caesar, it's a stray cat I feed. He likes you. What do you want me to say?" Caesar felt like being mad, but he didn't know what he expected from the phone call. Holding a lighter up, ready to strike, he said, "I don't know, man. Your stray cat's gonna be late for dinner, I guess. That's the message. I just wanted you to know, so you weren't up all night *worrying*."

Edmond sighed again. "Is that sarcasm?"

Caesar lit the cigarette and huffed. "I don't know. I think so. You know what? It's my cat now." He hung up and rolled his eyes at Tux, giving him a long eye-to-eye look before confessing, "You should know that I'm an alcoholic if you're really going to be my cat. I mean, I don't mind, you know, you hanging around. You can do what you want. It's just you should know what you're signing up for, is all. I want this thing to be transparent."

Tux just kept purring.

Caesar scratched his ears and explained that he could keep following him around, but he'd have to do his business outside because he wasn't going to mess with litter boxes. The bartender yelled in the middle of the conversation to say, "Hey! Is that a cat? Can't have cats in here."

Cesar picked up Tux and reflexively hollered, "Why the fuck not?"

122

The bartender and the patrons all turned to Caesar, silent. Caesar stood tall with Tux in his arms, a cigarette burning in his lips, alcohol bleeding in his eyes, and thought he might have yelled too loudly. The bartender, slightly annoyed, shrugged and just said, "Because you can't." Caesar slowly shook his head and apologized. "I didn't mean to yell. I just had some unplaced emotions, and... never mind. I'm leaving now." Caesar flipped his flops out of the bar and back to the road to carry on with his hunt.

A road beer was had.

Caesar pulled off at the next exit and picked up food, a water dish, and some toys for Tux. In the parking lot, he set Tux on the roof of his car along with a dish of water. Tux drank while Caesar asked him if he wanted fish or chicken. Tux kept drinking, and Caesar nodded his head. "Chicken it is." Tux was in his face the moment he peeled the lid off the can, sniffing and pawing at him impatiently. Caesar laughed a little and set the opened can next to the water. Tux ate it the instant it landed.

Caesar talked to Tux while he dug through his shopping bag. He pulled out a little felt mouse with a bell on it and shook it.

"You like toys?"

Tux didn't move from his food, and Caesar watched him. "Well, it's here when you're done eating." Reaching into the back seat, he pulled out a beer and popped the top, thinking about cigarettes. He put his chin on the roof close to Tux and watched him. It felt good to have a purpose.

"You think we'll end up driving all the way to California today?"

Caring for the cat reminded him of painful memories, and he almost started to cry, but then he remembered he had an open beer in his hand. With an emotional sigh, he rose from the car and froze. Across the parking lot, just outside the strip club, a distraught woman dressed in all black caught his attention. She had a sweatshirt on, hood up, and a serious look on her face.

"What's this?" Caesar said to no one, taking little breaths from the bottle as he watched. The woman was walking around a car, although walking wasn't really the word for it. Her motions were more primal, as if she was circling some sort of prey. She was noticeably distressed. Caesar took a drag from his cigarette and spotted a peculiar metal can in her hands. *Not something someone tends to carry around*, he thought, especially the way she was carrying it, fierce and savage-like. Like it was a weapon. Looking closer, he thought, *Shit*. He even said it.

"Shit."

Looking closer still, he thought out loud, asking no one, "Holy shit… holy shit, is that gasoline?"

It was.

It was a big red can of gasoline.

XII
DIRTY BATHROOM

Vivienne was peering over her knees. Uncomfortably slouching on a public toilet. Staring at the odd stains decorating the floor under her feet. A sticky floor with sticky stories. She hadn't realized how filthy the restroom was until she sat down. Her mind was preoccupied when she entered. Vivienne wasn't there to use the toilet. The seat was still down. She just needed a place to sit. All she wanted was a quiet space to think. A bit of solitude to digest the unbelievable situation her life had arrived at. A moment away from the magic. From the drug-entangled mayhem. From the rather troubling dilemma Cupid had senselessly fallen into. It seemed the fun ride she had tagged along for was departing and something dark was boarding. This was her chance to cut loose. To part ways before things got rough. There was a lot to think about. A lot to consider.

Only now her thoughts were being invaded by the stains she couldn't identify. A reddish-yellow splotch edged with a burnt green hue shaped out a rather disagreeable image before her. One too many bodily fluids had convened in this stall. If that wasn't enough to derail her thoughts, the smell of the place was becoming more and more apparent as the ruler of this public domain. With each regretful breath she took the smell came with. The stench hitched a ride with every bit of oxygen the room had to spare. Was it a foreshadowing of things to come, she wondered? Was her ride with Cupid a hopeless descent?

Where would it lead?

Where *could* it lead?

Hopeless was the word she was stuck on. At a glance, Cupid seemed to embody the very essence of the word. Of all the beings in the universe to be so lost, it left Vivienne feeling off. What tragedy could be so remarkable to spoil the hand from which love itself is gifted? Was it time that chipped away at him? Had the novelty of love wilted? Or had he himself suffered the sting his power holds in its shadow?

More presently, where were his friends?

Cupid's shape-shifting roadies were clearly taking advantage of him. At times it seemed Cupid knew this. But she could never really tell. Was he just that lonely? Was he so desperate for company? Had they always been around? Had the drugs taken their companionship down a dark road? How was it that nothing caring found itself drawn to help Cupid's suffering? Vivienne couldn't help but wonder, what could she do to help?

Should she help?

Vivienne was well aware of her ignorance with every facet of Cupid's world. Well aware she had long since departed from her element. A fish couldn't be any farther from water than she was at this moment. She was a fish skimming the surface of the sun. Still, she was intrigued. There was something compelling about Cupid's misfortune. It was somewhat intoxicating. Cupid's bow was missing.

What a thought.

The power to inflict unquestionable love upon any beating heart was just out there for the taking. One could redirect history with such an instrument. Vivienne pictured it lying unnoticed as countless people walked by clueless and unsuspecting. A snake coiled out of sight as feet carried on from place to place.

The way Vivienne saw it, Cupid had lost his grip on the bow long ago. Cupid lost grip of himself. There was so much more to return than just his bow. Cupid's heart was out there. And that, she told herself, that was what needed to be restored. Love's messenger was broken.

There was a knock at the door.

Vivienne cleared her throat. "Occupied."

A scratchy and confident voice called back. "You know we have a crapper on the bus, right?" It was one of Cupid's shorties. They were all gathered by the door. Huddled up and talking over each other.

"Of course she knows, she's used it."

"Yeah, she's just ditching us."

"Well Cupid wanted me to check on her, so I'm checking."

"Great, we checked, she's ditching us, can we go?"

"She isn't ditching us."

"Yeah, why would she do that?"

"Hold on, is she?"

"Wait... what's her name again?"

"Some French name."

"Hey, French lady, are you ditching us?"

Vivienne dropped her head into her lap. Cupid's strange little minions had come to collect her. She hadn't finished having the much-needed moment with herself. The shorties presence validated what she wanted to do. She felt a pull. Felt Cupid was reaching out for help. She was a life raft. A plane flying over the shipwreck that was Cupid's life. The desolate drug-entangled island he had been stranded upon.

Vivianne opened the door. "I'm ready. I just needed a bit of air."

"Air?" A shorty sniffed its way into the bathroom. "Not much air to breathe in here at all, French women."

Another sniffed in. "Yeah, just smells like shit. Shit and blood."

"Yeah, I smell blood too. Are you on your period?"

"Vag blood doesn't smell like that, you dim wit."

"What would you know of it?"

Vivienne gasped, "How dare you ask me this. Not that it is any of your business, but no I am not. I do not know whose blood you are smelling." There was blood on the sink and an alarming smear on the mirror. With a closer inspection, she discovered a few lost teeth resting in the sink. She hadn't noticed it until then. Vivienne sprung out from the bathroom with a look of shock. "I think someone has suffered a rather unfortunate moment in here."

A shortie looking in inquired, "Is it cute?"

Vivienne's eyes popped with a dead glare. "Cute?" She asked, not fully sure what she was even asking. All the shorties bunched up at the door. Their eyes reaching over one another.

"I don't see anything cute in here."

"Yeah, what's cute?"

"How is a period cute?"

"She said she wasn't bleeding?"

"Well, whose bleeding then?"

"Someone cute I think."

Vivienne rolled her eyes. Speechless, she walked away from the strange little creatures. Walked back to Cupid's love bus, ready to help however she could.

XIII
FRIENDS IN LOW PLACES

Gasoline was guzzling from the red metal can. Caesar was watching in awe. The woman poured it over the car with a passionate and furious emotion. She was crying. It was an angry cry. Puffy wet eyes pissed and pinched under her stiff, narrow brows, and pursed, tense lips murmured out frustration. She had a real serious stomp to her step. She chucked the can at the car when it emptied and paused. Arduous breaths held her in place as she stared at the slick, wet car, reflecting on whatever inspired her to bathe it in gasoline. It seemed to Caesar that she was trying to spark the petrol ablaze with nothing more than her look.

She wasn't.

He considered that she might be rethinking what she was doing. This was certainly the time for it. No going back once she took the next step. A moment of clarity may have caught her ear for a chance to back down. She wasn't. The woman was simply relishing the calm before the storm. She pulled out a matchbook, and Caesar leaned in close with two big, bright, gazing eyes to watch as she struck the match, tossed it, and the car quickly dressed itself in a fierce inferno.

Tux just kept eating.

The car was now a burning furnace.

Caesar stood with his mouth open, his eyes sparkling with the reflection of the flames. The woman seemed caught off guard by the power of it all. Caesar didn't sense any regret in her backward stumble, just surprise. It was a hell of a fire she summoned. When she spotted Caesar, however, was when notes of regret started working their way into her posture. It was obvious she had assumed she was alone. A witness changed the atmosphere.

Caesar straightened up, coughed, and thought, *Oh fuck, she's looking at me.* With her first step towards him, Caesar jumped. Beer spilled onto his sleeve as he scooped Tux up along with his things and rushed into his car. She was running his way now, her hood falling off her head. Fumbling with his keys, he could see the woman quickly closing the gap between them. She was a strong-looking Black woman, maybe two-hundred pounds, with dark walnut skin. Pain and fear shaped her round face.

Just as the car started, the woman slapped her gloved hands onto Caesar's hood. Caesar screamed a single-note yap in response. The woman was slightly out of breath with fire blazing behind her, outlining her form with an appropriate intensity. Caesar held his breath. The woman, stricken with an obvious mix of pain and panic, pleaded, "Please don't say anything." She leaned around to Caesar's window with her hands up in defense. "I'll pay you, just forget you saw me. Please."

Caesar gulped and absorbed the sincerity in the woman's requests, her demeanor, and the emotional strain shaping her face. With a quick nod of his head, he told her to get in. She paused for a brief second to register the offer but quickly accepted. She climbed into the back seat, and Caesar drove off the moment the door shut. Peering through the back window, she watched the car burn as they fled, her heart thumping with a frantic tempo.

The drive was silent for a mile or so. The woman would occasionally sort of sniffle and sort of laugh in shock, her mind still with the burning car. Tux sat in the passenger seat, staring at her with a curious wince. Caesar had opened a new beer while investigating the woman in his rearview. Caesar held the beer out for her and said, "You look like you could use a drink."

The gesture pulled her back to Earth. Clearing her throat and wiping her eyes, she chuckled and said, "You got anything stronger?" Caesar pointed to the seat next to her. She turned and laughed. "Where you going with all this?"

There was a box of liquor bottles buckled in next to her. Lifting a bottle of tequila, she asked if she could have some. Caesar nodded. Told her to go for it. The seal was cracked, and she took a healthy swig. She looked out the window, and took another, then looked back at the bottle. She held it up for Caesar.

"You want some?"

With a little smile, he told her, "You hold onto it for a while. I got my beer."

Caesar raised his bottle to gesture a toast and asked her if she smoked. She didn't. "Mind if I do?" he asked. She didn't. But she did roll the window down. The woman had caught her breath. The warmth from the tequila relaxed her shoulders.

"You usually drink and drive?"

"Yes. You set a lot of cars on fire?"

She laughed, but it was brief. Caesar pulled off the road into a turnaround next to an empty roadside stand. It looked like it sold produce when it was being used.

Caesar turned the car off and blew some smoke out of the window. His seat belt came off, and he turned around, put his hand out, and introduced himself. She shook his hand and said her name was April.

"So, what's the story?" he asked her.

She focused herself, arranged her emotions. Embarrassment glowed in her eyes a bit as she explained, "My man's been fucking behind my back." She said it like it was obvious, like, of course, what else happens to people?

Caesar sighed with sympathy. "Sorry to hear that, April."

April huffed, "Yeah, well, that's life, ain't it?"

She wiped more tears from her eyes. Emotion sniffled in her nose. Another drink from the bottle was had. Caesar opened his glove compartment and handed her a box of tissues. She thanked him and took a few. Blew her nose and wiped her face. Cleaned up.

Had a drink.

Silence returned to the car. April stared at the bottle in her hands. Caesar could see she was resisting the urge to cry. To weep and scream.

"How long were you two married?"

"Six years we been married. And he loves that car, fucking asshole…"

She took another swig of tequila, laughed a bit, complimented the bottle, and told him, "This is my favorite tequila."

Blowing more smoke out of the window, Caesar said, "Me too."

They tapped bottles and had a few sips. April's nerves were calming down. With a shameful smile, she apologized and said, "Thanks for the ride. I'm sorry I just climbed into your car."

Caesar smiled back. "No worries, I offered."

Blowing her nose again, she asked, "So where you and your cat going with all this liquor?"

"In a sense, we're off to burn a car of our own."

April chuckled. "No shit. Your wife sleeping around, too?"

"No. Divorced. Haven't seen her in years. I'm on a mission to kill Cupid, so no one ever has to suffer another broken heart. So, I suppose I'm burning all the future cars before they get a chance to need burning."

April started laughing.

"You're funny," she told him.

Caesar smiled, pointed to the bow, and said, "No, seriously. That's Cupid's bow and arrow." April looked at the bow and arrow, impressed. She reached for the bow with a careful hand, assuming by the look of it that the thing was expensive. Her breathing shifted when she held it in her hands. The power of the bow swelled her heart as it did to any who held it. The pain which guided her to burn her cheating husband's car was now a flavor she could taste in her mouth — ginger and cinnamon. Looking to bury the feeling, she commented, "Where'd you get this? Some old-time shit. I've seen that *Antique Roadshow*. This is the kind of thing you'd see getting a serious price tag."

Caesar sipped his beer, "I don't think they would know what to think about this one." He stared at the bow, enchanted by it, but also broken by it. April glared at him. It was a good act he was putting on. She smirked. "You really think I'm gonna believe this is Cupid's bow? There is no Cupid." Caesar shrugged and said, "Makes you feel funny when you hold it, doesn't it? Pulls at your heart. Can't deny it." Despite the truth to his words, April made a face like she wasn't buying it, and said, "*Please*. I just set my husband's car on fire. My heart is not a reliable resource at the moment. Bow *is* fancy, I'll give you that. Gotta be worth some money. But Cupid? *Come on*." But she didn't fully believe herself. The bow did have a feeling to it. But that feeling was silly, and Cupid wasn't real, so she set the bow down, cleared her nose, relaxed a bit, and thanked Caesar again for the ride. "This is a fucked-up day," she said, a slight hint of a laugh in her tone. Caesar raised his drink and smiled. "This is a day to remember. And I get the feeling we were supposed to meet."

"How's that?" April asked.

"Because of my mission to find Cupid. You're a sign I'm on the correct path. The universe, or whatever — it supports my crusade. I usually don't believe in those types of things, but given the existence of Cupid, well, seems life is nothing what I thought. Could be our intentions pulled us together. Like magnets or something. Or it's just the bow doing what the bow does."

They were both feeling rather open, a little more secure in their thoughts and feelings. It had everything to do with the bow. One didn't have to hold it to be closer to their heart, but only needed to be in the proximity of its magical aura.

Feeling and accepting were two different things, however. April wasn't quite ready to put her head completely underwater. She looked to the bow with a skeptical squint. "What is it, really?" she asked, rubbing the pristine etchings that shaped the curious relic. Caesar started the car and looked ahead, and told her the same thing as before. "I told you, it's Cupid's."

Caesar drove back down the road. April asked him where they were going. Caesar told her he was hungry, and he figured since he was now an accessory to arson, they should get to know each other over a meal. "Unless you just call the game here, I can drop you off somewhere, and we can go our separate ways," he added, his tone suggesting he'd rather not. April happily shook her head and said, "I'm invested now. Drunk-driving white man with a thousand-year-old bow-and-arrow gives a car-burning Black woman a ride to safety. I wanna see where this day goes."

Caesar smiled. "Good. You like chicken fingers?"

"Love 'em."

"The pub up here has the best fucking fingers. Plus, they let you smoke inside. They have other shit on the menu, too, that isn't bad, but I'm craving those fingers."

XIV
STORY TIME

Dead cigarettes perfumed the pub. April didn't smoke but said she didn't mind. Didn't really notice it, she told Caesar. Caesar kept an ashtray close and did his best to keep his smoke away from April anyway. Two orders of chicken fingers, some spicy jalapeno poppers, and two baskets of fries got the conversation started. April asked about the bow. Caesar had it lying next to him, Tux along with it. He had his head poking out of a bag and was purring. Caesar said, "I saved you, so you go first."

"Fair enough," April replied, taking a bite and gesturing with her food for him to ask something as she chewed. Caesar started with, "Stop me if I'm being too forward, or if it's too soon. It just seemed pretty early in the morning for someone to be at a strip club having an affair. I didn't know strip clubs opened up so early." April nodded her head and told him, "Some have breakfast buffets. But he wasn't doing his bullshit at the club. He was at work. It's my club."

"How do you mean?"

"I own it. It's my club."

"No shit."

"Shit, yes. Previous owner was a little motherfucker. Got himself locked up for selling sex out of the place. Court seized everything, and everyone went outta work. Now, I own a bed and breakfast and two liquor stores. I got my MBA, and I don't fuck around, Caesar. So, I got myself a grant, bought the land

and the club from the city, and turned the place into a woman's house of power. I love my girls. With the exception of Miss Panther. That slut's gonna wish she never crossed me." April scarfed down a few fries, nodding to her words. Caesar sipped his cocktail and said, "You have a dancer named Miss Panther who slept with your husband?"

April swallowed her food and washed it down with a swig of booze. "Her stripper name's the Pink Panther. She dances to the theme song. You know the one, *da-dun, da-dun, da-dun-da-dun-da-dun, da-dun, da-du-u-u, dun-dun-dun*. Bitch comes out in a pink trench coat. Had a magnifying glass early on in her set, but we felt she was making a joke on the male anatomy that didn't work in her favor, so she ditched the prop for a big pink boa. The song's a real sexy piece of saxophone. Gets the club's attention quick. My unfaithful piece-a-shit husband is one of my bouncers. Seems that saxophone was too much for him. Shit, I'll see to that. I'ma shove a motherfuckin' sax up his cheatin' ass and show him *how* it's too much. I'ma break his ass with that shit." She was grinding her teeth, trying to calm her anger.

Caesar sighed. "You must really love him. I'm so sorry, April."

April wiped a tear from her eye and took in a heavy breath to say, "I was good to that man, Caesar. I was so good to him."

"I bet you were. I get the feeling you're good to everyone."

With a big drink, April cleared her nose and said, "Well, now that you're my partner in crime with this arson shit, tell me about you."

He laughed. "Where do I begin?"

April smiled. "I shared my broken heart. Give it up."

Caesar sighed and huffed, "If we're going to talk about that, we'll need another round." April waved for a waiter and said, "Oh, we're getting drunk. I'm already fuzzy. But fair warning, when I drink, my tongue gets pretty colorful. I hope your ears aren't too sensitive. My mouth is a dirty place for words." Caesar raised his glass with a smile and said, "April, I think we're going to be good friends." They tapped glasses and had a happy drink. They told the waiter to keep the drinks coming — even ordered shots.

Caesar was cautious about his approach to the subject of his broken heart. It had been a long time since he'd even said her name aloud or said the other. He chugged his drink to prepare. April noted his hesitation, observed the dismal shift in his mood. The bow was easing Caesar into opening up, encouraging him to speak. Warming up, he commented on how long it'd been since he talked about it. Couldn't even bring it up the last time he spoke with his mother, he told her, which was almost four years ago.

April stopped him there, eyes wide, setting her drink down to say, "Shut the fuck up. You haven't spoken to your mother in four years?" Caesar sighed and slowly shook his head. April crossed her arms and told him, "You need to call your mother." Caesar sort of shrugged a lost gesture and flicked some ash from his cigarette.

April shook her head and waved her hand at him. "Motherfucker, she made your ass." To which Caesar replied, "Well, I don't remember asking to be made, so technically, I'm her responsibility, right? Maybe it's the moms who should be calling, don't you think?" April rolled her eyes around the entire building and back. "That's some stupid ass shit. Something fucked up with you, saying a thing like that." She rolled her eyes again and added, "You need to call your mother. Just saying."

"Fair enough," he said, holding a fry down for Tux. The cat gave it a few licks before snatching it and retreating into his bag. April waited for the rest of his story. Caesar took a shot and ordered another. Puffed his smoke. Failed to find the words to open up. April could see it was going to take a few more drinks to get Caesar to share, which only made her more curious. So she changed the subject, for the time being, and asked again about the bow.

Caesar told her about meeting Cupid and fighting him, pulling the arrow from his chest, finding the bow, trying to destroy the bow. "And he drinks," he told her. "He's a fat drunken asshole."

Feeling a bit tipsy, April listened to Caesar's tale with an open mind. She wasn't yet ready to believe anything magical, but she did think there was something significant about the bow itself. So she asked him what the plan was. Putting another shot back, Caesar shrugged. "The plan is to chase after the plump prick. I know he's going this direction in a big bus."

"Find him, and what?"

"I told you. I'm going to kill him."

They stared at each other in silence after that, Caesar's drink hanging in the air, Tux's head poking out for another fry. April squinted and asked, "Is this some cosplay shit? You two some fantasy role-playin' nerds?" Caesar burst into laughter. It was mostly forced, but genuinely inspired. April took a drink and continued, "I'm not judging. What's that roleplay shit people do where they dress up in a field and cast spells on each other?" Caesar chuckled into his drink and said he didn't know.
Sipping more of her own, April probed, "For real, though. Whose is it? Is it a family heirloom or something? Too heavy to be a prop. Shit is definitely real. I'm curious to know, but I'm more curious about this Cupid roleplay you got going on. This friend playing Cupid, he just a buddy or like a *buddy-buddy*?"

Caesar smiled. "It's not a sex game, if that's what you're implying. If you want to tag along, I'll eventually find him, and then you'll see for yourself. You can even help me rid the world of him. Two broken hearts sparing the future of humanity from suffering our fates."

April leaned back and said, "Tempting. I don't really know what I'm supposed to do now. The fire was a little impulsive, so I am looking to get away so I can process."

"What was the plan post-fire?"

"No plan. The idea just sort of came to me last night. Couldn't sleep. He was with her, told me he was with a buddy. I marched my ass to the club on foot to catch him starting his shift, fucking steaming. If you weren't there to bring me back to reality, hell, I might've killed him."

Caesar smiled. "Glad to be of service."

They both toasted to new friends and took another shot. April was sucking mercy from a lemon to soothe the liquor burn. With her face pursed from the citrus, she carried on, asking, "So you have Cupid's bow and arrow, and *you're* chasing after *him*?"

"Yeah, why do you say it like that?"

"Well, I mean, come on... wouldn't Cupid come back for his bow?"

Caesar sat in awe for a moment, taking a drag from his cigarette and shaking his head. With a subtle laugh, he smiled. "Son of a bitch." April gave him a wink and sipped her drink. She motioned for a cigarette. Caesar tossed his pack on the table and said, "Thought you didn't smoke."

She shrugged. "Only when I'm drunk."

She took a long drag and eased her posture as she exhaled, and asked, "Why *did* you help me back there?"

With a shrug, he told her, "Because life is tragic. We should all look out for each other. Especially when our emotions bring us to the places you found yourself this morning."

"I just set a car on fire, and you offer me a ride... a complete stranger?"

"Yeah, but I could see in your face you weren't crazy or dangerous. Maybe a little troubled. You just needed a hug."

April smiled, watching Caesar drink and not think much of his words, like what he was saying was so obvious anyone would have done the same.

With her glass tipping back for another drink, April ordered, "Alright, Mr. Tragic, let's hear it. Heartbreak time."

Caesar took a long breath, ready to share, his eyes welling up at the thought of saying what he was about to say. He couldn't look her in the eye when he spoke, his gaze lost in the table, hands nervously poking about. April focused. She could see he was working pretty hard to stay composed.

A lump formed in his throat. With a smoke, he started his story. "Five years ago, I was in a car accident. My pregnant wife was with me. She was nine-months... ready to burst at any minute. A woman on her cell phone ran a red light. She was texting her friend important 'lol's' and 'OMG's.' Baby died in the emergency room, didn't suffer. Didn't... didn't even know what life was. I, uh, I woke up the next day with some broken ribs and a headache. My wife... was, uh, she was in a coma for a couple of months. I slept at her bedside, waiting for her to wake up. Planned our unborn child's funeral during the day, slept beside my comatose wife at night. Buried the baby. Couldn't manage work. They gave me time off. But eventually, too much time went by, and I was let go. Then, miraculously, she finally wakes up. Seeing her eyes open, my god, my heart pumped for the first time since the car crash. My last good memory. See, she wakes up, only she has no idea who I am. Suffered some unique brain damage, they said, which hilariously erased me from her memory. Me, our baby, our lives. Apparently, amnesia is pretty rare, and hers is, well, hers is super fucked, I guess. We won the fucking lottery on rare amnesias. She woke up, not recognizing me, not feeling anything for me. In fact, I irritated her. Her brain damage causes her to reach anger rather quickly with things. Me being at the top of the list. What a fucking joke. We stayed together for a few months, and she tried, but there was nothing there. It was an obligatory pity. I just annoyed her. Like I was some con artist or a bad salesman she was politely trying to dismiss. To her, I was just this sad person she didn't know crying around her all the time. Hard not to be emotionally unstable, given the circumstance. She met someone pretty quickly, and so I moved out. Started drinking because I'd dream about them every night — horrible dreams where she was leaving me, and I just couldn't stop her. I wake up in a panic reaching out to her sobbing. But no one's there. Dreams where the baby just dies over and over again, ripped out of my hands every night. I lose them *every fucking night*. I wake up covered in sweat, out of breath, my heart racing, fucking miserable, tears just burning out of my face, and I can't breathe. *My god*, I can never breathe. I'm just choking. Wailing like an infant for mercy. But if I'm drunk when I fall asleep, I don't dream. That was such a gift to discover. To silence the relentless nightmare with a little brandy." Caesar blew his nose, wiped his tears away, and cleared his throat. He did a sort of laugh-cry before adding, "She was just erased from me, hollowed out. Like God reached down into my life and pushed me out of it. I could touch her, talk to her, ask her how her day was, but it was someone else. Left to grieve the loss of our child alone. She'd come to the grave and stand around like a child herself, or a pet. Apathetically hovering around in the shape of what was the love of my life. We were going to name him Oscar."

Caesar choked down a lump of tears and raised his glass, summoning April to do the same. April's mouth was slightly agape, eyes seeping with empathy. Caesar was struggling to hold himself together, waiting for her to tap his glass. Instead, she got out of her seat, pulled Caesar from his, and squeezed the life out of him. His feet dangled in her grip. Caesar hugged her back and started to cry. Tux watched with a curious tilt of his head, sniffing for fries. April didn't let him go, and even rocked him a little. His flip-flops fell to the ground as his legs swung from side to side. She didn't know what to say, so she just kept saying she was sorry. "You poor man," she said.

Caesar appreciated it, and let himself hang loose in her embrace. His head rested on her shoulder. Tears darkened her shirt. It felt good to let it all out, especially with the assassination that lay ahead —the justice which was finally upon him. Expressing the pain in detail felt like his testimony to the universe. Caesar felt that April's reaction validated Cupid's death sentence.

With a few pats on her back, he thanked her. When she set him down, April made a joke about his weight, telling him he needed to eat more.

"Cigarettes are slimming," he told her.

Getting drunk was easy, with the day's events being what they were. Sharing their broken pieces, allowing themselves to be vulnerable, they drank themselves into slurry words. Drank themselves into the late evening. Drank themselves through their entire life stories. Drank themselves across the street into a hotel lobby.

Caesar was outside smoking while April got the room. She stepped out and waved at him. "I got us a room. There are two beds, so don't get any ideas." Caesar held his hands up in defense and told her, "I was only thinkin' how trusting you are. Sharing a room with me like this." April laughed. "Please. Scrawny white man driving around with a cat looking for Cupid? You're harmless. Shit does have a serial killer vibe to it, but I get that vibe from most white people." Caesar smiled and said, "I sort of do, too."

Laughter led them to the room.

Arm in arm.

A wonderful and stumbling new friendship.

Inside they kept drinking, April happy to have company for her fire escape, and Caesar happy to be drunk and still drinking. April still had a glass from the pub in hand, the ice cubes dancing around as the two crashed.

"You didn't bring my drink," Caesar complained.

April huffed, "You finished your cocktail. Besides, you got that whole fucking box."

Sitting on the floor with his back against the wall, Caesar lit a cigarette and hugged a bottle of liquor. Smoking and drinking, he thought out loud, "Why do you think they call it a cocktail? Strange image, a cock with a tail."

April squinted at the thought, imagining such a thing as a cock with a tail. She smiled a little, suggesting the tail would probably have to grow from behind the balls and tuck up in the crack of your ass. They both discussed with great detail how it would make the dick look like a fleshy alien dinosaur with testicle feet.

They drank themselves into statues, eyelids cementing over. Weak laughs filled the spaces between their drunken banter. Before they could pass out, April managed to turn the conversation back around, asking that if he had been with his wife for fifteen years, "Then you started dating in high school, yeah?"

With a big drink, Caesar explained, "That's right. Married for ten of the fifteen. Shit, we'd be celebrating fifteen years of marriage if life wasn't such an asshole. Kid would be five going on six." With a heavy sigh, he carried on. "I'm fucking thirty-eight. Been dead for five years. Drunk for four. And I apologize."

"For what."

"Something we ate gave me gas. It was silent. I don't smell it yet."

April smiled and farted in response. A big rumbling storm from under. Caesar gave a little chuckle and farted back. Childish laughter volleyed between farts. After a silent moment, April lying on her back, half asleep, said, "So that means you started dating when you were eighteen." Caesar nodded and mumbled a yes. April, her eyes closed, asked, "No breaks in the middle?"

Caesar, eyes still closed, raised his cigarette, and said, "Only person I've ever been with."

April smiled and said, "Shut up."

Caesar put his cigarette out and huffed, "One and only." April opened her eyes and turned on her side to look at him.

"You tellin' me you only fucked one person, ya whole life?" With a nod, Caesar took a breath from his bottle.

April sat up in disbelief to excitedly say, "Your drunk ass is pushing forty, and you've only smashed one set'a legs?" Caesar shrugged, his eyes closing. April kept at him, "You haven't gotten any since, what? Since it happened? Fuck me, Caesar. Five years without any pussy." Caesar laughed and shook his head. April laid back down and smiled. "Your ass needs to get laid."

Caesar laughed again.

April grinned, her eyes closed, voice softening to her exhaustion as she told him, "I'm gonna get you some pussy." Caesar said he didn't want any. Shaking her head, eyes still closed, April declared, "That's what you need — some warm, juicy pussy. Fix your sad ass right up."

"You offering?"

April chuckled. "Ain't my type, sorry, Caesar. I got some good pussy, but, ain't my size, ain't my shade. You get a few more cocktails in me, and uh… *ha-ha-ha*, you might get your cocktail in me." April started laughing at herself. Caesar laughed as well, opening his eyes to get a look at April cracking herself up. As her laughter faded and she gave in to her drunken state, she apologized. "I'm sorry. I'm just playing with you." Closing her eyes, she exhaled a tired, "Couldn't help myself."

Caesar was asleep. Bottle in his lap, back against a wall, head hanging over his chest. April passed out shortly after. Tux was in the other bed, purring in his sleep. It was peaceful for a couple of hours — the three of them sleeping.

…

April didn't hear the screaming until it was outside. She sat up, still drunk, the hotel sign creeping a disorienting red light in through the window. Someone was outside shouting. Working to her feet, pushing through the red haze, April focused out the window. Caesar was in the middle of the road, shouting into the night.

"Oh my fucking god," she uttered.

She was outside running his way immediately. Caesar was in his underwear and nothing else. The room's television was smashed by his feet. Caesar, barefoot, agony twisted on his

143

face in painful directions, dropped to his knees when he saw April. He screamed at no one to get off their phone, screamed at everyone to stop texting and just drive their goddamn car. Screamed at April to make it stop. To kill him. To end it.

April wrapped her arms around him and tried to calm him. He was hysterical, grief melting him into hopeless puddles. Heaving sobs struck him like stones being thrown from an angry crowd.

This was why Caesar didn't talk about it.

This was why friends didn't bring it up.

Another hotel guest hung out their window and yelled for him to shut up. April picked Caesar up and yelled back at the man, telling him to fuck off before she came over and fucked him the fuck up.

Back in the room, April laid Caesar on the bed. She asked him if he was alright. Caesar was blackout drunk, face on fire with memories. He smiled at April, sniffled a little, and just said, "I like how you yelled at that man. You gotta real nice yell."

XV
JUST A DRINK OR TWO

Cupid had a map stretched out in his hands. Standing on the side of the road somewhere on Route 66, he strained his mind to recollect something helpful. A shorty stood by in the shape of a tall and slender fellow they met in England a couple hundred years ago. The shape was chosen mostly to be tall enough to peek over Cupid's shoulder at the map and offer some assistance.

They were lost.

It was frustrating.

Too many drugs carried them from one place to the next to make out the difference between their left and their right. Vivianne was watching Cupid from inside, capturing the moment in her sketchpad. A shorty watched her scratch his likeness into the paper with a blue ballpoint pen. The shorty was rolling a joint.

Another shorty was hanging out of the bus, stoned out of its mind, asking for an update. Cupid didn't answer. He just growled at the map. Growled and sighed.

Sighed and mumbled, "The fuck are we?"

Back on the bus, Cupid snarled, "Anyone even remember the name of the bar?" No one did. Vivianne was with them that night, but being the mortal she was and with all the partying they had been doing, she was passed out on the bus during the incident. Shrugs were tossed around, along with the joint. Cupid puffed away on the grass, telling the shorty on the wheel to just keep driving and stop at every bar until something looked familiar. Vivianne suggested that they try to conquer their quest sober. "You've been doing drugs nonstop since I met you. It's exhausting just to witness. You should've died several times over with how much you all indulge." A beer bottle popped open, and a cloud of smoke blew into the air. A shorty rattling a pill bottle shrugged and sort of agreed, "Clearer minds will prevail." Cupid laughed and gestured for the pills.

They stopped at a bar none of them recognized, but the owner claimed they had passed through. Still had a tab open to prove it. Cupid was in the parking lot, recreating the bout he had with Caesar. He was getting agitated with his shorties. Trying to orchestrate his reenactment with the state his companions were in was difficult. They took his plight seriously. The missing bow was dire. They were, however, drunk and stoned and horny and figured it would turn up like it always did. So being serious was low on their list of priorities.

Cupid rolled on the ground like he did that night, flopping onto his back, thinking to himself that this wasn't the place. With a huff, he motioned for a smoke. Still on his back, a shorty planted a cigarette in his lips. Another one lit it. Cupid smoked and sighed, "How far to the next bar?"

A shorty dug out a map and crossed its eyes to calculate the miles. Scratching its head, the shorty turned the map around, finding they were reading it wrong. With a laugh at themselves, the shorty corrected the number it gave while another shorty bumped them, shouting, "That's the wrong state."

"Fuck you. It's not."

They snatched the map and looked closer. "See here, this means water, and this means land." The two snickered over where they were. Lots of pointing and hand slapping. Laughing and teasing that got nowhere. Cupid heaved up to his feet, his little wings flapping about with great effort. Flicking his cigarette in their direction, he shouted for them to shut up. Screamed at them before stomping back into the bus. His head popped out shortly after to demand they get inside.

"We're leaving," he ordered.

More drinks were had along the way to the next bar. They were skilled at mixing and handing off. Little to no eye contact was made as beverages were crafted and distributed. It was impressive how symbiotic their use of drugs made them.

Despite the pristine execution of this performance, Cupid was festering, biting his nails and sweating. Vivianne was filling pages in her sketchbook with blue-ink cupids, studying his distressed disposition. Taking close note of how much substance Cupid and his troupe were consuming. She had a beer herself, partly for solidarity and partly to relish in the moment. "When in Rome," and all that.

Vivianne found herself pitying Cupid. He was awfully sad for being the God of Love. And with his bow missing, he wore a radioactive shade of humiliation. His anger did its best to hide his embarrassment, but shame like the cloud Cupid had cast above his head was hard to disguise. Cupid's little buddies did far more harm than good with their attempts to console their holy leader. Vivianne couldn't figure out if his loose-skinned companions were actually his friends or just freeloading tricksters high on love. They comforted him with drugs but offered little-to-no emotional encouragement. They mostly teased him in passive ways that fueled his anger. They were always clever about it. Cupid rarely got angry at them, but they got him steamed at everything else around him. They were either stupid or brilliantly sadistic. Vivianne was still analyzing. Either way, they weren't much help at all with Cupid's dilemma.

Their next stop was a biker bar. The shorties all reshaped themselves into the appropriate patrons to blend in, choosing the forms of big, Black bikers. At first, Vivianne thought nothing of it. But as they passed the bikes parked outside the bar, she spotted several Confederate flags, deciding then that these chameleons weren't stupid, but rather twisted instigators having too much fun at the expense of others.

While Cupid did his dance in the parking lot, Vivianne decided to enter the bar ahead of her group to procure a safe vantage point from which to view what might or might not turn into a fight. The few patrons inside gave Vivianne a look when she entered, the conversations dimming for a brief moment until she settled at the bar and ordered a vodka soda. A burly biker with curly blond hair, a long wispy beard, leather, and denim head to toe made his way to the seat next to her. His vest was bedazzled with little metal spikes.

Leaning in to catch her eye, he told her, "I like your accent. Where you from?" The burnt ash of a cigar was present on his breath. Vivianne smiled politely and answered, "I am from France." The biker turned to his friends and made a playful but somewhat patronizing face. His friends chuckled. As he turned, Vivianne noted the large Confederate flag on his back and worried over the potential racial tension the chameleons would soon bring.

"What brings you to the States, pretty lady?"

"I have been an American citizen for some twenty years now."

"Is that right?"

Vivianne smiled a big smile and spoke from her heart to say, "I love this country. From coast to coast, it offers such a colorful parade of cultures and breathtaking landscapes. I am here almost six months out of every year, seeing as much of it as possible."

The shapeshifters came in one by one. Their presence silenced the bar instantly. They were hamming it up, standing in the door sort of brooding, removing their shades at a dramatic pace. Gathering around Vivianne, they asked her who her new friend was, referring to the curly blonde brute perched beside her. The biker answered for her. "I'm Bruce," he told them, adding, "You all want a drink?" He turned to the bartender and snapped his finger, smugly saying, "A round of, uh. What's it called?" Bruce turned back to the shapeshifters and grinned, "What's that drink you all like, um, fried chicken?"

Bruce's friends all started laughing. It was a childishly rambunctious roar. The sort of obnoxious cackle that middle-aged adolescence inspires after pulling one's finger to pass gas. Vivianne winced at the joke. Apart from being appalling and racist, it was stupid and didn't make sense.

Cupid was still outside in the parking lot laying on his back with a joint in his lips, mumbling to himself. Mumbling lines he had remembered trading with Caesar the night of their fight. It wasn't helping any. Nothing about this bar seemed familiar. A crash and a muffled shout interrupted Cupid's meditation, and he turned his head to the bar. Bruce came crashing through the door with a shorty gripped to his vest.

Cupid rushed inside. Fists were flying, pool cues were breaking over backs, mugs smashing over walls, tables flipping. Cupid was unmoved by all of it. He'd seen enough bar fights to find this one more than underwhelming. It was Vivianne he was looking for, and Vivianne he found. Casually walking through the uninspired brawl, Cupid reached out for her with a tired smile. "This isn't the bar," he told her. A biker stopped her, grabbing her arm and saying something nasty with the word "Negro" in it. Vivianne tried to pull her arm free, but the man only tugged harder. Cupid's eyes turned red, and he did a rehearsed motion with his hand before tossing a flurry of pink, sparkly glitter into the biker's face.

Vivianne watched in awe.

The man immediately let go of her and stumbled back, weeping. Falling to his knees, he began sobbing and apologizing. His cries infected the bar, and the fight halted, everyone watching the weeping biker melting into a string of confessions, regretting all of the hurtful things he had done to women over the years. Cupid was unaffected by it. He was on his way out the moment it had begun, holding Vivianne's hand, tossing a sparkly, glittered spell into each biker's face on his way out. Vivianne smiled, her eyes wide with wonder as she watched the big, leather-bound brutes crumble into tears.

Outside, Bruce was rolling around with a shorty, trading blows. Cupid knocked Bruce off the shapeshifter with a pink emotional splash of magic and marched onto the bus. Vivianne had a seat on the sofa while Cupid plopped into the driver's seat and started impatiently honking the horn.

His big Black bikers filed in, shrinking back into their shriveled testicular shapes. Cupid was on the gas before the door closed. It was a heavy foot heaving the bus forward. Those still standing stumbled over, desperate for something to catch and keep themselves from falling. A few complaints raced for the driver's ear, but Cupid only growled in response. Vivianne, feeling giddy after observing Cupid's pink sparkly spell, was finding her curiosity in the plump god growing ever more, and her sketchpad filled with more and more Cupid.

Cupid ground his teeth while he sped up the road. Behind his anger, Vivianne could see the fear in his eyes. What was Cupid without his bow and arrow? But what other magical spells did he have hidden away? She needed to know.

With all the bickering and festering annoyance of the shorties moping around, Vivianne put her butt in the passenger seat and explored her new fascination. She told Cupid how impressed she was with how he handled the bigoted bikers — asked him if he had any other magical gifts.

Cupid almost smiled and told her, "I call that one Dust of Remorse." With a long sigh, he told her about his spells of lust, reflection, and misdirection. But none of them compared to the love which enchanted the arrows his bow gifted the world. Speaking of it saddened him. The fear Vivianne noted earlier had returned. A piece of Cupid was missing. There was an infectious desperation to the incomplete Cupid. Vivianne wanted to reunite him with his bow, like putting the universe back together. It seemed far too important a thing not to want. Too wondrous and fantastic and outrageously unbelievable to pass up.

Talking with Vivianne seemed to tamper Cupid's anger. Her interest in his work and his magic was genuine. It was refreshing. Cupid couldn't remember the last time anyone showed an ounce of fascination in his direction. Everyone was always taking. Always asking and grabbing, and thrusting, and humping, and *There are no more drugs, Cups,* and *Yeah, Cups, we need more speed.* His loyal travel companions, such a sore. Sad to think they were all he had, and for longer than he'd care to admit. But now here was Vivianne. A weathered yet still attractive French woman, more or less arriving out of nowhere, and with a smile on her face. A smile with questions that took him back centuries.

When a shorty leaned into the conversation with an attempt to ease his burden, the embers of Cupid's tamed rage quickly stirred back into a roaring fire. With a handful of sparkling remorse, Cupid slapped the wrinkly shorty in the face. The glittering strike sent the creature tumbling backward, sobbing and cowering from feelings it could never reach on its own. The scene set Cupid's other shorties on their best behavior. Silent and still, they kept to themselves for the rest of the ride. Vivianne preferred them this way. She hadn't any inkling to the length of time Cupid had spent with them, but it was obvious they were nothing but trouble. Friends or not. If she was going to help Cupid, they were certainly her first obstacle.

...

Some distance away, back in Caesar's room, Frances and Teddy were smoking some cigarettes. They'd been waiting for Caesar for a while. Teddy was thinking he should let housekeeping have a go with the room, even though Caesar made it known he didn't want his place cleaned. Shaking his head at the mess, Teddy huffed, "How does someone live like this?" Frances shrugged. "Caesar ain't doin' much livin' in here, just drinking." Teddy sighed and slowly nodded his head.

"Do you think he'll ever... snap out of it?" Teddy asked with a heavy breath. Frances did his sucking-thinking thing with his tongue and said, "I mean, if they can put all those thousands of satellites in the sky, I'm sure our little buddy can pull through this."

Teddy's face scrunched, and he uttered a confused, "What?"

Frances belched. "I don't know, man... I've been drinking."

They both had a beer in hand. Teddy lifted his a bit, some guilt bending his lips funny as he did.

"You think us drinking while we wait for him is maybe not the most appropriate thing given the circumstances?"

Frances sipped his beer and took a drag. "I think us just, like, coming into his place and sitting down uninvited is inappropriate. But that's love, ain't it?"

There was a pause and a moment of reflection from Teddy as he considered Caesar's boundaries. Frances sipped again and said, "But I see what you mean. Does sorta feel like we're bringing a drink to an intervention. Caesar's the type, though. I think the only way you could get him to take his intervention seriously is if you gave him a drink for it." Teddy set his beer down, asking, "Is that what we're doing?"

"Doing what?"

"Is this an intervention?"

Frances sighed a long breath. "Uh... I'd rather it wasn't."

Cupid parked at a bar called Pit Stop. On his way to the door, he didn't bother doing his memory dance in the parking lot. He just made his way to the front. His shorties were still nervous Cupid might splash them with his funny dust. Pushing him to reenact the fight. They were over-acting and excessively encouraging the god.

"Come on, Cups!"

One fell over, saying, "Was it like this?"

Another jumped over the one on its back, asking a zealous, "Yeah, didn't he jump on you after he knocked you over?"

"Bopped you in the nose, right?"

"That's what you said, remember?"

They were all tangled up, gripping throats, mocking punches, smiling big, wrinkly, eager-to-please smiles. Cupid rolled his eyes on his way inside and said nothing. Vivianne followed after, watching the troublesome creatures sharing looks of failure and pointing the blame at one another.

Cupid sat at the bar and ordered a drink. Vivianne smirked at his nude cheeks, buttered up on the barstool. She gently pulled on his wing when she sat down, smiling at him in hopes of cheering him up some. Cupid puffed his brow at her, playfully expressing his exhaustion. A Long Island landed in front of Cupid. He attacked the ice with a straw and asked Vivianne if she wanted a drink.

"God, no," she said, asking, "Don't you ever stop?"

"Oh, god, no," he said with a detached smile.

Vivianne asked if this was the bar where he left his bow. Cupid sucked his drink down, shaking his head no, and said, "Try not to mention it too loudly. If news were to get out, I'd, well, I'd be in a lot of trouble."

Vivianne zipped her mouth shut as the shorties entered. They were each in the shapes of Cupid's favorite people. There was an Irish woman named Fiona O'Clery who ran a pub in the late 1700s. She'd made a purple moonshine that always made Cupid giggle uncontrollably. Nebuchadnezzar II of Babylon, whom they found naked in the woods foraging for food. He traveled with Cupid as his pet wolf for nearly a decade before succumbing to dysentery. Monty Python's Michael Palin was holding hands with Cleopatra. Cupid seemed to light up when he saw them.

They ordered drinks, changing shapes around Cupid to please him, putting on an act. At first, Vivianne thought it was nice. Figured it was something they did when Cupid was feeling down. Cleopatra leaned past Vivianne with a curling smile and reached over Cupid's glass with a funny red cut of paper pinched between her fingers. "Want to add a little color to your sulking?" Cupid raised an eye to the tiny square of mind-altering papyrus. Vivianne asked what it was. Cupid smiled at his Egyptian-shaped temptress, tapping on his glass to accept the red addition to his beverage which dropped into the drink and began dissolving. Lifting the glass to his eye, watching the thing bubble and fizz, Cupid told Vivianne, "It's a groovy painkiller." With an approving sip, Cupid offered his glass to Vivianne. She refused and asked when they were going to leave. The bow wouldn't find itself, after all. The shape-shifting bunch all rolled their eyes at her. What's the rush, they wondered.

"Yeah, Cups, we could use a little lunch break."

"Been at it all day."

"All day, Cups."

"Nonstop since before breakfast."

"Besides, maybe it'd be easier to remember this place we are hunting for if we got twisted like we were when it happened."

"Brilliant idea."

"Oh, that's worked before."

"Makes sense, Cups. Get in the same mindset."

They were already ordering shots. Vivianne tried to speak up, but the shorties were too much, filling Cupid's head with flattery, distractions, and drugs. They weren't in any rush to find the bow. They just wanted to party.

"This place got a kitchen?" Van Gogh asked the bartender.

Menus were set on the bar, and the bartender told them it wasn't much, "But with how much you're drinking, it's all amazing."

Shots, bumps, and music.

The party had officially begun.

The four shorties were comfortable at the bar. Van Gogh was now Henry Paget, Cleopatra was still Cleopatra, and the other two changed into Ingrid Bergman and an elf called Shoeless. Vivianne posted up in the corner with her sketchpad and a basket of fries. The group was getting on her nerves. They muted Cupid's distress with nothing more than a costume change and more drugs. Did Cupid even really care? She was doubting her ability, and necessity, with helping the big lump of love.

She didn't notice the shift, but at some point, the barstools turned into lounge chairs. The lighting also seemed to have changed. Things were easier to look at. Two white women had joined Cupid and his party. They were middle-aged with heavy makeup and high energy. They both had a loud laugh and let it sing with almost everything they said. Vivianne was annoyed with them, and annoyed with Cupid. She sketched his eyes as they were now, comparing them to the fear she saw in them earlier. Where there was something adoring about his sadness, that passion that affected him before, there was now drunk lust and a shallow light. Eyes that were giving up. It was not going to be easy to help him, this she was sure of.

"Make me fall in love!" A woman sang out, hanging off Cupid like an STD dressed in lipstick. Vivianne thought again about leaving. She realized she was frustrated traveling with them. There had only been a short window where Cupid opened up to her. Was it too brief to consider, she thought? Was he a lost cause?

They were all a mess.

How could she even begin to help him at this stage? Who knows what that red tab did to his drink? She would have to wait till it wore off. But these creatures were addicts. This party wasn't going to stop for days, and it was only going to get out of hand. It would only turn into another party. Maybe she should get more on his level, she considered. She *was* curious to see what that red tab did. Things the God of Love thought were groovy probably grooved a great deal more than the average person's groovy.

154

Vivianne got a red tab from Cleopatra, and down the hatch it went. "How long does it take to kick in?" she asked. Mozart shared, "You got twenty minutes."

"And then what?"

"Who knows."

Best get the big sketchpad, she thought. Out of the bar and back onto the bus, Vivianne wondered if she would even notice a difference once this groovy red tab started working. With how strange everything was with Cupid and his shifting ensemble, everything was already on drugs.

Inside the bus, Vivianne touched the machine that gave love orders with a sigh. She ran her fingers along the magical device. A troubled smile ran across her face thinking of the disdain Cupid expressed toward it. Why was the God of Love such a mess? It was sad to think she might not be able to help him. He'd only been sober for fifteen minutes of their time together and only recognized her as a presence after a week of being onboard. With all the drugs he did, how long would it take someone to get to know him truly? She only then realized that the bus was empty.

Vivianne poked her curious eyes into the hall and wondered, was Cupid's room locked? Her lips nervously pursed, her brow high on alert. She wasn't fond of snooping. It took her a minute to work up the first few steps toward the door — anxious steps, high up on the balls of her feet. Sure enough, it opened right up.

Cupid's room was a mess. His bed was a raft floating amongst empty bottles and worn books. The bed itself was overgrown with flowering vines. The walls were dressed in old rose-tinted love orders — love orders covering every speck of wall and ceiling with all the hearts Cupid had brought together. It seemed as if it was more than just a job to Cupid. Or had been once. There were thousands upon thousands of them overlapping around the room. Kicking her way through the bottles, Vivianne took a knee on Cupid's bed. It was just about the most comfortable thing she'd ever touched. She immediately let herself fall into the flowered bed. It was so comfortable she began laughing. Reaching out, she plucked one of the many books that towered about the countless hollow bottles. It was a steamy romance novel. Vivianne rolled over, giggling. Towers of trashy erotica and sentimental love tales were growing like weeds through Cupid's messy bedchamber.

She was feeling more pity for the plump god.

Holding the silly love book against her chest, Vivianne let go of her doubts. She had to help him. It was too much to walk away from. Cupid was underappreciated. What he needed was a voice of reason. What he needed was a friend. Not drug-and-sex-addicted shapeshifters using him to party.

The supportive friendship would have to wait until morning, however. This groovy red experience was soon to take center stage. She could feel a warmth edging in around her perception. Threads of liquid now stitched the fabric of her surroundings. With her big sketchpad underarm and a box of pastels in her grip, Vivianne stepped out of the bus ready to commit whatever she saw to paper.

Two steps out of the bus, she stopped.

The bar had a bouncer standing out front where there had been no bouncer before. A bouncer and a red velvet rope. There was no red velvet rope when they first came — she was sure of it. Was this the drug, she wondered, the red tablet working its magic? Approaching the bouncer, a muscular giant of a man in a muscle-tight shirt, Vivianne gingerly smiled. The bouncer gave her a look but remained silent. Vivianne reached out and poked the large man. "You real?" she asked. The bouncer chuckled a bit, lifted the red velvet rope, and stepped aside. Opening the door, Vivianne wondered if she would ever return.

XVI
VANISHING ACT

Caesar woke to a purring, wet nose pushing at his eyelids. He opened his eyes to see Tux perched on his chest. His little wet cat nose hummed up close, pleased to see him. Tux pushed his face into Caesar's and started purring. There was nothing gentle about it. He had a head-butting approach to getting pets that didn't complement hangovers. Caesar sat up, head throbbing, staring at the outline left on the wall from where there used to be a television. He asked Tux if there was a TV in the room last night. Tux just purred and smashed his head into Caesar's hands, asking for pets.

With a cigarette planted in his mouth, Caesar ached his way to a warm beer, popped the top, and took his first breath of the day. Patting his pockets, he asked Tux if he had a light. Tux just scratched rhythmically at his ear, shook his head about in a violent tussle, sneezed, then meowed. Pulling a lighter from his pocket, Caesar gave Tux a pet and told him not to worry about it. He found his.

April stepped out from the bathroom. Her head was wrapped in a towel. Steam from a hot shower evaporated into the room. She asked Caesar if he was going to shower before they checked out. Lighting his cigarette, Caesar shook his head.

"Nothing better for a hangover than a hot shower," she told him. Caesar took a swig of beer and sat down with Tux. April had a look on her face that wanted to say something.

Caesar figured he had probably made a scene, gotten emotional, and made an ass out of himself the night before. Or worse, maybe he had gotten angry and said something awful.

But April held off on saying whatever it was she seemed to be thinking and just smiled at him. It was a reassuring smile. She asked, "You hungry?"

"Starving."

...

Dark, glowing maple syrup flowed over a tower of pancakes as lumps of butter melted down the fluffy stack with the thick sugar ooze. Caesar drowned his plate in the gooey sauce.

April chuckled. "You gonna use the whole jar?"

Caesar looked up from the task with a serious face. "Actually, I may need another to get the job done right," he told her, his eyes exploring the diner, taking note of the building's syrup supply. April laughed and poured a modest amount of syrup on the side of her plate. Caesar gave her a stink eye, asking, "That's it?" She cut a piece of pancake and dipped it. Said she didn't like to cover them because they get soggy. "I pour a little, do my dip thing. Pour a little more." She took a bite and smiled as she chewed and swallowed, and added, "Keeps the ride fluffy all the way to the last bite."

"Fair enough," Caesar said, stuffing his mouth, telling her he loved it when they were soggy.

"Sugar-logged cakes, sign me up."

Two Bloody Mary's landed on the table. Celery, a stick of bacon, an olive, and a little glazed donut ball decorated the drinks. April had ordered them with the works. She was pleased with the order.

"Look at that," she praised, inspecting the drink.

Caesar leaned over for his straw. April told him to be cautious — "I ordered them spicy." Caesar smiled and sucked up a healthy first-go at his drink. Sitting up quickly, he coughed and slapped his chest, choking out, "Fuck, that is spicy." April laughed and clapped her hands, picking up her drink and preparing herself for the kick. She coughed a little with her drink, but she fared better than Caesar.

April didn't usually drink with breakfast. Given the circumstance, it seemed more than appropriate. Caesar was quick to eat his toppings, leaving the olive on his plate. April pointed to it, asked him if he wanted it. Caesar shook his head, said he didn't like olives. April reached for it with a smile. "I fucking love olives," she told him, popping the bitter fruit into her mouth. Caesar cringed and said, "The olive is the foot of food." April chewed and smiled. "I must love feet then, 'cause I could eat these all day."

They laughed at each other, teased and joked about their hangovers. Caesar enjoyed April's mannerisms. She spoke with a lot of life. Her motions complimented her words. It was like she danced with herself when she talked. Her face was rich with expression. And her laugh almost always caught her off guard, as if she never expected to laugh. It was a rewarding accomplishment to get her to chuckle. She would mask her mouth sometimes with her hand and look away, like she was trying to hide until the laugh ended. Or she would look around as if she needed the world to recognize the humor in the moment that had captivated her so.

April was enjoying Caesar as well. He was more reserved in his expressions. His face was just as animated, but he managed it closely. Things rarely caught him off guard, but he would act like they did to play up the moment. Like he was letting himself express his feelings, and not the other way around. It was his smile that she admired the most. It was the one part he couldn't always tame. When it opened up without his permission, his teeth would show. There was a strain in his cheeks where his muscles would fight him, and he couldn't deny the smile its moment.

It was something Caesar was usually shy about. But, unwillingly, the bow had him feeling more open. It made them see each other with more clarity than their typical observations tended to observe. The influence the bow emitted, while it opened up their hearts to sharing, also ripened the pain their hearts harbored.

Caesar was the perfect diversion from April's cheating husband. His story had made an impression on her. His Cupid hunt only added to her interest in his life. She figured, whatever it was he was really doing, it must be his way of coping with his loss, and she wanted to talk about it more. She wanted to know more about the man.

"So, I wanted to thank you for sharing your story with me last night. It's a heavy bag you're carrying." Caesar put on a half-smile, awkwardly sort of nodding as he said, "Yeah, I don't usually talk about it. We got pretty drunk... I didn't make a scene, did I?"

April made a funny smile. "Actually..."

"What'd I do?"

Giving him a focused look, she told him, "The TV in our room? Yeah, you threw it in the street. Smashed it to pieces."

"Fuck, I'm sorry. I'll pay whatever they charge you."

"Tell you what. You let me tag along with you as your Cupid-hunting sidekick, and I'll let that shit slide."

"That invitation was already offered."

"Yeah, well. You're keeping my ass out of a lot of trouble by letting me tag along, so the fee doesn't bother me. My cheating piece-of-shit husband doesn't know that I know he's a cheating piece of shit. I sorta told him I was with you." April made a funny face and sipped on her Bloody Mary. Caesar stopped eating to ask her to explain.

April shrugged. "Said you were a chef, right? Well, I've been talking about opening a restaurant for years. Always been on the back of my mind. So I lied and said I was meeting with a chef. Told him we had a few too many drinks, and I crashed out. I've been known to get excited during business meetings, and more drinking happens than actual business." April swayed her head thoughtfully and commented, "Sort of a half-lie when you think about it. You are a chef, and we've been hanging out. Who knows, maybe I'll open a place one day you'll be cooking at. Call it the Heartbreak Café, or some shit."

Caesar dug into his pancakes, asking her when she spoke with her cheating piece-of-shit husband. April told him he had called her yesterday while they were drinking and carrying on and had left a message. "So I called him back," she went on to explain, saying, "I called him back this morning and pretended I didn't know anything. Acted all shocked and supportive." She sucked down some of her drink and smiled at herself. "You should've heard me, Caesar. *'Oh no, not your car. Baby, I'm so sorry to hear that.'* Yeah, I played his ass." April sat up, pleased with herself, taking a big sip from her drink. Caesar could see she wasn't actually happy. This was a victory in a war she never wanted to fight. It was a painful phone call and a painful act she put on. Her life was just freshly falling apart. She had yet to have time to live in it and see what all was different. The moment of impact was still shaking through her.

"I'm glad I met you, April the Arsonist."

Caesar wanted to cheer her up. Remind her of something he had too often taken for granted. Even though we're alone, we aren't alone.

"What's the plan now? You have to let him know you found out he's a cheating piece of shit."

April finished her Bloody Mary, nodding her head as she slurped up the last bits of spicy tomato and vodka. "I was thinking of burning his car again when he got a new one. Maybe just keep doing that for a while 'til it gets old. Or until he could no longer afford to get another car."

Caesar laughed, sensing she was joking. She smiled and sighed, letting her head down on the table, somewhat defeated. Saying she didn't know what she was going to do. She looked up to him. "I'm sorry about your family."

"Thanks. Sorry about your husband."

"Thanks."

They got the check and left. April asked where they were headed. Caesar looked up the road and smiled, asking, "You really coming with me?" She smiled back and rocked her head. "Hell yeah. I'm starting to think this Cupid is your therapist, and he's got this little game cooked up as a means for you to, like, work through your pain."

Caesar cracked a laugh and lit a cigarette. Pointing up the road, he told her they were going to the Inn. Opening the car door, April stopped him.

"Let's hold up a second. Yesterday I wasn't in my right mind, but I'm fresh now. And you've been drinking... heavily. I'm pretty toasted, myself. I know you and your cat are used to drinking and driving, but if I'm joining your adventure, one of us has to be sober."

Caesar took a long drag. Blew his smoke out in an aimless direction. Scratched his head and said, "So... we what? What do we do right now?"

April gave Tux a pat and scratched under his chin. "I'll sober up enough in about thirty."

"So, you're cool if I keep drinking?"

"Not that I think I could get you to stop, but no, I don't mind at all. Besides, the Inn isn't far."

"Great, so we have a little time to kill. What's there to do around here?"

April smiled. "Wanna shoot that bow?"

...

April set up targets behind the diner. She was excited. She liked guns, and found herself at the shooting range some weekends. She had never fired a bow and arrow before, though. Tux was watching from atop a pile of cardboard. April stacked milk crates at different heights and propped bottles and boxes onto them. Caesar was drinking a beer.

"So, where do you work? Anywhere I eat?"

"I work at the Inn, actually. Line cook, and I sort of manage the kitchen, sort of."

He was kneeling with the quiver. It was covered in pockets, with more inside. April asked, "The fuck you mean by sort of?"

"Well, I'm a drunk, so I sort of do everything ... sort-of-ly."

In the quiver, he found weed, a bag of coke, some dice, playing cards, and a picture of a Spanish woman. She was pretty. There were hearts drawn on the back with a note written in Spanish. Caesar didn't think anything of it. He kept digging around while April stepped away from the targets, telling him she was pretty sure it was sticks with points on the end that they needed. Caesar put on a laugh. "Ha. Ha. Ha. You're hilarious," he told her. She smiled at herself and couldn't help but chuckle. With his cigarette bouncing on his lips, Caesar told her about the things he was finding. April winced. "Maybe we should leave the drugs, just in case. Never felt good around Blow. People

162

always bring that shit into my club, and it bugs my girls out. Get all sniffy and twitchy."

Caesar put his cigarette out, giving one pocket in the bag a funny look. He reached in and grabbed hold of a funny little cord, giving it a tug, and showed April. "It's some cord." He told her. April asked him, "A cord?" Caesar let go of the cord, which retracted swiftly into the bag. Instantly Caesar disappeared.

Vanished into thin air.

Effortlessly removed.

April froze. Her eyes stuck wide open. Tux jumped a little, spooked by the vanishing Caesar. April turned around and turned back. She looked to the cat, but Tux couldn't explain it. He was just as confused as she was.

XVII
SOMEWHERE ELSE ENTIRELY

When Caesar let go of the pulley, everything around him changed. The world around him was yanked away like a sheet. A rippling flash revealed he was now somewhere else entirely. The shock of it paralyzed him — eyes beaming open, limbs frozen in awkward positions, his mouth slightly agape.

Caesar was in a room unlike any he had ever seen. The walls weren't walls so much as they were trees. Twisting branches swirled around the room towards a window view of something he wasn't yet ready to experience. Handwoven rugs stitched with hearts were spread across the floor in a haphazard fashion — old dusty rugs. Everything in the room was neglected. Wax candles melted up and down shelves and tables amongst books and bottles. It smelled like nothing he knew. Felt like nothing he knew. Above him hung hundreds of hearts, each carved from wood and painted every color imaginable.

From under a mess of papers, a little furry face appeared. Plump, fluffy cheeks with dirty, wispy whiskers caked with muck. Big, dark, slanted eyes shining about with a curious hunger, a wiggling snout sniffing at Caesar with a hyper fervor. Caesar had no idea what it was. It looked harmless. When he moved, the creature fled in a panic, knocking books over in its path. The commotion sent a frenzy of phantom feet scratching across the floor overhead, and the walls around him rattled and shook with a swift storm of fretful claws. As the ruckus settled, Caesar let himself breathe. It wasn't a dream. It was real. He was somewhere far away from anything he knew.

Cupid's bow and arrow were both with Caesar. Hooking them over his shoulder, he eased his way to the window to get a look at what he assumed would also be far from familiar. His eyes adjusted to the bright light coming in from outside, and the new world he found himself in came into focus. Across a long, precarious path scaled down a hill into a wild forest. Twisting branches curled through the landscape with rich, vibrant colors. Greens, reds, blues, and yellows. Color like he had never seen. Beyond the forest was a city made of white marble and rainbow-colored glass. Waterfalls and moss-spotted mountains tangled with the city — slender mountains stood like watchtowers, topped with more marble and glass buildings.

Caesar's wide, unblinking eyes soaked it all in, his mouth still agape. This was not Earth. But where it was or what it was, he hadn't a clue.

Cautious steps carried him to a set of curved stairs. More books and melted candles crept up and around the stairwell. Nothing was straight. There were no right angles to be seen anywhere. Crooked curving wood shaped the building. With every step his foot landed came a loud creak. Downstairs was similar to the bedroom. Books and bottles and candles. Hearts were carved into every shelf and cubby. Sticky wax dripped over most surfaces, but none were lit. No one seemed to be home. Nothing more than a sheet hung between rooms. Every room opened to the next. The only door was a round block of wood that shut off what appeared to be the front of the house.

Cupid's home, Caesar thought — it had to be.

There was a kitchen shaped in stones that needed cleaning. The sink was full of dirty dishes and bottles. Twisting tubes and cauldrons coated with dust sat sleeping in a room untouched. Caesar poked at a bottle of something gently swirling with color. Dark shades of green clouded around a dim light of blue and violet cream. His touch seemed to scare the substance in another, as it had filled with a solid mass of gray when he tapped the glass. The only room that didn't look like a party was had in it was still a mess of candles and wax. The shelves were lined with powders, gems, liquids, crystals, and stones. Everything was held in place with cobwebs.

Caesar felt uneasy around all the strange paraphernalia. Too much curiosity could lead to him setting fire to or melting down the building. He moved on. Careful steps carried him through the peculiar rooms until he found an opening to the outside. It was a heart-shaped doorway draped with some faded pink fabric. It was a wide mouth opening to a wild garden. Grass and flowers roamed around wildly. Blue and green flowers appeared to breathe a subtle light. A forest edge shaped the space into a cozy pocket, casting a spotted shadow from above. A swing hung from the branches, and a stream cut in from the forest and escaped under the house. Stones were set around with purpose, making seats, paths, and a pit with a small burning fire. Someone was standing over the fire. Caesar hesitated when he saw the man playing with the fire. Only he wasn't a man at all. He was made of ash, and his hand was stuck out, casually sucking the smoke from the blaze into his palm. His hand and the smoke had no divide. He and the smoke were one and the same.

The ash-being casually turned to face Caesar with a motion that suggested it knew he was there. "I smell a new friend, but no pesky shifter. Have you finally tired of their childish antics?" it said as it turned to face Caesar. But when it got a look at him, the thing seemed surprised by what it saw.

"Where is Cupid?" the thing asked.

Caesar gulped and said nothing. He moved his mouth as if words might find a way out, but nothing came. The thing gave him a curious inspection and ceased its magic with the fire. The bow and arrow hanging from Caesar's shoulder had peaked its interest.

Somewhat in disbelief, it asked, "Tell me, young man, how is it that you find yourself in possession of this bow and its arrow companions?"

In a brush of smoke, the thing sailed up close to Caesar — an effortless slide ignoring any obstacle a foot may have encountered. It smelled of fire. Its skin looked like burnt bark and silk. Flaking ash like scattered scales moved with waves of heat, yet it felt as cold as ice to be near. Caesar imagined a human shaped in paper, burning from the inside. It was difficult

166

to sense whether the being was fragile or dense. The ash figure wore an expression that revealed no threat, merely curious thoughts. Its eyes were black stones that told nothing of where it was looking. Hairless, it was dressed in a dark tunic that looked as if it were sewn from the embers of a fire. It stood on what looked like charred feet, and gray lumps of ash broke off with each step it took as it made its way around Caesar.

"Don't be shy, human. What's your name?"

Clearing his throat, Caesar introduced himself, and the ash figure grinned. It spoke with a slow worn timbre, its voice deep and crackly. "Caesar. Powerful name. They call me Whisper. Some refer to me as Whip, for short. Cupid and his lackeys often call me Midnight or Campfire. But all I am is burning. I have had more names over the millennia than I care to traverse. So, Caesar, the human with Cupid's bow, you are here all alone?" Whisper looked out, searching for others who may be with Caesar. But there was no one. The slightest hint of confusion curved into the thing's ashen forehead.

Caesar folded his arms and answered, "I pulled on something in this thing and … now I'm here. Wherever here is." Caesar was unsure of how he was supposed to feel. Suddenly his plan seemed beyond him. He hadn't considered what it really meant, Cupid being real. It made sense now that there would be other magical beings and a magical place they would call home. Suddenly, and overwhelmingly so, he felt in over his head. His brief, bright desire for vengeance was dimming back into his usual hopeless despair.

Whisper sort of smiled. With a relaxed tone, it told Caesar, "Well, where you are is not a place for unchaperoned mortals. Dangerous this realm is for the beating heart of a temporal chest. Amongst the righteous light, there walks much darkness through the roots of this boundless expanse. To trespass is to forfeit one's right to rights. Even gods have been sentenced to death for much less an act as a misplaced foot. A mortal with a leash is a sacred thing here, respected guests the flesh of short breath. But you have no guide tethered to your pulse, Caesar the Powerful. Instead, you possess a god's artifact. Not just any artifact, but the unbudging prick of love. Much weight it bears, this crime you have committed. Your face is lost, however. I smell from your breath, you are not a man of temperance. But what friend of Cupid could be? And whom but a friend would be trusted to care for such a *tool* as this?" With a gentle breath, Whisper gestured toward the fire. "Let's relax a while and trade stories, shall we? Cupid's company always fascinates me. Well, not always. Most of what sticks to him lately has been trash with holes and no substance but lust."

Smoke rushed under Caesar and lifted him from the ground. Whisper smiled as they were both carried to the fire and Caesar was placed on a stone seat. More smoke carried over a jug of gold liquid. The ash figure plucked two mugs from the fire. Caesar's mouth returned to gaping. His awe put a smile on the ash figure's face.

Whisper filled the mugs with the shimmering spirit. Offering one to Caesar, it told him, "If you are a fan of drinking, then this will please you greatly." With the mug in hand, Whisper toasted, "To stories." The ash figure took a drink and gestured to Caesar to do the same, and encouraged him not to be shy.

Caesar laughed, looking into the mug, completely mesmerized by everything that was happening. *Why not?* he thought. With a smile, he raised the drink and chuckled awkwardly. "To stories."

Down went the golden drink.

Caesar felt it rush into his blood immediately. He coughed, and Whisper smiled. He told him the drink was crafted from the finest berry it had ever discovered. And one of the rarest. "So tell me," Whisper said, filling Caesar's mug with more gold, "were you on Cupid's amusing little bus when you happened to find your curious fingers investigating his quiver?" Caesar took a hard breath and smiled. The drink was more than an alcoholic delight. It was also known by Whisper for the truth it inspired in those who consumed it. With some tolerance, one would need to drink a lot of the golden potion to be affected. First-time drinkers, however, only needed a taste to open up.

One sip and Caesar's eyes were spinning. Two sips, and he was laughing. Laughing and sighing and asking no one, "What's funny?"

Whisper smiled at Caesar, watching the potion take over. Realizing he had been asked a question, Caesar apologized. Whisper told him it was nothing to worry over, and he asked again how he had come to possess the bow and arrow.

Without a care in the universe, Caesar shrugged and said, "Oh man, I hate that motherfucker. I was fighting him, and the asshole dropped it. I found it in some bush the next morning." Whisper was amused to discover Caesar held such disdain for the god of love. It asked Caesar why he had been fighting Cupid.

"Because he's an asshole," was Caesar's immediate response.

"Can you elaborate?"

Caesar shrugged and told the ash figure, "I'm going to kill him. I have to kill him. Kill him to spare the future any more broken hearts. Stop him from spoiling the world any more than he already has. Kill him because he deserves it more than anything."

Caesar's words were unmistakably serious. There wasn't a hint of hyperbole in his speech. There was only emotion, only pain. Caesar was lost. Caesar was interesting. Pouring them both another round of golden persuasion, Whisper questioned, "So tell me, Caesar the Assassin. What inspired your undertaking? Are we on a mission of vengeance? I like vengeance."

Caesar took a crossed-eyed drink and explained plainly, "He shot me with his miserable arrow, and all I got out of it was a dead baby and an ex-wife who doesn't remember getting married. Doesn't remember falling in love with me. Doesn't remember the embarrassing things I said after she kissed me for the first time. The jokes we had between just us. The games we played with our eyes. The comfort and joy she filled me with so effortlessly. He shot me with this bow and arrow and turned my life into a nightmare."

This was the first time Caesar expressed such a thing without crying. He had the golden spirit to thank for that. The magical drink had his mind spilling out of his mouth, remembering the day he had that first kiss. He continued to tell Whisper, "I raced this guy in a Mustang that night. It was our first date. I drove this shitty sedan. Loved that car. Nothing anyone would race. I think they wanted to show off in front of her. I was already so nervous the whole date, but I fucked around in the car a lot, so I knew how to get it moving. The Mustang should've won, but the driver messed up his clutch, and I smoked him when the light turned green. I knew she didn't care either way, but she was smiling at my surprise. Smiling at me. Used to be a memory we shared. It's so fucked to sit with these things alone. This isn't a game for some sweaty, fat fuck with little asshole wings to just toss around at people. There are consequences. Life is not worth this pain. Nothing is worth this pain."

The ash figure thought deeply on Caesar's story. It was the fight that interested Whisper. Caesar's feud with Cupid. What would happen to the ebb and flow of the two realms if Cupid were killed by a human? Anarchy was an appealing thought. Just the threat of distress it would bring to the high and mighty council of gods was more than attractive. Caesar's intention was romantic, in a dark and twisted way. But hearts would keep breaking long after Cupid passed. Whisper didn't think it was important to let Caesar know that fact. Motivation is motivation. No matter how broken it gets, love never dies. It simply moves on. With or without you.

Caesar's mind was spinning. The golden juice had him drunker than ever. The flowers around him seemed to be reaching for him, sniffing at him for some insight he couldn't place.

Whisper dumped what remained in Caesar's mug and poured him something red. Whisper got serious while waiting for Caesar to take his first drink. It shot quickly through his system, the red magic sobering him up with a harsh transition. It was obvious in Caesar's posture that he was suddenly and uncomfortably aware of himself. Aware he was sitting in an alien world with a creature that shouldn't exist. Aware he may have just told one of Cupid's friends he was planning on killing him. Fear was painted across Caesar's face.

Whisper was quick to ease Caesar's trepidation by telling him, "I have been around for a long time, Caesar. A long, *long* time. And I have observed the worst exploits done in the name of love. Heartbreak such as yours holds but a candle to the horrors I have witnessed. The gods are far crueler than you could imagine. Cupid himself has even been stricken with the same curse. Poetic as it is for his infliction to be ironic, grace has slipped from his stride. Your deed would be more than just. It would be merciful. And to spare the future hearts such sorrow, you are truly Caesar the Great." Whisper smiled and lifted Caesar's mug of red potion, aiding him in his attempt to finish.

"Caesar, I will aid you on your quest. But I must know, I don't doubt your pain, but your conviction has not yet had the time to prove itself. Caesar, do you have it in you to truly kill this god? Passionate words aside, is there grit to your bite?"

Caesar finished his drink. Sobriety cleansed his mind, and the pain he harbored spoke for him. "I have to. There is no other option left."

"Then it is good you have found me. You can't just kill a god, Caesar, no matter how powerful you are," Whisper explained as it stood up. "Such a task by mortal hands must be done with godly gifts." It pulled a small sack from a bit of smoke and filled it with a rumble from its palm. The sack expanded with the sound of falling rocks. Whisper told Caesar to put a rock from the sack into a drink and then wait.

"Wait for what?"

"Wait for things to change."

Whisper pulled a slender crystal from its palm and warned, "Now, this may sting a bit." Caesar guarded himself, unsure of the ashen figure's intentions. Whisper broke the crystal in half, which instantly filled with a faint green light. "It is time for you to leave," the creature explained. "A mortal without an escort won't make it long without being chewed up by something around here, and you reek of mortality. Worse for you, this bow is not yours to have. The gods would punish you, Caesar. Something is already here to investigate your arrival. Your entrance made quite an impression."

Caesar heard the front door open. Fear slicked his skin with cold sweat, and he asked the ashen figure if this was really happening or if he was dreaming. Whisper stepped close to Caesar and smirked. "Takes a special constitution for a full-grown human to accept magic. Denial is an odd skill your kind has mastered to a fault. This is all very real, Caesar the Powerful. As is the threat coming your way."

Whisper put the crystal in Caesar's mouth and told him to swallow. Caesar began to protest, but the crystal was already going down his throat. With a bit of a sting, Caesar poofed away, vanishing into thin air, leaving behind an electrical cloud of red and charcoal smoke. The smoke spanned and thinned into the air just as an angel stepped out from the house, eyes glowing white. She stood with the doorway's drape in her hand, one foot out and one foot in. Seeing Whisper standing alone, she dimmed her glowing eyes to the perfect brown marbles they were. The angel sensed something off in the space around the ashen figure. Magic moved things. It perfumed the air. Left a print. And this was no ordinary angel. Her senses were the purest ever bestowed upon any being. She was an archangel of the highest rank. Some say she could smell truth and taste lies. Sense intent. Hear the clicking gears of a pondering mind.

Whisper bowed. "Azrael, always a pleasure."

Two more archangels emerged as Azrael spoke with a grimace. "The ashes speak. What are you doing here, *Whip?*" Whisper gestured aimlessly. "You know me, I prefer my solitude."

Azrael huffed with condescension. "Something has traversed here from Earth. It wasn't you, was it?"

"But of course not, that would be a crime. I know my place, my sentence."

Whisper smiled, wondering if the angels knew Cupid had lost his bow. The three archangels were sisters. Strong white wings rested tightly against their backs. They shared pearly skin, and black hair they wove into braids and dressed with flowers. Rings of light floated gracefully above their heads. They were dressed for duty, wearing light armor chest plates, pleated leather skirts, leather gauntlets, and leather boots. Each had a sword resting on their hip in a leather sheath. When the first gods took charge of the magic realm, they birthed the angels to uphold their laws.

Whisper was a criminal, cast out of their kingdom and shackled to a barrier it could not pass, left to wander the landscapes between worlds. It was a creature of chaos, born of the elements, physically bound to no single form. Most angels detested it. Some claimed it was older than time itself, and that it had grown legs to match that of the first gods to camouflage itself. Some believed Whisper was more powerful than the gods themselves. That it took every god's combined power to forge the magic that imprisoned the ash creature.

The only thing angels loathed more than the elemental being was humans.

"I smell something," Azrael said, her tone annoyed. Whisper shrugged. "Many things wander in from Cupid's careless troupe. You know this. One of them simply picked the wrong door as they often do, and I kindly helped them back out."

One of the sisters, Domino, was shorter than Azrael but just as pretentious. She made her way toward the fire, sighing. "You? Help? I'd wager you fed on the human who has left such a stench."

"Oh, I only feed on stories. I sent the lost shifter back home, don't you worry, oh holiest of birds."

Azrael sneered and pulled her hand through the air, conjuring a collar of light around Whisper's throat that stung the creature. Whisper fought not to expose pain in its expression. Azrael glared at it with disgust. "You're lucky the gods chose only to hide you away. If it were up to me, you would have been killed for your crimes the day you were defeated."

Whisper smiled through the pain around its neck and calmly told the angel, "If the gods knew how to kill, they would have done so. Goodbye, birds." Whisper dispersed itself into the fire, putting the blaze out with its exit, leaving behind a parting cloud of smoke and ash.

Waving away the smoke, Domino coughed. "I can't stand that savage beast. I'll never care to understand why the gods still work deals with such a thing." Domino's twin, Esther, was bored. She sighed, "I have no feelings towards it or this. Cupid's home is a dreary shack of dust. May we be anywhere else, Azrael?"

Her big sister took a few steps forward, smelling the air where Caesar had been standing. Her foot kicked around the ground, clearing the debris his departure had left. Dissecting the means by which the human traveled. She sensed a powerful magic and she told her graceful companions, "We are curious."

XVIII
SOME DRINKS HAVE A LOT TO SAY

April held Tux, still standing behind the diner where Caesar had vanished before her eyes. She was talking to the cat, asking him what had happened. The question wasn't aimed so much at the cat, as it was simply being offered to anything that may be listening. Her shock had not completely worn off by the time Caesar reappeared. As if from nowhere, he was suddenly standing directly in front of her. As if he had never left at all.

April gasped, her eyes rolled back, and she fainted, Tux trapped in her arms. Caesar lunged for her but came up short, and she fell on her back as Tux jumped from her arms into his.

Just like that, Caesar was back.

Caesar ran into the diner for a cup of ice water, rushing out to pour it over April's face. April sprung up with a yelp. Seeing Caesar, she immediately began swearing and pushing at him for an explanation. April wiped the water from her face, caught her breath, and pointed at Caesar with a frightful but excited finger. "Where did you go?" she asked him, eyes wide, heart thumping away.

Caesar suggested they have a drink somewhere quiet and talk about it. April shook her head. "No, you disappeared. You were gone. Shit needs to be addressed."

"I know. Let's go somewhere and talk about it."

April stood up and held her hand out, chuckling between words. "Motherfucker, *ha-ha*, we're somewhere now." Caesar

174

tried again to suggest a drink, but April shook her head, waved her hand, and laughed as she said, "You were gone. David Blaine'd your ass the-fuck-knows-where and then poof, fucking reappear out of thin air right *the fuck* back where you were. *Hell* no, we ain't going off for any casual drink and discussion time. Explain yourself, Houdini!"

April could see Caesar was just as perplexed about what had happened as she was. She didn't know if that made it any better. With a heavy breath to calm herself down, she started laughing again. Caesar laughed at her laughter, which made her laugh more. Laughter turned into April shouting out with excitement and confusion and a little fear. She bellowed, "WHAT THE FUCK?!" Clapping her hands to emphasize each syllable, she carried on, "You dis-a-ppeared."

Caesar started walking, waving April along to follow. "Let's go get a drink and talk about it. Please. Because after what I just saw, I fucking need one." April chased after, her nerves spilled her thoughts out as they came. "Caesar, I must be on drugs. You put some psychedelic drugs into my food this morning. Because that shit you just did wasn't right. I'm gonna tell you what, listen, because how'd you do that? Why did you do that? And how the fuck did you do that?"

Caesar opened his car and pulled out a beer, offering it to April. She declined, saying she needed to hear this story sober. Sipping his warm beer, Caesar leaned on the car and told her about the place he had just been, recalling Whisper and the crystal he swallowed. He finished the beer and opened another. He could hardly believe what he was telling her.

Tux was perched on the roof, purring into April's hands. April listened to what Caesar said with a furrowed brow. She wore a bemused grin, not concerned with hiding her disbelief. "*You're* the one who took the drugs this morning," was her response. Caesar shook his head and admitted, "I was a little fuzzy from drinking, but that had nothing to do with it. I told you, this is Cupid's bow and arrow. And I was just in… another world. I don't know. This beer isn't strong enough for this shit."

April thought for a minute. There was no denying what she saw. Caesar had disappeared and reappeared. She gestured to the small sack this magical being had given him. "Let's see it," she said.

They both looked into the bag. Inside were a couple of small rocks. April pulled one out and shrugged. "These are just some rocks." She was unimpressed. Caesar nodded his head, took a sip of his beer, and said, "Yeah, looks like it."

April put the rock back in the bag and asked if they were rocks or stones. Caesar shrugged, "I guess stones, right? Because they're smooth like that."
April sighed, "So what, we just put a rock or stone or whatever in a drink?"

"That's what it said."

"Then what?"

"Fuck if I know. You wanna just put one in a drink and see what happens?"

The rocks were too big for any of the bottles he had, so they went back into the diner and ordered a tall pint of light beer. They both peered over the bubbling beverage, shoulder to shoulder, eager to see what would happen. Caesar held out the rock, gave April a ready look, and let the thing sink.

Nothing happened.

April slouched in her seat and sighed, disappointed. Caesar sipped at another warm car beer. They both placed their heads on the bar. Heads down, they stared at the rock, resting at the bottom of the glass. Little bubbles swam up from the rock to the surface. Thinking about it more, April asked if they were pebbles. Caesar frowned a thoughtful expression, said, "Maybe. Pebbles are smooth, right? But stones are smooth, too. Or are they?"

April sighed, "So, is a rock a stone but not a pebble, and a pebble's a stone but not a rock?"

Caesar shook his head and laughed, "I don't know. Does it matter?"

The bartender chimed in, "I think pebbles might be smaller than this."

Both April and Caesar picked their heads up off the bar. Neither knew he was there. Tux poked his face out from Caesar's shirt, and the bartender gave Caesar a sour glare. Caesar shook his head like it was nothing and told him not to worry about it, saying the cat wasn't going anywhere. The bartender accepted with a passive shrug and asked again about the rock in their beer. "Is it like an essential oil thing?" Caesar told him it was a peyote button. The bartender laughed, and Caesar smiled, sipping at his warm car beer.

Seeing Caesar's foreign beer bottle, the bartender's brow narrowed again, and he asked, "Where'd you get that? We don't serve that."

"It's from my car," Caesar told him.

The bartender folded his arms and frowned. "You can't have that in here." Caesar shrugged. "But I bought a beer. I'm a customer." The bartender thought about it, and thought about the cat. Unfolding his arms, he realized he didn't care and shrugged it off. "Fair enough."

April finger-danced around the other rocks in the bag, bummed nothing was happening. Caesar poked the pint and suggested, "Maybe I should drink some of it." April leaned into the bar and leaned into her look at Caesar. Her eyes were studying him, skeptical. Caesar's disappearing magic trick had her mind excited. But it had to be a trick, something he was doing to mess with her. Fighting a smile, she asked him, "Are you fucking with me? This all just a joke?"

"I'm not much for jokes," a voice answered.

Caesar and April looked around, but the bartender was gone. There was no one close enough to own the words they had just heard. April asked Caesar how he had thrown his voice. Caesar shook his head and said he didn't throw anything.

"I did," said the voice they couldn't find.

"Down here," it added.

April and Caesar both looked down at the pint, leaning over and peering into the amber glass topped with frothy white suds with awe and wonder shaping their expressions. Bubbles fizzed wildly around the glass as the voice emerged from within. "Can you hear me?"

April, wide-eyed and mystified uttered, "The fuck?"

"Greetings, who might you be? And where is Caesar the Powerful? I'm quite certain I heard him speaking," the fizzing beer said.

"It's Whisper," Caesar stated, slightly mystified, himself.

Wild bubbles returned to the glass as the voice continued, "Indeed, I am. Now, about this Cupid business. If I am to help, I'll need you to find a mirror. You'll need to fill something with water, salt, and vinegar, and then place all the rocks in that bag I gave you into the mix. Set the mirror before the water and wait."

"What's that now?" April asked, leaning toward the talking beverage with a look of animated shock stretching across her face. The drink repeated itself and April nodded. "Yeah, that's what I thought you said." Caesar put his mouth close to the sizzling beer and asked what they were to do after that. Whisper told them the rest would work itself out. And that was all it said. The rock stopped sizzling, and the glass stopped speaking.

Tapping on the glass, April asked, "Hello? Hello, beer voice?"

"I think it's gone."

April threw her hands into the air, struggling to wrap her mind around what was happening. Caesar chugged his beer and burped. "Alright, so we need a mirror. Guess we're renting another room. Use the bathroom sink for this whatever-the-fuck we're doing, the mirror's right above it."

"Hold the fuck up," April requested, a bewildering smile buttering up her cheeks with awe and wonder as she pointed out, "This beer just talked to us."

"That it did."

"Can we talk about that for a minute?" April's eyes were as wide as wide as could be.

Touching the glass, Caesar asked if she thought it was okay to drink. She laughed and told him to go for it. She watched him think about it. Caesar bobbed his head and waved for the bartender. "I'll order another drink." April laughed and collected her thoughts with a calming breath. "I don't know what to say. I'm tripping. I mean, we just talked to your beer. We just had a conversation with this glass of fucking beer." Pointing to the glass with her eyes even wider, she added, "This is some trippy shit. Tell me this isn't normal for you."

Caesar shook his head. "This is far from normal." He put his hand on April's and gave her a reassuring look. "Really. My mind is spinning around in circles with how fucking nuts this is. Can't explain it, barely believing any of it. But I'm *definitely* going to do what the beer just asked us to do because why the fuck wouldn't I?" April chuckled and smirked. "I'm going to regret meeting you, aren't I? I mean, I'm dead. I have to be fucking dead right now."

The bartender stepped up, and April waved her hand at him with some excitement. "You just missed it. I mean, you wouldn't believe me if I told you, but, I mean, you just missed some freaky shit." With an awkward smile, the bartender asked, "What happened? You do a trick with that rock in your beer?" April just laughed and shook her head, and told Caesar to go on and order his drink.

"You want one?"

April swayed her head side to side and thought out loud, "I suppose we aren't driving 'til we do this mirror dance, and I can't wait to see what happens with that shit, so yeah. I'll have a mezcal on the rocks, side of pineapple juice."

The bartender went to work, and Caesar smiled at April. She smiled back, but asked him what he was smiling at.

"Interesting combo, with the pineapple chaser."

April smiled and nodded her head, saying, "Oh, it's delicious. You're gonna try some. Tastes like grilled pineapple."

With the arrival of their drinks, April asked if they could have a shot of vinegar and some salt to go. The bartender smiled with a peculiar expression and shrugged, but told them he didn't see why not.

"All I have is apple cider vinegar. That work?"

"That'll have to do."

With a curious toast, one drink turned into two, which turned into three. The silent beer was eventually drunk as well. A room was rented. Magical thinking was rewriting logic in both their minds as a sink filled with hot water, salt, and apple cider vinegar. April dropped the rocks into the steaming sink and jumped back. Nothing happened. Eagerly they waited. They waited and drank. Drank and waited.

Waited and drank.

...

Behind the diner where Caesar had disappeared and reappeared, the bartender was taking out a bag of trash. Opening the lid to a dumpster, he stopped his arm just before he tossed the bag inside. Standing with the dumpster open, trash sagging from his hand, he watched as a line drew itself over the asphalt. A white line that etched out into a long rectangle. It looked like chalk. Sounded like chalk. Only there was no one there. The shape drew itself. Puzzled by the sight, the bartender let the dumpster lid shut, trash still in his hand. The rectangle that effortlessly shaped itself sunk into a set of stairs moving downwards into the Earth. The ground rumbled slightly as it happened. The bartender felt uneasy. There was no one around to confirm what he was seeing. No one around to offer emotional support for the unbelievable happening. So, he pulled his phone from his pocket to document what he knew no one would believe. With an anxious breath, he opened the camera on his phone just as someone came walking up the impossible stairs. Three someones. Up came the three curious archangels, Azrael, Domino, and Esther. Frozen in shock, the bartender failed to take any photos. As the angels stepped up into his world, he fainted and dropped his phone along with the trash.

Azrael rolled her eyes at the collapsed man and turned to the road. Something was off. Domino poked around with her foot, feeling the same mysterious disturbance as Azrael, and said, "No god passed through here, but something beaming with a god's touch certainly did. Left a noticeable scent." Esther commented, "It's a familiar smell. Is it roses?"

"Cupid's bow," Azrael said, pulling a round compass from her robe. Silver dials rimmed the disc, and layers of blue crystals filled the heart of the magical device. The dials spun, and the crystals hummed. She glared at the compass and said, "Cupid's not far, but he wasn't here, and he wasn't just with Whip. Which may mean he has lost his bow."

Esther was pushing at the bartender's body with a stick. "Cupid, lose his bow? I know he's a mess, but it's hard to think he could screw up something so paramount. Imagine the stir news such as this would bring. Earth would be crawling with magical filth. Cupid's bow would be the poach of the century." Azrael laughed to herself thinking Cupid was more than capable of screwing up far worse. She pocketed her compass and stood over the unconscious bartender, thinking a great deal of thoughts. Domino stepped beside her. All three sisters looked down at the fainted man with crumpled brows. He stunk, but most humans did to them.

Domino sighed and asked if they should send word on Cupid's bow to the council. Azrael replied, "No, not yet. Let's find out what word to send." She was intrigued by the prospect of Cupid missing his bow. She opened the door to the back of the diner. Only it didn't open to the back of the diner. A door is only an intention, and to those who knew better, like Azrael, a door could open to wherever an intention was mutual.

"Where are we off to, Azrael?"

With a hint of a smile, she stepped through the doorway and said, "Let's have a chat with our beloved Cupid."

XIX
LONG TIME, NO SEE

Three curious archangels entered what had been the bar Cupid and his friends had stopped in for a drink. They had done some redecorating. From the outside, it looked like the same bar but inside, the ceiling had risen twenty feet. It was domed and dressed with murals. Swooping red drapes carried a subtle breeze. Candlelit chandeliers floated overhead. The bar was longer, circling around a new glowing tower of booze with bottles from both worlds. The crowd had grown as well and was now mostly occupied with magical beings. The few humans around were spellbound, drunk on both magic and substance. Everyone was drinking. Casual magic was cast from every corner. Instruments were filling the air with dance. Pixies fluttered around the growing crowd. Some were doing more than drinking. Most were dancing.

There was even a disco ball.

Azrael shook her head at the scene. Her sisters felt a mixture of derision and amusement. Esther sort of smiled as she commented, "A lot of magic being cast in here. They keep this up, it may cause another renaissance."

Domino laughed a little, remembering the parties Cupid threw in the sixteenth century. "The greatest thing Cupid ever did was inspire that renaissance." Esther sighed, "I do miss those centuries, so much promise."

Azrael yawned. "Yes, humans were almost interesting. Does anyone see Cupid? There's so much magic in the place I can barely separate my feet from the drapes." Domino smiled and huffed, "Too true, there isn't a stretch of this place that hasn't been conjured."

Esther leaned her head on her twin's shoulder and put on a bored smile. "So, what's our play, Azrael?"

Domino welcomed her twin with half a hug, turning them both to their older sister. "Yes, big sis, what is our play?" she playfully asked. Azrael smiled at her sisters. She had a lot on her mind. Straightening her posture, she turned to the crowd and said, "What is it the mortals say? When in Rome."

She stepped into the party, letting her wings open. They stretched out and caught the eyes of everyone in view. Her sisters joined her, wings out, drawing the attention of everyone around. Gods and magical creatures sober enough to recognize the wings weren't sure if they should be nervous. Magic was not permitted to be cast before mortals. Not without first getting authorization from the council. Worse yet was casting magic on a human without a permit. This party was in violation of a great many magical codes. Cupid got a pass with some of his spells because of his line of work, but even he would have to explain himself from time to time. A party like this would never get a permit. Not that any magical being cared to get permission for such things. Half the fun of a party like this was breaking the rules, and Earth was an easy place to break them.

The archangels enjoyed the tension they brought to the party. It was wise to fear the authority of the high-ranking sisters. Grapes were plucked from a passing tray as they stepped into the crowd. The bartenders were all humans under spells, powered with godly stamina so they could make drinks for a lifetime and never tire. They were so pumped with magic, their eyes were glowing and running light down their cheeks.

Azrael ordered three cocktails made from a fermenting heart plum she knew Cupid always traveled with. It was a clean drink, not too sweet, not too sour. It took a strong drink to affect the blood of immortal beings. The three sisters stood with the eyes of the room over them, sipping slowly. Domino counted all the magical violations shining around and said, "As fun as it is to fill a room with such discomfort, what are we doing?"

"We're investigating."

Esther smiled, excited by whatever her sister was scheming. Someone they knew stepped up to the bar. Azrael laughed when she saw the well-respected witch from their realm. "Of course you would be here, Helen. Always playing with the other side."

"Azrael and her sisters of majesty. Are we being raided, or is there a criminal sitting at the bar with us?"

"Fret not, Helen. Even if we were here for permits, we'd let you out the back."

"But why would the council send their perfect angels all the way across the universe for a party violation?"

Domino smiled. "They wouldn't."

Helen gulped.

Azrael hushed her sister. "We're just passing through. Wanted a drink."

Helen took a thoughtful sip of her beverage. She didn't believe the archangels. A wide-eyed human stumbled into the conversation. Azrael turned her nose from the sweaty creature. He was a lean man in a tank top. He was eyeing up Helen, drunkenly leaning into the bar beside her. Magic had him smiling big and bright. "What's your name, gorgeous?" he asked her, his eyebrows bouncing. Helen smiled and rested her hand on the human's cheek. "So sorry. I don't have any genitals."

The man laughed. "That's a shame."

Helen rolled her eyes, "Ah, yes, how I long for the irrational hypnosis of sexual hunger." Esther shrugged and commented from behind her, "Sex is all these things have to live for." The human looked at the sisters and smiled at their wings. He was so drunk on magic, his smile was lifting off his face. Looking back at Helen, he asked, "You look human. So what happened? Something here take your goods away?"

"I neutered myself."

"Neutered yourself? Why would you do that?"

"I'm a witch."

If the archangels weren't there, Helen would turn this human away with a mischievous spell. Azrael had a similar thought. If the room didn't have so many witnesses, she'd spin the human around. Might even kill him. Like pushing a careless thumb into a passing ant. The human turned to Azrael and smiled. "What's your story? Does the carpet match the wings?"

Azrael winced. "Are you asking me if the hair on my privates is white like the feathers of my wings?"

The human grinned bigger, nodding a stupid yes.

Azrael looked into the human's beady eyes with a vibrant grimace, and asked him, "And you feel this is an appropriate question to ask a stranger?" The fire in the archangel's eyes wore down the spell in the human. He sensed he had crossed a line and took an awkward sip of his drink. It was green and sparkled with an unearthly alcohol. When Azrael noticed what it was, she pointed and inquired, "Are you aware of what you're drinking?"

"Yeah, it started with a B. Brumble light, I think."

Azrael snuffed at his ignorance with an imperious breath. "This drink can permanently blind you. You're drinking Burtle Brite." The human's expression lit up with a crooked joy as he cheered, "That's what it was!" Shaking her head, Azrael told him, "You know when this party ends, and this drink of yours dissipates from your senses, all this will fade from your mind like a dream, and you won't know what to tell your wife when she asks where you've been." The man shrugged with quick acceptance and replied plainly, "She'll probably leave me. I've been super unfaithful today, so she should anyway. But how do you know I'm married?"

Rolling her eyes, Azrael uttered, "This place is a black hole." Turning away from the annoyance, she restrained her irritation to ask, "Helen, we've come to speak with the big queen. Have you seen our beloved Cupid?" Helen could sense Azrael's patience was waning. Being on her bad side was far from appealing. Helen put on a helpful face and told her, "Heard he stepped out back. Not like him. Parties like this tend to hold him center stage. Say what you will about the humans, Cupid's admiration for them is touching."

Azrael almost laughed as she responded, "I suggest you shy away from offering me perspective on the dust, Helen. Cupid is a drunken puppet born to love our creators' toys. There is nothing touching about him or the fleeting desperation that guides these simple beasts from their mother's filth to the holes they leave their bones." She finished her drink and half-smiled at the witch. "I like you, Helen. Do try and stay this way."

Azrael and her sisters stepped outside. They left out the back to find Cupid's rusting bus sleeping by the dumpsters. Making their way to it, Domino suggested, "You sure we shouldn't report our presence on Earth?" Her twin shared the thought and added, "Might not go over well for the council to learn we were here from someone other than us."

Azrael mocked responding to the council. *"But council, had we sent word, then rumors may have spread, and your precious Cupid could have been compromised."* She faked a smile and added, "The only reason they have so many rules for this awful place is to play their games. Without love, what game is there to even play? They will praise us for looking after their big dumb oaf."

A red heel shattered out from a window on Cupid's rusty love bus. The gaudy slipper tumbled before the three archangels, settling at their feet. Azrael raised her brow to the sparkling shoe and huffed, "Well, at least this promises to be entertaining, if nothing else."

Inside, Cupid was ripping everything to pieces. Vivianne was in the corner feeling groovy. Her hands danced charcoal around a sketchpad half her size. Two of Cupid's shorties were mostly hiding. Cupid's rampage held them in a fearful state. Everyone was feeling different levels of groovy. Bloodshot eyes, accelerated heart rates, wavering inhibitions, visual trails, slurred thoughts.

Azrael stepped on board and sighed. Cupid was bent over on all fours digging into the cupboards under a sink. His bare ass faced the royal being. Like a naked mole rat fussing about its burrow. Azrael made her way through the room almost unnoticed. Vivianne spotted the winged marvel but didn't fully register her as anything different. With her new groovy vision, the winged woman fit right into her surroundings. Vibrant trails followed after her like reflective tinsel dissolving into a cosmic sparkle. Vivianne simply added the image to what she was sketching. The changelings were too busy panicking over Cupid's rampage to do her vision justice. The drugs had hold of them all. Cupid's head was stuffed under the sink. The overall mood of the room was stoned panic.

Domino and Esther stayed in the doorway while their sister lifted the rose-tinted ribbon tongue of Cupid's love machine. She calmly inspected the names as Cupid raged on in the background. His sweaty ass wiggled in rhythm with the words he cursed as he tossed things away.

Gradually, the changelings' focus began to shift as they took in the image of the high-ranking angel standing in their bus, her wings out, but tucked close to her back. Their breath shortened, and their fretting over Cupid's rampage was overpowered by the fear of their new guest. A collective gulp passed through them.

Azrael leaned against a table as she cleared her throat. Cupid's orders in hand, she casually spoke up, saying, "Work's piling up over here, Phillip."

Cupid's savage motions halted the moment she spoke. Panting in the dark, hot space under the sink, he stopped to think. He couldn't place the voice, but he knew he knew it. Who would call him by his first name? No one had referred to Cupid by it for thousands of years. Never on Earth had he even heard it spoken. Most didn't even know he had a first name.

Slowly backing out from the dark nook, Cupid turned and was overwhelmed with reasons to be concerned. Azrael was an alarming sight on most occasions. Now, of all times, she could only mean trouble.

"Why so sweaty, Phillip?" She wore a smug expression, pleased with herself. Cupid didn't trust it. Why would an archangel be in his bus? And of all the angels, why Azrael? Sitting on the floor, his back against the cupboard, Cupid expressed his concern immediately, asking if someone had died, and promising he had nothing to do with it. "I know this gathering is my doing," he confessed, "but I am no conspirator, nor am I a murderer. I will take the punishment for my use of unlawful magic, but I will not accept responsibility for any blood spilled. You know how these things can get out of hand."

Azrael let go of the rose-tinted paper and told Cupid to relax. "No one has died," she told him.

"So, why are you here? Never took you as a sightseer."

"Well, there was a bit of magic cast in your home. Two different spells, both linking the same road. Some stairs going in and out of Earth. There and back again, as it were. Your scent was on them. Something had come and gone with a purpose. Only where the road leads does not line up with where I am finding you now. Something is off."

Cupid stood himself up, brushing dirt from his hands and knees. Who would have gone to his house, he wondered? Nervous, he asked if the council had sent her. Looking around the bus, she told him, "The council knows not of my travel to this rock. I am merely following instinct for the time being. So far, nothing to report. Unless you are privy to something they should know?"

Eyeing a bottle of a forgotten beverage, Azrael smiled and plucked it from a shelf. "You have Dandy Ale? Phillip, I'm impressed. I thought the last drop had been sucked away ages ago." Holding it up, she asked if she could have it. Cupid didn't care. Of course, he told her, take two. Azrael thanked him and tossed the bottle to Esther, who placed it in a pouch under her robe.

The shorties had huddled into the corner with Vivianne, who was starting to pick up on the uneasy vibe filling the bus. She continued to sketch, regardless. Only she slowed her hand, dulling the sound of her strokes as best she could.

Swallowing a lump in his throat, Cupid inquired further for motive, telling the three angels he was unaware his home had had any visitors. With another timid gulp, he asked, "Are you tracking someone dangerous? Should I be worried?" Cupid was hoping their appearance was merely a coincidence, and he could escape their interest before they discovered he had lost his bow. Azrael folded her arms and sighed dramatically. "No good leads yet as to what traveled to-and-from your home or why. I only wish to help where help is needed. Forgive me for imposing, but you seemed flustered when we entered ... *Missing* something?" Cupid swallowed another lump in his throat. Only this one was larger and harder to conceal.

Cupid thought quickly about what he could be looking for that would justify his desperate state. They had only just walked in on him in a tussle. They may know nothing of his bow. Azrael's question was simply searching for clarity. It was obvious he was looking for something. His answer needed to match the layer of sweat he was presently dressed in. Since it was already so obvious that he and everyone in the bus was stoned and drunk, Cupid confessed he was looking for cocaine.

Azrael turned an amused look towards her sisters. Cupid had found a rag and was wiping the sweat from his face. He even started sniffing to play up the lie. The shameful expression Cupid wore was easy to see through. Cupid was far too emotional to confess such an embarrassing truth and still manage such composure. Too much eye contact. Even if his act were more convincing, it wouldn't alter the fact that there was cocaine out and ready to play on the dining table already. There were even little rows lined up on the kitchen counter, ready to blow away any need for Cupid's hectic pursuit.

Azrael didn't bother pointing it out. Instead, she moved back to the rose-tinted orders and asked Cupid how he found the time to party with so much work piling up. Rolling the paper through her fingers, she asked him, "Where is your bow? All this work ahead of you. One would think your tools would be prepped. Your role in this realm is, as you know, valued above all the other gods. What is the world without love? And I haven't heard any complaints from the council. So I know you're meeting your deadlines." Letting the rose-tinted paper fall from her hands, Azrael took a relaxed seat and politely assured, "I don't mean to pry. I'll get back to my work. But before I part, may I see the bow? Still the finest artifact our creators have ever crafted. Be a shame to come all this way and not admire it."

Cupid strained for an excuse. Nothing he could imagine wouldn't provoke suspicion. But lying was better than the truth. He could lie until he found it. The best he could come up with was to claim it was broken and being repaired. "Should be back in a few days," he told them.
"Good as new."

Pushing at a little bag of coke, Azrael frowned and suggested, "Must be some power you encountered to break such a bow. Maybe you *are* in danger." Cupid shrugged with no response. The silence was too much. Cupid's awkward posture was too much. His shorties lost their nerve.

"It'll turn up," one admitted, their voice trembling.

Azrael looked at the little creatures with a stale expression and asked, "Turn up? So is it lost or broken?"

They were all shaking now. Cupid started to speak, but Azrael hushed him with a gentle gesture. One of the shorties sought to reassure the archangel that there was nothing to fear by telling her, "It always turns up."

Cupid snapped at the little creatures to shut up. Azrael stood between them, her wings opening wide, eyes glowing with a bright white light. The shorties cowered together as her wings caged around them. Cupid took a step forward, but Esther and Domino advanced into the bus, and he froze.

Towering over the wrinkly shorties with her bright eyes, Azrael asked them calmly, "Do you mean to tell me Cupid has lost his bow, and this isn't the first time?" Collectively they gulped and rattled their heads about in a means to say yes. Cupid began rambling about his encounter with Caesar. His fight with the disgruntled human. Azrael listened closely as he confessed about the fight. He explained waking up in a bush, battered and beaten. He was good at playing the victim. "Please don't tell the council," he pleaded, promising her he would find the bow.

Azrael relaxed her wings and dimmed the light in her eyes. Returning to her seat, she sighed and gave Cupid a little smile. She told him to relax. "I have no intention of informing the council. Nor do I wish for this gathering of yours to stop. Best to keep up appearances. All should remain copacetic, so as to not raise suspicion. Word of your missing bow could bring great distress and danger to many."

Cupid folded his arms and looked to the ground.

"This bout you had with the mortal. I assume you're parked here because this is the bar where it happened? Why else would you be here with all of these creatures potentially finding the powerful gift you have lost?"

Cupid's silence made her sigh. It was a painful breath. "So, are we digging around the bus because the bow is lost within these walls? I'm confused, Phillip. You told me you woke up outside. That you drove away from the bar where you left your bow. That you learned of your misfortune while on the road."

"We don't remember what bar we were at," a shortie confessed.

"Of course you don't." Azrael laughed under her breath. She looked to her sisters, pleased with Cupid's incompetence.

An idea was forming in her mind that pleased her greatly. She was going to find Cupid's bow. Standing up and smiling at Cupid with a reassuring grin, she told him, "Stay put, Phillip. We'll find your bow. It is our duty to keep the balance."

Once off the bus, Domino commented on Cupid's appearance. "The tales of Cupid's affliction do not do his decay justice." Esther agreed, "Had we stood in his presence any longer, I believe we may have become stoned ourselves."

Azrael got right to business. "We should limit our use of magic to just necessities for the time being. If Whisper has a hand in this, which I fear it does, best to remain anonymous for as long as possible."

Domino replied, "Whisper has no allies to reach in this realm. None that we don't own. What reward could it offer that we could not double?"

"True, we pay better. Anyone Whisper would try to reach would surely turn it in. Most rumors doubt the thing is even still alive."

Azrael shrugged. "We know too little to assume anything. Cupid is keeping the bow a secret, but news will get out eventually. The faster we work at recovering it, the better."

Domino raised her brow as she asked, "I get the feeling you don't wish to ever tell the council, even once we find the bow." Azrael said nothing. She stopped out front of the bar, near the road. Esther smiled and folded her arms, and confirmed, "We don't plan on returning the bow at all, do we?"

Azrael smiled and summoned a phone booth from the earth. As she stepped in, her sisters shared smiles. They both leaned into the booth and asked for Azrael to share her thoughts. Pulling a gold coin from her robe, Azrael told her sisters they were going to keep the bow. "The power of love has sat in those fat arms long enough," she explained. Pulling the phone from its hook, she expressed, "Just think how careless it was for our masters to have made the bow in the first place, let alone bestow such power in the hands of such a thing." She slipped the gold coin into the slot and grinned mischievously. "It's time things changed around here."

XX
A GUIDING WHISPER

April and Caesar were a little drunk. Caesar a little more so. They were lying on a bed, eyes closed but not asleep. They had tossed a few decks of cards into a bowl near the bathroom. The game had ended some time ago. Tux was perched on a pillow overlooking the room, purring and content. They had emptied a bottle of tequila and started working through a case of beer before they laid back impatiently.

Nothing was happening.

"Caesar, I'm too drunk to keep up like this. My eyes are getting heavy."

"Get some sleep, then. I'll wake you if anything happens."

Caesar took a breath from his bottle. Eyes remained closed. April huffed. "I think we did something wrong. We should put a rock in a drink again and ask this thing if we used the wrong vinegar." Caesar grunted but said nothing. They were both tired.

A gurgle popped in the bathroom.

Caesar's head popped up. His sight locked onto the bathroom but he saw nothing. Another gurgle sounded off and April opened an eye. "What's that?"

"I don't know."

Bubbles began brewing from the bathroom and they both sat side by side holding their breath. The sink started to steam. Caesar moved to get up but April stopped him. "What are you doing?"

"Something happening."

"The last time something happened you up and disappeared."

Caesar rocked his head and sort of smirked. "Actually, the talking beer was the last something that happened."

April slapped his arm, "Shut up, you know what I'm saying." Caesar took her hand and moved them off the bed, reassuring her he wouldn't vanish this time.

They both eased their way to the bathroom door. Steam was rolling off the surface of the water. The sink was boiling.

April squeezed Caesar's arm. "I'm too drunk for this."

The rocks started to glow. Tux had jumped to the edge of the bed, staring into the bathroom with dilated pupils. April reiterated, "I am definitely too drunk for this." The boiling sink intensified, and the bathroom filled with steam. The glow from the bubbling rocks covered everything in a dark blue light.

April's grip on Caesar tightened as lines began to smudge against the mirror, lines that wrote a big *Hello*. April pulled close to Caesar and whispered, "Oh my god. We're gonna die." A voice suddenly spoke up from the sink to say, "It's wild, isn't it?" April screamed and jumped, pulling Caesar closer.

"Didn't mean to frighten you," the voice said, and continued, "I need one of you to put one of those rocks against the mirror." Caesar told the voice the water was too hot. "So be quick," the voice said. Caesar shrugged and moved for the sink, but April kept hold of him. With a reassuring nod, Caesar separated himself from her. Shaking off his nerves, he struck quickly, pulling a rock from the boiling water. Caesar was confused by how cold the rock was. How nothing burned him.

"Very nice, Caesar the Powerful. Now, I need you to place the rock against the mirror."

Caesar thought about it, and April nudged him. So he raised the rock to the mirror, and it was sucked from his hand and stuck to the mirror like a magnet. The briefest moment of silence followed. The lights in the room dimmed. There was only the glow from the sink. The mirror's foggy reflection lost its luster. Caesar stepped back. April had her hands over her mouth. Tux hid behind a pillow, spying into the bathroom, ready to flee.

Gradually, the rock, which mysteriously held itself afloat, melted into the mirror. It liquified and filled the reflective space from top to bottom with a hard silver cover. April and Caesar both backed against the opposite wall, melting together in a form of comfort and support. The shine from the mirror mesmerized them. Its light dazzled in their eyes like faraway stars. Something began moving from within the silver window — a finger gently reaching out into the shape of a hand. April tightened the grip on her mouth to stop herself from screaming.

She tightened her grip on Caesar.

Now two hands pushed out. The silver covering wrapped around the fingers like paint. The hands grabbed a hold of the mirror's edge and pulled a face into the room next, then arms, then legs, and then a body. The silver covering left the mirror and wrapped around the bathroom's new occupant. The silver coating absorbed into the figure, and there stood Whisper. Its bare, ash-colored feet stepped off the sink, and the mirror shimmered back to its foggy reflection. The lights in the room illuminated. The sink stopped glowing. Everything returned to normal. Only now, there was an ancient being made of smoke and fire standing before them.

April looked up at the tall figure that had just entered her world from the mirror, her hand still over her mouth. Caesar instinctively picked up a beer and shook his head as he popped the top. Whisper smiled at him and asked, "May I have one?" Caesar handed the ash figure the beer he had just opened, and Whisper stepped out from the bathroom with a strong, eager posture. Breathing in deep, rewarding breaths, the godly being turned around in the room, smiling at its surroundings. It was easy to see that the thing was happy.

Caesar and April stood in the doorway to the bathroom, speechless. Whisper gestured to the case of beer on the floor as smoke chased out from its feet and lifted two bottles up for Caesar and April to take, which they both did.

Whisper sat down, and Tux, hiding in a corner, hissed at the new addition to the room. The smoky-being waved its smoky hand and the cat's fur puffed like a rug being dusted with a broom. Tux froze in a frightened pose like a statue. The ash figure frowned and gestured to the cat. "Is this loved by either of you?"

Caesar raised a nervous hand.

Whisper nodded and sighed, "Not much for animals myself. Not in your world. Everything to do with being made of what I'm made of, I'm afraid. Amongst my many flavors, fire, and ash are not easy things to befriend." With a sip of beer, Whisper shrugged. "Pity. I get on well with the wordless bunch back home." Caesar found his tongue and he asked with a bit of a bite, "Did you just kill my cat?"

"Goodness, no. Merely petrified the curious puss. The spell will wear off in a couple of days."

Spotting Caesar's smokes, Whisper smiled and snapped a finger, zapping a stick from the pack into its hand. Lighting it with a touch, Whisper took a slow, happy drag. Settling into a chair, Whisper exhaled a happier cloud and said, "Ah, this place tastes so different. I don't find one realm necessarily better than the other. It's just refreshing ... the nuance. Certainly a great deal dustier here, but dust is far from a problem. Substance here just holds so much more importance. It's so fleeting, so much more of a task to obtain and relish. Always on the move."

April and Caesar were still in the bathroom. Their heads peered out, mystified by the presence of the ash figure. April wasn't sure if she should be worried. It felt like she had just died. Felt like this thing was either going to point her to a welcoming escalator going up or a set of off-putting stairs tumbling down.

Whisper sat and smoked. Slow, methodical drags and slow methodical exhales. It was pleased with the smoke and pleased with the room. Pleased with its effect on Caesar and April. Getting comfortable, the ash figure smiled. Smiled, and got to business. "So, you want to kill Cupid."

Caesar and April were lost for words.

Turning to April, Whisper said, "Where are my manners? I am called Whisper. I am a being of the elements. I live in ash and sleep in the clouds. I breathe inside of fire and roam through the rocks that slumber beneath the earth." Whisper smiled with another drag of the cigarette and carried on to ask them, "Any questions?"

April folded her arms and popped her eyes at the figure, asking, "Yeah, the fuck you just come from?"

195

Whisper smiled and told her, "Where I am from is far away. It is so far away it sometimes overlaps with where we are right now." April and Caesar both sat down, and April said she didn't understand. "You're from a parallel dimension? Is that what that was with the mirror?"

Whisper shrugged. "'Parallel' is a funny thing. Think of the universe as you would a long hallway full of doors. Behind one door, you'll find a disco. Behind another, you'll find Cupid's home. You'll find us here and now. The pub across the street. A grocery store. Behind every door, in a sense, is every door. This hallway doesn't turn, doesn't slope down or up, it just goes on straight. If you walk down it long enough, you'll find yourself back at the disco." Whisper finished its cigarette, sucking it down to nothing and blowing a cloud up into the ceiling.
April and Caesar were still puzzled. Their looks made Whisper sigh. It wasn't an agitated sigh so much as it was just uninterested in the conversation. Sitting up, the ash figure told them, "Unless you have a passion for crafting maps, I recommend not bothering your mind with these things. The gods go just as crazy trying to explain it as your kind does. Best to just enjoy the dance."

April laughed out a short bit of astonished wind. She gave up trying to grasp what the thing was saying.

Adoring their silence, Whisper said, "I can appreciate your curiosity. Time, however, is against us. Killing a god is no simple feat, especially for a mortal. You will need a weapon made by a god to kill a god. For this, you will have some traveling ahead of you. Places that offer such tools are not as easy to find as a disco. I have arranged a guide for you, as I am not able to tag along."

"Where are you going?"

"I need to check in on Cupid. To do what I can to keep the distance between you. If he finds you first, the game is over. I'll be back at your side as soon as I can. I promise."

April gulped. "Why are you helping us? You got a fire buddy who broke your heart?"

Whisper laughed a little and smiled at April. "I am the only me there is, sadly. I am helping because Caesar's plight is just. The gods have beaten this horse long enough. Not to mention, Caesar the Great, you are the most interesting thing to pass by in a long time. To stand against this madness. To raise your bleeding heart and demand no more suffering. You're an inspiring man."

Whisper picked up the room's phone and added, "Along with Cupid, another factor standing against us is nature. Nature is nature. After all, it's always on course."

Dialing for the hotel's front desk, Whisper told them, "Nature will eventually return the bow to Cupid. It has been moving to remedy their separation ever since the thing left his hands. Just like a tree grows out from the shade to reach the sunlight, it will grow out to move the bow back into his hands. This, however, plays in our favor."

The front desk answered and Whisper asked for room service. Looking at April and Caesar, it asked if turkey was okay. They both nodded, and Whisper asked for five sandwiches, two to go. Hanging up the phone, it finished what it was saying. "Nature is patient. If all goes well, we will be long done before we notice the branches leaning our way."

Standing up, Whisper produced a small bag from the smoke of its arm. "We need to hide the bow from sight," it told them. "This is a special satchel. It can fit much and still remain small. More importantly, it does not reveal its contents. A rare item in itself — may draw an eye or two to those who know how to spot it." Whisper next extracted a yellow book bag and said with some amusement, "So, we put a bag within a bag. This one I got from a gift shop in Orlando."

Caesar took the satchel and looked inside. There was nothing — not even the inside of the bag was visible. It was an impossibly black illusion that hurt his brain. As he put the bow and arrow inside, the bag swallowed the items like a magic trick. They both shared an astonished look with each other. Caesar was feeling hopeful for their mission. The pain in his heart was a clenching fist, vengeance was within reach.

Whisper had stood up and grabbed the petrified Tux, asking Caesar if April was coming with him. Caesar had his eyes on the cat and nodded his head yes. Whisper put Tux into the satchel, and then the satchel into the backpack.

Caesar had questions all over his face as Whisper held the pack out to Caesar. "All you need to do is think of what it is you want and reach in. What you seek is what you get," it told them.

Room service knocked on the door, and Whisper dispersed. The cigarette smoke that lightly filled the air thickened with the motion. Caesar and April stood in awe. The knock returned to the door, and Caesar opened, his attention leaning more toward the smoke.

A chipper, bald man pushed a cart into the room. His name tag said, Roger. He greeted April and Caesar, and read their order from the receipt on the cart. They didn't say much back. They were looking up at the smoke clouding the air. Confused and worried about the smoke detector, the man followed their gaze. Suddenly the cloud moved and surrounded him. It even smiled at him. Smiled and rushed into the man's mouth, nose, ears, and pores. April and Caesar both jumped back as the man swayed. Then he smiled. What had once been Roger was now pushed down deep into a dream. Whisper controlled the man's body now — the smoke-stringed puppet master to a chubby Roger marionette.

With a stretch and a grin, Whisper looked at the man's name tag and said, "Hello, Roger." Smiling at April and Caesar, Whisper asked how he looked. In shock, April chuckled an uncontrolled breath and asked, "The fuck did you just do?"

Whisper dug around the room service cart and said, "I can't walk around your world looking all smoky, now, can I?"

Caesar scratched his head and asked, "What about, uh, the guy?"

"I'm only borrowing Roger."

Whisper tossed them both a sandwich and put the two to-go orders into Caesar's new magic satchel. Eat up, it told them, for the long road ahead of them.

Caesar zipped up a few bottles into the impossible bag and followed Whisper outside. April was over his shoulder, trying to keep her feet on the ground. "Caesar, I'm tripping. That thing took that man's body. Roger, it took over Roger, Caesar."

"I know, I saw."

"And what the hell even is that thing? Turns into smoke, eyes all black. You think Roger's dead?" Caesar shivered and shook his head. "It said it was only borrowing Roger." Nervous, April pulled at him. "I got a funny feeling about him."

"Me too."

April was happy to hear Caesar shared her distrust of their new guide, relieved to know Caesar was on her side and that this was all crazy, and she was not alone in the absurdity of it. But still, they were following him. Had no one else *to* follow.

Whisper led them around to the back of the hotel, out by the dumpsters. It snapped a bit of chalk into Roger's palm and drew a door onto a brick wall.

An old homeless man was watching from a pile of cardboard. Watched as the chalk outline opened up and swung inward. He had to sit up and wipe at his eyes. Tried to wipe the image away, but no matter how deep he dug, the image remained. A man had just drawn a door onto a wall and then opened that door.

April and Caesar wiped their eyes as well. Every step they took moved further away from the world they knew. And it only got more unusual. A bulky troll leaned in from the dark passage Whisper had drawn against the brick wall. It had green skin, pointy leaf-like ears, a protruding jaw, crooked teeth, broad, boulderous shoulders, a dark leather vest, dark lumpy britches, and a long, dark coat.

The troll's big head dipped under the top of the passage. It sniffed out before looking at Roger's body. Its green forehead scrunched into a curious fold, and it sniffed again, finding a scent it knew. Recoiling ever so slightly to the connection its nostrils had made, its big troll head bumped against the edge of the passage.

"Whisper?"

Roger's face smiled. "Indeed it is, Icarus. How have you been? Still bulging, I see."

Icarus laughed coldly and unamused. Looking at Caesar and April, he huffed an unconvincing threat. "I could make a pretty coin saying I saw you walking the Earth. These doors are already troublesome enough to work. Helping you could see my blood turn to stone."

"And after all these years of trouble, you stayed put working the same back door. I admire that."

Icarus huffed, "When a gig works, why look elsewhere?"

"Wise not to fly too high, Icarus."

The troll chuckled sarcastically, even putting his hand on his belly to emphasize his ridicule for the joke. "You're too funny," he said, then asked, "But seriously, what are you doing on this side of the door?"

"My friends here are to join a guide I have arranged. They have an urgent meeting they must make." Whisper smiled and leaned against the passage, peering into the darkness that lay ahead endlessly behind it.

Icarus shook his head. "You want me to let in two mortals … with or without you?"

"Without. I will not be attending this part of the expedition."

Icarus shrugged. "I prefer this. Still going to cost you something, though. How much coin you prepared to part with, *King* of the Shadows?"

Whisper pulled a pouch of noisy coins from the air and handed the bag to the troll. Icarus smiled as he shook the bag by his ear. His grin grew pleased as he uttered to himself, "If I were brave enough to share this story, *HA*! I'd sure gather some crowd. King of the Shadows drawing a back door, and from all places, Earth. Who'd even believe me?" With a low and pulsing cackle, Icarus stepped into the darkness. His new bag jiggled pleasantly in his hands. April and Caesar both looked into the black space and felt smaller than they had ever felt before.

Whisper held out two double-A batteries and asked them both to swallow one. April cocked her head and asked, exasperated, "Excuse me?" Whisper gave Roger's eye a wink and told them both, "Trust me. Easier to just swallow than for me to explain why." Caesar shrugged and took the battery, thinking it couldn't get any stranger than it already was. April sighed with a hard breath and took one as well, shaking her head at Caesar to tell him how crazy all this was. They each swallowed a battery with a painful gulp, and Whisper eased them toward the passage, telling them, "You'll be meeting a faun named Rugs. Follow his every word without question. You're safer walking the bottom of the ocean with only a suitcase full of air than you are walking this place without a guide. Do not doddle. Let nothing know what you are doing, what you have, or what you are after."

Sensing some hesitation in Caesar, Whisper asked, "You do still wish for this, do you not? A weapon to achieve justice for your wife and child? Redemption for all the hearts broken throughout time? Salvation for all those not yet inflicted with the poison?"

With a heavy breath, Caesar asked why the troll had called Whisper the King of Shadows. Roger's face smiled and just said, "I told you I have many names." Whisper left them, saying nothing else, marching into the night with Roger's pleasant grin.

With a frightened gulp, April took hold of Caesar's hand. She squeezed him and pulled in a strong breath. He gave her a supportive nod and a little smile, and asked her if she still wanted to come with him.

"I can't let you do this alone. And I sure as hell didn't just swallow a battery for nothing."

"Alright then," Caesar chuckled.

Caesar pulled a bottle from the impossible bag, took a deep breath from it, and handed it to April. She took the bottle and shook her head, saying, "You're crazy. You know that? With all this, you still want a drink. Did you see the big fucking green thing that just came out of this hole?" She swirled the bottle around, looking into the dark passage that lay ahead. Her thoughts collided with impossible speculations. She was more curious than afraid, but she was still afraid.

With a reluctant breath, April took a healthy swallow and emptied the bottle. She set the bottle down and laughed under her breath. "I'm seriously going to regret meeting you, aren't I?"

"I love you, too," Caesar replied, smiling a big bright smile.

Hand in hand, they stepped into the dark passage, slipping away into an endless sea of black. The brick wall sealed shut behind them with no sign there was ever a door, a troll, or anything other than brick and wall.

The homeless man watching from his cardboard corner had stood up, eyes wide in disbelief. He hurried up to the wall, feeling his hands around the brick, pushed at it, kicked it.

Nothing happened.

It was just a wall.

Walking backward, keeping it in view, the man scratched his dirty head. He stood and stared at the wall, convincing himself he saw what he saw. With a firm clench, the old man broke into a fragile sprint, and a frail roar carried him swiftly into the wall. His face bashed against brick, and he stumbled back onto his butt, stars swirling around his head.

XXI
CHECKING IN

With the sun rising at their backs, Azrael and Domino stepped off the road. They were following Azrael's magical compass. The device had led them to the biker bar where Cupid had recently cast his magic. They were hunting for the spot he had last shot his bow, the place he lost it.

Esther stayed back to keep an eye on Cupid.

She preferred the party.

Azrael's compass spun with a blue light, pulling her to the bar's front door. Bikes were parked outside, but the place was closed. Azrael pushed at the door, only to find it was locked. Her compass was certain magic was flowing from inside. Raising a brow, she touched the lock, and it snapped open. She pushed in and found the bar was vacant of all but the sound of blubbering men. The two sisters shared curious looks as they stepped around the counter to find a few big bikers huddled up, comforting each other and sobbing. They had candles lit around them and pictures of their mothers lying on the floor. Domino half smiled and said, "This is adorable."

The weeping men looked up to the two magical beings peering over them from behind the counter. The owner cleared his nose and sniffled, "Sorry, ladies, bar's closed." Azrael looked down at the wet-eyed men and asked, "Fat naked god made you cry?"

They all began sobbing harder. The owner tried his best to say yes through his heaving tears. Azrael turned from them, rolling her eyes, unable to tame her disgust. She moved a dial on her compass, and the colors changed red. She focused the tool's scope off the bikers. Dials spun and aimed in the direction of the nearest place magic had most recently been cast. Deeper in the compass, more dials curved and told her the potency of the magic, and how far it had been cast. Something new wasn't far.

Azrael stepped up close to the pitiful pow-wow and kicked at the owner. He looked up again, his lip quivering. Azrael put on a pained smile and inquired, "I see the bikes out front, but I'm wondering if any of you happen to have a car?" The weeping man pulled a pair of keys from his vest and told her there was a Ford Bronco out back. Azrael took the keys without a word and left the men to sob.

Domino rode shotgun as they drove onward. The compass sat on the dashboard with its guiding blue light leading the way. The sisters speculated as to why Cupid would torture those men with such a spell. It was an unlawful use of magic, although they would never charge someone for such an amusing act. It just wasn't in Cupid's nature to be so aggressive, unless they had attacked Cupid. It had them thinking Cupid could be keeping something more from them. Maybe he hadn't misplaced his bow. Maybe it was taken.

As they pulled into the Inn, Azrael's dial spun around with a wild rainbow of light. Domino smiled as they parked. This had to be the place. It had been a couple of days, but Cupid's bow wasn't just any kind of magic. Its presence would linger for weeks. Azrael followed the compass to the spot Cupid had fired his bow. The dial spun into a blur, and the crystals inside glowed white. She closed the device and tucked it into her robe. Pulling out a pouch of purple powder known as Reminiscence Dust, Azrael began to spread the substance around the parking lot.

The memory of magic shimmered in place around the purple powder. Like shards of metal on a magnet, they could see the faint outline of fallen arrows, outlines of a heart beating to the bright light of an arrow point sticking out from it. Domino admired Cupid's aim. "For a wasted god, he's a good shot." The violet reveal was brief. The purple powder worked quickly and thoroughly. Azrael chased more of the dust around and found the spot where the arrow was released. Cupid's form flashed on and off, the bow in hand. Streaks of motion led the angels along Cupid's post-shot stumble. They both looked into the ditch Cupid had fallen into. Azrael spoke with a demeaning air. "And here is where your fat ass fell. This is where you lost it, isn't it?" She tossed one more splash of dust, and the outline of the bow flashed and faded away. The dust showed the bow was left alone, that Cupid had stepped off without it.

But who picked it up?

Azrael and her sister had a seat at the bar. In their long, flowing robes they stood out, compared to the regular crowd. Lucky, the bartender, put out two coasters and asked them if they were models from some desert photoshoot. "You all look like you're from some fancy music video or something. Anyway, what are we drinking, ladies?"

The two sisters weren't fans of mortal spirits, but they knew blending in would play in their flavor. Since they were resisting magic, blending in was important. So Azrael ordered what she thought two human women who looked like they were on break from a fancy music video shoot or something would order.

"Two vodka cranberries."

"Coming up."

Tasting her drink, Azrael casually asked about Cupid. Said she heard people saying someone picked a fight with him. Lucky laughed. "I heard about it — pissed I missed it. I was here when it happened, too. He chased the, uh, Cupid guy, outside, and I didn't see either of them the rest of the night."

Domino stirred her drink and asked if Cupid had left anything behind. Lucky found the question odd, and told her he didn't know. Stabbing the ice in her drink with a straw, she asked, "So who was this person who fought Cupid?" From the end of the bar, Polly looked up from under his fedora and said Caesar's name. He laughed and told the sisters a buddy had found him on the highway with an arrow in his chest. He wasn't dead. Just had an arrow in him.

If they could believe that.

Polly added, "Boy, I sure wish I could've seen that fight. To see a man like Caesar throw down. If he ended up with an arrow in him, I mean, shit, that would've been a sight to see, man." Polly smiled at the two angels. His attraction for them was obvious — something they could use to get more information. Azrael asked, "Anyone know where this Caesar is?"

Polly wasn't in a rush. He picked up his beer and the coaster it was on, picked up his newspaper. Polly's grin folded his age over a few times in his cheeks. His tanned, Cuban skin resembled leather. His grin was as big as it could get as he made his way closer to the two angels. As he made the move, he said they had just asked the million-dollar question. He thought he sounded cool when he said it and didn't bother hiding the long trips his eyes made around their figures. Their robes hid their shapes, but Polly looked all the same, hunting for a leg or a curve.

Azrael faked a smile for his amusement and told him, "Good thing I brought my million dollars." Polly laughed and slapped his thigh. "You're a live one. I like that."

Lucky gave Azrael a funny look and lit a cigarette, asking her why she was so curious. Azrael smiled and answered with a shrug. "Cupid is out of this world. I'd like to meet the man who stepped up to a god and started a fight." Smiling at Polly, she added, "Must be some guy." Polly blushed and hid his face. "Caesar's a funny man," he said.

"Funny?"

"I never got the whole story, but he lost his wife and kid somehow. Buncha' years back. He's been drinking with us for damn near three years now. Not a real fighter. More of a, well, just a drinker. A quiet guy. A real sad guy."

Lucky flicked some ash into a tray and continued, "We all know Caesar around here. He works at the diner next door. Lives around back at the Inn. He may be a broken man, but he's a good man. And a good friend to everyone around here."

Polly rolled his eyes. "He's a crazy man."

Lucky snipped at him, "What do you know of it?"

Polly smiled and shrugged. "He went chasing after that big, naked lovebug. That's how come no one knows where he is. Teddy's been all manic, calling hospitals and what have you."

206

Domino asked, "This man Caesar went chasing after Cupid?"

Polly sat up. "Oh yeah, man's got a grudge. Saw him hightail it with a bow and arrow like he was going hunting." Lucky tossed a rag at him and laughed. "You did not. You're full of shit, Polly."

Azrael had heard enough. She got up from the bar with her sister, leaving their drinks. Lucky asked where they were going. Polly smiled and tipped his hat, trying to flirt as he asked, "We didn't scare you off, did we, ladies?" Neither of them looked back. They just closed the door behind their silent exit.

Lucky laughed at Polly, which prompted Polly to ask defensively, "What's so funny?"

"Your face is beat red," he told him, teasing. "You're a creepy old man, you know that?"

Polly picked up his beer and mocked a laugh back at Lucky, "Yeah, yeah. *Ha ha ha.* You don't stop recognizing beauty when you get old, Lucky. You'll see."

"I don't doubt that. It's just your privates were practically hanging out your mouth just now."

Polly smiled. "That obvious?"

"You're a creepy old pervert, Polly."

"Nah, I'm just ambitious."

...

The archangels took a seat at the diner, thinking to themselves how stupid it was that some human who worked in a place like this had gotten their hands on their Creator's most powerful artifact. They wanted to make quick work of finding him.

Amber brought over menus and water and a busy smile. A lunch rush was presently filling the seats. Amber told them what the kitchen was out of and what the specials were.

Azrael ignored the menu and said, "I saw a rather eye-catching display of pies on the way in."

"Just here for dessert, I like that. Yes, we have an apple, a cherry, a key lime, a custard, and a house-special chocolate cheesecake."

Azrael gathered the menus and held them up with a smile, asking her for two of the freshest pies she had. One of the only vices the Earth had over the angels was sugar. No matter how it was dressed, sugar agreed with angels. As Amber took the menus, Azrael apologized. "Sorry, just one more thing. I can see you're busy, but we didn't come here just for pies. We're sort of here looking for someone. A long-lost someone." Azrael was gifted at sounding sincere, sounding human. Summoning empathy in others was a gift all angels were naturally blessed with.

Amber was eyeing up her other tables, but said, "Oh?"

"Yes, I believe he works here. A man named Caesar."

Hearing the name struck Amber. The archangels noticed the spark. Amber held the menus to her chest as she told them he did work there and wondered why they were asking. Azrael sighed with well-faked emotion as she lied, "We've been looking for him... for Caesar, for... well, I don't know how long now. Years, Amber. We finally got a lead that he was working here and dropped everything we were doing." Azrael had a look of heartfelt loss and longing in her eyes. She could have fooled anyone with a look like that.

Amber felt light. Her chest scrunched around her heart slightly. Clearing her throat, she asked, "How do you know Caesar? Oh my god, you aren't... can't be." She looked the two over close and speculated, "You can't be his ex.... Are you related?"

Azrael smiled. "Yes, Caesar's our big brother."

Amber crumpled the menus and gasped, "My God, Caesar has sisters." She bounced her eyes around the diner, trying to find the order she should move in. She wanted to give her tables away. To quit and sit with the women and ask them countless questions. Stepping off in a hurry, she told them not to go anywhere. Her heart was racing. She had a smile so big, she was almost laughing.

Azrael watched the woman run into the back and smiled. Domino asked if this lie was the best approach. Azrael shrugged. "Seems reasonable. The man ran away from his life. We could be anyone. And we were told they are all such good friends." She turned back to her sister and added, "And he's an alcoholic who left his life behind. Reasonable to assume he has secrets."

Domino scowled over the hungry occupants surrounding them as she commented, "Do you think he even has siblings?"

"Who cares?"

"Why don't you just look into this woman and see what she knows, instead of playing games? Not that I don't enjoy games. It's just that our purpose here is time-sensitive."

"I suppose I could, but I'd rather use as little magic as we can until we figure out if someone is sniffing around. Suppose there is anything sniffing around. Not knowing we are involved gives us an advantage."

Domino rolled her eyes. "Oh, please. A vision spell leaves no more of a ripple than one of these thing's farts." Azrael shook her head. "The trace is not my concern. It's the conjuring I'm wary of. If something is waiting for it, any spell may alert them." Domino leaned into the table. "I admire your precaution, but I doubt anything is listening so closely. It is as you wish, though, and you may do as you wish. So far, the day has been more entertaining than most, so I'm not complaining. Simply eager to win."

Following Amber, Teddy came over to the table, nervous and excited, holding out his hand before they even knew he was there. Domino nudged Azrael and said, "Sister, a man is here aiming himself at us."

Azrael shook his hand and continued the act of pretending to be Caesar's long-lost sister. Teddy was a rambling mess and said he had many questions. Domino's expression was telling her not to waste time with this buffoon. Just cast a spell on him.

Azrael smiled at her sister and told Teddy, "Just start asking."

Teddy stood still and composed himself, motioned to start, but then second-guessed himself. Azrael patted the seat next to her. "Have a seat, Teddy. I'm sure we have just as many questions for you. Let's get to know one another." Teddy sat and sighed, asking the first thing that popped into his mind. "Does his ex still not remember him?"

Azrael didn't know what Teddy meant. Domino gave her sister a helpless shrug. Azrael shook her head and said, "We haven't kept in touch with her, sorry."

"Really? Damn. Well, do you know where she is? I don't know what I could do or if I *would* do anything. You know what I've always wanted to know? What's your last name? Caesar has kept it from us, if you can believe that."

The archangels shared a lost glance. Maybe they didn't know enough to make the lie work. Azrael gave herself a breath to think of her next move. Teddy's beady eyes were shining at her, eager to hear their name. She didn't like any of the answers she was coming up with, so she decided Domino was right. Enough games. Azrael put her hand on Teddy's back and worked a bit of magic. Her eyes lit up a little, as did Teddy's. It only took a swift combing through his memories to find what she needed — lots of reading and a little rearranging. Before she left the spell, Azrael nudged Teddy with a dose of persuasion.

"Would you mind not telling anyone we're here, Teddy? We're afraid we might chase Caesar off if he found out."

Teddy was all smiles. "Of course, don't you worry, we know Caesar all too well."

Amber set down two fresh apple pies. Azrael smiled at Teddy, and he smiled back. "The pies are on me." Domino grinned. "You're too sweet, Teddy."

Azrael picked up her dessert and suggested they go see Caesar's room. Only it wasn't a suggestion at all. Teddy was up without question. Pies in hand, they followed after him.

"We've been praying someone like you would turn up sooner or later," Teddy told them, adding, "Honestly, we've all been looking for you, or any family, really. But learning about Caesar is like pulling teeth. He had us convinced he was an only child."

With a scoop of her pie, Domino encouraged Teddy with a, "You don't say."

Unlocking Caesar's door, he continued sharing. "You know, we don't even know if his baby was going to be a boy or a girl. Caesar can't even find the peace of mind to say its name, or what it would've been named. Only heard him say the wife's name once." Opening the door, he sighed, "You can always see him thinking it when he talks about them. He just can't bring himself to say the name. Not that he talks much about it anyway."

Azrael and Domino stepped into the room ahead of Teddy, spooning moderate bits of pie into their mouths. They both found the room disgusting. Most did. Teddy defended the state of the space, expressing the pity he and everyone had for their big brother. They carefully made their way around the books and clothes and empty bottles that decorated the floor, all while picking at their pies. Teddy talked on and on about the family Caesar had made at the Inn, and that he was cared for. He mentioned again and again how happy he was that they had found him.

"We would like to stick around until he comes back," Azrael suggested, another bite of apple pie scooped up and swallowed. Teddy smiled and said he'd be happy to give them a free room for a few nights.

Kicking around at the mess, not looking at Teddy, Azrael said they would appreciate that. Domino looked into the broken microwave and yawned, "Yeah, Teddy, you're so sweet."

In the room they were gifted, Teddy handed them a set of keys and said someone would call their room if Caesar turned up. Domino took the keys and closed the door in Teddy's face.

Azrael sat on the bed. She bounced her butt on the mattress some, her expression disapproving of the quality. Domino folded her arms and stated, "This place is a dump." Azrael agreed but added, "This is where we set our trap."

Looking through the blinds, Domino asked, "Will you tell me the plan, now? What it is we are up to. I have grown tired of guessing. You don't wish to destroy it, for what would that change? They would only make another. We cannot use the bow. Only Cupid's own will can release the magic it bleeds. Cupid won't just hand you his bow. He would never step down from his role."

Azrael smiled at her sister. She was correct. When the gods made such tools as Cupid's bow, Thor's hammer, and Poseidon's pike, they bestowed the power only to the god to whom they gave the gift. Gods stuck to their roles. They had no incentive to rebel. But the great creators were merciful. If a god grew tired of their role, they could gift their power to another. Azrael, however, knew of a loophole in their maker's architecture.

"You see, like us, our makers think little of mortals. They never considered it possible that such simple beings would ever find themselves possessing one of their precious works. But a mortal can use them. Thor's hammer would likely kill them if they attempted to summon any lightning, but Cupid's bow? Well, any fool can shoot an arrow. The laws only address magic. Magic cannot take the bow. The bow must be given with clean consent. From one hand to the next. And what is written if a god should abandon their calling?"

Domino smiled as she rehearsed the law. *"If a god should forfeit their right, may their gift be passed to the first hands willing to find hold.* But the creators decide the new owner, regardless. It is still they who make it so." Folding her arms, she asked, "Are you saying that by this human's touch, the bow no longer has an owner?"

"I am saying that the human is the owner. There is no ceremony required to pass on the gift, for they are not of magical descent. They were never considered. They are hands that the bow has found. Unbound hands. We cannot steal it from this human. But…"

"It can be given."

"Correct. And as it stands now, Cupid has abandoned his role, and this, Caesar, has unknowingly taken it over. Cupid would never hand it over. But if a human were to gift us the bow, the power would come with it."

"But we cannot persuade a human with magic. How will you sway him to give it to you?"

Azrael sighed. "I will find a willing participant. In the meantime, we must control the space between Caesar and Cupid. Keep him from picking any more fights with the big drunk. Caesar would only lose, and the bow would be back home. We can sedate Cupid and keep him here in this room. Since the human is hunting him, it would be wise to keep the lure under our watch. The party is a good distraction, but it is far too messy for such a game. This needs to be clean and isolated."

There was a knock at their door.

It was Frances. He was in uniform. When he saw the two women, he blushed. "Oh, wow, you're a lot prettier than Caesar." Frances shook his head and bashfully looked away, apologizing. "Sorry, that came out wrong. I'm just surprised is all." Laughing and catching his breath, he said, "All of this is just such a surprise. Sorry, my name's Frances. Your brother is my best friend. Hell, he's like a *brother* to me." He was in the room shaking hands, shaking his head, giving hugs, and sitting down, laughing. Frances couldn't believe it. As he started to express his surprise in more detail, he stood up and apologized again. "I'm sorry, I just came right in and sat down. I think I'm in shock. I can't believe Caesar has sisters. And you found him! My god, this is fantastic."

Azrael gave him a smile. "It's okay. We understand."

Domino added a dispassionate, "Yes. This is big for all of us." Frances didn't notice her flat tone.

He was too excited.

"So, how'd you all find him? I know Caesar put a lot of work into not leaving a trail. I could never find out anything about him he didn't tell me. You hire someone?"

Ignoring his question, Azrael asked if he knew where Caesar was. Frances shrugged. "Your guess is as good as mine. Things have only been getting weirder around here. You may find this hard to believe, but, well… did you all know Cupid is real? I know it sounds crazy. I'm still trying to wrap my head around that. I mean, for real, real. The flying godly thing with the little wings that shoots people with love arrows… dude's real. I didn't see him, but I watched your brother pull one of his arrows out of his chest. I'm sorry. I must sound crazy."

Azrael sat next to him and put on another smile. "Did our brother happen to have Cupid's bow?" Frances laughed. "Yeah, we found it in a bush. Caesar had it when I left him. You don't think he'd do anything stupid with it, do you? I wanted to stick around, but I had to go to work."

Azrael stood up, ignoring Frances again to ask, "Is there a church nearby?"

XXII
A WOLF IN ANGEL'S CLOTHING

Roger's body got into his car and drove to the bar Cupid had filled with so much magic that it could be seen dazzling from space. Roger's body parked his car on the side of the road. There were a dozen or so other vehicles parked on either side. The bar was packed. Roger's body got out and looked at the line of people corralled by a red velvet rope, trying to get into the party.

Whisper watched the bouncers taking covers, making sure no deviants were getting through. There was a barrel on fire in the parking lot and a few critters dancing around the blaze. Cupid's parties attracted a few undesirables from the shadows. "Party poopers" Cupid would call them.

What caught the eyes of Roger's head was the smoke that leaked out from the bottom of the bar door. A thick fog covered the floor inside. Roger's face smiled a little, and Whisper slowly poured out from his ears, his mouth, and his pores. Smoke flowed down his body and sailed across the ground toward the booming party. It rolled right into the unassuming party mist when the doors opened.

No one noticed.

The doors closed.

Roger's smile slipped from his face as he returned from the dream Whisper had sent him. The sudden arrival back to reality startled Roger. He jumped and chased his vision around, lost in the unfamiliar space. He ran his hands over himself, and found he was in his own body. He looked around at the grungy bar parking lot and the people circling the dumpster fire. He had a look on his face that no one could help.

And there was no one around who could.

Lights flashed and lasers danced around inside the bar. Creatures swung over the crowd from vine-strapped swings. Whisper cruised through the fog, breathing around distracted ankles. Boots, heels, toes, and hooves. Dancing, tripping, flirting, fucking, loving, feet footing about in the unassuming mist. No one noticed the powerful elemental coursing through the smoke at their feet. Amongst the insignificant gods and goddesses, countless magical beings were riding the high of Cupid's pit stop. Whisper saw stoned humans shrunken into fish bowls hanging off the hips of nymphs and sirens. Minotaurs and satyrs were throwing darts soaked in fire. Laughing sprites floated about in bubbles. Brownies in a little boat sailed atop the fog, laughing around legs and drinking ale. Their tiny boat cut right through Whisper's vision, unaware there was anything there to pass.

Cupid was distracting himself in a booth that overlooked the party. Along with a few other attractive beings, he was sitting with a sphinx. Whisper had never seen one so close. They were doing more drugs than breathing. They seemed to be competing to see who could withstand more punishment. When Cupid was stoned, he was proud of his tolerance. A larger woman had her ass out and was shaking it for Cupid. Whisper watched him slap her rear, which excited the woman. Cupid sniffed something from a vile and cheered. Sniffed, cheered, and stuffed his face between the excited woman's bare cheeks.

Curious, Whisper thought.

Cupid didn't seem to care that his bow was missing. Did he even know? Rolling on through the party, Whisper searched for something out of place. There had to be a reason Cupid wasn't out looking for his precious toy. Cupid was nothing without his magic bow and arrow. He would leave no stone unturned to get it back in his hands. Then Whisper spotted someone unexpected. Pleasure warmed Whisper's dark and smoldering core.

Rolling up to Esther's feet, Whisper smiled. Had the archangel been looking down, she would have seen the curl from its grin shaping in the mist around her ankles. Like oil slicking the surface of a pond, Whisper gathered around Esther, collecting itself under her. She was drinking something from a leather pouch. But why would an archangel be at a party when such a thing was missing? Did she also not know? Her presence was more than just odd. No angel with a rank such as Esther's would be at a place like this simply to be at a place like this.

Whisper took its time climbing up the angel's legs. It needed to overwhelm her mind before she had a chance to react. Once she noticed the playful fog was no longer staying put, it was too late. Whisper rushed inside, and the world around her went dark. Esther's mind was swallowed and shut out from everything but itself. Trapped in a prison unaware anything had happened

Her face smiled, but it was no longer she who was smiling. Esther's wings opened, and the smile on her face grew. It felt good to wear something as powerful as an archangel. The youngest of the three holy sisters. Esther's blood was made of light, light which Whisper now swam through. Today, Whisper thought, today was a good day.

It took a swing of the potion Esther was drinking. It was a focusing elixir with a bite. Such a drink told Whisper she wasn't here to party. She was on guard duty. Blending in to watch. Azrael must be looking for the bow, so the council must think it's here. If Esther were alone, she would be checking in with her big sister at some point. *Best to make quick work of this opportunity,* thought Whisper.

Whisper strolled Esther through the magical gathering looking for more out-of-place beings. Whisper finished the elixir, using its power to gain an edge on its search. There were no other angels in sight, no other beings in the crowded flashing lights that were not there to party. This left Whisper more curious.

Esther's body stepped out back. Cupid's big rusted bus seemed lonely, but the lights were on. Whisper climbed the angel onboard and had a look around. It was a mess. Whisper had never been on the famous love bus before. Whisper had been banished from Earth long before the vessel was forged. It had heard many stories from Cupid about the adventures he'd taken it on back before it rusted, before it had an engine, back when it was a carriage drawn by horses. Back when Cupid would still visit his home while out on his travels. Back when Cupid was still interesting. Whisper often wondered if it felt pity for Cupid or for itself. With friends like Cupid, it wondered if it had any friends at all.

Vivianne stepped out from the bathroom. She stopped when she spotted the wings. Whisper put a smile on Esther's face and waved. The human was sorely out of place. Not just because she was a human alone on Cupid's bus, but because she was cold sober.

Vivianne bashfully approached the angel and apologized. "Sorry, I didn't introduce myself earlier. I was given this thing, and, well, I'm not used to drugs from other worlds. Not all that familiar with much of anything in Cupid's company."

"Been with him long?"

Esther's voice was as comforting as her looks.

Vivianne stepped over to her pile of art, contemplating a sketch as she answered, "A little over two weeks." Picking up a reasonably sized pad, Vivianne asked if the angel would mind if she drew her. Whisper sat down and smiled, telling her it would love nothing more.

As she began to sketch, Whisper asked her to share more about her time with Cupid. Vivianne smiled and sighed a loud, heavy breath. She didn't know where to start. Her face gave away a great deal.

"I feel bad for him," she confessed.

"How so?"

"Well, he may be the saddest thing I have ever met. Any man would've died a million times over with how many substances he abuses. It is hard to watch sometimes. He acts as if he has to drink the sea. My mother used to say, 'Mieux vaut etre seul que mal accompagné.'"

Whisper nodded Esther's head. "Better to be alone than in bad company."

Vivianne smiled. "You speak French?"

Whisper shrugged, "I speak every language there has ever been."

Vivianne stopped drawing and gasped joyfully. "How I would love to know everyone's tongue. To move to any part of the world, start a conversation with whomever was around without stumbling over words." Whisper told her it was a helpful discipline. It asked her about the company Cupid kept. "You think his little minions are not good companions?"

"Oh, please," she scoffed, saying, "They are the worst. They use him. My God, it's terrible. They know whatever this burden is, which pains him. And they do nothing to help. They only enable his destruction. Cupid needs to heal from something — I don't know what. But I am trying to figure it out. I was so relieved to learn you and your sisters are helping him return his bow. He is so much worse without it."

Whisper's attention focused. The three archangels were why Cupid was staying put. And if they were letting this party carry on, it was to mask their hunt. Whisper knew if they had told the council that Cupid had lost his bow, this party would not be attended by Esther alone. Cupid would be chaperoned, and the desert would be littered with angels. But why would Azrael keep this from the almighty? Sadly, there was nothing to pick out from Esther's mind. Whatever Azrael was up to, her little sister was not informed.

"Tell me, Vivianne, why do you care for Cupid?"

"I was going to leave. But he is the god of love. I can think of nothing sadder than for him, of all things, to be miserable. Seems only right to at least try to help. What is the world without love?"

She offered Whisper the sketch when she finished. Esther's hand took the work. "Thank you. I will cherish this." With the door in Esther's hand, Whisper told Vivianne that Cupid's pain was the same as anyone else's. It told her, "Just ask Cupid if it is better to have loved and lost than to have never loved at all. He can go on and on and on with that."

Whisper left the bus feeling good. It walked away from the party with a mind full of fun ideas. It stepped into the night desert, out of sight from anyone and anything. Standing alone with its thoughts, Whisper plotted. It was having a great deal of fun so far, and things were only getting started.

It smiled at the sketch Vivianne had rendered. "Looks just like you Esther," it said, letting the drawing blow away in the wind. With the thought of a match head snapping into purpose, Whisper turned itself into fire, burning Esther from the inside out. Her perfect pearl skin crumbled and cracked. She burst into flames, falling over into a rippling heap. Wings burned to ashes. The smoke that remained where she once stood took the form of Whisper's ashen figure. Its face stared blankly at the charred angel. That was naughty, it mused.

Smelling the air, Whisper sensed an approaching cigarette. Coming up the road was a truck driver puffing away on hand-rolled tobacco. Whisper's form blew into the wind, sailing toward the road, finding the smoke that chased the trucker's cigarette. Whisper swam its way through the burnt air and into the burning stick. The trucker inhaled, and Whisper pushed her into a dream. Her foot pushed on the gas, speeding down the road to Caesar's place at the Inn. There was so much more to learn, so much more to plot, and so much more fun to be had.

XXIII
NUNS

Azrael stood before a tall, pointed cathedral. She looked up to the cross aimed at the heavens and yawned. Inside the vestibule, she found a board greeting her with the nuns who ran the congregation. Four holy faces belonging to four minds primed with the will of God himself. Azrael scooped her hand through the baptismal pool and had a drink of the holy water. *Not much different from any sink*, she thought.

In the nave, Azrael danced her hand over each pew she passed, embracing the faith that kept the building breathing. It was a large room. Stained glass filled the open space with colorful light. Gracefully Azrael walked to the altar and looked up at the statue of Jesus dying on the cross. She winced at the symbol and uttered, "You. I forgot about you. Thought you were supposed to come back."

"Can I help you?" a voice gingerly called out from behind.

Sister Lynn was standing at the start of the pews, a bright smile on her face. Her hair was cut short with touches of gray sprouting with no sense of order. She was dressed in a black habit, the uniform of her lord. Azrael moved toward the casually dressed nun with a smile of her own. "Sister Lynn," she greeted, her tone pleasant and humbled. Clasping her hands gently, the angel looked down over the woman with a warm and innocent smile.

Azrael couldn't touch the woman with magic. A mortal needed to be unaffected by any supreme influence in order to pass on the power of Cupid's bow. The angel would have to be sweet and cunning. Good thing for her, this woman had spent her whole life convincing herself she needed to help Azrael. But why have one helper when she could have four?

"Sister Lynn, I need to speak with you and your other sisters, Dian, Madeline, and Gwen."

Lynn gave a curious look and asked what for. With a pleasant air, Azrael told her, "I have been sent by God, sister. I am an angel. And we have important work to do." Sister Lynn was confused by her. Her words were too sincere to be a joke. And she seemed far too put together to be crazy. Lynn assumed the woman was exaggerating. She didn't doubt the woman had something important to say, but she doubted this woman was actually an angel.

Smiling up to Azrael, Lynn asked what she had come to tell her. Azrael held the nun's gaze. "I'd prefer to tell all of you together. If that's okay?" Lynn's face clearly showed her annoyance. She didn't want to bother the others. They were busy planning a youth camping trip, she told the supposed angel. Azrael insisted, "Please, sister, it's important." Lynn smiled and sighed. She didn't like telling people no. Patting Azrael's hands, she told her to wait there.

Lynn poked her head into the room where Dian was working with Gwen. They were talking over a pamphlet layout, crossing sections out with a fat marker. Lynn hesitated to interrupt. Dian wasn't the sunniest of nuns. She was tall with short, fluffy, gray hair, and rosy skin. Her face was square with big, fierce, brown eyes and a pair of sharp, disapproving eyebrows. Dian had already noticed her as Lynn moved to tap on the door frame.

"Yes, what is it?"

"There is a woman in the nave claiming to be an angel."

This got Dian's attention. Gwen's as well. Dian capped her marker and asked with a troubled tone, "Is she homeless?" Lynn shook her head and asked them both to come with her. She insisted.

Gwen wasn't much taller than Lynn. Her hair looked like a faded blonde cotton ball. She had a wide face, a big smile, and wrinkly white skin. She was the only one brave enough to tease Dian for having a stick up her butt.

The nuns silently gathered, studying the supposed angel before making their presence known. Dian found her beauty surprising for someone she assumed was a nut. The robes made her curious. They did look angelic in some way. Dian had never seen an outfit like the supposed angel's. Still, she was skeptical. Dian always believed she was the closest thing to God she would ever encounter.

Forcing a cough, she said, "Hello."

Azrael turned and smiled with a warm greeting. "Hello, sisters. Where is Madeline?"

Impatiently, Dian sighed, "She is out buying a hot glue gun, I believe. Lynn tells us you have been sent by God. We'd love to hear why." Her smile was dismissive. Azrael took a few graceful steps forward, noting Dian's folded arms. "I have the most important task bestowed upon me, and I need your help. It'd be best to explain it to all of you at once." Azrael did not want to repeat herself. She was already annoyed with having to repeat her request. *Maybe three nuns are enough*, she thought.

Dian looked at her watch and tried her best to hide her lack of interest as she explained, "We may be waiting for some time. When it comes to Madeline, urgency is never a priority. And our need for a hot glue gun is rather insignificant."

"Very well. I am an angel, as Lynn has informed you. My name is Azrael, sister to two, cousin to many. God has sent me to Earth, seeking the help of a mortal. Only a mortal can fulfill the task I am set to perform. You see, sisters, the devil has possessed a man, and he is using his body to attempt the destruction of love."

A slender young pastor with nervous, blinking eyes entered the space, asking for Dian. Dian apologized and stepped over to him. He had come asking about plumbing. Dian rolled her eyes and spoke softly but sternly. Containing her fury with the dismissive human, Azrael glared with burning eyes at the hushed conversation.

The pastor awkwardly glimpsed Azrael and asked Dian who she was. Dian shrugged, uninterested, and said she was an angel sent by God. Dian turned to Azrael and apologized. "Miss,

I don't mean to be rude, but I have a great deal to attend to. My sisters can fill me in on your mission later. Now, if you will excuse me."

Done with the charade, Azrael unfolded her wings and spread them wide to shut the woman's mouth. Dian stepped into a stupefied slouch, her eyes wide, mouth open, hand over her chest. Gwen and Lynn wore similar expressions of astonishment. These were not props. These wings were real. Azrael even revealed the halo that floated above her head, letting its light shine and sparkle.

The pastor fainted, but no one looked away from the grinning angel. His body struck the floor with a hard, unnoticed thud. The nuns were speechless. They watched as Azrael walked past them, her ring of light floating overhead. Azrael kneeled over the unconscious pastor. Gwen and Lynn dropped into a pew. They could no longer stand. The sight was too much.

Madeline, the fourth and plump Sister, finally returned just at this moment. Azrael looked up from the pastor and smiled. Madeline stood in shock, throwing her hand over her mouth. She asked what was going on.

Dian pointed to the angel and started to answer Madeline, but her words escaped her as she joined the pastor on the floor, fainting with her own hard thud. The others flinched at the sound of her collapse, and Lynn and Gwen soon followed Dian and the pastor.

Azrael snickered at the room full of sleeping nuns, and said to Madeline, "Well, this is silly, isn't it?"

"You're an angel?" Madeline asked, feeling dizzy.

Azrael stepped over the pastor and took hold of Madeline's hands. With a heavenly smile, she told her, "I am. God has sent me to find you. I need your help, sister."

Madeline smiled and said, "Oh, good." Her eyes stayed open all the way down to the ground as she slipped from the angel's tender grip and fainted along with the others. Azrael looked around, pleased with her introduction. The nuns were perfect, and things could not have gone any better.

XXIV
NOWHERE & SOMEWHERE

A thin slice of light cut into the darkness. It was all Caesar or April could see. The troll was long gone. Their footsteps were all they heard. They were alone. Huddled together, they inched their way toward the light. Caesar reached for it and found it was soft. The darkness moved like a curtain. They stepped from nothing into the ruins of an ancient garden. Stone paths and archways crumbled between trees and neglected weeds. A dry fountain sat before them. The empty pool was overrun with moss and vines. Sunlight scattered in from the trees above. It was a forgotten place. Garden beds lay broken and overgrown. Roots broke through the stone path under their feet. They were both scared, but April was the first to express her discomfort.

"We died. I know it now. We had to have, because this is fucked up. This isn't real. Nothing about you is real. White people are supposed to be boring."

Caesar laughed and let go of her. She moved to keep him. "It's okay," he told her, slowly pulling away. April folded her arms and said, "Ain't nothing about anything going on here is okay. Don't even play like this shit is normal for you."

Caesar sighed. "You kidding me? I shit my pants."

"For real?"

Caesar gave her a smile. "Not really. Figuratively. I am genuinely freaking out. Being a little drunk is helping."

A twig snapped, and they jumped into each other. April shivered out, "Oh fuck, we're gonna die." From the overgrown path ahead, a figure stepped into view — two goat legs carrying a body concealed under a large, hooded cloak. April was quick to think out loud, "Motherfucker has goat legs ..."

Sensing unrest in the two humans, the faun put his hands out to calm them. Removing his hood, the face of a man assured them he meant no harm.

"I am Rugs. Your guide."

Rugs had a thick beard, a fat, goatish snout, pointy ears, short hair with a thin side braid, and two little horns atop his head. Rugs carried a long walking stick and an inspiring posture. Stepping close, Rugs wore a welcoming smile. April and Caesar kept their guard up, which he found amusing. Making his stance appear harmless, he said, "First time seeing a faun, I take it? Adapt quickly. You're about to see far stranger than me. All the shapes in all the worlds find themselves wandering about the twisting market of Nowhere. It can be the finest of places and the darkest of places. I myself find the whole thing to be rather absurd. Secrets always are. And when so many know of such a place, what secret is there?"

Rugs was relaxed. He stood with an obvious self-assurance, the kind of confidence that didn't get in the way. He set his stick down and dug into a pouch he had slung around his shoulder. Rugs pulled out two metal rings. With a peculiar slant, he addressed his new human companions. "Not much for words, are we? No worries, Whisper's done all the talking. Should be an easy run... if we're graceful. Simply keep your eyes to yourself, stay close to me, say nothing, and follow my lead."

Caesar asked where they were.

"We are as far away from anything as one could be."

April scrunched her face. "No riddle bullshit, please. For real, where the hell are we?"

"We are quite literally as far away from anything in existence as possible. The last stop before the edge of edges. The Lost Bazaar we call Nowhere is a market where one can find most anything. There are no rules here, but there is respect. Which is why humans must be leashed."

Rugs held up the two metal chokers in his hand and explained, "These look a great deal more serious than they are.

But they are more than necessary. They are everything." Still holding onto Caesar, April asked, "You gonna put those collars around our necks?"

Rugs nodded. "Afraid I have to. Humans are not safe in any realm of magic without a leash."

April shook her head. "Hell no."

Rugs lowered the chokers and shrugged. "If you wish to survive the road ahead, I insist." Caesar took a hard exhale and stepped toward the half-goat, half-man, giving April a confident look. He was willing to do whatever it took. Cupid had to pay.

Rugs smiled and stepped to Caesar with the choker open. Caesar sighed, and the faun took a swift step back, waving at his nose. "Odd occasion for spirits. To each their own, I suppose." When it clicked around Caesar's neck, two red lights on the choker switched on. Rugs played with a copper dial on a funny leather strap around his wrist, and the lights dimmed to a pale green. Caesar felt around the collar. It wasn't tight, cold, or heavy. It was just strange, but what happening to them wasn't?

As he held the other choker out for April, Rugs assured her, "I promise it doesn't hurt." April's nostrils flared, her eyes wide and alert. "This feels like some slave shit."

The faun shook his head. "I would never play in the slave trade. Stealing humans is a nasty business. And without this, you'd be vulnerable to such a snatching. If slavery is a concern, this will keep you from it. Think of it as a visitor's pass for touring a museum. Only it keeps you from being sold for your blood."

April was resistant, but she accepted the choker uncomfortably. Rugs dialed her in with the strap around his wrist.

The faun tapped his hoof and nodded. "There, see? Harmless." April pulled on the choker and looked at Caesar with a miserable glare. Caesar gave her arm a friendly squeeze and asked her if she was okay. April calmed herself and nodded with a half-convincing yes.

"Right, follow me, stay close, and absolutely do not do anything, touch anything, or talk to anything. Where we are going is no friend to a new face."

Rugs let his stick lead the way, stepping back out the way he came. Caesar and April rejoined at the hip, arm in arm, helping each other feel normal. April whispered to Caesar, "Are you sure about this?"

"Sure about what?"

"About what we're doing."

Caesar shrugged. "All I know is, Cupid has to die."

April studied Caesar's face. She read the pain, read the fear, but didn't know what to say. So April didn't say anything. She was in over her head. But so was he.

No one was ever going to believe her when she told them where she had been. If she lived to tell this story, would she even believe it?

Nervously, they followed the creature out from the overgrown garden into a narrow passage. Stone arched overhead, and it was dark once again. The passage was capped with a round wooden door. The faun stopped and gave his human company a funny smile. "Remember to stay close and don't talk to anyone. Someone asks you something, just point to me. And do your best to stop looking so surprised. You both look as though you are being mugged."

Rugs opened the door, and sunlight rushed in along with a barrage of sounds and voices. The path opened to a long wooden platform curving through a towering market swarming with life. The market was packed with vendors stacked upon vendors. Shops filled their windows with displays. Stands and carts cluttered up rows and took over the streets. The layered market was cut up with alleyways, ladders, ropes, and winding stairs. Platforms on pulleys rose above them, pulling the market into the sky well over twenty stories. Bridges and paths sprouted between platforms like branches in a tree. Below them, the market dropped another forty stories to a dark and sandy carpet.

Rugs locked the door behind them with a hard clank. April and Caesar pulled each other closer. Rugs smiled at them, his hood finding its way back around his pointy ears. Waving his walking stick to the wonder that lay ahead, he rejoiced, "Welcome to Nowhere. Where everything is and isn't. Stay close, humans."

April and Caesar were flabbergasted.

They made their way through the crowd of busy traders. Twists and turns brought them past steaming pots filled with new smells, colorful languages they had never heard, wares they had never seen, and creatures they couldn't name. They had never felt more out of place. And they never felt more grateful for a hand to hold.

Most things were too busy trading to notice Caesar and April with their funny collars. A few who saw them made them feel out of place. Caesar reached into the magic satchel inside his bag. April tugged on his sleeve. "We're supposed to keep that out of sight." Caesar pulled out a flask and smiled at her.

"You're seriously going to drink more right now?"

Caesar nodded and took a breath from the flask just as a big brutish ogre marched past them pushing a cart of bottled fish. It sniffed at them as it passed, and sneered. April reached for the flask, eyeing the parting ogre. "Give me some of that." She gulped the liquor down and coughed, then gulped a little more. Passing a vendor selling shrunken heads, April had to look twice before she could believe her eyes. Rugs commented over his shoulder, "Try not to look so surprised by everything. Confidence will play in our favor."

The paths they took were thinning out. The sound of the market slipped into the background. The looks they were getting became less friendly. Rugs brought them into a saloon. The place had a familiar cowboy feel, thanks to the swinging doors at its entrance. Most of the tables were empty. The bar held a couple of travelers sipping spirits and trading stories. Their drinks glowed and sparkled. The things they ate were both alive and not.

A creature that looked like it belonged underwater was tending the bar. It gave Rugs a sketchy nod. At least April thought it looked sketchy. The environment seemed familiar, and simultaneously, not at all. She knew she could go to the bar and order a drink, but she wouldn't know what to order, or probably even how. Everything was like that. The functions all made sense. The substance, however, was completely foreign.

Rugs pulled out chairs for his human companions, and the three had a seat. The seats were normal — wooden chairs like any they'd find back home. Rugs told them this was where they would be getting what it was they came to get. Told them he didn't know what it was, and didn't want to know. But this was the place where it would come.

There was a long open window overlooking the market outside. April looked out to the foot traffic, pulling at the collar around her neck. No one would believe any of this. The thought stuck with her. People will look at her the way she looked at people who claimed aliens had abducted them. Caesar didn't care. He didn't need to tell anyone. He just wanted Cupid to pay for the broken hand he had dealt him. It was all he could focus on. It helped keep the unfathomable nature of it all manageable.

The bartender came up to the table, looking part human and part octopus. April couldn't help but stare, and Caesar couldn't help but stare at April staring. The bartender spoke a different language. Rugs spoke back, and a minute later, a round of ale landed on the table, along with a bowl of some type of roasted nugget. Caesar asked what it was. Rugs lifted his pint and said, "This is us blending in. It's all harmless. Worse case, you may experience a little gas."

April picked up a nugget inspecting the thing up close. She pulled in a courageous breath and smiled at Caesar. "Fuck it. I'm embracing this. No one's ever gonna believe us, Caesar. And we ain't coming back. I'm gonna eat this freaky nugget, and I'm gonna drink this … whatever the fuck this is. And when this is over. Well, we will just have to see." April dropped the nugget in her mouth, and her face instantly lit up. "Fuck, this is good." She chewed and laughed. "Caesar, you gotta try one." Caesar popped one into his mouth and was immediately surprised. The comfort the tasty nuggets brought put them both at ease. For a moment, everything was almost normal.

Rugs kept looking at his timepiece. Caesar couldn't figure out how the faun was able to gather any information from the device. None of its gears and dials revealed anything helpful, as far as he could tell. April could see the creature was getting tense and asked, "Can I ask you something?"

Rugs shrugged. "Go for it."

"How dangerous is what we're doing?"

"Honestly, it's best if we don't discuss it."

Not much was said after that. Rugs kept looking at his timepiece. Caesar finished his drink. The bubbles in his head grew into a heavy buzz. Breaking the silence, Caesar asked Rugs how he knew Whisper. The question rang a bell that Rugs couldn't seem to silence quickly enough. He leaned into the table with a sharp expression, his finger pushed against his lips. Head low, Rugs told them he didn't know what they were talking about. What little normalcy there was had vanished and was replaced by only tension. Tension and Rugs looking at his odd timepiece, making things more tense.

A shadow came over the device, and Rugs looked up. A big weasel-looking fellow in a poncho pulled up a chair next to Caesar with a look of fear in his eyes and long, dark hair like snakes running wet down his weasel face. The moment he sat down, he dropped a heavy wrapping into Caesar's lap. Dropped it and whispered, "Check it. Make sure it's what you want." His voice was worn and phlegmy and his breath stank of sewage.

Caesar grabbed it, and the weasel-man nudged him. "Discreet, be discreet." The thing was wrapped in a dark canvas sheet. Caesar pulled at the fabric, working his way to the lump it concealed, nervously checking the sightlines of the other things around the bar. The weasel was smiling at Rugs as they pretended to talk. The weasel chewed some nuggets, trying to act like it wasn't sweating. April was having trouble blinking. Thinking again, *no one will ever believe me.*

Peeling away the folds, Caesar found himself looking at an old brass revolver. The handle had a subtle curve. It looked more like a baton than a gun, like an ornate stick with a trigger, cylinder, and what he assumed was the hammer. It felt old. Looked old. It wasn't what he imagined he would use to kill Cupid. Covering the weapon, Caesar cleared his throat and nodded. The weasel swallowed a nugget and pushed from the table in a rush. April laughed at his departure, saying, "Twitchy thing."

Rugs was up shortly after. A look of urgency contorted his posture. April tried to speak, but Rugs stated, "Nothing is going on, nothing happened, and you are not in possession of anything." Caesar gulped and slipped the gun into his impossible bag. He could see the petrified Tux float by his hand as he let the weapon go. The empty space was eerily hypnotizing. It made him feel like his pain would never leave him. Even after all this was done, he worried he would still be left with the empty space where his family once was.

Before Caesar could close the bag, a hand had grabbed ahold of it, tugging it from him. "What are we playing with, human?" said the brute who snatched the bag. Caesar fought back, clawing at the bag. The brute put an arm out, keeping him at a distance, laughing at Caesar's lame attempt to fight. The thief was his height but wider, stronger. He looked human, but didn't. His bone structure was too wide to be a human's. That, and he had a subtle blue hue to his skin. Dark, trimmed mutton chops fuzzed up his cheeks. He had a ruby-capped tooth that shined red with his grin.

The brute dug into the impossible darkness of the bag, saying as he did, "Icarus tells us a big deal is being made. That true, Rugs? You bring these humans shopping?"

Rugs swung his walking stick, whacked at the thief's arms, and the bag hit the floor. He kept his stick pointed at the big brute, but the large fellow had his eyes on the floor. Rugs glanced at the bag and then turned to Caesar with utter surprise.

"You have Cupid's bow?"

The bow lay on the bar floor. It had fallen from the bag. Lightning struck the group. April rushed to it and tried to stuff the bow back into the bag. Rugs stood between her and the brute. The big creature lunged for April, and she tensed up to guard herself. Caesar pushed her away and took the strike — a strike that sent him crashing through the swinging doors. Caesar slid across the floor, his arms protecting his face as he crumbled to the ground, the wind completely knocked out of him. Up on all fours, he coughed, his eyes spinning around his head seeking to establish forward.

Rugs pulled April behind him and pushed Caesar up with his stick. They ran back into the crowded market. The brute was close behind. Running with hefty steps and grunts. Rugs plucked a melon from a stand of produce and lobbed it into the air. An orange arc of light danced up his stick connecting some type of magic to the melon. He swung and it flew toward their large assailant. The melon multiplied in the air, quickly becoming dozens of melons, and the path behind them became a twisted mess of feet and fruit. The brute collapsed into the growing pile, and Rugs pulled his human company around a bend.

They returned to the door where they had started. Rugs put his key into the hole and gave it a strong turn. But the door didn't unlock. Instead, the key was sucked out of his fingers into the hole. Rugs was quick to reach for it, pawing at the hole with desperate swipes, but it was hopeless. Frozen in a moment of deep meditation, Rugs stared into the hungry keyhole. Caesar asked if something was wrong. April reinforced the concern with, "Yeah, why isn't the door opening?"

Rugs turned around, heavy thoughts folding troublesome lines in his forehead.

"What is it?"

"My key has been taken."

"Is that normal, or is that because of what we're doing?"

Rugs chose to remain silent. Pulling a ring of keys from his pouch, he began to thumb through them, recalling the role of each as he did. April was clutching the magic bag, her face tense as she asked, "What are you doing?"

"Something knows we came this way and enchanted the lock."

Finding a key he liked, Rugs smiled. Putting the key into the hole, he told them, "The older and more obscure the key's destination, the less likely..." Rugs was silenced as the second key was also sucked away.

"Fuck."

"What do you mean, 'fuck'?"

Rugs returned to the frantic search around his loop of keys. A roar called their attention from down the way. The brute had managed to clear the magical pile of melons. Sticky bits of fruit dripped from his figure along with rage.

"Hurry up."

"I am working on it."

Another key was sucked away, and Rugs kept trying. Caesar started to ask if he should use the weapon they had just picked up, but Rugs silenced him before he could finish, his tone gravely serious. "Don't tell me. I do not wish to know what you have come for. I am only paid upon your safe return home. This is my only concern."

The brute stomped ever closer, but his savage expression became a look of fear. Caesar and April both shared a confused glance as the brute's march to pummel and rob them was abruptly abandoned, and he turned away, walking into the crowd as if he never cared. Caesar peeked around to see what had convinced him to part with his pursuit. Baffled by what he saw, Caesar commented, "There's an angel walking towards us."

Rugs jumped in a panic and looked back. His face paled with fear, appearing almost ill from the sight. An angel named Gabriel was approaching. His halo glowed overhead, his wings up but tucked back. His robes draped over his shoulders with his armor visible. What was most alarming was the sword he had pulled from her hip. The sword was relaxed by his side, but it was still a sword.

"How bad is this?" Caesar asked.

Unresponsive, Rugs was back at the door, trying every key he had. April turned to Caesar and shook her head. "Seems pretty bad." The angel had begun speaking, his voice calm but powerful.

"By decree of the secular law, I am in my right to take possession of your wares. Lay them down before me now, or I will have to respond accordingly to your disobedience."

April inched back and asked, "The fuck does that mean?"

"Fascist dogma," Rugs declared, his voice firm but shaking. More keys were being sucked out of his fingers. Edging closer, the angel's eyes filled with light. Caesar reacted to the gesture with a frightened adjustment. April noticed that he had put himself between her and the angel. He was guarding her. April could see in his face he was more afraid for her than himself. The act made her feel the same for him. She wanted him to make it home. She wanted them both to make it home. To laugh about all this years from now over a stiff drink. As the angel closed in, Caesar reinforced his position, pushing April behind him. April grabbed his arm, supporting their link for whatever the angel intended with his sharp, shining blade.

A click and rumble sounded off behind them. Rugs had found a successful key and was pulling his companions with haste. The three rushed through the door, the angel filling the passage behind them, reaching out for Caesar. He stumbled back, crashing into April, who crashed into Rugs, who crashed into a wall partially finished with stone, and partially with drywall. They were between worlds. Mysterious hallways twisted and turned around moments. On the other side of the wall, a man on Earth with a small basket of groceries was startled. The canned food that sat on the shelves before him had all been knocked off with a mildly violent jolt. He couldn't see or hear Rugs to know what had happened. The older woman behind the register peered over her counter with a furrowed brow. The man looked at her, lost. She spoke Portuguese, and asked him what he had done. The man shrugged, and told her he had done nothing. Cautiously picking up one of the fallen cans, there was another jolt. This bump was calmer but just as unusual. The cans on the shelves all jumped. Out from behind the register, the woman scratched her head. Another bump was followed by another. Shortly thereafter, a sword came slicing through the shelf like a hot knife through butter, sending cans through the air, some cut and spilling out their wet contents. She and the man screamed, both jumping back.

Back in the magical hallway, the angel chased the three down a long, dimly lit passage, his sword now glowing and slashing after them. Rugs blew into the end of his stick, sending a fierce wind in the angel's direction, keeping his strikes from removing anyone's limbs. He had given April one of his keys and pointed to the door ahead of them. Letting her and Caesar pass, he kept blowing into the stick, angering the angel.

April hurried the key into the ordinary-looking door. The door opened, and Rugs turned his walking stick toward the wall, the force of its wind pushing him into Caesar, who crashed into April, sending the three tumbling into a cluttered office. The walking stick blew the door shut in the angel's face with a final gust of wind. He reached for the knob, but the key was sucked away, and the door vanished. He cursed and struck the wall with his fist.

Rugs was laughing, lying in the pile of Caesar and April along with some cardboard boxes. Rugs helped them up and opened the door they had just flown through, but it did not open to a dimly lit hall with a ravenous angel. It led them to a small convenience store, ravaged by an otherworldly assault. The older woman and the confused shopper stood with each other overlooking the mess. They were speechless as Rugs and his goat legs stepped out from the back office, April and Caesar close behind him. April clutched the bag in one arm and Caesar in the other. Rugs waved at the startled humans and made a gesture for a phone. The woman silently nodded to the faun and pointed behind her at the phone hanging on a wall. Rugs smiled and thanked her, making his way around the register.

As he picked up the phone, Caesar asked him where they were. Rugs dialed a number, answering plainly, "Brazil, I think." April's jaw dropped. "Brazil!?" Rugs didn't say anything on the phone, just dialed and hung up. Caesar and April chased him around with questions, but he was silent, making his way around the messy floor to the front door. Sure enough, a busy Brazilian street sat just outside of the store's windows. April shook her head. "I've always wanted to visit Brazil." Rugs smiled over his shoulder at her. "Beautiful country," he told her. Then he turned the open sign on the door around. No one protested.

"What are we doing?" April asked.

"We are waiting. I'd prefer to do so in silence. We aren't safe yet."

The clock ticked away, and no one dared speak.

When the bell above the front door rang, half an hour had passed. A large woman in overalls stepped into the store and smiled. "Are we having fun yet?" she said, looking around at the haphazard group. April and Caesar were two deers dazed by oncoming traffic. The woman frowned and asked, "Don't recognize me?" She winked. Her eyes were black, filled with the dark coal that belonged to Whisper. Whisper gave the faun a noisy bag of coins. "I hope it wasn't too much trouble." Rugs put the bag away with a shrug and a tired smile, saying nothing. He bowed to Caesar and April. "It has not been a pleasure, none of which is your fault. May we never meet again." He returned to the back office and shut the door, and Rugs was gone.

Whisper waved the puppeted woman's arm and joyfully told his April and Caesar to follow. The front door opened, but not to a street in Brazil.

The bell above the door rang as it closed, and they were gone. The startled woman leaned out the front, poking her head up and down the street, finding the sight just as unbelievable as everything else she had just witnessed. The man who was shopping left his basket and stepped around her, leaving her store with no intention of ever returning.

XXV
ICE CREAM & BONDAGE

Azrael packed the four nuns into a van. They had all woken up from the dizzying sight of a real-life angel and entered the vehicle of their own free will. They were now on a mission from God and could not be bothered with anything else. Azrael stopped to get them all ice cream. Everyone had a cone in hand, happily licking the cold, creamy treats on their way to do God's work. It was a bonding gesture of solidarity that Azrael felt was important. She also found it amusing. Her opinion of humans was less than desirable, but religious humans were even more pathetic in her eyes — not just because she knew the gods who made them saw them as expendable, or that she knew the holy books they recited were all props that those same gods had taken no part in fabricating, but because life was so much larger than the scriptures that held them prisoner. These things lived their entire lives in service of something that would never come. So afraid it could be worse, they denied themselves the only thing they would ever get. Worst of it was how obnoxious some were about it. So self-righteous and patronizing. And so she gave them ice cream cones because to her they were stupid children. And partly because of her affinity for sweets.

While enjoying the ignorance of her new recruits, Azrael made up a story for the bow. Cupid was a few too many myths removed from the book these women worshiped. So she told them God placed the power of love in a bow to test some profit's goodwill, only the Devil had stuck his big red nose into the affair and possessed the man. Caesar being the man. The nuns were to post up at the Inn and wait for Caesar to return. They were to take the bow and give it to Azrael. God commanded it must be a human hand to restore love.

The nuns kept licking their desserts while the angel explained to them, "Only the four of you know I am what I am. We will need to keep it this way. We don't want the Devil knowing we're here."

Dian peeked up from her ice cream to ask, "We?"

Azrael smiled for her new soldiers and told them there was another angel with her. "She is at the motel blending in, as it were. Something you will all need to do. We need to blend you into the background so we can get the jump on the Devil. I'm going to give you all a job at the Inn so you can watch and wait for the possessed man without drawing any unwanted attention."

Lynn gulped and joined the conversation. With the Devil on her mind, her voice was a bit shaken. "This bow he has, how are we supposed to get it, exactly? I mean, he is, you know…"

"I know this can be frightening. But I wouldn't look at the possessed man as anything but a man. He won't be shooting fire out of his eyes or anything. There won't be anything inhuman about him at all. Just a man possessed. Not much different than any man."

"And what do we do with a man possessed by the Devil?"

"I'm glad you asked."

Azrael parked the van at the Inn. The nuns stood around her, the back of the van open. Opening a bag, she told them all, "I can't gift you any magical device to aid in the physical harnessing of the bow. Magic cannot break the spell. This is why you were chosen. You are holy women, blessed by God. It is your hands alone that must break the hold the Devil has on Caesar. Being as you are nuns, I am giving you pepper spray and a self-defense baton. Use it carefully." She handed each of them a canister of mace along with a retractable metal baton.

Lynn shook a can of mace, then looked at the metal weapon and asked, "So we spray the possessed man and take the bow? This seems … I don't know. A little bit out of our wheelhouse." All three nuns looked confused.

Madeline held the baton like she was looking for the clean end of a turd. "What is this thing?"

Gwen made a somewhat playful gesture with the baton still sheathed, mocking a few swings at Madeline's head. Unamused, Madeline folded her arms. "What are we supposed to do with this? Violence?" Lynn added, "Yeah... he is still human, right? So, we can't really, um, hurt him, right?" The nuns all nodded their heads, looking at one another with self-conscious expressions. The angel's story, and her plan, didn't feel at all biblical. It felt and sounded like a cheap plot in some silly mobster thriller.

Azrael whipped her wrist to extend a metal baton as a demonstration. The defensive tool snapped into shape, its crack blasting the nun's eyes wide open. Azrael smiled and said, "This is meant to make you feel safer. The spray will be more than enough. I only want you to feel prepared for anything. Say you spray him, and he runs away blind. You can hit him in the back of the legs with this to stop him from escaping. His legs will heal, and the Devil will be foiled. And God will be proud of you."

Dian tried her hand at her new baton. It whipped into shape, and she held it steady. Her fellow sisters gave her a frightened but impressed look. Smiling proudly to Azrael, Dian said, "We will not let you down."

"I would expect nothing less," Azrael said as she closed her baton.

Madeline swung her wrist but nothing happened. Frustrated, she tried a few more swings, progressively increasing her force with each swing until the baton flew from her hand and hit a car. She crossed her heart and asked for forgiveness. The other nuns tried to hide their smiles.

Kim was working the check-in desk while watching a movie on a small TV-VCR set. Azrael and the nuns stepped up to the counter, and Kim greeted them with a smile. Azrael asked for the owner. Teddy was in the next room, working the small convenience store, his mind roaming around another magazine when Kim summoned him.

Teddy gave Azrael a curious look when he entered. "You're one of the sisters, right? How's the room? Can't begin

238

to tell you how happy I am that you're here. Caesar's part of the family."

Azrael put on a smile and asked if her *brother* had returned. Teddy shook his head, looking to the nuns, ready to hear why he was called over.

Azrael explained, "Well, these fine ladies will need to be put into uniform and given some jobs. I would like one to run the front desk here, and two of them to do your housekeeping."

Teddy sort of laughed. "What?"

Azrael looked into Teddy's eyes with a quick and subtle flash of her own. Teddy's scrunched brow un-scrunched, and he smiled, saying, "Of course." This confused Kim, and she looked to Teddy, ready to comment in protest to his acceptance, but Azrael was quick to suggest Teddy give the rest of the staff a week's paid vacation. This confused Kim more. As she turned her confusion toward the angel, Teddy was already accepting the proposition, which pulled Kim's confusion back onto him. Kim shook her head and let out a bewildering, "What is happening?"

Teddy smiled at her and asked, "You cool with that? Week of paid vacation?"

Kim shook her head in disbelief and agreed with a stupefied, "Sure."

As she left, Kim smiled at Azrael and told her, "I like you." Her head kept shaking as she walked to her car, laughing under her breath and laughing all the way home.

Teddy was already digging out uniforms from a closet, saying he would train them herself. The nuns were watching everything closely. They were there to stop the Devil, after all. They needed to be vigilant. Teddy set the uniforms on the counter and asked with a smile which two would be housekeeping. The nuns each straightened their backs, all waiting on Azrael's word. The angel smiled at her silly children and delegated roles. Madeline and Lynn were to clean the house, specifically Caesar's room, while Gwen stayed put at the front desk. Dian was quick to inquire where this left her.

"You'll be coming with me," Azrael told her.

...

Domino was in the room Teddy had given them. She looked distraught when Azrael entered with her new holy companion. Skipping the introduction, Azrael asked her sister what was wrong. Domino was on her feet with a heavy breath, telling her sister the bow had been spotted in a saloon Nowhere, and that their brother Gabriel had tried to stop the two humans seen fleeing the market leashed to a faun. The news was troublesome. While Azrael sat with the update, Domino pointed to Dian and asked who she was.

"This is Sister Dian. Dian, this is my sister, Domino."

Dian bowed with a professional, but timid, motion. "You're another angel?" Domino hid her amusement as she realized what Dian was, admiring the cross around her neck. Playing along with the game, Domino let her halo shine to life as she reached out to greet Dian properly. Dian felt her heart rate increase. Domino was taller than Dian, and she let her height lean over the nun as she smiled and thanked her for heeding the call of God's will. Dian cleared her throat and told the angel she was born to help.

Moving for the door, Azrael told her sister, "We're going to get Cupid now."

"You and Dian?"

"Yes."

"I'm coming with."

"What for?"

"I can't reach Esther."

Azrael paused silently with the news, worrying that there was something Cupid hadn't told her. She hoped her younger sister was only preoccupied with the rare spectacle she had been asked to watch. Azrael nodded. "Okay, let's check on our sister. We have to go the long way. A door would attract too much attention."

She handed Dian the keys she got from the biker and told her, "Come, Dian, you're driving."

Dian scratched her head, "Did you say Cupid?"

. . .

Lynn stood outside Caesar's room, nervously gripping her new cleaning cart. She couldn't find the strength to let go.

240

The Devil had stood on the other side of that door. It was all she could think about. Some poor man was suffering to find the Lord and the Devil rose within him. She knew the Devil's temptations were always around. It was simply a fact of life. But to know for certain that the beast had physically stood where she would soon stand, well, that gave Lynn the willies.

Madeline stepped beside her with an audible gulp, and asked her if she wanted company. Lynn laughed uncomfortably and let go of the cart. Madeline wasn't going to let her sister post up in a room like that by herself.

Crossing her chest, Lynn slowly pushed the door open, whispering for God to stand with her as she entered. Madeline turned the light on behind her, and they both noticed the stench, both reaching for their noses.

"What is that smell?" Lynn asked.

Noses gripped tight, the two absorbed the mess, the piles of dirty clothes, empty bottles, disheveled books. Lynn found the source of the smell. Caesar had left his cheese out on the counter. She poked at the funky, open container. It was fuzzy and spotted. If it sat out any longer, it might've grown legs and walked off.

Madeline pulled the cleaning cart into the room and shut the door. "If we're supposed to wait in here, then we might as well clean a little. Maybe at least clear a spot to sit." Lynn sprayed the air with a scented mister and sighed. "You take on the kitchen. I'll... I'll work on whatever this side of the room is supposed to be."

Once they started, they couldn't stop. Trash bags filled with Caesar's long and lonely nights. Lynn peeled a bottle from the floor. Part of the carpet tore off with it. Wrappers and molding containers were carefully excavated from dark corners.

Long, green, rubber arms carefully snaked around the messy room, scrubbing and scraping and picking. Cleaning kept their minds off the Devil. They pitied Caesar. With a home like this, it was no surprise the Devil took him. They prayed for his soul, prayed for their mission.

Madeline was standing in front of the fridge with a trash bag. She shook her head and said, "How does someone drink so much and not have any food?" Lynn was in the bathroom, scrubbing the floor. She had filled a whole bag with bottles just from the bathroom alone. Scrubbing away with a tired breath, she replied to Madeline with a laugh. A laugh she sucked back into her lungs as fast as she could.

Someone had knocked on the door.

Lynn's head shot out from the bathroom, her eyes beaming in fear. Madeline had shrunk herself a bit, not entirely sure what to do. Looking at Lynn's head peeking out from the bathroom floor, she asked, "You think it's Gwen?"

Lynn gulped, a glimmer of hope easing her expression to something less electric. That was when Teddy spoke up. "Caesar, you home? Lights on?" Lynn's expression zapped back to fear, and Madeline attempted to shrink even smaller. Silently, they mouthed to one another for a plan.

Teddy hadn't the patience for Caesar's typical hermit status. The prospect of Caesar's return, given the arrival of his newly discovered sisters, made Teddy forget his manners. He opened the door, too excited to wait. "Caesar, I'm coming in." Madeline dropped behind the counter, her hands wrapping tightly around her mouth. Lynn sucked herself back into the bathroom, rolled over into the bathtub, and pulled the shower curtain closed. Teddy heard the curtain. Closing the door behind him, he stepped toward the bathroom. "Caesar, sorry to just come in, but, well, how long have you been back? A lot's going on around here."

Madeline put her eye to the edge of her cover. She watched Teddy make his cautious steps towards Lynn. Teddy wasn't one to barge in on a person in the bathroom, but there had been no response. Caesar could be passed out drunk for all he knew. Wouldn't be the first time he had found him floating unconscious in bottles.

"Caesar? I know you're in there."

Lynn was balled up in the tub, praying to God to protect her. Teddy's footsteps walked up to the door, and the hinges started to squeak.

"Caesar?" he called out again, his face easing into the bathroom. Madeline was up on her feet, her heart throbbing in her chest, hand crossing her heart, thoughts and prayers reaching up to God.

"Caesar?" he called out again, his hand on the shower curtain. Lynn saw his fingers reach around, saw his hand grip and pull.

Teddy jumped when he saw Lynn lying on her back, a canister of pepper spray aimed up. Lynn screamed, and Madeline swung a pan into the back of Teddy's head. He yelped and fell forward just as Lynn sent out a fiery breath of pepper. The hot cloud burned in Madeline's face, and she cried out in pain. Teddy fell against the side of the tub, his forehead bouncing off the hard, ceramic edge. Madeline stumbled back, coughing and spitting, her hands clawing at her eyes. Lynn tripped out of the tub, pulling Madeline into the bathroom, apologizing profusely. The new bathroom spice was lingering thickly, and Lynn had begun to cough, her eyes watering to the burn. They both struggled to balance as Lynn brought Madeline into the bath. With her arms reaching out from Madeline's underarms, Lynn turned the shower on. A cold blast of water rained over Madeline's face. She gasped and hollered a "Sweet Jesus!" Lynn kept her upright while she held Madeline's burning face under the water, which slowly turned hotter than the spray that had impaired her senses. She shrieked and jumped back, slipping into Lynn, who slipped in response, and they both went down. The scalding water beat them out of the tub, like a fresh-caught fish flapping its way off a boat, back into the cool embrace of the ocean.

Laying on the floor with the unconscious Teddy, the nuns both caught their breath. Their slap-stick routine settled into itchy, wet panting, and they sat up against the tub, dazed and confused.

"Is he dead?" Madeline asked, her eyes wincing to get a look at the stiff man by her feet. Lynn turned away from him as she gave his body a little nudge. "I don't think so," she moaned, disgusted and terrified.

Gwen stepped into the room. Closing the door behind her in a hurry, she asked, "What's all the racket? I can hear you two screaming from across the parking lot." She caught an eyeful of the sleeping man, and her hands went up, one over her chest and the other over her mouth. With a frightened gasp, she asked, "What did you do?" The wet and disoriented sisters looked up to Gwen with swollen red eyes, but said nothing.

...

243

Azrael had sent her sister into the bar to find Esther while she and Dian walked around back. They stood outside of Cupid's rusty bus and waited.

Dian was curious. "Why didn't we go in with Domino?"

"The one we call Cupid has been compromised, Sister Dian. I'd rather not subject you to the sights and sounds a distraught god can summon. It's no place for mortals."

Dian was not content with the answer. She wanted to see inside. She wanted to see everything. She tried to ask more, to get some more information about what she was being spared from, but Azrael dismissed her inquiry. Dian couldn't tell if the angel was being condescending or protective.

Domino stepped out the back with a frown. There was no Esther to find. Azrael sighed and moved for the bus, telling Dian to wait outside.

"I can help," the holy woman assured.

Azrael gave her a big grin. "I know you can. And you will. But this is not the place for you. Please wait here. Trust me. We will be quick."

Cupid was sitting at the round kitchen table. He was smoking a cigarette and watching one of his shorties sort through a bucket of pills. Another shortie was in the shape of a Vegas showgirl, done up like a peacock. It was casually singing Billie Holiday's "Blue Moon" to no one in particular. Vivianne was hanging over the sofa, talking to Cupid. Everyone looked to the two angels coming aboard, Azrael greeting them as she did. "I hope this is not a bad time, Philip."

With an anxious drag from his cigarette, Cupid huffed, "Of course not. I'm sort of waiting on you. You here with good news or bad news?"

"Always good news. But first, have you seen our sister Esther?"

Cupid shrugged, and Vivianne raised her hand, unsure if she should just start talking or wait. So she waited. Azrael smiled at her. "Yes?"

"Last I saw her, she went off into the desert."

"Did she say why?"

"No. And nothing we talked about would suggest she would go anywhere. Regardless, I have not seen her since she left."

Azrael motioned for Domino to go look. Domino shrugged. "You want me to just wander the desert?" Azrael turned to Vivianne and asked her to show her sister which way Esther had gone. As they left, Azrael had a seat next to Cupid. The big love god and his shapeshifting comrades were all silent, more or less frozen. Azrael gestured for the pill-sorting shortie to carry on with whatever it was doing. It gulped and slowly returned to organizing its bucket of drugs.

"Philip, I don't know if word has found you yet... but your bow has supposedly been spotted in, of all places, Nowhere."

Cupid put his cigarette out, scrunched his brow, and asked, "The fuck's it doing there?"

"Two humans were leashed to a faun and escorted to some back-door trade. Too many unknowns to say for sure what was happening, but this little adventure got out of hand. The humans with the bow fled back to Earth."

"So, what does this mean?"

"It means you're coming with me."

"Am I in danger?"

A shriek from outside interrupted the conversation. The door flew open, and Dian came running in, screaming about a demon. A shorty chased her in, its bare skin appropriately flushed with a demonic red hue. It had even sprouted little horns to entertain Dian's outspoken fear. Pinching at her ass, the little chameleon giggled and grinned. Its bouncing red-hot erection was the real show-stopper. Azrael stood up and stepped between them, her wings spreading wide, stopping the wrinkly freak in its tracks. Dian hid behind her, rosary beads tangling around her shaking fingers, wailing, "It's a demon!"

Glaring down at the shriveling creature, Azrael sighed. "It's not a demon." Dian spotted the shorty sitting with Cupid and she jumped. "My God, another one!"

"They aren't demons," Azrael snipped, looking over her shoulder to Dian, her patience thinning. Dian was mouthing a prayer, fingering the beads in her hands. Everyone on the bus stared at her.

Cupid took a few pills from his shorty's hand and asked Azrael if the spooked woman was with her. The archangel lowered her wings and exhaled. "This is Dian. She's helping me." Cupid tossed the pills into his mouth and swallowed them down with a big swig of beer. "What's she helping you do exactly?"

Dian kept fingering her rosary beads, reacting to Cupid with a shocked, "You're drinking?" His wings and halo left her thinking he was another angel.

Cupid chuckled, an expression of humorous disbelief playing across his eyebrows. "What are you, Mormon?" he asked, chuckling and drinking more. Dian studied the god of love, her judgments lining up single-file in her mind as she focused on telling him, "Catholic."

Cupid choked on his beer as he laughed out, "Jesus Christ, Azrael, did you bring a fucking nun here?"

Dian cried, "My God, he's possessed."

Azrael rolled her eyes. "He's not possessed."

Cupid laughed, took another drink, and said, "Once these uppers kick in, I'll be nothing but possessed." Turning to Azrael, he asked, "Why would you need a nun's help, Azrael? What's going on? Am I in danger?"

The shorty that had chased Dian was staring at her, sweating and smiling. Erection still stiff and red. Azrael pointed to it with a subtle head motion and asked, "What's wrong with this one?" Lighting a fresh cigarette, Cupid casually explained, "Took some ecstasy with breakfast."

Domino returned with Vivianne. Her face was stricken with bad news. Vivianne's, too. Azrael didn't say anything. Everyone on the bus knew the look. It was one of those serious looks that said *your plans are changing*. With the door still open and one foot out, Domino told her big sister, "You need to come with me."

...

Esther's scorched remains lay twisted in the sand. Azrael and Domino stood over their dead sister, silently weeping, hand in hand, heads bowed. With each tear that fell from their eyes, anger took its place. Rage focused itself from within. Scorn had never looked so calm. Vengeance never sharpened with such clarity. Azrael would invent Hell and craft a chair for each soul responsible. Whatever mercy the two angels ever possessed was, at this moment, lost forever.

"We have no choice but to inform the council," Azrael began, adding, "Take Easther's body home, and prepare for the deposition."

Domino sniffled. "What do I tell them?"

"Tell them I'll explain once I have secured Cupid. Tell them we have everything under control."

They held each other for a moment, Domino looking at her twin's charred figure, and Azrael looking up into the sky.

A hole opened by their feet, and a set of stairs lowered in the sand, each step carrying Domino away, her dead sister in her arms. The hole closed, and the steps were gone. Turning to Dian, Azrael calmly told her, "Wait in the car." Dian obeyed without hesitation.

...

Azrael shoved Cupid onto his sofa, hard. She spread her wings out, closing off the world around Cupid. Her finger pushed firmly against his forehead, she demanded, "Who is the human to you?"

Sweaty and trembling, Cupid asked a stupid, "What?"

"Esther is dead."

Her finger pushed harder.

"She's what?"

"Dead. My sister was burned alive paces from your sad, little bus of self-loathing. This human who has your bow, tell me who he is to you."

Cupid didn't know what to tell the angel, but he feared the wrong answer would have him suffering the same fate as Esther. He didn't know any more than Azrael did. So, frightfully, he told her just that — he didn't know.

Azrael glared at the stammering god, her eyes shining with a scowling flare, ready to strike him. Ready to beat him unconscious and drag him to the Inn so she could prepare her trap and begin to construct his seat in the Hell she would make for him. Taming her fury, she asked, "Why are you so fucking sweaty? What did you take, Philip?"

Cupid's eyes were practically crossed. Fear and confusion swirled through his expression with more stuttering nonsense. Azrael lowered her wings and moaned, "Fuck this. I need you sober." From her robe, the archangel pulled a red vial, uncorked it with her thumb, grabbed hold of Cupid's face, and forced the sobering potion down his throat. Cupid's skin pulsed with an odd shine, and his pupils shrank. A painful sound shrieked from his gut, and he dropped down to all fours to puke up a mess of bile and confetti.

Discarding the empty vial, Azrael stood back and sighed. It was a breath to realign her composure. Silently she stood in Cupid's eyeline, letting him know that she was all he should concern himself with. That she wasn't going anywhere. As Cupid caught his breath, Azrael gave him a subtle smile, and calmly asked, "Who knows your bow is missing?"

Cupid thought it was a trick question. He gulped and uttered, "Um, you." A swift brush from the back of Azrael's hand shook his fat cheeks with a red stinging mark. Cupid cupped his face and whined. Azrael's expression remained poised. Again, she asked the same question, this time adding, "Don't tell me those you already know I am aware of. The faces in this room, for example — do not list them... Philip, who knows your bow is missing?"

Whimpering just enough to notice, he told her no one. Azrael's little smile began to gain a sharp edge, a crack in her otherwise graceful composure.

"The man who attacked you, his name is Caesar. A drunk. A lonely, drunk, waste of life has your bow. Do you know how pathetic this is?"

Cupid nodded his head.

"Who would aid such filth between realms, Philip? What thing would be so bold as to murder an archangel? To burn a firstborn? Do you know what kind of magic can even do such a thing?"

Cupid was silent.

Azrael inhaled a troubled breath. Her eyes turned to the others on the bus.

"This is a sad life you lead, Philip. A sad and selfish destruction I can barely stomach. You have compromised everything. Do you realize this? Are you in danger, you ask me?

Because of you, you fat waste of magic, we are all in danger. And if I find out you are lying to me about anything, or keeping something from me, I will peel the flesh from your bones and watch as you eat it bite by bite until it regrows so that you may feast again."

She put her hand out and told Cupid he was coming with her. Cupid gulped, looking around at the others as if they could help. Scratching his head, Cupid suggested, "Where are we going, anyway? I mean, we can just follow you."

Azrael sneered. "Just you. Now"

...

Cupid plopped into the back seat of the Range Rover. Fear kept his skin slick with sweat. Dian was in the passenger seat, looking back at the god with a shaming eye. Cupid looked nauseous. Dian felt pity for him. She found it curious that such a thing could be so weak. Not that she fully understood what he was. Or how an angel could get fat.

Azrael climbed behind the wheel, her magic compass set on the dash. Cupid asked where they were going. Azrael drove off, not answering him. Nervous questions kept coming, regardless. A broken spout of rushing queries overflowed the car. Azrael asked him to be quiet, but he was far too terrified for silence.

Dian was still clutching onto her rosary beads, her eyes stuck to Cupid's reflection in the rearview mirror. Finally, Cupid turned to her and barked, "The fuck are you looking at me like that for? You're freaking me out."

Dian turned to him with a vial of holy water from her fanny pack. She chanted for Christ to help her remove the poltergeist from Cupid. The big love god batted away the water the nun was flicking into his face, complaining to Azrael to do something. "Make her cut it out."

Dian wasn't stopping.

Azrael looked ahead with disdain, wondering if she could resist the urge to kill them both.

...

Frances was at the Inn, sitting in his squad car. He was on duty, so he was in uniform. He couldn't stop thinking about Caesar's sisters. He had a bouquet of pretty flowers for them. He felt silly about it. Unsure of what impression he was going for with the flowers. Was it too much? Did it suggest the wrong thing? What was he trying to suggest? When he got out of his car, he saw Caesar's light was on. This was a surprise. Maybe they were all together, he thought. The family finally reunited. If so, he figured he should give them some time to themselves before he stumbled in with his flowers. Easing to the window, he tried to peek in. The blinds were shut. With his ear against the door, he could hear voices, but couldn't make out what they were saying. His hand went up to knock, but he held it still. *I'll wait in the car*, he decided. *Give them a moment, wait, and see if they come out.* Sitting on the hood of his squad car, Frances lit a cigarette and thought about how attractive Caesar's sisters were. How they didn't look anything like him.

Different mom, maybe, he thought.

Things were tense in Caesar's room. Teddy was sleeping on the bed, hands bound together with a dress tie, feet bound with duct tape, and a big lump on his head. Gwen stood over him with her arms crossed, and said, "I really think we should tape his mouth shut."

Lynn was sitting on the futon, shaking her head. "He's the manager. I don't think the angel told him anything about our mission. He's just a person."

"Then he'd understand the precaution on our end. Don't you think so? We *are* fighting Satan."

Madeline chewed her nails. "I agree. We tape his mouth shut just to be safe. When he wakes up, we explain ourselves. The angels will be back eventually. They can fix all this."

Frances' patience had run out just as Gwen unrolled a long strip of tape and put her knee on the bed to get close to Teddy's mouth. He knocked on the door, and Gwen fell over, sticking the tape to Teddy's head. From his nose, over his eye, around what little hair he had, and then to the bed it stuck. She yelped on her way down, which sparked a similar sound from Madeline. The yelp pulled her hands up to her mouth, knocking a mug from the counter that shattered over the floor.

Frances shouted in, asking if everything was okay. "It's me," he said, "Frances. I heard a scream. Buddy?" The nuns tensed, feeling a sense of hopeless dread cut them off from the world. His knock disengaged their life support, and they drifted into space. Three holy women floating about a faceless void, their limbs no longer able to function. Lynn gestured for Gwen to hide the body. Gwen was partly taped to Teddy's head, mouthing a scared, *How?!*

"Roll him over behind the bed," Madeline whispered with a fierce hiss.

In his best police officer tone, Frances repeated himself, genuinely concerned about the silence that followed the crash his knock inspired. Gwen began rolling herself to the edge of the bed, attempting to gracefully bring Teddy with her. Her effort resulted in a rocking motion that unraveled more of the duct tape. The tape rolled off the other side of the bed, sticking to sheets before it found the floor with a small thud. Frances could hear her grunting, along with the squeaking of the bed, and he feared Caesar was drunk and face up with a throat full of puke.

"I'm coming in," he announced, turning the knob.

The door swung open and Gwen heaved herself off the bed with Teddy in her arms. His body flopped onto her as she hit the floor. Frances rushed in but stopped. He looked to Lynn who stood on the other side of the futon with her hands over her head. The place had been cleaned. Recognizing Teddy and the housekeeping uniforms, Frances raised his head and demanded, "Just what the fuck is going on in here?"

A pot swung against the back of his head, and Frances hunched over, guarding his skull and cursing at the pain. It was a serious whack. His vision went dizzy and he missed a step. Turning around to see Madeline readying another swing, he put a staggering arm out to stop her, but Lynn dove over the futon with a bottle high in the air. The bottle cracked over his skull, and he stumbled into Madeline's second swing, which hit right across his jaw. Frances spun around, his eyes closing as he collapsed on the floor next to Lynn. The bouquet landed on her chest.

No one moved for a few long breaths.

Lynn looked up and panicked. "Close the door." Madeline dropped the pot and slammed the door shut.

"Lock it!"

The deadbolt slid into its pocket, and Madeline dropped to the floor, her back against the door, fingernails pressed into her mouth. That was where they stayed for a moment of reflection — Gwen pinned under a sleeping stranger tangled in tape, Lynn lying next to an unconscious police officer, flowers in her hand, and Madeline sitting against the door chewing her nails.

No one noticed the whistle. At first, they all thought it was in their heads. When the kettle boiled into a scream, everyone returned to Earth. Madeline rushed to the kitchen and pulled the screaming kettle from the stovetop.

"Who's making tea?"

Gwen emerged from under Teddy, peeling tape from her face to say, "I was. Anyone want some?"

XXVI
THE ALMIGHTY'S

Azrael hadn't blinked for miles. Cupid was bouncing in the back, tugging on Dian's seat. He was rambling out demonic nonsense to torture the woman. Dian was bunched up, fingers in her ears, praying to God.

Like children, Azrael thought.

Cutting the wheel, the angel had had enough. She rushed off the road and slammed the brakes. The abrupt stop silenced the two, both searching for the right apologies to calm the frightfully distraught angel. Azrael wasn't pulling over to have any sort of dialogue. She stopped the car to shut them up. She flashed her eyes at the nun, and Dian's mind rolled back into a dream. Cupid jumped back with his hands out, pleading, "Wait, wait, wait — " but Azrael flashed her eyes at him as well, sending him into a dream of his own.

She took in a slow, centering breath and looked back to the road. But she couldn't see. Dust had kicked up and surrounded the vehicle. A sudden storm removing the world around them for a loud moment. But this was no coincidence. This storm was here for her.

It was Whisper.

But how on Earth did such a thing manage to get to Earth, she wondered.

Slithering lines of mist worked their way from the storm along the road toward the car. Smoke poured in through the air vents as a thin shape of Whisper formed in the lap of Dian.

"Azrael, Angel of the Firstborn. Leader of the adored, benevolent sister-trio. The great transporter of souls. What are you and sleepy Cupid doing with this spiritually-tainted human being?"

With a subtle smile, she answered, "Just working."

"On the top side of Earth, working. Who died?"

There was a noticeable elation in how Whisper chose his words. *Died.* Azrael wasn't in the mood for games. She spoke out clearly.

"You killed Esther. Didn't you?"

"Me? I would never do such a thing."

Azrael knew it was Whisper. Knew this smoke was here to pick a fight.

"You've broken your treaty by coming to Earth – you know this? I should take you in. Let the makers finally put an end to your disrespect. Or I could kill you myself."

Whisper sighed. "I was bored. Wanted a cigarette. No harm in that. You're the one with the curious actions. Why do you want the bow?"

This question caught her off guard.

"What?" Azrael played dumb. She was convincing, too, but Whisper already knew. It waved a smoky finger at her. "Come off it. With all that magic behind your fingers, the only reason you'd drive in one of these combusting boxes is to hide. I've been listening to the holy radio. Council didn't send you. You're being a bad dog, keeping secrets from your owner. Be easy enough to bag the bow and return it to Cupid. Shouldn't need a human assistant. Don't know what you're up to, but it sure seems fun." Whisper looked at the nun, its smoky hands around her cheeks as he asked, "Tell me. Did you lie to this poor woman? Take advantage of your appearance to manipulate her faith? Does she think you are from her fantastical book?"

Azrael sneered, "What is it you're after, King of the Shadows?"

Whisper leaned back and smiled. "There is something in the way the air moves on their end of the playground. Just can't help but want to *swallow* it all up sometimes."

The angel threatened, "I'm going to kill you for what you did to my sister. And I'm going to make it last."

Whisper nodded his head with a little smirk and said, "I've always wondered, with all those fancy tricks you can do, who's more powerful?"

"Would you like to duel... Whip?"

Whisper chuckled. "Always."

"I can arrange it."

"Maybe someday. For now, duty calls. Seems someone spilled the beans."

Azrael looked in her side mirror. A figure she would never confuse was walking toward the car. Whisper laughed and patronized the angel. "Your divine temple has sent a messenger. Must have found out about the bow, looking to put their brightest apostle on the case ..." Whisper started sliding back through the air vents as it teased the angel, "Will you tell them you're already looking, or will you act surprised? How does it work these days? I'm not up on the latest gospel. Do you have to please them before you are allowed to speak to them?"

Azrael snapped at the fleeing cloud, "Why are *you* after the bow, Whip?"

It smiled. "I'm not."

Whisper reeled the vapors out from the car, dissolving itself to dust and wind, shaping out a big taunting grin as the wind blew it off with a kiss. Azrael growled. Her hands squeezed the steering wheel tightly.

The messenger tapped on the window and Azrael rolled it down. It was a tall marble statue holding a tray, and on the tray was a golden ringing telephone. Azrael looked up at the mindless sculpture and told it, "This isn't a good time." The messenger pushed the phone closer but said nothing.

Azrael sighed a heavy breath and picked up the phone. There was nothing said. This wasn't a phone for conversation. When the phone found her ear, she vanished. The messenger vanished. The phone, however, remained. It fell, along with the tray, the receiver dangling over the door by its golden, curly cord.

Cupid and Dian continued to nap.

...

The creator's palace was a visual mastering of form. An architectural wonder that never ceased to impress. Even Azrael spotted something novel every time she laid her eyes upon it. Sections moved so organically, it challenged the mind to grasp how it wasn't alive. Layers to a churning crystal cake rimmed in gold towered like a dream that one was endlessly waking from. Breathing with the light of diamonds, edges so smooth one could drag a spoon through its perfectly-coated icing and take a bite. There was more space within its walls than the outside universe could dream to fill. A labyrinth of perpetual possibilities unfolded with an ever-changing nuance so gracefully altering one would never find themselves in the same place twice. Getting lost came simply from moving forward, and just as easily from standing still. Trust was how one moved throughout such a space. To attempt the impossible and deny the structure its unparalleled sanctity would send any guest into an endless voyage to nowhere.

Surrender yourself and trust.

Azrael appeared from a cluster of pink, prickled clouds. Wings spread wide, halo glowing brightly overhead. Her feet gently came to rest on a pristinely polished pathway. Slick emerald stone rolled onward, beckoning Azrael to walk. She growled before beginning. Her eyes closed. She hated to look upon this place. She sighed as she looked ahead at the palace and found wonder sparkling through her thoughts. She knew once she looked away her mind would feel molested. She wanted to despise the marvel of her makers. Wanted to hate its ephemeral charm. It possessed the viewer without effort. Subjected them to obeying. The sight gripped Azrael as it always did and denied her the ability to feel how she believed she felt. *Why*, she always wondered. *Why and how?* How could beings so remiss to the beauty they enveloped around the stars live within something so pure? It was a lie. They were an infestation callously hiding behind what they could never be themselves. But she could not hold the truth while she took in the view. She was a victim of her makers' narrative in these moments. Spellbound by their power, hopeless before the heavenly composition of form and material, of depth and texture. No one deserved to live within it. This was not a place to own. This was the heart of possibility. Ethereal in every stretch of the imagination.

Azrael could weep if she were to take in the sight for too long. How she wanted to look at it and spit.

The gods who claimed its celestial chambers were malignant growths sticky and soiled in apathy. If there were ever hearts warming their spirits they had long since frayed with atrophy. As her gaze pulled from the magnificent subterfuge and pulled down to her feet, her true feelings rose through the fading carbonation of delight and she growled once again. The creators made everyone walk the same path. Everyone who entered to bear witness to their greatness would first be mystified by the walls they called home. Intoxicated. Consumed. Stolen.

Forcing a smile, Azrael began walking with her sights first fixed on her feet. She prepared her mind for what was ahead. This would be the last walk she would make beneath them. Their reign would soon end. Her eyes returned ahead, and the palace tangled around her thoughts with endless wonder. Fellow angels fluttered about. Her cousins, aunts, uncles, her children. Moths to a flame, they circled the castle, lost in its cunning aura. Along the path stood giants. Loyal guardians strapped with silver armor, wielding spears of ivory. Each of them bowed when Azrael stepped into view. Azrael, the Firstborn. The shape from which all life was inspired. High from the magic of it all, Azrael smiled at the towering figures. She was revered by all magical beings. Those who did not truly love her, feared her all the same.

The green stones under her feet rolled up into ruby bricks stacking into a pair of shimmering stairs. Azrael ascended to a doorway dressed in a golden sheet. It rippled like liquid as she approached. Azrael closed her eyes before stepping through. Closed them and let the spell fade from her mind. Her true feelings returned. The loathing and disdain.

Azrael stepped into the chamber of her makers' council, her wings out but at ease, halo glowing above her head with pride. She wore a forced smile. The round chamber was larger than any room needed to be, especially for the seven seats it held. Seven thrones faced the vast opening that lay before them. Golden rings circled the floor, each ring descending from the last to a white circle where Azrael was meant to stand. The gods who claimed the thrones looked like men. They were dressed in the finest silks, decorated with the richest jewels, and capped with the most prestigious of crowns. Golden trays of food perched around them in abundance. Decadent displays of culinary gifts didn't fail to amuse, and the gods' beards were littered with stains and crumbs, like almighty bibs no mother would dare change. Slime and froth they were too careless to address crusted around the corners of their almighty mouths. Pixies buzzed overhead to refill wine and entertain. Their nude, giggling figures distracted some. Gods would look up with their glazed eyes to the glowing, miniature breasts floating about and kiss the air before them.

They were always eating and drinking.

Chewing and slurping.

Azrael found her place in the center and kneeled, as was expected of her. The towering gods kept chewing as they greeted their most prestigious of creations.

"Azrael, our Firstborn. You've made it safely. Good, good."

"We have heard the most distressing news."

"Most distressing, indeed."

Smacking lips, crunching teeth, slurping mouths – it was all hideous. The angel couldn't even remember the days her gods possessed grace, decency, or respect for anything they weren't stuffing into their mouths. Their indulgences were treated so obscenely, the angel preferred their human derivatives.

"Your sister has fallen. What say you?" a god asked, his slimy fingers poking around for what to eat next.

Azrael kept her head down. "She died serving you, my lords."

"Died, how?"

"Yes. How?"

Azrael chose to lie. If they knew Whisper was free, she might be reinforced with others who may get in her way. A war that she had no interest in fighting could start. A war that would take the bow and return it to Cupid. "Dark magic," she told them, explaining, "The culprit has been dealt with. Suffered greatly for the act, I assure you."

A god growled with a low, disapproving rumble. "Heard a whisper that it was Whisper who saw to her demise. Is this true? Has he found some way to break the treaty and pass between worlds?"

All seven gods stopped chewing to listen to her response. *Did they truly fear the elemental?* Azrael wondered.

"Rumors, my lord. Jesters claiming to be more frightening than they are." Azrael was good at lying. Her creators were too arrogant to ever consider an angel would dare deceive them. The gods accepted and moved on, sucking meat from bones and slurping down wine from greasy goblets.

With more focus on the cake he was cutting, a god snorted and asked, "Cupid's bow? Do we hear correctly that a human has taken possession of it?"

Azrael looked up to see no one was looking at her now. Too busy eating, picking their teeth, and guzzling grapes. Taming her disdain, she answered, "This is true, my lords. It is why I was on Earth. And why I held my motives from you. We feared news of the bow would arouse unnecessary danger. So we sent no word until we understood the weight of Cupid's plight."

"Danger?" a god spit, his tone arrogantly dismissing that he could ever know danger. The gods who still had half an ear in the conversation chuckled. What was there to ever fear? All there was, was there for them.

Azrael sighed. "Many ill-hearted beings may see opportunity in such a moment. We simply wanted to end matters before the wind began filling curious ears with ideas. We wouldn't want to alarm your kingdom, is all."

While the gods deliberated amongst themselves, Azrael imagined what it would be like to shoot them all with Cupid's bow. What should she have them do once they fell to her feet with undying love? Would she have them fight over her? Fight to the death before a crowd of spiteful eyes? Would she keep one as a pet to crawl around her feet and eat her scraps? Would she have them eat every single human one after the other until they burst?

A god belched and began to pick his teeth as he said, "Very well then. What news do you have to speak of your progress in the matter?

"My lords needn't worry. I have found the culprit, and I have Cupid safe. I was en route to remedy this misfortune when I was summoned."

A slew of approving murmurs filled the round chamber. It was a welcome pause from the incessant consuming.

"You'll want to see your sister off?" a god offered.

"I'd prefer to postpone her ceremony until after the ordeal is over. Her remains are safe in our chambers, but unrest still befalls your Earth, my lords. Best to end it first. Then we may seek closure with a proper ceremony for my late sister."

A god choked and pulled a bone from its greasy lips. "No, no. We do not wait for such things. There is no danger on Earth. Cupid's bow can be reclaimed by another. You must burn the sacred torch for your sister. The time you have already allowed to pass we find most offensive."

"Yes," another god proclaimed. "Esther's ceremony must begin promptly."

Azrael forced a smile. Their eagerness for the ceremony had nothing to do with their love for Esther. It had everything to do with their image. A fallen angel must be mourned, for the maker's creations were sacred and were to be respected above all. They did not seek the grief of lost life, but rather, a lost piece of their property. Azrael concealed her motives well as she spoke back. "Of course, my lords. I apologize sincerely for the delay. May I request that no one be sent for the bow in my place? Since there is no danger, there is no rush. I would prefer to finish my work myself, if it pleases my lords. My sister would have wanted it so."

With an emotionless, sloppy, and careless wave of a wrist, Azrael was dismissed. "Very well." The callous gesture stung the angel. She could hear the rattling of her makers' gold bracelets bouncing around her thoughts as she left the repugnant audience of the so-called *Almighties*. Domino was waiting for her outside the chamber, a foul expression on her face. She had listened to what was discussed, equally appalled with their gods. Time had made them obnoxious. It had worn them away and, tragically, left them hideous. A revolting nuisance upon the senses which the angels could no longer endure.

"I want to cage them and starve them. See how long it takes for them to turn on one another," Domino expressed.

"We will make their death last, my sister. Worry not. We will make their decay a spectacle no one will forget."

Esther's death would not be in vain. The kingdom would soon be theirs. They would force some to love the spirit of Esther, to wallow forever in her absence. They would have their creators follow them on all fours, chained at the necks like dogs. They would rule with power, with grace, and with a clean fucking face.

XXVII
GOODNIGHT ESTHER

It was a kingdom of white marble and colored glass, of golden lace and honey perfume, of rich green foliage and vibrant gardens groomed and thriving with life. A city built into a valley of slender mountains and enormous, lush trees. Waterfalls rained down from the moss-spotted mountain tops and ivory towers, filling the paths below with clear, glistening rivers. Nature blended into the architecture with a grace that suggested the buildings themselves grew from the rocks below.

The kingdom of magic was in mourning. The sound of horns carried a low, ominous pitch that hummed through the intermittent ringing of bells. Perched on high walkways, standing on bridges, in doorways, and lining the streets, all who lived in the kingdom were present, dressed in their finest black cloth. All were silent and holding hands. No one would work this day. Those who lived outside the kingdom gathered around the walls and perched themselves in trees to get a glimpse. Those who cared, and those who were curious.

Azrael and Domino arrived by boat, a slender pearl vessel guided by the hand of an angel. An angel with a long white pole. Walking the pole through the water, pulling the boat along at a calm pace. Esther's remains rested silently in a dark stone coffin that lay between the sisters. Each angel had a hand resting on the coffin, and a hand holding the others. The kingdom passed them by as their boat entered the central canal, flowing with crystal clear water. The canal floor was lined with white stone and rich green grass, spotted with flowers that swayed gently in the current. Patches of blue and red, trails of white and yellow. Things were always in bloom in the kingdom. The season, perpetually perfect and never changing.

The mourning horn pulsed through the chiming bells. Its rhythm helped the sisters remain present and take the moment for what it was – a time to push their frustration with Cupid's bow aside and say goodbye to the youngest among them. Being home, despite the circumstance, was refreshing. Being amongst their own kind in the kingdom they helped build was calming. Flower petals fell from the high reaches above them, soft floral lips filling the air with a departing sense of love and grace. The sisters looked up to the hands that were setting the petals free. Amongst their fellow angels were a mix of magical beings who came to pay their respects. Those who did not love the angels knew well enough to fear them. It was their kingdom after all. They made the rules.

The sisters were met at the dock by two others from their bloodline. Distant cousins born from distant cousins, unlike Azrael and Domino, who were manifested by the hands themselves. The first born. Angels born of other angels weren't necessarily seen as inferior, but there were contemptuous murmurs often traded between shadows of lesser beings. It was something that only pulled the angels closer together. Made them all the more prejudice against everyone and everything beneath them. Angels were angels after all. They were the highest class one could dream of being next to the makers themselves, and royalty is royalty. Angelic offspring, however, were forever subsidiary to the direct hand of the Almighties. "Second born" they were called. A powerful insult if the inflection colored the title just so. From the first born, there was no condescension, though. They were their children. An angel's pride was not an easy thing to break. But it had been, on rare occasions, broken. Azrael knew there were still some who favored the maker's light above their own. How many angels would resist her climb to power? Who amongst her kind were so blindly loyal to the clowns who made them that they would betray their own? And would they be so foolish to think she would hesitate to push them out of her way? Azrael was making note of those she'd spare and those she'd make suffer once she and Domino ruled.

The two angels on the dock who took Esther's coffin showed no signs of betrayal. Their faces were ruined with devout grief. A true and unmistakable pain watered in their eyes. The silence they each shared as their looks met seemed to agree on everything. An angel had died, and there was nothing more tragic.

Azrael and Domino followed their fallen sister's coffin hand in hand through the marbled streets that snowed with heavenly petals. The path they walked cut through the center of their kingdom. A line of angels filed in behind them. No one flew. The pain was seen as too great to carry into flight. To fly on this day would be disrespectful. An angel would lose their wings if they dared to lift off. And so, droves of angels marched onward toward their sacred temple. They stood along the path, waiting for Esther to pass, waiting for the line of angels to pass so they could join the ranks. The sound of their feet would bond into a lamenting march onward to pay their respects.

The temple was carved from their world's whitest stone, polished to a shine that would make a pearl blush. Trimmed and capped in gold, there were seven towers and seven bells. Azrael wondered how many times they would ring before the war she was bringing was over.

At the temple entrance, Gabriel stood with his two sons. Gabriel too was a first born. There were twelve in total, and Gabriel was the twelfth, nicknamed the last born – a name he didn't care for. A name that often strayed his commitments from his fellow first born. The title bore no ill intent when it was first cast upon him, but time sharpened the label's edge into a patronizing echo. Manifested without brothers or sisters, Gabriel was the only angel brought into creation alone. Further isolating him, he was made centuries apart from the others, manifested long after their traditions had come to life. Gabriel always had something to prove where there was no need. Azrael knew he would be trouble.

Most angels had not seen the makers in their chambers, the grotesque state they gestated within. Some did not wish to believe such divinity could recoil into something so unsightly, so revolting and offensive. What did it say of an angel, if the hands that made them could be so unworthy? Gabriel was one who could not accept the sisters' word about the Almighties. Domino suspected his doubt was born from jealousy, for Gabriel had never been summoned to meet their makers. Never welcomed into the chambers of his supreme creators, he reduced all ill chatter about the first gods to treason. And he had many ears keen to lean in and agree.

Gabriel and his sons offered their condolences. He entered the temple alongside Azrael, asking if they could talk after the ceremony. She couldn't quite place his tone. Azrael remembered it was Gabriel who had confronted the human she was hunting. Could he have known about the missing bow? With a firm hand on his shoulder, Azrael guided his path away from hers with an unassuming nudge. She offered a silent nod to his invitation but wasted no breath on words. Domino looked at her sister with a scrunched brow as she couldn't hear what Gabriel had asked. Azrael made a subtle gesture to suggest it was nothing significant.

Domino wasn't convinced.

The temple ceiling stretched into the sky above. Arching columns curved into a web of sculpted angels. Thousands of marble limbs and wings extruded from the ceiling as if a mass of angels were frozen in flight, frozen and forever falling from above.

As the temple filled with angels, the bells and horns halted with a fading reverb trailing off into a powerful silence. It was an open space. No seats, benches, or pews. Each angel held a candle unlit for the moment. Each angel held their impermanence in earnest. Forever felt so fragile whenever one of them fell. A grim reminder that eternity was just as temporary as anything else.

The sisters stood hand and hand, Esther's remains lying before them upon an altar. An angel with braided silver hair stood at the head of the chamber. Her name was Uriel. The ninth born from the Makers' hands, she had given birth to well over three-hundred second-borns. She was often referred to as the Mother.

Uriel read from an ancient text words of pain and love, words of purpose and hierarchy, words that empowered Azrael's hunger for the war ahead. The candles all held a fire for Esther while Uriel read. A few passages were chanted. It was the same for every fallen angel. A rare ceremony, but one none ever forgot.

Centuries past, when Whisper brought the last great war to the magic kingdom, many angels had perished. Why he was never executed for the act Azrael could never figure out. The true meaning behind the war had never been clear either. Thinking on it then, she replayed her Makers' pause earlier when Whisper had been mentioned. The shift in the room had been unmistakable. If they truly did fear the elemental being, then how cautious should she be of the thing? Whisper had spent so much time in his shackles, tethered to the outskirts of the magical realm, that her sisters had diminished his status to a common prisoner. An outcast. A worthless pariah no more interesting than fading graffiti that had lost its meaning.

But who set the thing free?

Was Cupid hiding something?

Looking over her shoulder, Azrael spied Gabriel. His expression failed to conceal his annoyance. He was clearly absorbed in thought. Where was the grief? Where was his loyalty? Azrael wondered. Would the famous *last-born* expose her for not reporting her work on Earth? Would he aim to ridicule her and Domino? To blame them for their sister's death? Or would he want to offer his help? Did he want to tag along to help catch the humans he'd already tried and failed with? Which was worse? A needy Gabriel, or an enemy Gabriel? She would have to tread carefully in the conversation he sought with her and Domino. What if he knew about the bow? What sparks would that fact ignite in Gabriel? Whisper... her thoughts kept creeping back to that foul beast. What were the odds Whisper was using Gabriel? What were the odds Gabriel was the one who set the King of Shadows free?

With the angels dispersing to carry on with their grieving, Azrael and her sister made their way to the catacombs beneath the temple, accompanying Esther to her final resting place. Every twenty paces the path was lit by torches flickering warmth from above. Tiny embers dropped to the ground trailing dying breaths of red smoke. Domino kicked at some as they passed by, imagining what it was like for her sister to perish at the hands of Whisper.

The catacombs were a maze of rounded ebony stone stitched with gold. Its halls were wide with shallow ceilings. Before the war, it had been just a room, a small space to hold the few, rare passings. But now it was tangled like roots with nothing to grow but death. It was a reminder of Whisper, the infamous King of Shadows, and the unthinkable evil it possessed. It was a reminder of the Makers' failings. To let such a thing carry on breathing after such an act was weakness. Unforgivable weakness.

Along the way, Domino leaned into Azrael's ear, "What did our dear Gabe ask of you?"

"We shall know soon enough, as he wishes to speak to us both."

"Now?" Domino's tone was offended. "What is so pressing that it's necessary to part with our sorrow? And he wishes for this to happen here? As we push Esther's ruined figure into a hole? Has he no sense?" Azrael sighed. "He may be an obstacle in the days to come. We should hear what he has to say so we can better assess the weight of his stupidity. To lose the element of surprise could impede our chance to strike. Our Makers can't catch wind of our intentions."

Domino thought about what they were working towards, and all the ways Gabriel could slow them down. "You think he knows something? How could he?"

"I don't know what he knows, all I can do is speculate what he *may* do knowing the bow is missing, and that we did not report it. Not only did we not report it, but we got our sister killed doing whatever it was we were doing while not reporting it. Gabriel, the Boy Scout he is, would be writhing in joy to bow before our Makers with the chance to put a pair of high-ranking corrupt angels on trial. It doesn't matter what we are doing. I'd wager he will fight tooth and nail at any chance to pry our opinion of his precious Makers from the kingdom."

Domino recoiled at the thought, "Oh god, no. What an awful image. Can you imagine? Gabriel in court working feverishly to suppress his itchy need to be the good little boy?" Azrael chuckled under her breath. "I'd cut my eyes out before such things could poison my vision."

Esther's coffin was set in a tomb dug out just for her. A pocket in the wall with her name on it. Azrael and Domino were left to mourn. This was a pain they never imagined would come for them. If their sadness was greater than the anger they felt, they couldn't say. Anger certainly seemed more and more prevalent the longer this new horrible reality made itself at home. To make matters worse, one of their own had weaseled themselves in the middle of this moment. Filled their thoughts with dreadful suspicions of betrayal.

With a troubled sigh, Azrael huffed, "The only thing worse than an angel standing against another angel is one sucking our gods' off while he does It. If Gabriel stands with our Makers when we step up to claim this kingdom, I will tear his wings from his back and let him fall for ages, blind to the ground he will never know is or isn't coming."

"We could pluck his feathers and have him parade about for our amusement. Or make him fall in love with the sun."

Azrael smiled at that, offering, "Leash him to the ground so he is stuck reaching for it. Flying out to embrace his death only to be tugged back. All the while slowly burning under the heat of his longing."

Domino composed herself and looked down the hall. "Speaking of, here comes our thorn now. Will he prove predictable, or will he surprise, dear sister, and admit his mistake?" She began to mock him then. *"Oh my sweet sisters, please welcome my apology. I was such a fool. Our Makers' cocks were buried too deep within my throat to see the truth."*

"Yes, I can see so clearly now. They were flaccid. Flaccid cocks laying limp in my mouth. It was pity I held onto. Pity that had me arguing against the light you so graciously offered to our people. Pity, for such soft, floppy cocks."

Azrael turned to see Gabriel making his way toward them. All their jokes departed rather abruptly at his sight. Gabriel's presence was nothing to laugh at. Never had he looked so serious. His presence made the war instantly resolute. They truly were going to enslave their gods. And they were going to kill anyone who stood in their way.

Azrael pondered, *Who will you be in the days to come, Gabriel?*

"Sisters, again I offer my sincere condolences. Esther was by far the most beautiful angel our gods ever made. Her departure was unexpected and hard to accept." Gabriel's demeanor was stiff. Something in him was harboring a subtle defensiveness. There was too much on his mind to convey a believable sense of empathy. Even if he was saddened by Esther's death, whatever he was there to discuss was far more pressing than grief.

Azrael offered a small look of appreciation for his words, but was quick to pull on his intentions. "Given the circumstances, we'd quite like to be alone with Esther, you understand. Could we hear what's on your mind?" Gabriel seemed proud of himself then. His eagerness to share was not far from physically percolating out of his flesh. It had Domino listening with a mild grimace.

"I wanted to speak to you before rumors started spreading. Give you a chance to explain yourself so I could sway with the approaching tides, so to speak."

Azrael smirked and asked him gently, "Elaborate."

Gabriel folded his arms as he answered. "Well, you are obviously up to something rather significant, as you kept it secret for who knows how long. And now your sister has fallen in the name of whatever it is you are doing on Earth." Azrael almost laughed at his smugness. "And what do you know of our... secret and significant something?"

Gabriel shifted with a disarming sense of pride. "I know that a human was led across realms through an unregulated passage. Two, in fact. Two humans. Guided into the heart of Nowhere to buy a weapon."

Azrael and Domino both concealed their surprise. Why would they need a weapon if they already had the bow? Azrael sunk deeper into her suspicions that Cupid was not telling her everything. There was more to his story. His sister's blood was on his hands.

Domino stepped into the conversation. "And do you know what this weapon was, or if they obtained it?" Her question made him smile. Gabriel liked knowing something they did not. And to make it all the more delicious, it was obvious to him this had everything to do with their secret and significant something. Happily, he shared, "It was an old relic from the Shadow King's war. One of its... *God Killers*, I believe they called them. A concept itself outlawed long before it was ever fully conceptualized. To grant any hand such a talent. Wicked magic."

"Interesting," was all Azrael said. Four syllables expressed with no emotional nuance. She was a master at concealing her feelings. Gabriel drew himself back. "Interesting?" His disappointment was striking. *How quickly he loses his righteous composure*, both sisters noted. He had expected his news to provoke more emotion from them. Expected it to reveal some insight into their secret actions. How it pleased them to unnerve him so.

Gabriel's expression tightened as he began his attack. "There is rumor spreading that Cupid's bow has been destroyed. That you are aiming to make a fool of our creators. That you plot to jest at their expense, or worse. To ridicule them for some sadistic amusement. Was it you? Did you destroy the bow? Have you led these humans into our realm?"

Azrael burst into laughter. "*Hahahaha!* Have you come up with this piffle all on your own?"

Domino smiled. "They mock themselves, sweet Gabriel, hiding away in their waste. And who are you to shine in such gossip? Have you forgotten your place?"

Gabriel clenched his fist. "Enough! I will hear no more of your incessant dishonor. I am not the only one who can see the lies you spread when you speak of our Makers. You mettle in acts behind your power. It's *you* who has forgotten your place. We are *their* children. And I have had enough of your ill favor towards our Makers. Your actions in this matter are teetering on treason. You disgrace our kind with this talk. And your game with these humans, whatever it is you are playing at, has gone far enough. If the rumors are true, and this relic has been unearthed under your watch, mark my words, sisters, I will see you hanged."

Azrael pushed herself into Gabriel, her eyes beaming with a harsh white light. Gabriel stumbled into Domino, who was ready to stop him from falling over. They were far stronger than he gave them credit. Pinning him just so that he couldn't free himself. Their motions were so graceful he feared to even try. Azrael stood in his face, scowling. "What would you do if we aimed to do far worse than *mock* your precious Makers? What if I told you we were going to kill them?"

Gabriel's eyes widened. "You lie. No one would be so bold."

Domino pushed her lips towards his ear. "Will you cower at their feet as we behead them one by one?"

Gabriel gulped, but said nothing.

Azrael's expression went cold. "Will you whimper over their headless shapes while we clean our blades of their unworthy blood?"

"You go too far, Azrael. You both do."

"We will go where we damn well please, Last Born."

Gabriel pushed himself from Domino and drew his sword. Azrael matched his motion, disarming him with an effortless swing of her blade. The strike was so quick Gabriel almost didn't notice she had taken three of his fingers along with his sword. He pulled his dismembered hand to his chest, shock pulsating from his face. Domino rushed in from behind, her blade sticking into his back. His breath stuttered as the edge punctured his lung. Azrael moved toward him at the same moment, sticking her blade into his gut. Gabriel gasped for air. His eyes raced hopelessly around the catacombs for escape. Azrael was calm as she spoke to him. "Foolish Gabriel. Don't you know how to play war?"

Gabriel coughed and began to lose the strength to stand. With what little strength remained he asked them why.

Azrael rested her head on his shoulder, slowly pushing her blade further into his belly as she answered, "Because, we are better than them." The sisters pulled their swords from Gabriel and he fell to their feet, lifeless. Another fallen angel. Only this one would not be buried among his kin. Gabriel would hang in the streets a traitor. When the war begins, he will be their flag.

Azrael and Domino turned to Esther's tomb and held each other, the fire within them spreading in all directions. It felt good to kill, to spill unworthy blood before their path to greatness.

...

Cupid and Dian were still asleep, uninterrupted on the side of the road.

XXVIII
A STRIP CLUB THAT WAS SOON TO BE A TREE

A tent full of bottles was pitched in the desert somewhere between Doesn't Really Matter, and No One Cares. Inside that tent, a phone was buzzing with twenty-eight unread messages. It was April's phone. She and Caesar were parallel, each in a sleeping bag floating in a small pool of empty bottles. Whisper had set them up in the tent and told them to wait until it returned. They drank all night. The longer they sat with the memory of their otherworldly adventure, the easier it was to drink. To laugh at the impossibility of it all and drink.

Drink and drink.

And drink.

The buzzing phone had finally opened one of April's eyes. Although bloodshot and glazed over with a thick, oily film, it was alive enough to register the vibrating light was for her. She opened her other eye and sat up. Thumbing through the messages, she muttered, "Fuck, fuck, fuck…"

Wiggling out from her sleeping bag, she tripped on Tux, still petrified and stiff. As she fell into one side of the tent, the other end flew up. Caesar's head popped up along with a noisy wave of bottles. His eyes opened, and he snorted awake. April's legs were searching for the ground in front of him, kicking at his feet.

"I'm awake. I'm awake. I'm awake. Stop kicking me."

April's face was smashed up against the tent, her arms seeking leverage. Caesar helped her turn herself around, and she sat on her butt. She held the phone up and huffed, "My man figured out I burned his car."

Caesar yawned a half coherent, "What?"

"Listen, I know we're supposed to hunker down and wait for the smoke thing to come back, but I need to see my girls and manage some damage control."

Caesar dug a used cigarette from his shirt pocket and perched it on his lips, nodding his head to April, but not fully putting her words together. He stopped nodding and asked a more coherent, "What?"

April sighed. "My man — he flipped his shit this morning. Someone had the cops come and he was escorted out of my club. I need to go see my girls."

Caesar returned to nodding as he lit his cigarette. April gave him an impatient look. "We can leave the thing a note, yeah? If we don't get back before it does." Puffing away, Caesar nodded once more and shrugged. "Yeah, why not?"

They zipped out from the tent, April's hair looking like an abstract sculpture. Caesar had the stiff Tux under his arm, a warm beer in the other hand. Both were hungover. April dialed a cab company and exhaled a painful breath.

"Caesar…"

"Yeah?"

"Where are we?"

They both looked around the desert that spanned out in all directions. Caesar took a drag and a swig and said, "Somewhere between Doesn't Really Matter, and No One Cares."

April sort of laughed. "Shut up. It's a campsite. Gotta be a sign somewhere."

…

A cab dropped them off behind April's club. She used the backdoor — the door her girls used to avoid creepy customers. Caesar stopped when they entered, holding his cigarette up, and asked if he was allowed to smoke in her club.

She pulled him on. "Yeah, you can smoke. Hard to run a smoke-free joint when your business is tits and ass."

April was proud of her club. She made a show of opening the door for Caesar, smiling big as she held it, and said, "After you." Caesar liked that she was excited. The whole ride over she had been nervous. It was nice to see a real smile. She believed her girls would be on her side, but she had also left them with the wrath of her man.

The club was still opening up, so all the lights were on. April kept it clean. The lights didn't reveal anything unsightly. A runway stage ran up the middle. The booths had poles wrapped around little side stages. A dancer was stretching on stage, warming up on a pole. The bartender counted cash in his registers. April's tour ended when she spotted the wrath her soon-to-be ex had brought to her club. The wrath was a barstool sticking out from the mirror that dressed the back wall of the main stage. "Motherfucker," was her immediate reaction. Caesar gave her back a friendly pat.

"I kinda like it. Sorta sets the mood for excitement."

April gave a half-hearted chuckle. "Shut up. That's a couple-thousand-dollar repair bill is what the fuck that is."

Finishing his cigarette, Caesar reminded her how expensive a car is. April gave him an eye. "Yeah, yeah, yeah. How about you park your skinny white ass at the bar while I talk with my girls. Unless you want a dance?"

The offer was real, which made Caesar chuckle.

"No dance for me. Drink would be nice."

April told the bartender Caesar could have whatever he wanted, on the house. The bartender gave Caesar a funny look and then asked April how she was.

"Oh, I'm fine. Just playing *Lord of the Rings* with this skinny man here. You wouldn't believe me if I told you. And I don't have the time to even think how to start with this shit. Don't let him get too drunk. I'll be in the back for a bit."

The bartender was a lively man named Moses. He was muscular, his face equipped with a wide range of expressions, and he wore glitter like his skin naturally produced a shimmer. "So, how do you know April? You some strange kind of exotic rebound?" he asked in a deep, yet feminine, voice, his expression animated and guarded.

274

"Her rebound?"

"You know? To get over someone, people go off and tag something strange to move on." Moses made a casual, humping gesture to accompany his words. It made Caesar laugh.

"Oh. No, it's not like that. Just friends. She'd break me in half. I'm fragile."

Moses smiled. Letting his guard down a little, he asked, "Okay, April's 'just friend.' What are we drinking?"

"Old fashion, neat. Please."

Moses started mixing the drink, asking what Caesar knew about the fire. Caesar played dumb. He could tell Moses liked to gossip. As he made his drink, he shared everything he knew about April, her man, and the car fire. When the stories ended, Moses asked, "So, what's in your cute yellow bag?"

With a heavy sigh, Caesar looked at the sack as he answered, "My cat."

Moses laughed. "Your cat, huh? So's that what you call your pocket pussy?"

"A little early in our friendship for a joke like that."

"Bitch, please, you're drinking in a strip club, and it ain't even noon."

"Fair enough," Caesar said, a little smile on his face. Caesar complimented a small bonsai tree that sat on the bar. Moses poured his drink and thanked him. "It's my little buddy. Boyfriend got it for me. Supposed to bring a calm energy. I'm always complaining about the dickheads I serve here, so he wanted to help."

"Does it?"

"It does, yeah. It reminds me of him, so it calms *me* down, at least. People are still dickheads."

Caesar thanked him for the drink as he reached for it. Moses told him to wait. He poured himself a shot and tapped it to Caesar's glass, asking, "What are we drinking to?"

Caesar raised his glass and thought about it before saying, "To my first time in a strip club."

Moses raised his shot and rolled his eyes. "You ain't missing nothing."

One drink turned into two, which turned into three. Caesar and Moses quickly found they had a similar sense of humor. Moses shared wild club stories. His admiration for

April's no-bullshit manner of running a business was obvious. He was happy she had burned her man's car. "I would've helped her do it if she told me what she was up to," he told Caesar, claiming, "Shit, I'd'a burned his car on my own for her. You ask me, the car wasn't enough. And him coming here and fucking the mirror up like that, *hmph*. He's lucky I wasn't here when it happened. If I had my chance with him, I would—"

Moses stopped talking.

Caesar set his glass down and asked, "You would what?"

Moses' expressive face went cold, and he seemed to set himself on the shelf with the bottles, fading into the ambiance. Caesar looked back around to Moses, confused, and asked again, "You would what?"

"BITCH, I KNOW YOU'RE HERE!" a big, booming voice roared out from the front of the club. Caesar turned around to see a big Samoan man carved from stone stomping into the club with his chest puffed, eyes beaming, his upper lip hitched up on one side by some unseen string of hostility. Caesar picked his drink up, nervous for the show that had just begun.

"WHERE YOU AT, APRIL?"

April came out from the center stage entrance with calm, deliberate steps. Strong disgust shaped her ready composure. A few of her girls followed and stood with her as if they had rehearsed the entrance — arms folded, shoulders slanted, eyebrows raised to fierce arches.

Unblinking, April greeted him. "You got some nerve coming here, *Darrel*." Her girls all swayed in support. Darrel moved his arm sharply, and a leather whip sprung out and cracked the air. April and her girls all made exasperated faces at the action, their brows scrunched and eyes wide. Looking at one another, their faces asked, *Did he just do that?*

April chuckled. "The fuck you bring a whip for?"

Caesar mumbled to himself, *"Who the fuck has a whip?"* Moses looked to Caesar and shrugged the sort of timid gesture you might find present in a chihuahua. He seemed to shrink. It was obvious he wasn't going to help out in any way if things got out of hand. Looking at the barstool sticking out from the mirror, Caesar asked how dangerous Darrel was. Moses made a subtle shift with his eyes as he pulled the spout from a bottle and took a drink, setting it on the bar for Caesar when he was done.

This is going to suck, Caesar thought.

"I know it was you who set my car on fire. Maybe I should burn some of your shit." Darrel was looking around the club, pushing his threat into every corner of the room.

April smirked. "Go for it. I got insurance that covers crazy. Your wallet deep enough to back up crazy?"

"Bitch, you fucked my ride up."

"First of all, you're gonna cut the 'bitch' talk. Now, I know you were here this morning, and the cops already took your ass out once. I don't know who the fuck told you I was here, but you need to be on your way."

"You're gonna pay for the car."

"You gonna pay for that mirror?"

"Fuck your mirror."

"No, fuck your piece of shit, cheating ass. Get the fuck out my club before there's a problem. 'Cause there will be a problem. You and your dumbass whip. That shit's assault, by the way, you know that? Swinging a whip around like you're Indiana-fucking-Jones."

Darrel growled and cracked the whip at April. It didn't come close — it was just meant as a threat. Regardless, it scared Caesar. Afraid and drunk was a funny combination. He was afraid for April, and acting on impulse to stop a whip. Acting on impulse to stop an enormous, enraged man. But he wasn't physically equipped to assist. This man could blow him over with a huff and a puff. So Caesar did the only thing he could think to do.

Darrel cracked the whip again, shouting more demands when an arrow shot into his back. Everyone gasped. Moses bent back into a frightened arch, hand on his chest, eyes wide on Caesar and his bow.

Instead of moaning in pain, as everyone expected, Darrel seemed okay. The heart-shaped tip sunk into flesh, and the magic that enchanted it flushed his heart with an overpowering sense of desire. His anger melted into a dizzy, innocent expression. A longing, aching ecstasy took him stumbling forward with grief and joy as he wept out, "Sasha!"

It was at that same moment that Azrael's magical compass shimmered to life with a rainbow of colors. It shook so wildly that it began spinning around on the dashboard. Azrael's face lit up, and she swerved off the road, screeching to a halt outside of a gas station.

Domino, Dian, and Cupid all braced themselves as the car stopped abruptly. The nun gasped and asked what was going on. Azrael pulled her from the car, shouting, "The bow was just used. Domino, stay with Cupid." Dian was an accessory stretching out in the angel's grip as she bolted for the closest door and pushed it open, glowing compass in hand. What should have been a gas station bathroom opened to a strip club. The scene inside slowed the angel's pace. She stopped to observe. Dian, taken aback by the angel's special use of doors, stood close and pinched herself.

Sasha was hiding halfway through the doorway to the backroom looking worried, using the door as cover. Darrel was on his knees, hands clasped in front of him, reaching out to her. The arrow protruding from his back. April and her girls were still up on the stage. April was pissed, her hands up in the air conducting an orchestra of emotions as she hollered, "*Sasha*? I thought you were fucking with the Pink Panther bitch."

Hearing this pained Sasha. Her worried face turned sad. "Hold up, you and Tammy? You tell her the same shit you told me? Huh? Tell you her you were a neglected man? You get her to play with your balls, too?

Darrel wept, "Baby, I was just having fun with her. Man's gotta eat. I *love* you."

April shut her eyes before she reacted. "*Love?* Oh, *hell* no. You cheated on me because I wouldn't suck your balls? You for real right now?"

The arrow's spell had no use for lies, and saw no need for silence. Darrel was quick to express, "I like it. I like having my balls sucked on."

April shook her head. "Man, you're fucking sad."

Sasha was fighting back tears now, still holding the door, asking, "How long have you been with her?"

"Tammy? It started before you, baby. Honest."

April snapped, "Baby? BABY!? Asshole! *You! Live! With! Me!* And Sasha, you need to fuck off right now. Fifteen years I've been with this man, you don't get to be hurt if he cheats on you. You're both fucking cheating on me!"

The fight kept on. Things started getting tossed around. Shoes and bottles. The yelling got louder. From the doorway, Azrael spotted Caesar zipping his bag, and saw the bow going in. She pushed Dian. "That's him." Dian pulled her attention from the heated argument and focused. It was time for God's work. Azrael pushed her toward Caesar, demanding. "Get that bag. This is your moment. God is watching." If Dian was the one to take the bow, the link that Caesar had would break. There was too much to risk in Azrael's own hand getting near it — a truth that agitated her deeply. How simple it would be to just pluck it from his weak little arms and be done. To stick his heart with her sword and end the hunt.

Dian walked towards Caesar with a nervous but assertive posture, a small crucifix in her hand. She held the cross outright as she moved toward the Devil. Azrael watched her, bewildered, shaking her head and muttering, *"Jesus Christ."*

Caesar was noticeably confused by the woman moving toward him. If things couldn't get any more out of the ordinary, now there was a nun walking his way, aiming a cross at his face. Plucking the bottle from the bar, Caesar drank in preparation. The nun then began to say, "I know the Devil is in you. But you do not have to obey him. God can forgive you. There is still a place for you in Heaven. Resist the serpent that has taken refuge in your body and give me that bag." Caesar's confusion became a great deal more noticeable. He made a quick look at Moses, who was backing away from the bar. Moses hadn't even noticed the nun. Moses was making a break for the front door. It was his bonsai tree he was running from. The thing was moving.

"The Lord is here with me. You have nowhere to go, Satan," Dian told Caesar, her face terrified, yet fierce. Caesar put his arms through the straps and pulled the bag snugly to his back before asking, "Who the hell are you? And why do you want my bag?" Stepping closer, she continued, "I'm a servant of God. And I am here to take back what you have stolen from our Lord.

Resist the evil you are possessed with, and give me the bag. Begin your atonement."

Caesar backed away from her. His one eye remained on April as she yelled, "How many of you have been sucking this asshole's balls?!"

"Resist the Devil," the nun pleaded, her cross still outright, pushing closer. Caesar's hand worked along the bar to keep balanced as he moved back. Startled by a change in texture, his hand recoiled. The bar was half-covered in short, green blades of grass. It seemed like it was reaching for him, like it was taller where his hand had just departed. Stepping away, Caesar stumbled on a vine growing out from the bar.

This can't be good, he thought.

Azrael was watching Dian's failure with troubling contempt, but her dimming faith in the holy woman was a frustration she would have to set aside, as the bar was continuing to grow a rather noticeable green thumb. A sense of urgency pushed through the angel. Caesar's use of the bow had gathered more than just her attention.

Nature had arrived.

Azrael jumped onto a table, put two fingers in her mouth, and whistled. The shriek stole everyone's attention. Azrael pointed to Caesar and shouted, "Everyone see that man with the yellow pack? The first person to get me the bow inside of it gets fifty thousand dollars." The dollar amount was arbitrary. She would have said anything to convince them. It worked. Everyone stopped arguing. They all looked to Caesar. Only April kept looking at the Angel. *Who the fuck is this bitch?* she thought.

All of April's girls sprung after Caesar. Darrel reached out to Sasha as she ran by, but she pushed his arms away. The fifty-grand reward was more pressing than their relationship status. The flock of strippers was an alarming sight. Caesar turned to run, but his foot snagged, and he fell. A vine had grown around his ankle and was quickly winding its way around his leg.

This is definitely *not good,* he thought.

The rush of women halted their assault as the small bonsai tree that claimed the bar grew a great many times larger than it should've ever grown. The bar broke apart under its twisting trunk. The vine that had Caesar's leg was now a rising branch lifting him into the air, his head swinging upside-down, blood rushing to his skull like an overflowing glass of wine. April's girls abandoned the prospect of a quick buck and fled out the back, Darrel chasing after.

April was off the stage, cautiously assessing a way to rescue Caesar. Dian was on her bottom retreating backward across the growing floor, convinced the Devil had conjured the tree that now towered over her. Azrael sighed and let her wings free before lunging from the table toward Caesar with a graceful glide to her feet.

Caesar shouted for April, but Azrael's wings obstructed the view of her upside-down friend. The angel's halo had beamed to life, and her eyes were filled with light. She looked up to Caesar with disgust. "Give the woman the bag," she demanded, pointing to the frightened nun on the floor behind her.

I'm going to die, Caesar thought.

The angel's glowing eyes blazed. Her teeth slashed a sharp slice across her face. "Drop the bag," she urged.

Smoke blasted behind the upside-down Caesar as if a bomb had gone off. Azrael crossed her hands over her face as the force of it pushed her back. Fists formed within the smoke and drove their way down her throat. More fists shaped around her neck, her arms, shoulders, legs. Azrael fought the restrictive, dark cloud and the onslaught of smoky hands, pawing and squeezing, gripping and pulling, all the while miserably choking as the smoke filled her lungs.

The other end of the smoke chewed at the nature around Caesar's leg like acid. Caesar saw the branch that was holding him severed. He felt himself embrace the air, embrace the mercy of gravity, and the ground against his back. Coughing out the impact, he hoped Tux wasn't crushed.

Smoke rolled by April, forming part of Whisper's face. It told her to get Caesar out of the building, its voice straining as the fight with Azrael carried on. Azrael, who had managed to free her sword, found a solid bit of Whisper to stick. Her sword cut in and swung out. An ashen hand fell from the violent cloud and broke into a pile of rocks as it hit the shifting ground below. The magical brawl was exciting the bonsai tree which had twisted into the ceiling. The bar under it no longer existed.

Branches curved around the walls and swung out in search of the bow. Nature covered the floor. Flowers bloomed alongside shrubs and twisting roots, weaving in and out of the ground with an impressive power.

April rushed to Caesar, struggling over the wilderness at her feet. Grabbing Caesar, she pushed at the door, but the vines had grown too thick. April put her body into it, heaving as hard as she could to break free. Caesar began kicking drunken thrusts that did nothing. The twisting branches behind them began bending toward the bow. April saw the reaching wooden limbs and intensified her strikes at the door, occasionally locking eyes with Caesar, both terrified for themselves and for each other.

Whisper pushed itself from Azrael, slipping free from her throat. She gasped for air as the dark cloud rushed away and crashed through the front door with a gust of wind that lifted April and Caesar off their feet and through the hole it made to the outside.

April and Caesar tumbled into the parking lot like clothes blowing free from opened luggage. "Hurry up," Whisper shouted as its ashen feet found shape across the asphalt. It ripped a door free from a truck. Lightning from its finger sparked the ignition, and the truck rumbled to life. Whisper backed up immediately, the truck's bed beckoning for April and Caesar to board. Grass rushed from the club like flooding water, bringing more vines and weaving roots. The hole Whisper had created was already sealing over with wild growth. Caesar and April hopped into the truck bed, pushing and pulling each other up as best they could to help, the rushing nature reaching after their feet. Whisper stepped on the gas, and the truck kicked up grass and dirt as it sped away.

Azrael cut her way through the thickening vines, emerging from the club too late. The truck was too far away. Caesar and April both watched her accept defeat, wondering all the while who she was. They watched the bonsai tree twisting up through the roof and opening April's club to the daylight. Neither of them could believe their eyes.

April's insurance didn't cover this kind of crazy.

Azrael sheathed her blade and returned her wings to beneath her robe. The truck was a vanishing dot on the horizon. The fight was lost. Dian struggled her way through the forest to rejoin the angel. She was out of breath and annoying Azrael with questions, fear rattling her winded voice.

"What was that smoke? It had hands. I saw it. Hundreds of hands." She was looking at her own hands as she trembled. The spectacle of Satan's power was greater than she had ever imagined.

Azrael didn't look away from the road. She stood brooding in her defeat, speaking more so to Whisper than she was to Dian, as she answered, "That was an Elemental. A creature with no honor. Nothing but chaos. We banished it from your realm when it decided it was the true god of all things. We banished it to the shadows where it lived only in the winds of rumor as a whisper. Something has freed it."

"The Devil?" Dian offered, brushing dirt from her pants and pulling a twig from her hair.

Azrael rolled her eyes, tired of Sister Dian. Frustrated with her human incompetence, but mostly with her own need for a human altogether. "There is no Devil," she told the nun with a hiss, adding, "There is no Heaven, no Hell. Your scriptures are babble meant to make shape to a game my Makers lazily fuss about like it is all there is to do." Dian shook her head. Surely she had heard the angel wrong.

Azrael stepped to the nun with fire in her eyes, and told the holy woman, "You are a toy for aloof gods who are so detached that they haven't the grace to finish chewing their food before speaking. They carelessly expect absolute obedience. '*Do as I say, not as I do.*' They may be even more pathetic than your kind. Or maybe they are no different than you. What would a human be like in their position, but electrified garbage?" Azrael stepped closer to Dian, and kept stepping. Dian, frightened, stumbled back. Azrael kept pushing at her with scowling eyes as she spat, "You don't ask him nicely for the bow. You just take it. What were you thinking when you were failing me just now? If your God *were* real, he would surely dismiss you for such a pathetic display. You are weak, Dian. You are a sad shit stain polluting this world with fear and ignorance." Dian's feet scuffed and tripped about as she backed into the overgrown club, stammering a failed attempt to defend herself. Azrael shadowed over her as she tripped and fell into the grass.

"What do you have to say for yourself?"

Dian pleaded, "I'm sorry."

Azrael laughed and shook her head, "No, you're not."

The angel kneeled over the sobbing woman, gripped her throat, squeezed her face purple, and pushed her into the newly formed earth. "You're nothing," she told Dian as she pushed the woman's choking, thrashing shape deep into the dirt, burying her alive. Dian's face was swallowed by dirt, silencing the shallow screams her final breaths summoned. Azrael growled as she held the woman in the earth. Dian's choking breath was barely audible – slight, subtle puffs that faded with her passing life.

Azrael sighed and pulled her arm from the ground. She wiped the dirt from herself. Disappointment carried her through the wilderness of the club back to the door through which she had first arrived.

It opened back to the gas station.

Domino was sitting on the hood of the car, waiting with her legs crossed. Seeing the state of her sister, she frowned and asked what had happened. "Whisper," was all Azrael said. Domino sighed an agitated breath. Sliding from the hood, she asked, "And the nun?"

"What nun?" Azrael dismissed as she climbed behind the wheel.

XXIX
MUDDY HOT TUB

Whisper wore a funny grin. It held an arm out the window, enjoying the wind rushing around the truck as it sped down the road. April and Caesar were still looking back, processing what had happened in the club. It was more than enough to distract from any heartache, at least on April's end. Caesar was quicker to accept the impossible situations unfolding around them — not that he knew where to place any of it or how to define what was happening. The perplexity of it all simply helped him remain focused on the point. The less he understood about Cupid's place in the universe, the easier it was to maintain a hateful narrative around him. The only thing that needed to make sense was the only thing that did — the pain.

The truck swerved, and April bumped into Caesar. They both fell into each other, startled, helping the other to balance. Whisper was at the wheel, laughing. He had swerved on purpose. He swerved again. Caesar and April toppled over. Caesar opened the back window, poking his head into the truck to complain.

Whisper smiled. "Just having a bit of fun, no need to fluff your tail."

"Is this really the time to be fucking around?"

Whisper's smile sharpened. It patted Caesar on his cheek while it slammed on the brakes. April closed her eyes as she slid on her butt, crashing into Caesar and pinning him against the cab of the truck. Whisper pushed Caesar through the window the moment the truck stopped and came towering over the dazed and confused pair now lying on their backs.

"Not the time for it?" Whisper laughed and said, "When is it ever not the time for a laugh? We are alive. We should always seek to keep our spirits up. Especially after such a close call as the one you aroused with your careless act."

Caesar sat up, annoyed with the thing's behavior, and asked Whisper to explain. Whisper sat on the frame of the truck bed and calmly asked, "Why did you use the bow?"

Caesar shrugged. "How do you know I used it?"

Whisper shook his head. "Caesar, everyone and everything that knows the bow is missing is aware you used it. You shook the heavens when you let that arrow loose."

Caesar scratched his head. It was hard to tell if the ashen figure was upset. Still, there were more questions. "I thought you said nature was slow? That was what was happening, yeah? That tree? Nature trying to restore balance, like you said."

Whisper shrugged. "Usually it is slow. But when the unlawful magic *said-nature* wants to restore is cast, well, there is a tendency for motivation. Magic begets magic. Nothing uses energy more efficiently than nature. There is no singular mind full of thoughts that hinder decisions. It has only a constant reaction with no concept of choice. And the love in that bow is more powerful than anything will ever dream of becoming. It is, truthfully, the most irresponsible creation in the history of history itself."

Caesar huffed, "Well, shit, I'm sorry."

Whisper jumped to its feet and smiled. "Fret not, Caesar the Powerful. Your lapse in good judgment offered a rather rousing engagement." Hopping off the truck, Whisper brought their attention to the hotel it had parked out front of. With its arms out, it smiled and said, "Shall we get a room?"

...

Whisper had filled the body of a plump man in his late forties with a room to himself which Whisper opened with the man's key. April went right for the bed. She was still hungover and trying not to think about her club or Darrel. Caesar dropped the bag and made a gesture to join her. It was the only bed. April smiled at Caesar and patted the spot next to her, welcoming him to rest. Caesar slid into a pillow and sighed an exhausted breath. Their fatigue was far greater than their concern for what was next.

Whisper stood puppeting the plump man at the foot of the bed and asked, "Comfy?"

April was hesitant to speak. She propped herself up on her elbows and asked about the woman with the wings. The plump man's face smiled with a thoughtful expression before telling them both, "Her name is Azrael. Azrael, Archangel of Death. The first angel made — first creature made, in fact. Angels, the gods' precious soldiers. She is here to return the bow to Cupid, so she claims. But I suspect she has no interest in restoring anything. Most curious, the choices she has been making. Perhaps she has found a way to harness the bow for herself. *Maybe that was the nuns' purpose?* One could reshape the universe with that fancy bit of wood you have, Caesar the Great. Could rule all without opposition. All the more reason to end Cupid. Leaving such power to irritate the hearts and minds of desire — irresponsible, wouldn't you say?"

April didn't like the expression Whisper was wearing. Or the tone of its voice, the lofty manner in which it played. She asked, "So we broke some magic law? Is that what this means? Nature itself is against us? We're in some serious trouble, aren't we?" Whisper sighed and shrugged, "In so many words, yes. But it is Cupid's incompetence which has allowed for this event to unfold, which stands as more proof that Caesar's quest is a righteous endeavor. Cupid's carelessness has put the universe in danger. This situation alone is proof there is a flaw to be mended."

April wasn't convinced. "That was an angel going after Caesar. Why would an angel be bad?"

Whisper chuckled. "Is that a serious question? Your world's most famous angel is the Devil." April let herself fall onto her back with a tired huff. She didn't like Whisper, but she didn't know what to do about it. The mention of the Devil had Caesar thinking, and he said, "There was a nun with a cross. She was waving it in my face asking me for the bow. She kept bringing up the Devil. Thought I was working with him." Looking up, Caesar asked Whisper, "Are you the Devil?"

The plump man's face smiled. "There is no Devil, Caesar."

"But there are angels?" April was back up on her elbows. Her brow hung with a serious curve.

Whisper found their suspicion amusing but was tired of questions. It smiled and told them both, "Angels are not what you think they are. They are glorified police of the magical realm. Think of your kind as you do the dwindling species your people protect in wildlife reserves. I can appreciate the bewildering effects our adventure is having on you both. And I understand your doubts in trusting me. But I am all you have, and all I want is for Caesar to succeed in mending his broken heart. And more so, for love to no longer burden the hearts and minds of tomorrow with the same pain that ails you both."

April winced. "What *will* happen if Cupid is killed? For real?"

Whisper covered one of its eyes as it explained, "Love will no longer be a game. That is all."

"The fuck are you doing?"

Whisper smiled. "I have an eye watching over Cupid. I am looking through that eye now."

Whisper had left a bit of itself in the car Azrael was driving, but Cupid was asleep in the back, so it couldn't see him. Where had he gone? Shifting its sight, Whisper had left another bit at the bar where Cupid's party was still happening. To Whisper's surprise, it saw Cupid with a drink, having too much fun. Leaving this line of sight, it told Caesar and April what it saw and that it was going to get Cupid and bring him here, to the room.

"I will be using this man's car," it said, looking through a wallet. "Gregory — I will be using Gregory's car to escort our target here, where you will be hiding, say, in that closet. You, and your fancy pop gun. He will come in, *pop-pop-pop*. Heartbreak is forever abolished from the universe. Any more questions?"

April didn't like any of it. But she didn't want to talk about it with whatever Whisper was. So she said nothing. Caesar didn't want to know anymore. His doubts were frustrating him. He just wanted justice. Wanted it to be over.

Ready to move on, Whisper asked, "Any more inquiries."

April stayed on her back as her arm shot up. "Yeah. I got a question. With all your smoke magic shit, why couldn't you just swoop us up and carry us the fuck outta there?"

"Bread crumbs. Magic leaves traces. Carrying you both like that and this far would leave one hell of a trail."

No one said anything.

Whisper clapped the hands it possessed. "Wonderful. Sit tight, my wonderful companions."

Gregory's body opened the door, and Whisper left.

April and Caesar lay together in silence, composing their thoughts. It wasn't until Caesar needed a cigarette that anything was said.

"You mind if I smoke?"

"Go ahead."

Caesar sparked a used cigarette, and April sighed. Caesar could tell she had more on her mind. "What is it?"

"It's just... this doesn't feel right."

"How do you mean?"

April sat up and started to explain, "Magic being real is one thing. That shit's gonna take a while to sync up. But killing love?" Caesar didn't want to hear anymore. He smoked and turned away from her.

April stood up and said, with her tone sympathetic and concerned, "Listen, I get your pain, I really do. But to remove love? You can't kill love. Shit ain't up to you. It's not up to anybody."

Caesar winced. "So why'd you tag along? I told you what I was doing." April chuckled and said, "Motherfucker, I didn't believe you. Who the fuck would, seriously? I thought it was a game you were playing with some experimental therapy shit, like in one of those stupid Lifetime movies. How else would I explain the crazy shit you were telling me?"

Caesar got defensive. "So what, then? What do you suggest? You want to stop me?" April sighed. She didn't want to upset Caesar. She just knew everything was over their heads and out of control, and killing wasn't right. Killing a god seemed even more immoral. Doing her best to sound on his side, she told him, "I think you should give up the bow, and we cut our losses. There is more to all this than we could possibly understand."

Caesar shook his head. "There is no going back for me. Cupid has to pay. That's it."

April sighed. Her compassion for Caesar was obvious in her face, but her fear for their lives was greater. Her fear for what would happen.

"Do you really trust this Whisper thing?"

Caesar took a long drag and exhaled. He didn't want to think about how scared he was, how much more scared he'd be if April wasn't with him. But she was trying to stop him. It hurt to say it, but he had to do it. He told her, "If you want out, then go."

April didn't want to upset Caesar anymore. And she wasn't going to leave him. She stepped for the door and told him, "I'm gonna go see what the deal is with food around here. We should eat. Anything specific you're craving?"

Caesar took another thoughtful drag and said, "Tuna salad sandwich."

April paused. "A tuna salad sandwich from a hotel in the desert?"

Caesar sort of scowled, "Yes, a tuna-fucking-sandwich from a shit hotel nowhere near water. Thank you."

April nodded with agitation and left. The door closed, and Caesar thought about what she had said, and about his own doubt with trusting Whisper. Thinking about why he was there, about *her*, Caesar reached into the bag and pulled the weapon from the impossible darkness. It was heavy. He turned the cylinder around, trying to find a way to open it, so he could count the bullets. But he couldn't figure it out. Tossing the relic onto the bed, puffing away on his cigarette, Caesar reached back into the bag for Tux. Still stiff, the cat came out, the bow hooked on his paw. Caesar shook Tux, dropping the bag as the bow fell to the floor. He didn't care about the bow at that moment — he just wanted the cat.

Caesar sat on the floor with his back against the bed and Tux in his lap. Smoking and petting his petrified buddy, Caesar started to cry. It wasn't much, just a few runaway tears, the building tremor in the back of his throat like an emotional warning. An imminent meltdown was a few memories away.

When his cigarette ended, he looked for a place to put the butt. There was nothing left to smoke from it, so he didn't want to pocket it. But he did anyway. There was an arrow half out of the bag on the floor that caught his eye. Setting Tux aside, he reached in and pulled the quiver free. Poking around the arrow bag, he inspected the pockets looking for the picture he had found before, careful not to pull the wrong thing this time.

Along with a little bag of weed and a heart-shaped key chain, Caesar found the picture. He couldn't tell how old it was, but he knew it was older than him. There was a handwritten note on the back in a language he couldn't read. The woman in the photo had a dark complexion, and she appeared wealthy. She was smiling. It was a real smile, not a fake smile for the camera's sake.

. . .

Cupid was tossed onto the bed in the room the angels had been given. Don't speak, she ordered. Cupid was shaking. He gestured his fingers over his lips as if sealing a ghosted zipper. Azrael shook her head at him before turning away. "If he talks, hurt him," Azrael told her sister. Domino pulled a chair up to the bed and smiled at the frightened Cupid. "Are you going to play nice, Phillip?" Cupid blinked with a nervous breath and Domino shook her figure at him, "Don't answer that, I'd have to hurt you if you spoke."

Azrael used the front door to connect directly to Caesar's room. To her surprise, there were new faces.

"Who are your friends?" she asked as she closed the door behind her, amused by the sight. Teddy and Frances were both awake, tied back to back, with tape over their mouths. The three nuns stood up right away. Gwen greeted the angel with apologies. Azrael smiled, letting her halo fill with light as she walked around the bound men and said, "I'm sure there is a wonderful story to explain this. But I'm not interested in hearing it now." Frances recognized her, but the halo was hard to believe. It was just as confusing to Teddy.

Azrael smiled at the two confused men. Soon they would love her, and their confusion would forever be over. She put her hand on Teddy's head, petting it as she explained, "We have

Cupid in our room. When the man comes, the man with the bow, I need you to take it from him. Do not give him a chance to speak. He will only trick you. You must be swift. Don't even let him know you are coming for him. Grab the bag and run to me. Do you understand?"

They nodded.

"Good. Gwen, you should return to your post. We need eyes everywhere." Azrael returned to the door, and Madeline asked where Dian was. With the doorknob in hand, Azrael told them, "She is in Heaven. God bless, sisters."

. . .

Whisper was a rolling vapor, easing its way to the steam that poured from a hot tub where Cupid was presently relaxing. The party was still alive and well. It was not as booming, however. These parties always worked in waves before they finally washed out. It was low tide. The dance floor was resting. The party-goers were gathered in little herds charging their batteries for the next wave.

The big love god had a martini in hand, his feet propped up out of the hot tub, getting a pedicure from a horned succubus. Another was massaging his scalp. Cupid was flirting, telling the creatures pampering him about all the sexual miracles he was going to perform on them once he was rested. They giggled and blushed.

"Can't wait," a voice close by whispered.

Cupid popped a cucumber slice from his eye and uttered uncomfortably, "I know that voice." The steam before him slowly took the form of Whisper's smiling face, and said, "You do know me." Cupid flinched, his feet dropping into the hot tub, head springing up into the nose of the succubus behind him. She slapped his head and stomped away. Cupid apologized, but she was already gone. And he was being pulled at. Whisper was becoming a muddy version of itself as it turned the hot tub into a thick sludge. The mud slid in close to Cupid, wrapping its arms around him and grinning.

"You look nervous. I didn't mean to startle you."

Cupid gulped. "Really? Find that hard to believe."

Whisper laughed. "Old friend, my apologies. It was just that I could have sworn you left this place. What did Azrael want with you?"

Cupid was trying not to shake. His eyes lied before he could even start to say, "Yeah, that whole thing — just talking. You know angels."

"I do."

Whisper's grip tightened. Cupid chuckled a quick, nervous laugh and said, "Oh man, you want anything? I can get you a drink."

"No, thanks."

Whisper let go of Cupid and casually slid around to the opposite end of the hot tub. "So, what were you and the angel talking about?" Its fingers playfully patted the bubbling mush.

Cupid scratched at his head, trying to sound calm as he answered, "Ah, shit. It was nothing. Azrael was just at my place and thought I was there, and I wasn't, and so she was just checking in on, ah, like a fucking trespasser situation. *Possible* trespasser. It was nothing."

Whisper wasn't smiling then. Its directionless stone eyes were locked onto the nervous lovebug. "Why are you lying to me?" it asked.

Cupid gulped. "What?"

Whisper's face remained cold. "You know the thing about changelings is the smell." Cupid turned white, and Whisper grinned terribly.

Cupid's form shriveled quickly, wrinkling back into the chameleon it was. "Where is Cupid?" Whisper asked, its tone deadly. The shorty tried to flee, slipping against the muddy wall of the tub, whimpering and pleading for its life. Whisper pulled the shorty into the muddy water. Hands forming around its neck. Whisper was a tall, wet bog looming over the captured shifter. A deep, rumbling growl vibrated from its throat. The shorty was choking on mud, squirming and crying for mercy. Whisper tightened its grip, ignoring its pathetic cries. "I don't appreciate, being lied to." The shorty face sunk under the muddy, bubbling water. Whisper took a deep breath while it thrashed. A breath to calm itself. The shorty resurfaced and gasped for air. Whisper's shape melted into the mud, its face washing up close to the changelings. Hands wrapping around its wrinkled cheeks.

"Please don't kill. Please, I've done nothing wrong. *When the boss is away, as the boss, I will play.* Wasn't trying to fool you. Just enjoying the party was all, I swear. We do it all the time."

Whisper smiled. "Relax. You're fine. I just wish to know where your chubby leader has gone to." The shorty paused for a breath before telling another lie.

"I don't know."

Whisper sighed and then growled. Climbing from the tub, Whisper dragged the wrinkly creature by its ankle. It grabbed at everything it could, begging for its life as Whisper dragged it outside.

Cupid's bus blasted open as the shorty was thrown in, crashing and tumbling into the sofa. Whisper stepped aboard, looking like a swamp creature. Sloppy steps gradually dried behind its ashen feet. The shifter curled into a ball on the sofa, shaking and begging for its life.

Whisper sighed and sat next to the frightened creature, petting and hushing it like a puppy. Whisper assured the shorty, "Calm yourself. I'm not going to kill you. I just want to know where Cupid is. My friend, Cupid, I'm worried about him, that's all. I know you are only wanting to protect him, this is why you lie."

With a relaxed shrug, Whisper cradled the frightened creature and said, "You and I want the same thing. Cupid's safety. Our deer friend. So, where did the big important archangel take him?"

The shorty covered its face, trembling as it spoke. "They're trying to get his bow back. Went to that guy's place. Caesar, I think his name is."

Whisper put its hand over its chest. "Heavens no. Cupid lost his bow?"

"He did, and the angels were only trying to help."

Whisper pushed the shorty to its feet and yawned. "Well, little buddy. Let's not waste time here. Lead the way."

"To Cupid? You want me to bring you to Cupid?"

"Yes," Whisper said, as if answering the dumbest question ever asked.

The shorty stepped towards the driver's seat, but Whisper grabbed it, saying, "We can't take this, now, can we?

Would raise suspicion. I have a car out front to keep us inconspicuous. Come now, we must not keep Greg waiting any longer."

Whisper pushed at the creature to keep the pace up, and stepped off the bus. The door shut, and from the cupboard under the kitchen sink poked Vivianne's frightened and curious head.

...

An average tourist couple was checking into the Inn. A timid Gwen was doing her best to remember what Teddy had shown her. The couple was thin, tan, and aging. They had that *"kids are all at college and we're finally free again"* vibe. Big vacation smiles carried their suitcases to their room, and in they went. The door closed, and they both took in a pleased breath, approving of the room. They were husband and husband. The taller husband let the suitcase fall. It opened when it hit the ground, and the real Cupid came spilling out, sweating and gasping for air. "Fuck me, it's a swamp in there."
"Sorry, Cups," the shorter husband said.

"Yeah, best case we had for the job," the taller husband added.

"Meant for one of us."

"Yeah Cups, we compact easier than you."

Cupid rolled over onto his back, catching his breath. The shapeshifters shrunk into their shriveled forms and continued to unpack. They had a cooler filled with booze and were eager to start drinking.

"Wanna drink, Cups?"

Cupid sat up with a yes. A cold beer found his hand, and he chugged it down. Peering through the blinds he asked what room the angel was in.

"Two down from the check-in," a shorty answered, jumping onto the bed with a beer at his lips.

"But we saw her going into another," the other shorty mentioned, joining the first on the bed.

"Right. Decoy Cupid is in one, but don't know what's in the other."

Cupid pulled a chair up to the window and perched himself with a slit in the blinds to a view of the parking lot. His shorties were jumping up and down on the bed, asking what he wanted to do while they waited.

Cupid shrugged. "I don't know. How much beer did you bring?"

XXX
EARLY CHECK-OUT

The hotel had room service, but April was out of the room, so she ordered at the front desk. She told the clerk she'd prefer to bring the food up herself. She and Caesar needed a moment alone.

Caesar was still sitting against the bed. An empty bottle sat by his feet. Another bottle was tucked in his lap, helping him breathe. A family photo had surfaced. His pregnant ex was frozen in his hand, smiling at nothing. Silent tears burned in Caesar's eyes. He could feel the tears in his heart ripping deeper into his chest, the sensation locked in a constant loop. The thumping nuisance seemed to regenerate the moment it was snatched away, just to be snatched away again and again. He was falling forever away from her hands, always just out of reach. Never fully vanishing, never there. Always hopelessly lost. Always pain. Always the screaming lament hollowing out his mind.

Killing Cupid had to silence this relentless howl.

It had to.

He needed to be free from it.

Tux's tail freed Caesar from his pity parade. Realizing it almost inspired a laugh, a fast little rattle of joy that was chased with a final flurry of tears.

"You're awake."

Tux was pawing at something he couldn't see. Whatever he was batting at was humming. Caesar moved to look and he saw the cat pawing at Cupid's bow. His little white paw strumming the string that hung magically taut from end to end. The strum sent out a little tune that magical things found arousing.

Things like nature.

Caesar pulled Tux from the bow feeling uneasy. The room felt like it was moving. Caesar nervously looked up. The nice plant that once decorated the space was now crawling up the wall.

Caesar panicked, spilling his beer as he rolled away from the bow with Tux in his arms just as the plant sent a long leaf whipping down. With his foot, he pulled the bow away from the plant's reach. The wall was covered in green. Vegetation claimed the ceiling. Dozens of monstrous leaves sprawled out, ready to attack.

Caesar rushed into the hallway. Stuffing his bag with the magical items, he put his back into the door, severing a searching leaf as it slammed shut. Tux had jumped into April's arms. She dropped the food she was just bringing for them to eat. Everyone looked down as the squirming green leaf flopped and shriveled. Relieved breaths calmed their panic enough for words. April addressed the scene. "What the fuck did you do?" Caesar shook his hand and pointed to Tux. "Wasn't me. He did it." April pulled Tux close and winced. "Did what?" Caesar moved to begin explaining but was interrupted by a thud that shook the door.

The plant wasn't done.

Caesar turned with caution to face the room. Another thud slammed against the door. April reached a hand around Caesar's arm, no longer interested in knowing what the cat did. "Shouldn't we be checking out?" *Thud*, the door rattled louder. Caesar and April inched closer together, their eyes fixed on the room. The sound of scrapes and squirming vines clawed from behind the door. "Caesar, I don't like this," April said, pulling his arm with a bit of force as the door was violently ripped from its hinges, crumbling wood vanishing into the furious jungle the room had become. Tux leapt from April's arms as she shrieked, pulling Caesar into her chest, her arm around his throat squeezing his face purple. She was running before Caesar could pry himself free. Like a helpless bag hanging from her shoulder, April pulled Caesar down the hall. Vines filled the passage like a wave of green snakes. Climbing the walls. Slithering up and around the ceiling. Rushing along the floor toward their fleeing feet. Wiggling tentacles whipped out and caught a foot. April stumbled and Caesar's throat was free to gasp for air.

In the lobby, the man attending the front desk was looking toward the racket he couldn't identify. His head was slightly cocked, brow pinched in the middle with a troubled fold, and his ears leaning out to place the peculiar rumble. The sound of feet stomped ever vigilantly his way. To his surprise, the first thing he saw come around the corner was a black cat – a scared black cat that hurried past his feet toward the door. There was no cat door for Tux to escape through. His only option was to paw at the door and meow for support. The man gave the cat a quick look before his gaze went right back to the approaching rumble. When April and Caesar stumbled into the lobby the man raised his voice. "Please don't run in the halls." They ignored him. Didn't even give him the slightest of looks. They were too frightened to notice him. To notice his arm reaching out as they ran past.

"What did I just say? *No running!*"

The sprawling growth of aggressive vines fed into the lobby. The man at the counter turned to yell at whoever it was to stop running. Only there was no one to yell at. The man at the counter was lifted into the air by the green mass, screaming as it swallowed him. The front desk disintegrated as the wild growth twirled and stretched itself out further. April and Caesar were rushing to the parking lot. A tidal wave of green exploded through the doors after them.

The truck they had come in was still parked out front, the key Whisper generated still in the ignition. They were driving away the moment they entered the truck. Racing away from the expanding greenery.

Pulling onto the road, they both shouted, cheering and slapping their hands in victory. Caesar hit the horn in excitement, his heart beating too fast to count. Tux jumped into Caesar's lap, and aggressively pushed his face into his jaw, purring like a lawnmower.

Watching the horticultural nightmare vanish in the side mirror, April laughed and asked where they were going. Caesar didn't have an answer. Where could they go? They weren't even safe from plants.

Caesar dug a cigarette from his shirt pocket and said, "Well, Whisper left for Cupid. So that's where we'll go. I've been a few times – shitty little bar like any other. But they have curly fries, so we go sometimes. Place ain't far."

April winced at him. "Curly fries?" She found it amusing that he felt the need to share that detail. Caesar didn't pick up her tone, and so he answered, "Yeah. They have regular fries, too, but I mean, when there are curly fries, why would you order anything else?" April shook her head at Caesar. He looked at her, looked at the road, and then back at her.

"What?"

...

Vivianne was sitting at the bar. Some of the building was back to normal, but most of it wasn't. Mostly it was a mess, like the streets of New York City in the first hour of the New Year – desperately in need of a cleaning. The bartender was on the floor, overdosed with magic, glowing from his eyes and humming something unidentifiable. So Vivianne served herself.

She had made herself a few drinks.

With everyone gone, she didn't know where to go. So she drank and waited. They would come back eventually. But eventually was taking its time, so she was getting a little drunk. Getting drunk and questioning once again her capabilities to help Cupid. It all only seemed to get more out of control. More over her head.

Tux hopped onto the bar and rubbed his head into her hands. Vivianne laughed at how aggressive he was. "Hello, Mr. Kitty. Where did you come from?" Caesar came in through the front entrance, asking what happened. Vivianne kept petting Tux. "Oh, well, that is not so simple to explain, I'm afraid. Do you believe in magic?"

Caesar stepped behind the bar, asking if Cupid had been there. Viviane smiled. "Oh, so you know already. Ah, yes, Cupid was here. But he is in trouble, I suspect. Some angels came and took him away. Only it was not him."

Caesar poured himself a drink, and one for April. He held a bottle up for Vivianne, who nodded her head. He asked her to elaborate. Vivianne swayed playfully with her answer, saying, "I told him he would only get into more trouble. But they were on a lot of drugs, you see, and were very paranoid. So one of his disgusting little shapeshifters turned into Cupid, and, well, the angels took the fake Cupid away. Would not want to be around when they find out."

She smiled at Caesar and April and asked, "How do you know Cupid?" Curious that they were both human. "You are human, are you not?"

"Yeah, we're human."

Vivianne smiled with a long and troubled breath. Pouring herself another drink she huffed. "What a funny thing, all of this. So much trouble. So much pain."

Caesar prodded. "So, where is the real Cupid?"

"Went chasing after his decoy, to see what the angels are up to."

Caesar took a drink and sighed. "I'm sorry. Who are you?"

"My goodness, where are my manners? I am Vivianne," she said, holding her hand out with a welcoming smile. Caesar shook her hand and introduced April and himself. Vivianne lit up. "You are *the* Caesar? You have the bow, do you not?"

Caesar nervously pulled at his bag. "I do."

Vivianne got serious. "Well, what are you doing with it? Cupid needs his bow back. He is a mess without it. Not that he wasn't before, but it's so much worse. Come, we must return it." Vivianne got up off the barstool, but Caesar wasn't moving.

"What are you doing? They went to where you live. Let's go. Take us there."

Caesar didn't want this woman to get in his way. If she knew what he was up to he worried she would stop him. But he also didn't want to lie to her. He wanted to believe people would understand. He needed people to understand. He couldn't be the only one who wanted Cupid dead. Vivianne was too drunk for patience. "What is it? Why do you keep his bow? You have so much in your eyes. You look as if you will explode. Spit it out."

Caesar sighed and told her about his plan to kill Cupid.

Vivianne laughed. "That is the stupidest thing I have ever heard. Are you pulling my leg?"

April clapped her hands. "Thank you. I tried telling him. Shit is dumb as hell."

Caesar crossed his arms. "You were agreeing with me when I first told you."

"The sentiment, yes. But for the record, I did not believe you were serious at first. Now, I feel your pain, Caesar. You have every right to feel what you feel, to be pissed the fuck off. And I agree it's fucked some drunk god is running around forcing people to be in love. I'm not about that. Love should be a natural thing. But killing the guy? I don't know. I just don't know."

Vivianne laughed. Caesar asked what was so funny. She took the bottle from his hand and poured them all another round before saying, "You want to end heartache. This is a romantic thought, but, Caesar, that is part of what it all is. Love is not worth it if there is no fiery pit of turmoil hidden beneath each wonderful kiss. Everyone knows this. Children know this. I don't mean to offend you. But we need love, and we cannot have it without the risk of suffering lurking around it." Vivianne pushed the refilled glasses toward her new friends and smiled. "Drink and let's be gone. Whatever will happen will happen, but we should go to where it will happen, so we do not miss it."

"You're not going to stop me?"

"I don't think you will do this. But no, I will not try to stop you. This stupid idea of yours is between you and him."

...

Cupid's big love bus was rolling down Route 66. Caesar was driving. April sat with Tux on the sofa. Vivianne was in the passenger seat, observing Caesar. His assassination mission intrigued her. She had a small sketchpad in her lap and drew Caesar while she dug into his story. Caesar held a beer bottle over the wheel while she probed him with questions, taking little breaths from it as he revealed the motivation for his hunt. She watched as he took bigger breaths from his bottle and took note of why. She took some time to think it all over before saying, "I can see in your eyes you are more than this. This pain you are fighting. I think I can appreciate why you think killing Cupid will help. But I still know it is stupid. And I think you and Cupid should maybe just talk."

Caesar rolled his eyes. It made Vivianne smile. She told Caesar, "You know what? I have seen the same pain you have in someone else's eyes."

Caesar winced. "Who's?"

"Cupid's."

XXXI
ABRUPT CHAOS

Gregory's car was approaching the Inn. One of Cupid's wrinkled shorties sat behind the wheel. Gregory's body was sitting in the front passenger seat, filled with Whispers smoke. Whisper was leaning over the dash, asking what room Cupid was in.

"Fuck if I know," the shorty huffed.

"They didn't tell you the room number? What good are you?"

Whisper poured out of Gregory and slipped into the engine, overheating it to a stall just before the Inn. The shapeshifter pulled the parking brake and cursed at Whisper, who steamed into the air outside with a subtle chuckle. The shapeshifter was relieved it left, thinking it should do the same. Wishing it had the balls to just run. Whisper was far too frightening. So, it just sat there and worried.

The wrinkly creature spent so much time worrying it had forgotten Greg was there. When the human woke up his screaming caught the shorty by surprise. The changeling screamed back at him, and they both sat screaming at each other. Screaming and slapping and pushing and screaming. Screaming as Whisper returned through the vents. Screaming as Whisper climbed its smoke into the shapeshifter, taking control. A sight that had Greg gasping for air. Whisper smiled and mimicked the man with another scream. Screamed and shook the shapeshifter's head around like a maniac. Greg shrunk into himself, his back pressing against the door as he screeched in fear. Whisper stopped the insanity abruptly, and Greg froze with his hand on his chest, terrified, heaving breaths, his mind racing. Whisper leaned the wrinkly creature's face close and smiled at Greg. Nose to nose, Whisper reached the shorty's wrinkly arm around and grabbed the door handle as it told Greg, "Run away." Whisper opened the door and Greg fell out of the car. Fighting to his feet, he took off down the road as fast as he could. Whisper waved to him and joyfully sighed. "Farewell, Greg."

…

The angels both stood over the fake Cupid. It was snoring and drooling. Azrael raised her nose to him. "Disgusting creature." Domino laughed. "I don't remember him being so big." Azrael sighed. "We should have him fall in love with aerobics."

"You're funny. We could have him run himself to death."

Azrael slapped Cupid across his face. He sprung up in a panic, not knowing where he was or what was going on, morphing immediately into the shape of the handsome Black cowboy he was just dreaming of. The angels' faces struck with alarm and outrage. The sight was so upsetting it frightened the shorty into pissing itself. It was still somewhat in the dream Azrael had slapped it from and couldn't quite place how it was where it was. But the shapeshifter knew it had done something wrong. It recognized the two powerful angels, both of whom were now looming over it. Noted their disdain. In a purposefully pathetic voice, the malleable being asked, "What did I do?"

Azrael flared with rage, her sword sinking into the creature's heart before it knew there was a sword to fear. Its death was quick. A sudden burst of shock and pain. A flinch and an aching breath. Azrael left her blade where it was, pinning the chameleon's lifeless shape to the bed. Turning from the act without pause, Azrael opened the front door, connecting it to the bar that had been hosting Cupid's big party. Only, the party was over. The place was empty. She had no words. She had been duped. And of all the creatures to be tricked by, how disarming it was. They were worthless hooligans. Dimwitted, drug-addicted, sex-depraved hooligans.

Azrael stomped into the bar with a heavy foot. She kicked stools and tossed tables, her eyes glowing white with rage. She pushed the back door from its frame, sending it to the ground with a heavy crash. Azrael sneered with an ill-composed frown.

Where the hell was Cupid's bus?

...

Cupid's big, rusted love bus pulled into the lot at the Inn. It was too big for a spot. It stopped in front of the check-in counter that was parallel to Caesar's room and parked. Across the lot, two fat and sweaty fingers were stuck between a pair of blinds. Two eyes burning behind them.

Cupid watched from the window. His face hid in the blinds as he commented in a confused tone, "My bus just pulled up." A shorty shaped as King Edward VII, also known as "Dirty Bertie," was sitting on the bed wearing only a robe and holding a mirror. Another shorty shaped as the Roman emperor Caligula was sitting behind him dabbing lines of cocaine onto the mirror. "Your bus, you say?"

"How strange."

"Yeah, Cups, very strange indeed."

King Edward VII bounced off the bed and pranced to Cupid's side with the mirror in hand, a glass straw tapping Cupid's shoulder. Cupid took the straw and inhaled a line. The white spice hit him hard and he winced, coughed a bit, then beat his chest with a cheer before turning back to look through the slit in the blinds. "Who the fuck's driving my bus?" Cupid uttered, sniffing and rubbing his nose. The king shrugged and blew away a line of his own. Smudging the tray with his finger and rubbing his gums, he told Cupid they were running low on blow. Cupid sniffed hard, trying to clear his nose while he glared at the shorty. "We have plenty of everything else. Can you focus on the fucking... the fucking goddamn thing we're doing? Why we're here and all that?" Cupid turned back to the window, muttering to himself, *"Fucking Christ."*

Cupid tensed, his hand tangling in the blinds a little as he attempted to compose himself with what was going on outside. Another one of his shorties was walking by. It wasn't hiding in human form. The short, pink, shriveled testicle marched bare-assed across the parking lot for all the world to witness. This wasn't a part of the plan. Cupid rubbed his eyes. "What the fuck is it doing?!"

"What is it, Cups?"

"It's... I don't know which one...." Turning to the two shorties behind him, he waved his hand around trying to place the creature's name. Giving up, he finished his thought with an agitated, "It's one of you."

The king tossed his robe to the side and asked in a bratty tone, "Cups, do you not know our names?"

Cupid rolled his eyes. "Fuck you," he said, then returned back to the scene unfolding outside.

The shorty entered the bus and Cupid cursed. "God-fucking-damnit, the fuck is going on?"

. . .

The shorty took two steps onboard the bus before it fell flat onto its face. Whisper effortlessly pushed out, as if the creature was nothing more than a discarded coat. Finding Caesar in the driver's seat, the ashen being said curtly, "I thought I told you to wait."

Caesar shrugged. "Plans changed."

Whisper smiled. "For the best. Everyone is here, it seems, even Cupid. Somewhere. I'll find the angels first, and then we can lure the lovebug out. Too risky at the moment. We need you to remain out of sight for the time being."

Vivianne gave Whisper a judgmental look. Whisper curled an eye toward her. "What's the matter? Do I have something in my teeth?"

. . .

Domino held her eye to the peephole in her room, peering at the view of the bus. Looking back at the dead cowboy pinned to the bed, she figured there was nothing to guard anymore, so she might as well investigate.

...

Back on the bus, Whisper was pulling the god-killing relic from the impossible satchel and forcing it into Caesar's hands. "You wait here for the big guy to emerge and then make your move," it told him. Caesar seemed timid, but Whisper leaned close to him. "You aren't doubting yourself, are you? Think of what he did, Caesar. Your wife and child. He will only continue this if you let him."

Vivianne stood up from the passenger seat. Tux ran to her and jumped in her arms. Assertively shaking her head, she expressed, "Why are you helping Caesar to murder that sad creature? And just who the hell are you anyway?"

Whisper ignored her, stepping back to the door with a finger on the little curtain that blocked the little window. With a calm flick, the curtain opened and Whisper's stone eyes looked out. Domino was making her way to the bus. *Oh joy*, Whisper thought, as it grinned with a pleased breath. "Who am I?" the ashen being asked Vivianne. Its ember-kissed form flaked into smoke as it answered, "I'm just the wind, having a bit of fun." The smoke that was Whisper sucked into a round cloud which hardened before their eyes and dropped from the air. A dense ball of darkness hit the floor with a harsh whack.

...

Domino reached out to open the door to the bus when a loud crash popped from inside. It was a deep thud that played a heavy game with the vessel's suspension. The angel paused for a brief calculating moment but couldn't think of what the sound could be. She opened the door and saw the dark ball lying in the dent it made on the floor. She looked at April, Vivianne, and the cat. With a stiff brow, her eyes returned to the ball asking a question she would never finish. *What the fuck is that?* was the question.

What the fuck? was all she said.

Whisper flew from the floor in a blur. The force of it shattered every window on the bus. It punched into Domino, sending her soaring through the air. Its speed was remarkable. She smashed through the wall of Caesar's room almost the moment the ball met her gut. The bus swayed from its swift departure, and everyone on board felt around to make sure they were still all in one piece. Tux had fled, leaving Vivianne with a serious scratch across her face.

From the dust and debris of the crash site, Whisper strolled back into the daylight, brushing bits that didn't belong from its shoulders. Smiling a big pleased grin, it formed itself into the dusty air and blew away.

Caesar was in the passenger window of the bus watching the dust settle from his room. Vivianne's question bounced around his mind. *And just who the hell are you anyway?* Who was Whisper? What was going on, really?

As the hole revealed Caesar's room, it revealed Frances and Teddy. The image started Caesar's heart with a sense of urgency.

The crash in the room had left everyone stunned. Madeline and Lynn were lying on the floor beside Caesar's futon. The wall that once held the front door was now folded into the room. The kitchen was mashed under the bit of it that still held onto the building. The front door was in pieces scattered across the floor. A ceiling fan was swinging overhead. It was the first thing the two nuns noticed. The second was the pair of legs sticking out from the wall beside the bathroom. They recognized them as an angels, only they didn't know which angel. They held onto one another, wedged themselves closer to the dusty futon, and silently prayed.

Footsteps entered the room, hurried feet kicking around debris. Lynn braved an eye over the edge of the futon and quickly recoiled.

"What is it?" Madeline asked in terror.

"It's him!" Lynn whispered with a harsh and frightened voice.

Caesar stepped over his disheveled mattress and pulled the tape from Frances' face. He threw his face into Caesar's chest and thanked him. "Jesus-fucking-god-damn-Christ, little buddy! Just what the in the actual fuck is going on here?"

Caesar untied his arms. Teddy was bouncing himself close, mumbling under his taped mouth. Caesar asked if they were hurt. Frances grabbed hold of him. "Am I alright? I don't know, man. Am I? Are you? What the fuck just blew through the goddamn door, the big bad wolf?" Teddy was pushing himself into Frances, who reached over and yanked the tape from his face. Teddy yelped and began yammering the most broken English he had ever spoken. Frances agreed with him as he untied his own legs, Caesar untying Teddy. Frances stood up. "You know your sister is looking for you? She's into something freaky, man."

"I don't have a sister."

"You what?"

April stepped into the room, asking if everyone was okay. Frances found himself momentarily distracted by her. She noticed him checking her out and gave him a *not-the-time* look before doubling back and giving him a *not-so-bad-yourself* nod. Teddy was still rattling off a million unrelated words. Frances pulled Teddy to his feet and asked, "Caesar, buddy, what the fuck is going on? Pretty sure these women are nuns. One of 'em hit me upside the head with a pan." Caesar looked around at his ravaged room. "Nuns? What nuns?"

"Women of the cloth, man. Listen, something fucked up is going on. Now, where the fuck have you been? I mean, fuck, Caesar. There's a giant fucking hole in the wall."

Caesar started to explain but stopped. A box of memories had blown open from the angelic missile. Pictures of his lost love were scattered around the floor. The last pieces of her he had were now strewn about in dirt. Relics of his life tossed around like trash. Letters she had written. Notes. Little drawings. Proof that love was real. That he had it. That it had him. Caesar didn't know if he should give up or push on. Was Vivianne right? Was this stupid? Frances had found Domino's legs. He reached for the radio on his uniform, wondering how the hell he was going to call this scene in.

The two nuns were holding each other, searching for the inspiration to strike. This was their moment. The man Satan had possessed was standing before them. The mission God himself had bestowed upon them was here. God was watching. God was judging. Lynn jumped up and pulled out the baton Azrael had given her, shouting for the world to hear, "Stop right there!" Everyone turned just as she whipped her wrist and the baton slipped from her hand. Caesar ducked as the thing flew out of the broken room and skipped across the parking lot.

April was at her right away, growling a serious, "Hell no." Lynn tensed up and closed her eyes as April tackled her to the ground. Frances, still trying to call the mess in over his radio, reached out to pull April off the nun as Madeline appeared. She screamed and closed her eyes, unleashing an aimless cloud of pepper spray.

...

Azrael stepped back from the bar into her motel room, frustration unfurling from her posture. She was ashamed she had been fooled by Cupid and his wrinkled little perverts. The angel didn't wear humiliation well. Her pride demanded revenge. She pulled the sword from the dead cowboy and returned the blade to the inner folds of her robe. She could hear screams and moans from the room next door. Already annoyed by it before seeing whatever it could be, she stepped outside, stopping immediately when she saw Cupid's bus. *Tame your temper*, she told herself. More screaming and moaning from next door pulled her attention around. The hole in Caesar's room was concerning. *How long have I been gone?* she wondered. Making her way to the crater to observe the mess, Azrael shook her head. Everyone was weeping with red, wet, stung eyes, coughing and whining. The sight was pathetic. April was holding Lynn in a chokehold, both crying red. Caesar was blindly digging around the dirt for pictures. Frances was stumbling about and hacking into his radio. Teddy was in the fetal position. And Madeline was blinking through her tears, warning everyone with the threat of more pepper spray. She was facing no one. The whole room was in ruin. Then she saw her sister's legs. Azrael stormed inside, pushing Frances to his ass as she passed. Domino's top half was missing. Guts spilled out from her legs in a pool of blood and dirt. Tears cut into Azrael's face like a cold blade. She would burn them all. She would turn her Makers into pets and force them to watch her burn their precious Earth and all the people they let fill it.

"I will burn you all," the angel muttered.

Azrael roared, her eyes glowing white, halo burning, and wings out. She shouted and demanded the bow be given up. "Enough of this. Give them the bow, Caesar." She marched up to him and repeated the order. Caesar, still on all fours, looked up to her through his burning eyes, confused. The angel pushed her foot into him, sending him onto his back. Caesar tried to protest but the angel stepped on his chest. "Madeline!" she ordered. "This is your moment. God is watching." Madeline stumbled close. Azrael pushed her foot into Caesar and demanded, "Now, give her the bow."

Wincing through his stinging eyes, Caesar felt around himself. His bag was gone. *I must have left it on the bus*, he thought. He coughed, "I don't have it." The angel sighed with frustration. Her fists clenched. She was tempted to cut them all down. "What do you mean, you do not have it?"

"I don't have it."

Azrael could picture her blade swinging through Caesar, then effortlessly dissecting the useless holy women. She could make quick work of everyone in the room. Why stop there? She could dance her blade around the motel, drag blood across the globe, exterminate the entire human infestation. *Screw the bow*, she thought.

"Azrael, my spoiled adversary. How about that duel?"

Whisper appeared in the parking lot. Azrael turned and stood guarded, smirking as she drew her sword. Whisper puffed its brow. "Cute stick." An ashen hand opened, and a sword burned into shape. The King of Shadows held its weapon up and examined the sharp black edge with an arrogant smile. "This should be fun."

And it would have been fun, too. A fight for the ages. An epic tale told around countless campfires for centuries to come. Had Vivianne not found the bow and arrow, the world would have shaken under their legendary swordplay. She put little thought into her choice to use the bow. She didn't care for how this fiery creature had been acting. A little love would do it some good.

The magical arrow stuck with a hard thunk. Whisper stumbled forward and dropped to a knee, dazed from the hit, dazed from the enchantment fusing into every fiber of its being.

Azrael relaxed her sword and took a calm step toward her foe. She smiled with a, "Tsk-tsk-tsk. And what will we love, oh King of Shadows? What could you hold dear in that dark rock of a heart?" Whisper looked up with a crystal blue tear jumping from its stone black eye. Azrael's proud grin slipped away with the look it gave her. It was her it wept for.

"Oh, Azrael, Archangel of Death. My sweet adversary. I—"

Azrael swung her blade through its words, severing its head clean off its shoulders. The ashen crown met the ground and broke into a pile of lifeless rocks. The angel sneered as the rest of Whisper crumbled into stones. *What a pathetic thing*, she thought. The dust would talk no more.

Cupid stepped out of his room, eyes ablaze with coke. Sweat slicked his forehead. He jogged to his bow, ecstatic to see Vivianne with it. Azrael aimed her sword at him and he skidded to a halt, hands up, eyes wide and darting back and forth from his bow to the angel to Vivianne. His nose was snow white with blow. Sniffing and snorting.

Azrael ordered, "Go back inside, Phillip."

"What? But my bow."

"Now."

"The fuck, Azrael? You said you were helping me."

"I am. I'm helping everyone. Now go back in while I—"

Another arrow interrupted yet another promisingly worthwhile moment. Vivianne shot the angel right in the heart. If she had known the bow never missed, she would not have felt so proud of her aim.

Azrael dropped her sword and started to weep gentle tears that surprised her at first, but quickly settled into her heart. The arrow felt good. As if a knot untwisted in her chest and she was breathing for the first time. Azrael's love was for everything. The mere truth of existence itself filled her with endless bliss. She felt shame for her hatred but joy in her new acceptance.

Caesar had been sitting in the rubble of his home with his thoughts during all of this. His eyes burned from the pepper spray, but he was also crying. This felt like the end. It felt like everything he had ever loved was just as his room was then – a messy pile of shit, ruined beyond repair. He could hear Cupid, the reason for it all, the thing that dealt him the cards his heart would forever bleed from. His sadness turned back into rage. Caesar stepped out from the rubble with the loaded relic in hand – the god killer. It was hard to see through the pepper taking up residence in his vision, but he knew the big, fleshy blur ahead of him had to be the asshole he wanted. He raised the weapon, squinting to focus as best he could. He held the last five years of pain in his fist.

Enough is enough, he thought.

Azrael stepped toward Cupid with open, repentant arms at that same moment, a glowing smile on her face. She was ready to forgive herself and accept the personal perils of those around her not as weakness, but as life. Things were going to be different. She was going to help. When the gun went off, everyone flinched. The magical bullet popped out with the roar of thunder. The angel didn't even know it hit her. She burned to ash before the spectators could hear the ringing in their ears.

Cupid wept and ran for the bus.

The shriveled shapeshifter on the bus cried, "Fuck, fuck, fuck…" as it crawled into the driver's seat. Vivianne turned and shouted, "What are you doing?!" It started the engine and yelled, "It's a god killer!"

It stepped on the gas, the bus fleeing the parking lot, and Cupid running after. Caesar shook off the disorienting recoil and aimed again through his blurred vision. A second clap of thunder fired but hit a stranger's car, ripping it open like tissue paper. Vivianne yelled for the shorty to slow down. "Cupid is trying to get on!" The thing panicked, cutting the wheel. Cupid tried to slow down, but he was moving too fast. The bus turned, and he ran right into it, bouncing off and falling to the ground. Vivianne held onto the door, yelling at the driver, "You fucking idiot, you hit him."

The shorty's nerves were out of control. The bus screeched around in a circle. Vivianne leaned out of the door, reaching for Cupid, shouting to Caesar to put the gun down.

314

Another roar of thunder put a hole in the ground next to Cupid. He was up on his feet quickly, running in circles after the bus, reaching for Vivianne, begging her to save his life. Vivianne yelled to the driver once more, "For fuck's sake, stop turning the goddamn bus!"

The bus straightened out, and Cupid ran right into the steps, tripping into the bus with his legs dangling out like worms. Vivianne pulled at him, keeping him from falling out. Thunder struck again, the magical bullet striking the bus. Everyone on board felt the impact. The bus stalled and the driver cried, "Fuck, are we hit?!" The shortie behind the wheel fought the clutch before getting the engine back on. No one knew where the shot had landed. The bus kept on going down the road, increasing speed. When the door to the back bedroom opened and Caesar stepped in, everyone saw the road pouring away behind them in the hole the gun had made. Caesar raised the weapon, his face stricken with madness.

Vivianne begged, "Caesar, please don't do it."

"I have to," he cried, pulling the trigger once more just as Cupid dropped to the floor. The bullet ripped out of the front of the bus. The dashboard blasted into pieces, the steering wheel lost. The shapeshifter's hands waved about in the air with nothing to grab. The bus went swerving into the desert, out of control. The shorty hopelessly yelled, "HOLD ONTO SOMETHING!"

The bus toppled over, and everyone onboard desperately held on as it crashed into the desert, rolling onto its side, scraping along the sand and rock with a violent and arduous groan. They hadn't made it far from the Inn. Everyone still alive gathered around watching the madness. Every customer, bar patron, motel guest, and employee. Everyone except for Gwen. All the magic had excited the plants at the front desk, and she was stuck in the overgrowth of nature, her cries for assistance unable to be heard.

Slowly, eyes began to open from within the wreck. Moaning voices pushed around in search of others. Everyone was okay. Okay enough, anyway. Vivianne helped the shorty up from the twisted seat it had been folded into. The creature pushed her away when it was freed. Agitated and steaming with regret, it shook its head at her and marched down the road, turning into a man in a suit, and putting its thumb out to hitch a ride with anyone who wasn't Cupid.

Back on the bus, Caesar was far from done. He'd come too far to quit now. Pulling himself up from a pile of romance novels, Caesar aimed the gun at Cupid, who was laying on the kitchen wall, too bruised to fight. Cupid gave Caesar the finger. That was about all the energy he had left. He flipped him off and readied himself for death. Caesar pulled the trigger. But the gun was empty.

He pulled it again, and again it clicked with nothing.

Caesar let the gun fall. He felt as if he had failed her. This was his chance to do something for what they were. Justice for the pain. His once chance. Lost.

Cupid started to laugh short cackles of disbelief pulsing between long, exhausted inhales. He even managed a slow insulting clap. He laughed out, "That's fucking hilarious." Caesar began trembling, pain and anger and frustration, all screaming from within. Screaming for something to help.

Vivianne looked at him with sympathy and offered her hand, but seeing her just reminded Caesar of why all this was happening. How hopeless it always was. How stupid he was. Caesar picked the gun up. He shouted and swung the relic against the god's face. Cupid put his hands out to defend himself as Caesar struck him. Sobbing and hitting, they screamed at each other, bled on each other. They screamed and fought and then they did nothing.

Caesar gave up and fell off the battered Cupid crying, more lost than he was before it had all started. Cupid laughed with a painful breath, spitting up blood as he said, "Oh man, fuck you, guy. Fuck you so hard." Cupid held his face and sat up.

"The fuck? For real, man. In all my years of doing this shit, never has someone been such a fucking asshole to me. This is next level, fucking, asshole-ery. You tried to fucking kill me. ARE YOU FUCKING SERIOUS?"

Caesar was silent. There was no justice, no freedom, no true release from the pain. No closure. She was gone and that was it. Love broken. When the mint and cinnamon scent of his suffering heart found the magical little hairs in Cupid's busted nose, the love god gave Caesar a second thought. They sat silently looking at one another, thinking and re-thinking. Studying the details in one another's face. The lines that aged their eyes. The sorrow that darkened them. The melancholy that hung onto their skin like a permanent foundation. They knew each other. They were the same.

Caesar got up and made his way over to Cupid, who backed away in response, his arms up and ready to combat the next assault. Caesar waved his defense away, gesturing that the fight was over.

He lit two cigarettes from his pocket, gave one to Cupid, and told him he was sorry. "I just... I just don't fucking know. Something about you being real, just, I don't know. I'm sorry. I just want it to stop." Tears filled Caesar's eyes. Caesar held out the picture of the happy woman he found in Cupid's quiver. Cupid smiled when he took it, eyes welling up with old memories. He held the picture like he was holding the person in it. As he saw Cupid's reaction to the picture, Caesar shook his head at himself, uttering, "I had a feeling." Sullenly he made his way off the bus, stepping through the hole he had made in the windshield.

With a limp, Caesar took a seat against the overturned vessel. He smoked his cigarette as he looked at a picture of his own. It had been taken on the day they found out they were expecting. An old friend took it. His ex, him, and the belly to be, all smiling. It was a good picture. It was a good day.

It would have kept being good.

How do you move on?

How do you feel without feeling?

How do you let go without letting go?

His life post-tragedy was something like a ghost with unfinished business. Only there was nothing to finish. The pieces were all broken. The business was closed.

Cupid tapped Caesar on the shoulder with a bottle of something fancy. It made Caesar laugh. Cupid sat next to him as he drank. The bottle traded hands. They both drank and smoked. They reflected on the storm of events that led them to this moment beside each other.

"So, who is she?" Caesar asked, pointing his words to the picture in Cupid's hand. Clearing his throat, Cupid told Caesar she was his wife. "Only time I ever fell in love. I'm designed to love everything, but this was different. I was told I was a fool for marrying a human. But I was in love, so there was no talking me out of it. You don't get to negotiate with love. The, uh, the *righteous deciders* denied my requests to gift her magic, to prolong her aging. Said a life partner was not in the cards for my role. They said it would only be a distraction. Told me to enjoy her for what she was. And I did. I haven't looked at this picture for a long time. Try not to think about it. You get it. I can tell."

Vivianne was right. Caesar could see himself in Cupid. In a way, it was like looking at an overweight reflection. With a long sigh and a big breath from the fancy bottle, Cupid asked Caesar, "You must have some story. You mind if I—" He held his hand out, letting it finish his question. Caesar didn't quite understand what he was asking for. Cupid put his hand on Caesar's chest, saying, "I'd like to know what inspired all this destruction."

With a subtle buzz of electricity, Cupid's hand warmed, and he choked on the pain Caesar lugged around in his chest. Tears rolled down his chubby cheeks. His lip quivered and he wept with Caesar's pain. Caesar was in awe of it. Cupid pulled his hand from Caesar, understanding all too well why things went the way they had.

Cupid wiped his eyes dry and said, "Whoa. That's a rough ride. I'm sorry, man. I really am." Tossing his cigarette away, he added, "But you weren't one of mine."

"What?"

"I had nothing to do with your love for this woman. Or hers for you. I'm contracted fifty to eighty orders a year. Some years I only do about a dozen. None of them are my call. Most love has nothing to do with me at all, man. Shit is just part of the cosmic debris. I'm the god of love, but I don't own it. It's just a job, and one I can't quit. Believe me, I fucking want to." Pulling a cigarette from a pack, Cupid added, "Love was here long before I was created. And it's not going anywhere when I'm gone."

Lighting the cigarette, he said, "So you were trying to kill me in revenge for something I didn't even do. Sorta fucked up." Cupid smiled and pulled in a long drag from his cigarette. "Not that I blame you. I've done pretty similar shit."

318

Scratching his head, Caesar told him, "I was thinking if you die, then love dies, and then no one has to suffer this shit anymore." Cupid chuckled, "That's cute. And sort of the dumbest fucking thing I have ever heard." Caesar sighed, thinking about *her* and what *she* meant to him. He wondered what she would think of him in this moment. The her before the accident. What would she have thought of any of this? What a mess he had made of everything. Shaking his head, Caesar huffed, "This really was stupid of me." Cupid patted his shoulder, "Don't dwell on it. This is nothing. Just another broken heart working through the pieces. Not the first asshole to come after me. No one's gone this far, or been this crazy."

They both laughed a little, shared more stories, drank and smoked some cigarettes. It was a real bonding moment.

XXXII
AFTER THE DUST SETTLED

Teddy's insurance saved him from the strange damage of that most bizarre of days. The whole thing was written off as an act of god. Ironically enough, in many ways it was. The magic of it all faded from most memories. Everyone who witnessed it all struggled to recall the details of what happened. As time went on, they would remember it all as nothing more than some bad weather. Just another blur in countless blackouts of Caesar's downward spiral. Only he resurfaced with a new friend. The parts of it all he really needed to remember he shared with April. A serendipitous meeting over a burning car. A drunken road trip riddled with hard-to-place dreams of magical creatures and talking rocks. Bonding and letting go. Their great surrender to the damage done.

Caesar stopped working at the Inn shortly after the bad weather. He took Henry up on an offer to help out around the cemetery. Henry even talked him into putting up a little something for his lost past. Something outside himself he could reach out and touch that was just for him. A place he could put the pain. A tiny tombstone for the kid who never was, and the wife who came and went. Caesar refused to drink when he sat with it. He was pretty sure it helped in some way to have the space set aside for them. For himself.

April took advantage of the overgrown bonsai tree and turned her property into a novelty hotel. The place was always packed with people who wanted to sleep in a big tree. With the profits, she finally opened the restaurant she had always wanted. She put clothes on all her girls and had them waiting tables. Caesar accepted her invitation to be her head chef. He opened a bank account and moved into an actual apartment with Tux and a new cat he named Tux's wife. He started bathing regularly and got car insurance. He still owned flip-flops, but added a few pairs of actual shoes to the things he owns. Frances got him to stop driving drunk, although they both took his squad car out occasionally on moonlit tussles through the desert after they'd had a few too many deep breaths.

Frances started dating April. They moved in together and quickly found out they were expecting twins. Cupid had no involvement in any of it. Although, had Caesar never tried to kill the plump god, they would have never met.

The biggest achievement of them all was getting Caesar a phone. April bought him several over the years and finally managed to get him to use one.

Use it to call his mother.

She didn't pick up, and her voicemail was full, but it was a start.

Going to bed sober was hard at first but Caesar welcomed the return of his wife to his dreams. As painful as it could be, sometimes it was nice to see her. Sometimes they hung out like nothing bad had ever happened. Made the mornings lonelier than usual. But for a moment they were together again, smiling. Those dreams were nice. They reminded him of why life was worth waking for. Caesar knew she would always be there, somewhere inside of him. Always being what shaped him. Always sitting in the first seat of his heart. He didn't care to make room for another seat. Caesar believed that feeling only came once – that big, all-consuming, grand sense of purpose for another. The odds of Caesar, the odds of her. The odds of it all. Of meeting and falling in love. The physical companionship had ended. The experience was over. But the truth of it, the memories, the effect, those were real. *They* were real. *It* was real. For Caesar, that was a moment in which the universe felt invincible. For a moment it had been. For a moment there were only two sets of eyes. Two hearts beating joyfully together. Two minds dreaming the same dream. For a moment it was everything it was supposed to be. For a moment it was eternal. And that was more than enough. No sense in drowning in it anymore. Instead, it was time to start celebrating that it happened. The pain was only there because it was real. The pain did not own the feeling. It did not own the memories. It would take someone truly remarkable for him to ever move on. To give someone else the pieces he held onto. Until then, he had his cats. Caesar was always telling the cats stories about her.

They were really good listeners.

The great war never happened. The idea of it died with Azrael and her sisters. The Almighties held a vigil for their lost angels and just kept eating. Some of them still feared the shifting dust that moved around in the shadows. The whispers it made in the wind.

No one knows where the hell Dian is. They keep looking for her, but they don't even remember why they left the church in the first place to even lose her. It's really sad and fucked up.

As for Cupid, he still roamed the globe with love orders. The remaining shapeshifters all went their separate ways. Vivianne became Cupid's assistant in the love trade. There was nothing romantic between them. They both just loved love and were happy spreading it around. As for Cupid's substance abuse, he started meeting with a group every Tuesday and Thursday to share stories that always began the same.

"Hello, I'm Cupid, the god of love, and I am an addict."

THE END

Acknowledgments

Thank you to Madeline Talbot, a talented editor without whom this book would be riddled with errors and too many unnecessary characters. Thanks also to my grandfather, Gerald Fraser, your investment in this book helped push it out the door and reach a wider audience than I would have managed on my own. Thank you to everyone who took the time to read my advance prints and offer feedback. Your responses were flattering, helpful, and most delicious. Thank you also to my family and friends who always encourage my creative outlets. Thank you to everyone out there offering help and advice for indie authors.

Thank you to everyone who shared their broken hearts. I mixed them all up into this story. Every last shard of pain that moved me is melted into this work of fiction. Our heartache is now a few degrees more playful. At least I hope that was the effect.

And thank you as always to my wife, Allise Blackman. These stories would not happen without your love. Your support is immeasurable and I am forever grateful that you continue to encourage this passion of mine.

For more stories by Willie, visit:

Woollywillie.com

And follow the podcast

Our Story Begins